Virginia Woolf's

Jacob's Room:

The Holograph Draft

Virginia Woolf's

Jacob's Room

The Holograph Draft

Based on the holograph manuscript in the Henry W. and Albert A. Berg Collection of English and American Literature at the New York Public Library

Transcribed and Edited by
Edward L. Bishop

PACE UNIVERSITY PRESS

Pace University Press
One Pace Plaza
New York NY 10038

Printed in the United States of America
British Library Cataloging in Publication Information Available

Library of Congress Cataloging-in-Publication Data
for the hardcover edition

Woolf, Virginia, 1882-1941
(Jacob's room)
Virginia Woolf's Jacob's room : based on the holograph manuscript in the Henry W. and Albert A. Berg Collection of English and American Literature at the New York Public Library / transcribed and edited by Edward L. Bishop.
p. cm.
Includes bibliographical references.
1. Young men—England—Fiction. I. Bishop, Edward. II. Berg Collection. III. Title.
PR6045.072J3 1998b 823'.912—dc21 98-14724 CIP

ISBN for hardcover edition 0-944473-45-8

ISBN for paperback edition 978-1-935625-00-1

The paper used in this publication meets the minimum requirements of American National Standard for information Sciences—Permanence of Paper for Printed Library Materials, ANSI Z39.48—1984

CONTENTS

ACKNOWLEDGEMENTS

I am grateful to Professor Quentin Bell, and to the Henry W. and Albert A. Berg Collection, New York Public Library, Astor, Lenox and Tilden Foundations, for permission to quote from the manuscripts, and to The Hogarth Press for permission to quote from The Hogarth Press edition of *Jacob's Room*. I also wish to acknowledge the Social Sciences and Humanities Research Council of Canada for the grant that made this research possible.

I wish to thank Eric Savoy for suggesting the project to me in the first place; Gerald Wandio, whose keen eye and devoted labour in the initial stages of the transcription made him more a co-editor than a graduate research assistant; Ray Siemens Jr. for his invaluable help in formatting the initial transcription on the computer; Jean Richardson for her excellent proof-reading, and designer Nada Zeljković for her painstaking preparation of the camera-ready copy. For help and encouragement I also wish to thank Susan Dick, John Graham, Louise DeSalvo, and the librarians at the Berg Collection, Stephen Crook, Philip Milito, and the late Dr. Lola Szladits. To editor Mark Hussey thanks for his patience, guidance and persistence in seeing the project through. Finally, thanks to my children, James and Erin.

INTRODUCTION

I
Composition

In early January of 1920–the first month of a decade that would come to be identified with literary experiment–Virginia Woolf was excitedly considering "a new form for a new novel." She was not yet sure exactly what shape this new work would take, but she knew it would leave behind the traditional form of her two previous novels, *The Voyage Out* and *Night and Day*, and move in the directions suggested by the short sketches she had been writing: "Suppose one thing should open out of another–as in *An Unwritten Novel*," she wrote in her diary on January 26, "only not for 10 pages but 200 or so–doesn't that give the looseness & lightness I want: doesnt that get closer & yet keep form & speed, & enclose everything, everything?"[1]

She began in April and wrote steadily through the summer, though pressed by her work for the Hogarth Press and by the reviews she was writing for the *Times Literary Supplement*. By August, along with reading Don Quixote, reviewing Gorky, and discussing Roger Fry's translation of Mallarmé with him, she had taken Jacob through Cambridge and on to London (chapter V). Feeling alternately oppressed and abandoned by the *TLS* (for though she refused some book reviews she felt slighted when they were not offered), and saddened by the departure of her friend and rival Katherine Mansfield, she forged ahead with *Jacob's Room*, hoping to finish by Christmas.

In September she told the *Times* she would do no more reviews, only leading articles and those she suggested herself. But then after two months of steady writing she found herself halted in the middle of Mrs. Durrant's party (chapter VIII), intimidated by her new friend T. S. Eliot and by his praise of Joyce. A few days of illness followed, and Woolf concluded that it was headache and not Eliot that had affected her, but afterward she worked less exclusively on the novel. She always had more than one project on the go, and now she wrote a paper for the Memoir Club (probably "22 Hyde Park Gate"), reviewed, among other works, biographies of John Evelyn and Jane Austen, and D. H. Lawrence's novel *The Lost Girl*, set type for Leonard Woolf's *Stories of the East*, and fired off a letter to the editor of the *New Statesman* on "The Intellectual Status of Women." As Christmas approached she noted "Everyone's book is out" (*D* II, 78)–T. S. Eliot's *The Sacred Wood*, Roger Fry's *Vision and Design*, Katherine Mansfield's *Bliss*, and John Middleton Murry's *Aspects of Literature*. She was only about half-way through the first draft of *Jacob's Room*.

Her thirty-ninth birthday, 25 January 1921, found her at a "crisis" with her novel. Perhaps goaded by the laudatory reviews of *Bliss*, she wanted to "finish in 20,000 words, written straight off in a frenzy" (*D* II, 86). This did not stop her from taking Russian lessons, though trying to keep up with Leonard was like being "attached to an express train" (*D* II, 90). March was broken up by trips to Manchester, where Leonard was to be adopted as Labour candidate, and to Cornwall where Virginia read but deliberately did not write. In April she was cast down because her book of short stories, *Monday or Tuesday*, rated only a short review in the *TLS* while Lytton Strachey's *Queen Victoria* received three columns of praise. She was losing momentum, and in early May found herself at a "full stop" in *Jacob's Room* after reading T. S. Eliot's essay "Prose and Verse." Nevertheless, in a few days she was writing the scene of Jacob on the Acropolis (chapter XII), and later that month was beginning to think about the shape of her own book of essays: her "Reading-book" that would become the first *Common Reader*.

In mid-June, however, she came home after a concert and was unable to sleep; it was the onset of two months of ill-health. She did no writing. She confined herself to one visitor a day, and read Scott's Waverley novels, as well as D.H. Lawrence's new book, *Women in Love*. By early August she was well enough to work on her own novel again, making good progress through a busy fall that included visiting with James and Alix Strachey, who were just back from studying with Freud in Vienna, buying a new second-hand printing press, and discussing literature with T. S. Eliot who, she was disappointed to find, no longer intimidated her. On November 4, 1921 she finished the first draft of *Jacob's Room*.

She relaxed by reviewing Henry James's ghost stories, stitching the edition of Roger Fry's woodcuts for the Hogarth Press, and following daily politics. Early in 1922 she was ill with influenza, and concerned that Mansfield's new book, *The Garden Party and Other Stories*, would soon burst upon the world in glory, reducing *Jacob's Room* to "stale acrobatics" by the time it appeared. She consoled herself by arguing violently with Lytton Strachey about Percy Lubbock's recent book, *The Craft of Fiction*, which she felt wrong-headed.

Finally in early March she began work on her novel again, cheered by visits from Clive Bell, and from E. M. Forster, just back from India. A month later she was beginning to have the manuscript typed, and was already enthusiastic about the opening chapter of *The Common Reader* and a short story, "Mrs. Dalloway in Bond Street"–new writing that helped quell her growing anxiousness about the reception of *Jacob's Room*. At last in July, in between helping to organize a fund to provide an income for Eliot, and visiting doctors who disagreed about whether or not her lungs were infected with tuberculosis, she finished *Jacob's Room*. As was her custom, she gave it to Leonard to read; he pronounced it a work of genius. Virginia noted with satisfaction in her diary for July 26, 1922, "There's no doubt in my mind that I have found out how to begin (at 40) to say something in my own voice" (*D* II, 186).

II
The Manuscript

The manuscript of *Jacob's Room* is contained in three bound notebooks in the Berg Collection of the New York Public Library. As in most of her manuscripts, Woolf has ruled a blue pencil line down the left side of each page to create a margin. She writes on one side of the page only, in black ink, reserving the verso side for the occasional note, calculation, or sketch.

Volume I consists of 215 pages and two blank leaves. The cover is of shiny paper with green, orange, and olive-coloured diamonds. A white label with *Jacob's Room* written in blue pencil is pasted on the front. The volume covers the period from 15 April to 24 Nov. 1920, and it contains scenes from chapter I to the opening of chapter VIII, Betty Flanders' letter to Jacob in London.

Volume II consists of 273 numbered pages and ten blank leaves. The cover is disintegrating–one third of it is gone–and the gummed label has "Jacob's Room 2" written in blue pencil. There is a blank square of blue construction paper glued below. This volume covers the period from 26 Nov. 1920 to May 1921. It picks up the narrative in chapter VIII and carries it to the end of chapter XII, leaving Jacob and Sandra on the Acropolis. It also includes four short sketches: "Romance," "The Telephone," "Written for a picture: A letter to a lady," and "A death in the newspaper," as well as a portion of the ending of "The String Quartet" (MS 148-153).[2]

Volume III consists of 223 numbered pages; there are nine blank leaves and several have been ripped out. The cover has a leaf and flower design in burgundy. The label bears the title, "Book of scraps of J's R. & first version of The Hours." It only contains twenty-two pages of material related to *Jacob's Room*: the closing scene of the novel, and revisions or additions to chapters II, IV, X, and XI. It is dated March 12th 1922. I have not located additional manuscript material, nor have I found typescript (except for the eight-page fragment in the Monk's House Papers) or page proofs.[3]

III
Revision

The sequence of the manuscript corresponds to that of the published text, but many of the scenes are quickly sketched. Much was expanded and added in intervening drafts. There are innumerable small alterations within the manuscript and between the manuscript and the published novel, and these details range from the apparently whimsical to the deliberately symbolic. Name changes, for instance, are often made casually, along the way. Mrs. Flanders' maid is first Alice but Rebecca by the end of the next page (MS 12), and Captain Bingham becomes, without cancellation or comment, Captain Barfoot (MS 19). Arthur Bonamy becomes Richard Bonamy (MS 84), and the young man at Cambridge who stays behind in Jacob's room to talk of Julian the Apostate is Headicar at the beginning of the discussion, Simeon by the end (MS 46-7). Sometimes, however, the decision is not so easy–the Countess of Rocksbier is so named only after Rockhand, Rocksway, Rookham, Rockscave, and Rockhold have been considered (MS 137-

8). The change seems insignificant, though the final designation captures the sense of solidity, as well as a hint of the moribund and the rapacious, appropriate to this aged rider to hounds. Less subtle is the original first name of Mrs. Wentworth Williams: initially "Sabine," after a page she becomes the more innocuous "Sandra," perhaps so as not to cast Jacob's diffident wooing in an ironic light (MS 214).

Jacob's exotic uncle (last seen in Penang, in the draft) is Uncle Eliot in the manuscript but becomes a more robust-sounding Uncle Morty in the final version (MS 36). Eliot in turn becomes the last name of the tall, gray-haired Miss Julia, the guest of the Durrants who looks at the stars through Mr. Clutterbuck's telescope. In the draft she murmurs, "Aldebaran," but later Woolf chooses a different name from her list of constellations, one more in keeping with Julia's situation in life and her melancholy view of astronomy, and so for the final version the lady murmurs, "Andromeda" (MS 64). Mr. Clutterbuck is cheerfully deaf in both draft and final text, but in the manuscript Woolf toys with the idea of having him take opium. However, she cancels the passage (MS 66), reserving his habit and his silences to develop them in the character of Mr. Carmichael in *To The Lighthouse*.[4]

Places change too. Mr. Floyd originally meets Jacob in the Strand, but this becomes Piccadilly (MS 15). The socially ambitious wife of a Cambridge tutor, Mrs. Plumer, is first begotten in South or West Kensington, but by the final version her birthplace has become Manchester (MS 31). Even time is altered, and once again the revisions embrace both the trivial and the significant. In the manuscript Jacob's sailing voyage takes three weeks, but Woolf, possibly reflecting that she would have to justify taking that long to reach the Scilly Isles from Falmouth, reduces the duration to six days (MS 62). The church clock, which is slow in the manuscript, becomes fast in the published novel (MS 12)–perhaps to accord with the general speeding up of the narrative? At any rate, Florinda becomes younger: 25-30 in the manuscript, but 20-25, closer to Jacob's age, in the final version (MS 86).

She also reads different books. She leaves Jacob's room with one of Jane Austen's novels, but by the time she gets home it is one of Peacock's, and by the time *Jacob's Room* is published the volume has become Shelley's poems. In addition, "Adonais" becomes, along with

Shakespeare, one of the "sovereign specifics for all disorders of the soul" (MS 92-3). Other cultural references are quietly altered. The bust in the dining room on Guy Fawkes day is at first Greek, but Woolf changes it to Roman, no doubt to preserve for Jacob himself the associations with Greek statuary (MS 87). At the Durrant's party Elsbeth Siddons originally sings "Drink to me only with thine eyes," but in the final version she sings the equally famous, but more ambiguous and provocative, "Who is Silvia? what is she? / That all our swains commend her?" from *Two Gentlemen of Verona* (MS 113).

These alterations are intriguing, but more interesting are the larger conceptual changes that occurred in the course of writing. Virginia Woolf had been turning over the ideas for "a new form for a new novel" for three months when she sat down that rainy April morning to sketch out a plan.[5] The preliminary note (MS 1) seems to indicate that the focus and the structuring principles were clear in her mind from the outset. But Woolf's intentions were not at all certain: she will "perhaps" call the book "Jacob's Room"; she says, "Let us suppose that the room will hold it together." And further, what is "it"? *The Voyage Out* was about the maturation and early death of a young woman. *Jacob's Room* is more elusive. The book was not written simply as an experiment in style, but neither–to take the other extreme–was it conceived as an anti-war polemic. Whether one takes the book to be about a particular young man named Jacob (who resembles Thoby Stephen), or the generation lost in the war (epitomized by a figure who resembles Rupert Brooke), or about the relationship between the narrator and her subject, or about the process of perception and the nature of being, or all of this and more, one finds in the manuscript a gradual, and often very tentative, process of discovery as both the subject matter and the form evolve together.

What strikes one first about the manuscript draft is that Woolf is using rooms as an index of characters; Jacob's is not at first singled out. In fact the lyrical passage that introduces Jacob's room at Cambridge, "The feathery white moon never let the sky grow dark..." (MS 37), appears again at the opening of a section which deals with a young woman in her room at Newnham College. Woolf later deleted the vignette of female university life, and published it separately as "A Woman's College from Outside" in *Atalanta's Garland* in 1926.[6] Its appearance on the first draft of *Jacob's Room*, however, suggests that her statement, "Let us suppose that the Room will hold it together," was not a clear resolve but rather a supposition, one which only gradually came to be realized. The fact that Woolf used the introductory passage, "The feathery white moon never let the sky grow dark..." to place the two rooms in such obvious apposition suggests that her intention was not at first to make Jacob her exclusive focus, and that she was going to reveal him by the more expansive techniques of reflection and contrast she had used in her two previous novels.

The next chapter in the manuscript focuses on Mrs. Pascoe, the Cornish peasant woman, and again rooms seem to offer a partial solution to the problem of knowing another. Her character may be reflected in her face: as in the final text we are told that "Her face was assuredly not soft, sensual, or lecherous; but hard, wise, wholesome rather, signifying in a room full of people the flesh and blood of life" (MS 58). But in the manuscript, the heavily cancelled description of the atmosphere of the room creates an impression utterly different from the wholesomeness implied by her face:

> An earth closet out in the rain - sickness - a woman's period [copul] copulation upstairs in the double bed, [or here before the fire perhaps]–<childbirth> [the] birth–[all all that veils & places in the shadows the natural functions of the body are all bodies] as the room filled with bodies. [these functions & desires would assert themselves. all these functions & desires press become prominent,] it would be impossible not to think solely of these functions & desires. [& Whether The small room is altogether filled with the body.]
> Yet the room was scrupulously clean. (MS 57-8)

"Yet the room was scrupulously clean": in this set of rooms Woolf emphasizes the disjunction between antiseptic exteriors and the animal functions of the body. Woolf seems to be exploring the interpenetration of psychic and physical space, and one can perhaps see a pattern emerging–Jacob's room contains hints of his intellectual self, Angela's room reflects a social self, Mrs. Pascoe's room captures the physical self, and each has implications for what constitutes life and being.

The appearance of three prominent rooms in the first fifty pages of manuscript (and three months of writing) indicates that initially Woolf was thinking of structuring her novel around the rooms of several characters, not Jacob's alone. However, from this point on in the manuscript there are no rooms with the same significance as Angela's and Mrs. Pascoe's, as if Woolf saw that she would lose the suggestiveness of Jacob's room by surrounding it with others. By cutting the passage on Mrs. Pascoe's room, Woolf associates the discrepancy between wholesome appearance and the unmentioned functions and desires of the body specifically with Jacob, not simply with peasants, and thus it is reserved for the scene between Jacob and the prostitute Laurette, in which the nature of their relationship, "the whole bag of ordure," is covered by polite conversation (MS 145, *JR* 103-04).

The deletion is part of a comprehensive pattern of post-draft revisions that sharpen the focus on Jacob. For example, Woolf cuts a passage in which Nick Bramham, the painter who is jilted by Fanny Elmer for Jacob, reaches a profound and lyrical despair. In the published version Woolf describes Nick and Fanny as "impetuous spirits" who, "believing implicitly in the truth of the moment, fling off, sting the cheek, are gone like sharp hail" (*JR* 120). There is a space break and then the short passage in which Fanny bursts into the studio saying, "I'm afraid I'm late" (she has been "hanging about" Jacob's neighbourhood in the hope of seeing him). The scene is brief, to the point–Fanny leaves Nick for Jacob. In the manuscript, however, Nick is not the stoic who ends the relationship with a curt "Don't, then." He becomes (by implication, for the passage is narrated) one of those like Peter Walsh, with his dream of the solitary traveller, for whom death is a temptation as well as a last resort (here, and in most of the subsequent quotations, I omit cancellations):

> Nick, perhaps, or Fanny Elmer ludicrously supposing that this is the worst, the last, the end; leap, snatch knives, take drugs, or, prevented, drift like wreckage across the track. {Riding the crest} fling off, {sting the cheek on a with sharp hail &} are seen no more, & Perhaps–perhaps. For life, this dark eyed mother, with all her violence, spurning us, bidding us fly, vanish, never learn to grow old, yet if you press

> {close}–to her murmurs; some secret.... Life, life, booming: & the lightning; I say, how vast it is! How musical! She draws us on. (MS 178-9)

The scene, however, had to go, for it lends disproportionate stature to Nick, and such reflections on "life, this dark eyed mother" could hardly be imputed to the bluff, no-nonsense Jacob. Woolf's problem throughout seems to be that although her subject is Jacob she is continually sidetracked by other characters and, like the passenger on the train in "An Unwritten Novel," starts making up stories about them. In fact, the fat Italian Jacob meets on the train in Italy is, in the manuscript, Guiseppe Bandelli, a horse dealer with a whole history of his own (MS 207-8).

Her stories about minor characters also reveal her giving way to impulses that she curbed in revising the book. Mrs. Plumer, the working-class wife of the don who invites Jacob and some other undergraduates to lunch, is, in the manuscript, judged harshly: "Creditable though her action was... it is impossible to acquit her – No, no, no, Mrs. Plumer was not a nice woman" (MS 31). In the published novel Woolf seems more tolerant of the grasping impulses which follow inevitably from Mrs. Plumer's background. And the description of Pascoe's cottage quoted above reveals (particularly if one reads through rather than skips over the cancellations) a revulsion uncalled for by artistic necessity. Though such outbursts are rare, later when she comes to describe the old women eating lunch, whom she contrasts with the "impetuous spirits," Nick and Fanny, Woolf has in her final text this touch of the grotesque: "Damp cubes of pastry fell into mouths opened like triangular bags" (*JR* 119). The manuscript, however, reveals a stronger distaste:

> But oh, when stout suburban women satisfy nature's needs how unnecessary it appears! So equably could we let that fire be quenched. [The however is opened wide & damp clods of pastry dis And] No fire can come from damp clods of pastry. It is [prettier] <better far> to see lions with bloody bones in their paws than these cheap lunching women. (MS 171-2)

The revised version preserves the repulsiveness but renders it abstractly: "clods" have becomes "cubes" and the mouths, no longer bestial, have become "triangular bags." Where the manuscript heaps epithets on the women the final text transforms them; the overt outrage is filtered through a cool but remorseless cubism.

Another passage that was excised is this brief exchange between Jacob and Florinda when they first meet:

> Oh Jacob, said the girl as they pounded up the hill in the dark, 'I'm so frightfully un-happy!" You're not a Jew, are you? she said. "I <do> hate Jews".... {Oh Jacob your Christian name is it–} And she told him how a Jew had played her a dirty trick, leaving all his dirty clothes scattered over the room, & she having to pawn her mothers watch to pay the rent. (MS 87)

The revised version (*JR* 73) omits the reference to Jews and leaves us with a Florinda who is more pleasantly empty-headed, repeating, "I'm so frightfully unhappy," for no specific reason.

I spoke of Woolf curbing certain impulses in revising these passages, and it might be tempting to identify them as simply contempt for Jews, peasants, and the working class, or distaste for things of the body. However, in the manuscripts of the novels and the essays the attitudes expressed are apt to be blunter, the positions taken more hard-edged, than in the published texts. (In a discussion of the revisions to *To the Lighthouse*, Susan Dick notes how in the manuscript Lily's commitment to art is more aggressive than in the published text.[7]) The fine control comes in revising. Unlike the leisurely *Voyage Out* or the voluminous *Night and Day*, *Jacob's Room* is pared close to the bone, and Woolf was, of course, working in a more elliptical mode from the outset. Yet much of the compression comes from the fact that where she described in her earlier novels, she now dramatizes, and the change occurs after the draft. Between the manuscripts and the final text, she consistently reduces authorial comment and exposition, letting her scenes suggest. When the Rev. Floyd proposes to Jacob's mother she is annoyed, but the reader is left to infer the causes of her reluctance. The only reason she offers is that "she had always disliked red hair in men" (*JR* 19). The manuscript is much more explicit:

> "How could I think of marriage!" she thought to herself almost bitterly as she fastened the latch with a piece of wire.

> It was, probably, that the idea of copulation had now become infinitely remote from her. She did not use the word; & yet as she sat darning the boys clothes that night it annoyed her to find that it was so. "And [I've always disliked] red headed men" she said; pushing away her work basket. (MS 14)

And looking back on the incident as she strokes the cat, she thinks,

> how she had had him gelded & how she did not like red headed men–both thoughts coming on top of each other & making her smile, though she had not used the word gelded or–indeed she never used word, when she thought indecent thoughts. Smiling she went into the kitchen; Jacob smiled. (MS 16)

In the revision (MS 277) Woolf lets the coordinate structure make the connection for us; instead of telling us Betty does not put thoughts into words, she dramatizes the mental evasion.

In the scenes dealing with Jacob's infatuation with Clara, and later with Sandra, Woolf again revises so that the crosscurrents of emotion are only hinted at, and in doing so she substantially alters the effect of the scene (MS 70, 258-266). In this first passage Jacob is saying goodbye to Clara:

> The children were whirling past the door throwing things into the air.
>
> "Little demons!" she cried.
>
> ["I haven't said it"] Jacob thought to himself.
>
> [I want to say it. I can't say it. Clara! Clara! Clara!"]
>
> "They're throwing the onions," said Jacob." (MS 70)

In the manuscript Woolf's first thought was to have Jacob struggle to declare his love, crying the name of the beloved silently, as Terence cries aloud in *The Voyage Out*. But the cries from "Rachel! Rachel!" to "O Death!" remain exclusively elegiac in Woolf's novels, and here she may have felt them inappropriate. In any case, the lines take us into Jacob, stating his emotions, where her concern in revising is to engage us in the narrator's act of inferring them. In the final version the tension is rendered by movement: while Clara keeps moving in order to forestall an intimate moment, he stays rooted to the spot, his strangled emotions evoked by his immobility.

Even more radical revisions were made to the climactic scene in which Jacob and Sandra experience a moment of intense but indefinable meaning on the Acropolis (MS 258-266). At this late stage in the manuscript, and after extensive rewriting in the draft, Woolf still seemed to be thinking in terms of some sort of consummation (the kiss), and still seemed to be trying to specify that elusive "thing" that Sandra and Jacob are hoping to discover and create. Between the draft and the final version Woolf cut significantly. Jacob does not attempt to express his emotions, Sandra's motives are not analyzed, and it is the wind itself that conveys the emotion: as the tension between Sandra and Jacob increases the narrator moves further and further out, and the single line, "Sandra's veils were swirled about her" (*JR* 159), carries the intensity of the moment. The changes also eliminate the earnestness of the manuscript scene. In the published text there is no talk of their agonizing over whether or not to kiss, and the narrator is almost sardonic, observing offhandedly, "There was the Acropolis; but had they reached it? The columns and the Temple remain; the emotion of the living breaks fresh on them year after year; and of that what remains?" (*JR* 160). The versions of the scene show Woolf striving for greater suggestiveness, trying by indirection to capture something beyond language, teasing the reader toward the ineffable. But further, the initial inclusion of Jacob's attempts to express himself reveals that after writing almost two hundred and fifty pages of manuscript Woolf had still not firmly settled on the means for presenting her central character. It is only after the first draft that Jacob becomes a figure seen primarily from the outside, whose thoughts and emotions remain a matter of speculation. Significantly, the manuscript opens with Jacob lost and crying "Nanny! Nanny!": Archer's searching cry, "Ja-cob! Ja-cob!" that goes "out into the world, solitary, unanswered" (*JR* 7), was added in a subsequent draft. This is consistent with the manuscript version as a whole, which is an account of Jacob trying to find himself, rather than what the novel became, an attempt by another to know Jacob. The drama of the narrator's search, which dominates the final text, is here less urgent.

The book is, as readers have been quick to observe, concerned in part with questions of knowing, particularly with the difficulty of knowing another human being. In the published text these questions are tied to Jacob; they rise out of the narrator's love for him, her attempt to know him. In the manuscript, however, they appear in connection with other characters, even minor figures such as Mrs. Pascoe (MS 56). Further, Woolf altered the quality of the narrator's comments. What distinguishes the published novel is the fact that it is not only an attempt to know Jacob, it is the narrator's own quest, an intimate relationship which we are privileged to share. Yet originally the narrator was much more collusive, always conscious of her audience. "But you know how anyone reads who's worth anything, just what he likes" (MS 37-8), she says in the manuscript, where in the text she simply asserts, "Any one who's worth anything reads just what he likes" (*JR* 37). In the final version the reader is most often acknowledged indirectly, through the imperative mood, and the relation between the narrator and Jacob becomes a private one.

Finally, to turn to questions of spatial form, Woolf often sharpened scenes as discrete units, using narrative structure to impart her sense of the "chasms" in our lives (MS 130-1). At the finish of the episode in which Jacob and Jinny and the sculptor Cruttendon walk in the gardens at Versailles, Woolf takes them back to the train station for a sentimental parting:

> The hyacinth smell; or the frilled waxy flowers; or all these new names; or Cruttendon & Jinny & himself marching up & down up & down; made Jacob feel a new kind of person: And as they were all about the same age that was what they all felt. And Cruttendon knew that he was a very great genius. And Jacob gave Jinny a bunch of violets. And they never met again. (MS 196)

The next day she tinkers with the passage, but retains the main elements, ending as before with the narrator's summary: "Then up they got & went to the station, & Jacob bought violets from a girl & gave them to Jinny. They never met again" (MS 198). Then she rewrites the whole episode and recasts the ending, dropping the violets and the overly dramatic, "They never met again," offering instead a scene which captures the awkwardness and bathos of such moments. Aside from a change in location from the Gare St. Lazare to the Gare des Invalides (with its ironic overtones), the scene is very close to the published version:

> And they stood in the Gare St. Lazare.
>
> With one of those queer movements which are so slight, yet so definite, which may wound, or pass unnoticed, but generally inflict a good deal of discomfort, Jinny & Cruttendon drew together: Jacob stood apart. They had to separate. Something must be said. Nothing was said.
>
> A man wheeled a trolley past Jacobs legs so near that he almost grazed them. When Jacob recovered his balance the other two were turning away, though Jinny looked over her shoulder, & Cruttendon waved his hand. Well, it was over. (MS 202)

The laconic, "Well, it was over," still summarizes but it also dramatizes, being midway between authorial observation and indirect speech. For the published version, however, Woolf went further, deleting even that line to end with action rather than comment, leaving the moment frozen in process as she did with the scene between Jacob and Clara in the garden: "And Cruttendon, waving his hand, disappeared like the very great genius that he was" (*JR* 129). The technique is similar to the cinematic device of the "freeze-frame": the action stops and after a pause a new action begins. In the novel the blank space on the page provides the moment of suspension.

In revising the conclusion Woolf again alters to achieve the effect of action suspended, broken off. She first wrote,

> "What is one to do with these, Mr. Bonamy?"
>
> She held out a pair of Jacob's old shoes.
>
> [They both laughed]
>
> [The room waved behind her tears.] (MS 275)

The next day on a separate page she rewrote the final lines, confirming her cancellations. The waving of the external world behind Betty's tears was shifted to the beginning of the novel where it introduces the united themes of perception and mortality. Left at the end the tears would have provided a resolution of the action, shifting the focus to the mother's grief. By breaking in mid-action Woolf emphasizes the impossibility of making sense of such a death; the closing leaves the reader with the absence which swallows Bonamy's cry, "Jacob! Jacob!"

The moment of arrest emphasizes the paratactic relation between events, but the tenuousness of the connections seems to have grown on Woolf as she wrote. The space breaks on the page which emphasize the sudden shifts in action, or in emotion, were not present at the outset. Woolf begins by designating the episodes as separate chapters, then part way through the first volume she starts to let her chapters encompass larger units, and she divides her episodes with rows of x's (MS 56). The first space break occurs at MS 44, but she continues to use rows of x's. Early in Volume II, however, she begins dividing the episodes more frequently with space breaks.

The breaks unite the formal and the thematic aspects of the novel and they also seem to be a product of that "unseizable force" that goes "hurtling through" the nets of novelists. Woolf's political sympathies were in place before she began the novel. But they grew stronger in the writing. The ironic, sometimes cynical tone of the narrator emerges much more strongly in the published text than in the draft, and revisions such as those to the passage on the "unseizable force" sharpen the social criticism of the novel. We are told repeatedly in the published text, with a phrase at first innocuous but finally bitterly ironic, it is "they"–the men in the clubs and Cabinets–who "say" these things:

> ...*they say* that character-drawing is a frivolous fireside art... These actions... oar the world forward, *they say*. It is thus that we live, *they say*.... *they say* that the novelists never catch it.... This, *they say* is what we live by... this unseizable force. (*JR* 154-55, my emphasis).

The indecisiveness of those who would draw character here appears superior to the decisiveness of those who would so efficiently obliterate it.

The tone has changed dramatically from the draft version, where the narrator herself appears faintly scornful of mere gossips, or of the ineffectual philosopher–those who fail to realize that "life is all action" (MS 239-41). The effect is crucial. Woolf is by these revisions deepening the element of political satire, implicitly suggesting that the impulse to create character is not as frivolous as it seems, that in fact the "fireside art," be it gossip or scrawls, is an ordering force (and a force of love, we know from the activity of the narrator herself), which runs counter to the "unseizable" will to power, and which belies what "they say," that this is all we live by.

Yet this force seems to be somehow connected with love as well as war. Woolf reworks the passage later in the manuscript (MS 256) and the force is now not something that drives an old woman to suicide and a young man to parliament but the fated impulse that leads Jacob to Sandra, a connection implied by juxtaposition only in the manuscript but made explicit in the published text: "Jacob (driven by this unseizable force) walked rapidly down Hermes Street and ran straight into the Williamses" (*JR* 156).

That this unseizable force which raises the pillars of the establishment should be the same force that drives Jacob to Sandra seems curious at first. But once we recognize that it is not the force of the institutions themselves, but a force in nature that is channelled through the institutions we can see it more clearly. It is the creative force in its dark aspect, the will to mate and to dominate that appears again in the mad fecundity of the "Time Passes" section of *To the Lighthouse*, or in the mingled lust and aggression that underlie the sexual and military politics of *Between the Acts*. Thus the force that brings Sandra and Jacob together is not materially different from the impulse that creates banks, businesses, and wars.

The counter agent to the unseizable force–or more properly the other side of it, for the two are not ultimately separable–is the Greek spirit. A central tension in the novel is that between "force" and "spirit," between the violence of institutions and the order produced by art. Jacob's life is shaped by both. In revising, Woolf makes more emphatic the distinction between character-drawing and political action, yet she is not at all reductive. In linking the predatory Sandra both with the Greek spirit–she is "the English type which is so Greek" (*JR* 141)–and with the unseizable force, Woolf is recognizing what Jacob does not: that inspired idealism and crude acquisitiveness are both present in the raw energy of society. Civilization is neither the pure design created by Jacob's Cambridge tutors, nor the embodiment of Commerce envisioned by the men in clubs and Cabinets. Jacob, like Julian before him, would like to preserve the Greek ethos unsullied by its base elements. His mistake is in thinking he can keep them separate.

However, Woolf was not writing to any preconceived formal or political program. The phenomenological and the political themes develop together, as if her sense of the contingency of life and of the madness of war reinforced one another, both structuring the text. The breaking up of the narrative on the page constitutes the most obvious departure from Woolf's previous work, but it is merely the spatial adjunct to the rhetorical shaping of the scenes. And this shape developed in response to the demands of the subject, the complex nature of which was only fully discovered in the act of writing. Led by intuition rather than theory, she was not trying out a new method but moving toward one. She sensed at the outset that the room might "hold it together," but she did not perceive at that point precisely how it would function. The movement toward the room as an enclosing figure and the concomitant movement away from conventional closure, from "holding it together" as she had in her first two novels, were both gradual. The final shape of the work and its true intent emerged only toward the end of the first draft, as Jacob (the public, the private, and the perceived being) and his room (the domicile, the psychic space, and the text itself) progressively defined one another.

IV
The Transcription

I am much indebted to the work of Professor John Graham and Professor Susan Dick, whose editions of *The Waves* and *To the Lighthouse* respectively have established the format for this edition. I have chosen to follow them in making a facsimile transcription, reproducing the manuscript page for page and line for line, because it conveys much more closely than any other method the process of the author's writing. If readers compare the brief manuscript passages quoted in this introduction with the main transcription, they will quickly see how the various kinds of brackets, while useful for maintaining a linear format, give no sense of how Woolf actually worked — trying different versions of a phrase, crossing out within the line, writing above the line or in the margin. Further, while an edited transcription may be easier to read, it gives a false sense of completion; again, if readers compare the passages quoted above where I have omitted cancellations with the main transcription they will quickly feel the distortion. Spelling has not been corrected or normalized in the transcription, and neither has punctuation. Woolf often omits quotation marks at the beginning or end of a quotation, and frequently shifts between double and single quotation marks, even within the same passage. She occasionally omits the second dash or the closing parenthesis with an interrupting element, and she uses colons or semicolons where we might expect a period. The *Jacob's Room* manuscript is a work still very much in process, and the energy and the sense of discovery that the manuscript conveys could not be conveyed by any other form.

The handwriting is, on the whole, legible and uniform, but as Professor Graham has pointed out there are characteristic difficulties in the hand that often make it difficult to decipher a particular word: initial upper and lower case letters are often indistinguishable, *r* and *s* resemble each other, and an initial *n* often has a longer ascender than a mid-word *h*.[8] Occasionally, working back from the published text confirms readings that could never be deduced from the manuscript alone. I have made educated guesses but have not imposed my reading on any passage.

The short sketches Virginia Woolf wrote in volume II of the manuscript have been included because of their implications for the composition of *Jacob's Room* (a novel which owes far more to her sketches than to her previous novel, *Night and Day*). The reviews and portions of *Mrs. Dalloway* from volume III, written after the main body of *Jacob's Room* had been completed, have not been included.

EDITORIAL CONVENTIONS

Pagination: I have numbered the pages of the manuscript consecutively from beginning to end. Virginia Woolf wrote only on the recto pages, occasionally making notes or computing the number of words written on the verso pages. The Berg Collection has numbered each volume of the manuscript anew and numbered both the verso and the recto sides of each page. As an aid to readers who wish to compare the transcription with the manuscript, these numbers are given within parentheses in the gutter margin of each page.

Marginalia and Interlineations: Marginal additions and interlineations are in smaller type to distinguish them from the draft proper. Most begin where they begin in the manuscript but occasionally adjustments have had to be made to keep them from running together.

Cancellations and other marks. Virginia Woolf used both horizontal and vertical lines to cancel words or passages. These, along with marks on the manuscript, such as a loop with a line to indicate an insertion, have been included, although because of the shift from holograph to print it has been impossible to reproduce them exactly. Square brackets have been used to indicate a doubtful reading [search?] or an illegible word [?].

NOTES

1 *The Diary of Virginia Woolf*, Vol. II: 1920-1924, ed. Anne Oliver Bell (London: Hogarth Press, 1978), 13. Further references will be cited parenthetically in the text.

2 References to both manuscript and the published draft will be cited parenthetically in the text, the former designated by MS and page number, the latter by *JR* and page number, e.g. (MS 61; *JR*, p. 36). References to the published work are to the Hogarth Press edition, London, 1971. For manuscript quotations in the introduction words within pointed brackets <word> are interlinear additions or emendations; words within braces {word} are marginal additions or emendations; and words within square brackets [word] represent cancellations by Virginia Woolf.

3 Later versions of three of the sketches in volume II, "Romance," "The Telephone," and "A death in the newspaper" have been collected in *Virginia Woolf: The Complete Shorter Fiction*, ed. Susan Dick (London: Hogarth Press, 1985), pp. 432-6. The other material in volume III consists of the following:
13-57, 67-73, "On Re-reading Novels" (*TLS,* 20 July 1922, 465-6);
75-95, review of *Love and Friendship* by Jane Austen, with a preface by G. K. Chesterton ("Jane Austen Practicing," *New Statesman*, 15 July 1922, 419-20);
131, "Thoughts upon beginning a book to be called, perhaps, At Home: or The Party" (outline of *Mrs. Dalloway*, dated Oct. 6th 1922);
132-151, "The Prime Minister" (*Mrs. Dalloway*);
153, "A possible revision of this book" (*Mrs. Dalloway*, dated Oct. 16th 1922);
155-167, "The Prime Minister";
169, 171, Royal Academy 155th exhibition (untraced and perhaps unpublished);
173-181, "Romance and the Heart" (*Nation & Athenaeum*, 19 May 1923, 229);
183-217, *Mrs. Dalloway*;
219, 221, review of *The Art of Thomas Hardy* by Lionel Johnson (untraced and perhaps unpublished);
273, review of *Maud Evelyn* and *The Sacred Fount*, by Henry James (untraced and perhaps unpublished).

4 "Mr. Clutterbuck" also appears in a list of names early in the holograph draft of *To the Lighthouse*, see Susan Dick, ed., *To the Lighthouse: the Original Holograph Draft* (Toronto: University of Toronto Press, 1982), p.3.

5 This section of the introduction draws on my article, "The Shaping of Jacob's Room: Woolf's Manuscript Revisions," *Twentieth Century Literature* 32.1 (Spring 1986), 115-135.

6 Virginia Woolf, "A Woman's College from Outside," in *The Complete Shorter Fiction* (London: Hogarth Press, 1985), pp. 197-201.

7 Susan Dick, "Editing the Original Holograph Draft of Virginia Woolf's *To the Lighthouse*," presented at the University of North Carolina, 24 Feb. 1983, and the University of Alberta, 11 May 1983.

8 John Graham, ed., *The Waves: The Two Holograph Drafts* (London: Hogarth Press, 1976), p. 42.

A Chronology of *Jacob's Room*

In the following chronology I have collated the dates on the manuscript with references in the *Diary*, volume II, and the *Letters*, volume II. Page numbers are indicated for the manuscript dates. Quotations are from the *Diary*. Chapter numbers refer to the chapters in the published editions.

1920

10 April	plans to begin *JR* next week
15 April	drafts preliminary notes (MS 1)
16 April	writes opening (MS 2)
11 May	the "sense of an impending shape" keeps her writing
20 May	the "most amusing" novel writing she's done
28 May	"11,000 in six weeks" (MS 34)
7 June	riding home sees a defiant beggar woman (cf. MS 75, ch. 6)
13 July	has not worked on *JR* for three weeks
19 July	Mrs. Pascoe (MS 54, ch. 4)
28 July	Mrs. Pascoe, continued (MS 55)
5 August	working every morning
15 August	Jacob in London (MS 71, ch. 5)
25 August	forging ahead and hopes to finish by Christmas
10 September	Jacob and Florinda in Soho (MS 98, ch. 6)
17 September	Mrs. Durrant's party (ch. 7)
26 September	halted mid-party, perhaps by T. S. Eliot
1 October	headache, not Eliot, has stopped her
25 October	writes to revive, feels life "a strip of pavement over an abyss"
10 November	neglecting *JR*
23 November	bags the phrase "strip of pavement" for *JR* (cf. MS 130)
24 November	Jacob in the morning (MS 118, ch. 8)
26 November	begins notebook II, Mrs. Flanders' letter (MS 121, 122; ch. 8)

1921

3 January	Jacob at Lady Rocksbier's (MS 138, ch. 9)
21 January	Jacob walking home from Hammersmith (MS 154, ch. 9)
25 January	wants to finish in 20,000 words, written "straight off in a frenzy"
5 February	beginning the "last lap"
1 March	Mrs. Flanders in the orchard (ch. 11)
13 March	too busy to start Jacob's "travels to the East"
5 April	Jacob at Versailles (MS 199, ch. 11)
8 April	depressed by reviews, unable to work
17 April	Italian trains (MS 205, ch. 12)
3 May	"Full stop," perhaps because of reading T. S. Eliot's "Prose and Verse"
6 May	Jacob on the Acropolis (MS 226, ch. 12)
10 June - 8 August	ill, no writing
2 November	hopes to finish on the weekend
4 November	finishes *JR*

1922

25 January	VW's fortieth birthday
14 February	concerned that by the time *JR* appears it will seem "stale acrobatics"
6 March	begins work on *JR* again, after six weeks of influenza
12 March	begins notebook III, Jacob sailing to the Scilly Isles (MS 271, ch. 4)
11 June	copying out *JR* for Miss Green, the typist.
23 June	*JR* being typed, to be sent to Harcourt Brace 14 July
17 July	finishing *JR*
23 July	Leonard Woolf reads *JR*
10 August	asks Vanessa Bell to alter her dustjacket for *JR*
6 September	correcting proofs
4 October	Harcourt Brace accepts *JR*
27 October	*JR* published in Britain by Hogarth Press
29 October	records reactions, notes, "One of the perquisites of Jacob seems to be society"

Reflections upon beginning a work of fiction to be called, perhaps, Jacob's Room: Thursday, April. 15th 1920.

I think the main point is that it should be free.
Yet what about form?
Let us suppose that the Room will hold it together.
Intensity of life compared with immobility.
20
60 Experiences.
To change style at will.

April 16th

Sept. 13th

April 16th
1920

Jacob's Room

. I .

Beyond the rock lay ~~a pool~~ ~~shiny green~~ something shiny on
the sand. A few small fish, left by the tide, beat ~~with~~ up &
down with their tails. On the edge of the wave, paddling
their feet, stood a single line of gulls; &, Jacob was trotting
towards them when the light came across the waves. ~~At
that moment he felt that he was lost~~. ~~He knew then that he was
lost.~~ ~~The light should have come in at his window.~~ ~~He looked
round & saw the~~ ~~The beach~~ He then saw that the beach
went on & on; ~~he saw the~~ ~~there was a churchtower among
the sandhills;~~ he saw that there was a new line of hills; above it;—
- in short he was lost. He trotted along by the waves &
& one after another the gulls rose ; ~~& settled again~~ & settled again. ~~he was
saw his nurse~~ ~~In the distance sitting in the sand.~~ ~~he saw a
dark woman sitting, sitting,~~ & but in the distance he saw a
~~dark~~ woman sitting; & as the gulls rose he ran faster & faster.
to reach her. But oh the waves came round her. She was a
rock. She was covered with seaweed that pops when it is
pressed. She was ~~immense~~. slimy. 'Nanny, nanny!' he
cried; ~~e~~ Nanny! nanny! ~~nanny! nanny~~! Now he
sobbed it out mechanically as he ran. Nanny! Nanny!

After him came the dark ~~fronds~~ shiny—things that took
two or three huge ~~strides~~ paces after him & then stopped. ~~But~~
Pointing at him across the sea came the light from the
lighthouse; ~~which~~ ~~when it had reached him~~ ~~it~~ ~~went out;~~ ~~Then it
came again~~ ~~which touched him & then stopped~~ went out. The light
~~was the worst most frightening,~~—— which, when it had
reached him went out; ~~& came again.~~ This was the
worst ~~of all,~~ for this light was the one that came in
at the nursery window. Here it was ~~loose~~ wild. Running,
running, running as fast as he could, & sobbing . . . . .
~~he~~ the waves came creaming up to him; the grey sand
seemed not to lie flat but to fly up ~~in~~ ~~his~~ at him . . . . & then, worst of all,
there were lights ~~on his left hand~~ one on top of another.

He was running quite alone lost on the beach
at midnight. The steamer which
~~had~~ Archer had seen come into the bay at dinner
had lights on it.- ~~only~~ but ~~they were~~
~~it was different then.~~ it was
horrid now —

~~Lights belonged to the other world, not his world,~~ meant ~~midnight.~~
~~But~~ ~~Quite~~ alone ~~he was running out on the beach — lost~~
all bright ~~& hostile~~. & hostile. This was what happened at
midnight; b~~ut q~~uite alone he wa~~s~~ running los~~t on~~ the beach.
~~"Well, I never~~—". "Well I never—" So she took him; Alice
covered hi~~m up~~; he lay in his own bed in the nursery.
(For lights belong to the world that goes on after bedtime)
And here was a jawbone with teeth in it. That must be
taken home.—If he could escape with it— But the light
again — "Nanny, Nanny! he cried; But suppose the
it was
teeth came out of the jaw bone, & ~~each was~~ allowed ~~by~~ that
each counted as a bone? Only he was lost; the others were
at home. Running, running, running as fast as he could &
~~sobbing — keeping out away from the curling froth~~ swerving
away from the waves when they came after him — so he ~~fell~~ ran
~~gasping~~ & grasping his bone into Nanny's ~~lap~~ — legs & butted his
head against them.
—"Well I never!"— So she took him; ~~& he lay in~~
~~his own bed in the nursery~~. ~~Alice~~ carried him up; & he
lay in his own bed in the nursery.

Of course it was the jaw bone ~~that lay at the bottom~~
~~of the bed~~. That he felt at the bottom of the bed. Archer would
Archer's jaw was & Archer's jaw
know how old the bone was. ~~The~~ ~~It was full of teeth~~. ~~But~~
ed
The blind was thin yellow; ~~like a~~ curv~~ing~~ cut, for the
nursery window was open. It curved fuller, & then ~~just~~
was sucked in
~~drew back slightly; just as the hush hideous~~
~~came from the sea — that was the wave breaking -hissed~~, &
At the same time the sea made that dull noise; so then ~~that~~
the water was drawn back; then it made the dull noise again.
filled with more sounded further
Now the blind was a ~~brighter~~ yellow; & the dull noise ~~was~~
~~away~~ ~~fainter~~. On the chest of drawers Jacob could ~~see the~~ just see
with all its teeth in it
the big flowers in the white jar— for it might be the
horrid jaw bone. ~~But~~ Oh no, that was hard at
that
the bottom of ~~the hard~~ bed. The little trailing noise ~~of the~~
made as it was drawn along the floor
again
knob on the blind cord ~~again~~ made him open his eyes. The
~~large~~ purple petals were falling from the flower on the
missed the chest of drawers - it fell
chest-of-drawers. One ~~fell down, — down - miss~~ fell down- down

x II

~~He saw the~~

~~several things~~ he saw ~~the edge of the chest of drawers, a corner~~ a line; & following it up, came to a bulging white shape, never seen by day; & following that up, came to purple things; Oh these were the ~~anemone~~ flowers that mother picked; the ~~petals were falling~~; one purple thing floated out & ~~missed~~ missed the chest of drawers fell down down —

.II.

M^rs. Flanders—dear Betty Flanders, poor ~~Betty~~ - ~~still~~ ~~Elizabeth~~ Betty - ~~Betty~~ ~~Betty is sti~~ she's very attractive still - odd she don't marry - these little boys might be a hindrance. ~~perhaps~~ No, I don't think thats it. I think she's one of those women — Elizabeth Flanders, ~~mother of Archer, Jacob, & John~~, of whom this ~~was said, was~~ & much more than this was said, was, of course, a widow in her prime. And Betty's prime was between the ages of forty & fifty, for though youth had been the season of grace, ~~he middle-age~~ she needed ~~ripeness~~ maturity to ripen the gifts she carried ~~in~~ with ~~her, unripened,~~ her through the ~~first~~ mute years of girlishness. Years & sorrow & between them; the death of Seabrooke her husband; ~~the birth~~ care of three boys; poverty; ~~then a~~ a house on the outskirts of Scarborough; | the attentions of Captain Bingham; all ripened Betty Flanders; her figure ~~was no longer good~~ enlarged; her face ~~was~~ with jollity; ~~sentiment came freely to her eyes; &~~ & flooded her eyes ~~upon the least provocation with the dews of sentiment. sometimes twenty times a day~~ for no reason that any one else could ~~see with the dews of sentiment;~~ see perhaps a dozen times a day.

[margin: poor Eliots ~~death,~~ downfall; & possible demise tinged her where was he? — what was he? ..]

True, there's no harm in crying for one's husband. & the tombstone — though plain— ~~certainly~~ was a solid piece of work, & ~~there~~ on ~~spring~~ summer days when ~~people saw~~ the widow ~~with~~ brought her boys, ~~no one could it was a help~~ to stand there feel~~ing~~ kind~~ly~~ to~~wards~~ her — Seabrooke lay six foot beneath; dead these twenty years; & sealed in three

[margin: right to make the]

shells, ~~presumably~~, the crevices ~~stuffed~~ filled with lead, so that had grass & earth & wood been glass, doubtless his very face ~~could have~~ lay before one.__ the face of a young man, ~~hale~~ whiskered, ~~taken accidentally~~ shapely, but if he looked in death what he looked in life, too quiet a face for / the face of a man of business. ~~S But M.D~~: "Merchant, of this city" the tombstone said; but why Betty Flanders had chosen so to call him, when, as many still remembered, he had only sat in an office for three months, & before that time had practised medicine, & trod the stage, & read many ~~Greek~~ books, & some said been in the East— well, she had to call him something. An example for the boys.

Had he, then, been nothing? It is the custom in ~~death~~ to close the eyes, ~~& it~~ as it is ~~through~~ in the eyes than we perceive ~~whatever it may be in men that dist stamps them - themselves makes them something, character or the something~~ whatever it is that makes men something, ~~we could no~~ An unanswerable question, now that his eyes were closed. Indeed, had Betty been given to thinking, she would have made out something dreadful in the ~~stages of t~~ process that took him from her; ~~day by day;~~ until visiting the tomb she herself At first, part of herself; now one of a company,- ~~the dead~~. ~~so he had left her, in~~ he had merged into the grass, the sloping hillside, the thousand white stones, slanting & upright, the decayed wreaths, the crosses of green tin the/ narrow yellow paths, & the laburnum that drooped in April over the ~~wall~~. churchyard wall. Seabrooke was now all that; & when with her skirt hitched up, ~~she carried meal~~ feeding the chickens she heard the bell for service or funeral, that was Seabrooke's voice. The rooster had been known to fly on to her shoulder & peck her neck, so that now she carried a stick, or took one of the children with her.

"Wont you use my knife mother?" said Archer Sounding at the same moment as the bell, ~~she~~ her son's voice — it would be impossible to say exactly what Betty Flanders felt ~~on that moment~~ at. ~~as she heard him~~.

a <u>sort</u> of relief perhaps; ~~that there was~~ "I'm younger than I thought,'- & sorrow, & pride ~~too~~.

"What a big knife for a small boy like you!" She took it, to please him

Then the rooster flew out of the hen house, & shouting to Jacob to shut the door into the kitchen garden, M[rs.] Flanders ~~did whatever she had meant to do with the meal.~~ set her meal down & clucked for the hens, went bustling about the orchard, was seen from ~~far off by~~. over the way by M[rs.] Cranch, who, ~~was~~ beating her mat over the gate, ~~was~~ held it one moment while she watched — & ~~reflect~~ thought

to herself

that ~~that~~ M[rs.] Flanders was ~~is~~ in ~~her~~ the orchard with the chickens.

~~&~~ For there were the Cranches, the Woolmans, the Beans, & the Garfits; ~~in~~ in ~~M[r]~~ Woolman's house ~~the a~~ a white mappie stuffed; in the Garfits an otter, in the Beans ~~w~~ a ~~carved~~ piece of carved ivory; & among them were two immensely old men, ~~a~~ one idiot girl; ~~& the post office was run by them, & the groceries-in-shop~~ & a ~~nu~~ number of children all able to play in the road;

strangely enough,

~~The post~~ though ~~baby in arms~~ ~~a baby in arms was seen~~ ~~it was~~ babies in arms ~~comparatively seldom that anyone saw a baby in arms.~~ were almost unknown.

"There's Captain Bingham" said M[rs.] Garfit one ~~week~~ Tuesday

"There's Captain Bingham" said M[rs.] Woolman one Thursday.

"There's Captain Bingham" said ~~Mr.~~ George Bean coming in ~~from his garden~~ with lettuces for for a "Captain Bingham —" ~~&~~ but old George mumbled his words ~~so that you could hardly hear them;~~ being ~~well over ninety~~; & what he thought was suspended by a trail of sound which hung about him ~~but after~~ he had spoken like the smoke ~~round~~ on an engine;

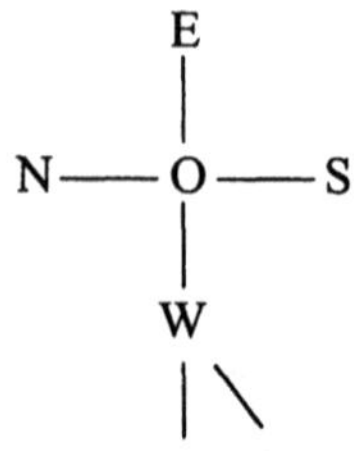

```
      E
      |
N-----O-----S
      |
      W
      | \
```

He had fought in the Crimea, & remembered Lord Cardigan.
M[rs.] Flanders could be seen in her orchard because the orchard was
a piece of Dodds Hill enclosed; & ~~from~~ Dodds Hill~~,~~ dominated
the village; ~~if a small hill & a small village that word~~
~~can be used of such a small hill & such a small village.~~
& though it was
~~if such a word of a~~ small hill & a small village ~~can be allowed.~~
~~an imp~~ no word can exaggerate the importance of Dodds Hill,
~~since so man the~~ It was the Earth; the ~~thing~~ world against the
sky; the horizon of how many glances can best be computed
the same for
by those who have lived in / village ~~of~~ eighty years & more.
The progress of the sun was measured by it; & the tint of the sky
laid to be
~~judged~~
~~matched laid~~ against it./ judged/~~H~~ Opening her orchard gate
Mrs. Flanders ~~would~~ would often walk ~~up~~ to the top of Dodd's
Hill holding John by the hand; Archer & Jacob ran in front, or
lagged behind. ~~They seldom kept pace with her; but~~
but they were always in the fortress before she came there,
& even shouting out what ships were to be seen in the bay.
For there was a magnificent view — moors behind, sea in
front, & the whole of Scarborough/ from the gas works, ~~to~~
~~lay exposed~~
laid out like a puzzle
at one extremity to the market gardens at the other. ~~open to view,~~
M[rs.] Flanders, who was growing stout, would sit down in
the fortress, & ~~wait, patiently, or~~ look round her. The
entire
~~whole~~ gamut of the views changes should have been known to
her: ~~the~~ winter aspect, spring, summer & autumn; ~~the~~
how storms came up from the sea; how ~~shadows~~ the moors
~~first~~ darkened & lightened as clouds went over; she should
have noted the pink spot where the villas were built; & the
~~how a plain green field was so~~ criss cross of lines cut
upon ~~a field by the~~ green fields by allotment holders -
Or, if details like these escaped her she might have let her
fancy play upon the gold tint of the sea at sunset.
lapping in coins of gold upon the shingle~~; whence all~~
~~the little pleasure boats shoved off~~ - Little pleasure
boats shoved off into it; the black arm of the pier
hoarded it up; the whole city was pink & gold,
~~&~~ resonant; strident; banjoes strummed; the

parade smelt of tar; goats suddenly cantered their carriages through
crowds; it was observed how well the Corporation laid out the
flower beds; sometimes a straw hat was blown away;
~~newspapers on win windy March afternoons swept swept the~~
~~gritty pavements~~; tulips burnt in the sun; triangular
hoardings were wheeled along by men in white coats;
~~the sunflowers the~~ & oh the smell of the whale in
spirits of wine! For it is well worth while to visit the
Aquarium. ~~A~~ a kind of well~~;~~ ~~&~~ sunk beneath our feet-
a diving bell, rather, in which we descend to mid-Atlantic — &
there ~~del~~ behold what nature does when ~~we are not~~
~~looking~~. ~~She is the strangest~~ left to herself. She is
nothing like so virtuous as we suppose. She made the
daisy — true, but kept the octopus to herself — a thought
she fondles in secret. The sea anemones may pass;
~~But the shark — the~~ but scarcely the shark. The
~~yellow blinds~~ sallow blinds seem to screen her indecencies;
then there's the ~~skeel~~ skeleton of a whale; & ~~lying back~~
sitting in bamboo chairs under palm trees we knock
ashes into ~~cigarette~~ trays, & ~~feel~~ smell ~~something~~
what appears to be the essence of sallow blinds.

fellows in bath chairs

Number of sponge bag trousers were to be seen; & ~~b~~ purple
bonnets fringing ~~old~~ in soft pink. unmarked obsolete faces on
~~women's the faces of elderly women who chose b~~onnets —
~~did they do more ? Knew shade from sun, & did they do more?~~
& ~~what was digestible~~. A monster shark had been caught.
~~The~~ One side of the triangular hoarding said so in red, blue
& yellow letters, each sentence ending with three notes of exclamation.
~~in one or other of those colours.~~ So that was a reason for
going down into the aquarium, ~~in~~ where the yellow blinds,
the stale smell, of spirits of wine & sea salt, ~~&~~ the bamboo
chairs, the tables with ~~cigarette~~ ash trays, the revolving
fish, the attendant ~~rolling chocolates~~, knitting behind
~~a~~ six or seven chocolate boxes, (often she was quite alone for

hours at a time

with the ~~octopus opposite)~~ octopus)- ~~fish, & must have the~~ known
the ~~octopus the~~ all ~~seemed signified that monster shark,~~

remained in the mind as part of the monster shark; he himself being
receptacle
only a flabby yellow ~~can of~~ empty ~~receptacle~~ in a tank.
Nobody had ever been overcome by the Aquarium; but the faces
chilled
of those emerging quickly lost their dim ~~quiet~~ expression when they
perceived that it was only by standing in a queue that one
could be admitted to the pier. Once through the turnstiles, every one
~~ran~~ walked for a yard or two with extreme rapidity; some
flagged at this stall, others at that; but it was the band that
drew them all to it finally — even the fishermen, on the lower
its
pier, ~~staking~~ taking up their pitch within / range. But why,
though speaking of the late nineties, use the past tense, since one is
speaking of a pier? At this moment, the band plays; the deck
chairs are drawn out; no 9 goes up on the board; it is a
waltz; ~~all~~ the young women dream; the young men too;
the pale girls — the old widow lady — the three Jews at the
same boarding house — the dandy — the major the
tired of looking at them,
[?] in the chair gets up
horse dealer —;& the ~~intellectual looking~~ young man / looks over
the ~~par~~ parapet, ~~& sees the green water beneath, &~~
into the ~~water & thinks~~ green water below. What does he
think about? Well, something quite sentimental. ~~Still~~
~~its all very pleasant by way of a change.~~
That there was a time when none of this had any existence ~~at all~~.
can be proved if, ~~shutting your~~ & fixing your eyes upon —
~~take~~ [~~?~~] t that ~~skirt~~ ladies skirt ~~for years~~ will do.
Look intently. Ah, it changes: ~~amplifies~~ drapes her ankles;
red -
then amplifies ; now its burnished ~~silk~~ ~~How lovely~~ —
stretched on a crinoline; how I wish I could see her face!
a tiny foot - black shoe . white stockings - emerges;
Still sitting there? Yes - ~~its~~ she's still on the pier—
the
~~pi~~ silk now is sprigged with roses, & ~~the stockings silk~~
but ~~I~~ somehow —I no longer see ~~the plank~~. so clearly-
They're playing a minuet for strings — & now thats over—
oh no, the heavy chariot may swing along the
turnpike road, but there's no pier for it to stop at.
Let's to the museum. ~~Roun~~ Cannon balls, arrow heads,
Roman glass & a forceps.

– The Reverend Jasper Pendleton dug them up at his own expense early in the forties from Dodd's Hill - see the little ticket with the faded writing on it.

Yet Mrs. Flanders thought of none of this, as she sat ~~in the~~
in the [spring?]
~~fort~~ on Dodds hill, ~~in the summer evening.~~ ~~&~~ John kept
grass or dead leaves
running up to her & slapping down into her lap ~~something he~~
~~had picked. "Tea" he called them~~ ~~the grass and leaves;~~
which he called 'tea'; & these she saw; for she arranged them
methodically; ~~thinking, as she did so, of~~ ~~&~~ as she did so thought
of
~~how Jacob different~~ her sons ~~were~~ - how she wished she could
buy Mr. Grays field - how the church clock was certainly slow-
how ~~the~~ it ~~was getting tim~~ James Garfit was getting too
old to ring the bells - how —
Thats an
"~~An~~ orchid, Johnny, ~~she said~~ Look at the spots on the
~~Where are t~~
leaves. ~~Go and find~~ ~~the others~~. ~~Tell them I'm going home.~~"
Come along
~~She got up, & We're~~ We must go home. ~~And~~ Ar—cher!-
Ja—cob!"
"Ar—cher! Ja—cob!" Johnny called after her & ~~he~~ as
he called he strewed round him ~~all~~ the leaves & grass he had picked-
~~almost~~ as if he were sowing seed.

'Captain Bingham's here', said Alice as they came back into the house.

big arm chair in the
He sat in the ~~armchair, reading a book~~ drawing room,
reading; & Betty Flanders took the boys up to bed &
gave John his bath before she came down; ~~& she~~
opened the drawing room door quietly; & Captain Bingham
took off his spectacles put them in their case, & said
Good evening Mrs. Flanders — all very sensibly. though

jumped up from behind the mound, where they had been crouching with the intention of springing upon their mother unexpectedly; & they
all
~~walk home~~ began . to walk ~~home.~~ ~~slowly home. Circle round~~ ~~Mrs.~~ slowly home.

"Who is that?" said Mrs. Flanders.

looking below.
"Thats old man in the road?" said Archer, ~~following~~

"It's not an old man," said Mrs. Flanders - ~~thats~~ He's- no, he's not, ~~" she said.~~ "I thought it was Captain Bingham
"children"
but its Mr. Floyd!" she said. "Come; ~~children~~; ~~we musn't~~
bother
"Oh / Mr. Floyd!" said Jacob swishing at a thistle's head, for he knew already that Mr. Floyd was going to teach them Latin, ~~& so he did, being the son of the~~ as indeed he did for

in his spare time, out of kindness,

~~in his~~——goodness,
three years, ~~being as a out as a great~~ kindness, for there was no ~~other educated~~ gentleman in the neighbourhood who could
elder
have ~~done~~ done such a thing, & the / boys were getting beyond her, ~~&~~ must be got ready for school, & it was more than most clergymen would have done, ~~after~~ coming round after tea, or having them in his own room — as he could fit it in- ~~for he~~ the parish was a very large one, & Mr. Floyd like his father before him, visited cottages miles away on the moors— & like old ~~Mr.~~ Floyd he was a scholar, ~~though not so much interested in antiquities. He was a~~
a
~~fond of his books.~~ ~~botanist.~~ Which made it so unlikely — she had never dreamt it— ought she to have guessed? But, let alone being a scholar, he was so much younger; ~~his~~ she knew his mother ~~;~~ old Mrs. Floyd, — ~~Ten years younger.~~ She had tea there. And it
very
was that / evening when she came back, that she found ~~In~~ the note in the hall, & took it into the kitchen with her ~~never dreaming, &~~ to give Rebecca the fish, thinking it was ~~nothing at all~~ — something about the boys.

Oh yes — no, no, — I left it - -

~~for~~ she ~~saw~~ was reading —

~~Fry the fish~~ Enough for fish cakes ~~for~~

tomorrow — Certainly ; — Perhaps Captain Bingham, Rebecca

so She went into the garden ~~with it~~, & read it through,

~~walking once only, since she could not keep back her tears~~.
carrying Mr. Floyd's letter, & under the ~~laburnum~~ walnut tree she
read it through. But once only. ~~Respect had deepened into love,~~ &
He wished indeed to marry her; ~~since~~ Up & down went her breast, -
she leant one hand on the bark of the walnut tree to steady
herself. Seabrooke came so vividly before her. ~~Then~~ Her tears fell.
She ~~nodde~~ shook her head very slightly, & raised the letter as if to
read it again, & then three geese half ~~flew~~ shuffled, half~~ran~~ unning, across the
lawn, & Johnny came trotting behind, brandishing a stick. ~~She~~
M~~rs.~~ Floyd was really angry.
"How many times have I told you" — she cried,
& seized him, & snatched the stick away from him;
"But they'd ~~they~~ escaped! — he cried, struggling to get free.
"You're a very naughty boy! if I've told you once, I've
told you a thousand times. I won't have you chasing the
geese" she said, & picking up Mr. Floyd's letter, & holding
Johnny fast, she herded the geese back to the orchard;
~~s~~ "How could I think of marriage!" she thought to herself
almost bitterly as she fastened the latch with a piece of wire.
It was, probably, that the idea of copulation had now become
infinitely remote from her. ~~She did not use th~~ She did not
use ~~that~~ the word; & yet as she sat darning the boys clothes
that night it annoyed her ~~that~~ to find that it was so.

She had always disliked redhead

"And ~~I've always disliked~~ do red ~~hair in men" she said,~~
headed men" she said; ~~She~~ Pushed ing away her work basket. she
fetched paper & ink. Already ~~that~~ she showed signs
of ~~the~~ ~~hapzh~~ her haphazard ways, ~~that became later so marked.~~
~~She could not concentrate;~~ & could not concentrate her mind
upon her letter, for she had to write to Mrs. Thompson too —
& then there were papers to be filled up — ~~she would have asked~~
~~Mr. Floyd to help her~~ — ~~dear, dear~~ — she sighed for weariness,
& read Mr. Floyd's letter again, & her breast moved up & down
~~again~~ when she came to the ~~w~~ sentence about marriage, but not
so fast this time, for she saw Johnny chasing the geese again,
& knew that it was ~~quite~~ impossible, ~~yet she was happy too~~,
~~& looked very~~ for her to marry anyone; let alone M~~r.~~ Floyd,
who was so much younger than she was — but what a
good fellow, & a scholar too. "Dear Mr. Floyd . . . .
Did I forget about the cheese? — she wondered, laying down her pen; taking it up she wrote ~~D I have~~ Your letter is . . . on

The letter that ~~Mr.~~ Floyd / found on his hall table ~~received~~ next day did not begin like that, but it was such in inconsequent, motherly, regretful ~~le~~ respectful letter that he kept it for many years, long after his marriage with Miss Wimbush of Andover; long after ~~his~~ he had left the village. For he asked for a parish in Sheffield, which was given him, &, sending for Archer & Jacob & John to say good bye, he told them to choose whatever they liked in the study, as a present, to remember him by. Archer chose a paper knife, because he did not like to choose anything too good; Jacob chose the works of Byron in one volume; & John, who was still too young to make a proper choice ~~w~~ chose Mr. Floyd's cat, ~~Topaz~~, which ~~was~~ his brothers thought an absurd choice, but Mr. Floyd upheld him. Then Mr. Floyd spoke about the public school to which Archer & Jacob were now going, & next day he went, - first to Sheffield then to Hackney ~~where he met Miss Wimbush & married her~~ ~~& finally,~~ then to Maresfield House, of which he became Principal, & ~~finally~~ ~~at this moment he lives at Hampstead,~~ finally, having edited a ~~theologi~~ series of theological biographies, he retired to Hampstead with his wife & daughter, & is often to be seen feeding the ducks on Leg of Mutton pond. As for Mrs. Flanders letter - when he looked for it the other day he could not find it but he never altogether lost touch with her. - Meeting Jacob in the Strand lately, ~~he~~ recognized him at once. must be ~~Thats [?] Mr. Floyd~~

"~~Dear me,~~ said Mrs. Flanders, ~~in the~~ when she read in the Scarborough & Harrogate Courier that the Rev. Andrew Floyd lately of ~~had been~~ of St Peters Hackney had been made Principal of Maresfield House. "That must be our Mr. Floyd - for after he ~~left~~ left Sheffield, I remember he went to Hackney - & now he's been made Principal of Maresfield House- " A slight gloom fell upon the breakfast table as she spoke, as if she had read ~~all~~ the news of his death. What a life to be sure! Sheffield, Hackney, Maresfield House! How meagre! compared, that is, with what was going on at the moment. For it was Monday, the 25th of April - the postman was still talking to Rebecca in the kitchen - lilacs & laburnums - all those things were of course in bloom, ~~in~~ but what everyone at the breakfast table felt was that ~~w~~ they were alive; & poor M~~r.~~ Floyd, ~~was only in the papers.~~ [going on doing things ~~in the papers~~ like that] It was the last day of the Easter holidays.

Mrs. Flanders & Jacob both looked at Topaz, ~~Mr. Floyd's cat; only he was the — yellow reddish cat now a very old cat, a~~ [kitten] asleep by the fender - for Mr. Floyd's kitten was now a very old, very large ~~cat, reddish~~ cat, still reddish yellow but a little mangy on the head so that Mrs. Flanders often began a sentence ~~said something about~~ 'poor Topaz' which meant that he would have to be killed. "Poor ~~old~~ Topaz" she said, getting up from the table, & ~~she~~ he stretched himself out, & she rubbed him, & smiled as she did so, thinking how she had had him gelded, & how she did not like red headed men - both thoughts coming on top of each other and making her smile, though she had not used the word 'gelded' ~~or consciously connected the two the idea, in her mind~~, - indeed she never used word, when she thought indecent thoughts. Smiling she went into the kitchen; Jacob smiled. Only last week, as they were finish~~ing~~[ed serving] ~~the t~~ potatoes he had ~~been sure~~ [felt certain] that Mr. Floyd ~~to~~ had ~~been in love~~ proposed to his mother.

"You won't go far this afternoon Jacob" said his mother, popping her head in at the door, "for the Captain's coming, & I want you to see him - . It was the last day of the Easter holidays.

Yet no one had ever thought that Captain Bingham ~~was going to~~ [wanted to] marry Mrs. ~~Flan~~ Flanders.

"There's Captain Bingham" said Mrs. Garfit.

"There's Captain Bingham, said Daisy Cranch, and old George Bean had ~~said~~ only stopped saying it a twelvemonth back, when he died, in his chair, of bronchitis, all in a moment~~.~~ The Captain was lame ~~missed~~ & wanted two fingers on the left hand: —— ~~if there were~~ for he ~~had~~ served his country; ~~but whether that was the~~ [his ~~lameness~~] ~~reason - whether it wasn't it was~~ - but ~~how were there sufficient reasons for~~ why should that make one certain that he did not wish to marry Mrs. Flanders?

Possibly this was one of those cases - how to account for it otherwise we know not - when the truth, for it was

the truth, is the truth; ~~so that no one~~ & every one knows it, ~~& as they know that~~ & the ~~inhabitants of the~~ Mrs. Mr. Cranch, Mrs. Woolman, Miss Garfit & George Bean would have been indignant if any stranger, seeing ~~&~~ Captain Bingham ~~it~~ waiting ~~it~~ for Rebecca to open the door had so much as wondered what the old gentleman came so often ~~for~~. to Mount Pleasant for.
~~Also~~, Captain Bingham / also was married.
If Betty Flanders was out when he came, Rebecca would bring him a tumbler of water & the newspaper, if it were summer, & he would rest ~~his lame leg, in by~~ in the arm chair, stretching his lame leg ~~in front of him~~. Straight ~~out~~ out. For he was a married man.

in front of him

~~There is no doubt that circumstances~~ His wife's name, before her marriage, had been Coppard; & the ~~fount~~ drinking fountain where West Street joins Broad Street is the gift of James Coppard; & it was James Coppard who was Mayor at the time of Queen Victoria's Jubilee & ~~there is the name of~~ Coppard is painted upon the ~~carts which~~ watering carts, & over shop windows & ~~on~~ upon the zinc blinds of solicitors.consulting rooms.
In spite of all this, ~~Jane~~ Ellen Coppard might have been a fresh chatterbox; mellowing into ~~buxom~~ motherhood; instead ~~of which~~, ~~she~~ ~~took~~ taking her airings in a bath chair, ~~was childless~~, having no children. & observ~~ed~~ing implicitly ~~those~~ the boundary lines which her position as the daughter of James Coppard had chalked in front of many doors, places of entertainment, & even right across the Esplanade. ~~For many years she had not been inside the aquarium, &~~ She was debarred from the aquarium; ~~& one of the piers was also prohibited~~.
& when the men came by with the posters she knew that she would never see Pierrots or Zincalis or Miss ~~Esther~~ Daisy Budd.
She knew many things & thus ~~& thus perhaps~~ ~~& was so completely barricaded by chair. lines of all kinds that~~ ~~for~~ so that perhaps we do wrong to pity her. Even her malady serving to support her, & making her quite certain ~~of many~~ when many points ~~which~~ her ~~for most people seem present two faces. remain~~ have doubtful to the end. which for most people ~~present two faces~~. remain doubtful to the end. Poor woman! Yes, turn it as we may, ~~the~~ certainty is damnable. To know things impossible. To

280
2
5,600

believe what we are told intolerable. And Ellen Coppard, ~~found~~ with her
bath chair in the sun, was ~~the most~~ ~~one of those prisoners whom we~~
~~see in such numbers~~ a prisoner - a prisoner ~~to~~ of civilization -
~~the church~~ all the bars of ~~her~~ cage falling across the esplanade
upon sunny days; when the ~~sun stood behin~~d church, prison,
drapery stores, swimming bath, & hospital, striped the ground
with shadow. ~~A mel melancholy topic! - Chiefly for this~~
~~reason~~.

"Move me" she would say to Mr. Dickens, her bath chairman.
or again, "That'll do, thank you Mr. Dickens." At the first
~~sum~~ command he would seek the sun; at the second, he would
stay the chair there, in the bright strip.

An old inhabitant himself he had much in common with
Mrs. Bingham. If his chair was not exactly on a level with her
hood, he was allowed to sit by her. She would ~~tell him~~
~~he might smoke~~ . ask him questions. - who people were,
~~what~~ who ~~had married~~ - whether ~~business were doing — well~~.
~~Then, how~~ fathers were being succeeded by sons - then
about the season - & had Mrs. Dickens tried - whatever it might be.
Oh the thin flaky conversation! Words issuing from the
purplin lips as if they were coins; Henry Dickens being
as much prisoner as Mrs. Bingham; & equally parched & prim; -
save that he played billiards at the Three Shells & never washed
himself.- ~~indeed, how could he?~~ -; ~~not otherwise, & had~~
as indeed in his his cottage there was scarce room.
She closed her eyes. M~~r.~~ Dickens would then take a turn. The
feelings of a man had not altogether deserted this ~~wizened light~~
dry powdery looking old gentleman, though as you saw him
coming towards you, you noticed how one knobbed black boot
swung round tremulously ~~to pr~~ in front of another; & ~~there~~ his were
shadow~~s~~ beneath his waistcoat, ~~& trousers~~, & how he ~~had the~~
leant forward unsteadily like an old horse, who ~~has~~
finds himself ~~suddenly~~ out of the shafts. drawing no cart.
~~Mr. Ah~~, But as Mr. Dickens ~~smoked, he~~ ~~drew~~ sucked in the smoke -
puffed it out again, the feelings of a man ~~made him~~
~~showed~~ were in his eye - he was thinking how Captain Barfoot
was now on his way to Mount Pleasant, & how
Captain Barfoot was his master - for at home, in the

55
42
—
13

little sitting room, with the canary in the window, & the girls at the sewing machine, & ~~the~~ M$^{rs.}$ Dickens huddled up with the rheumatics, at home where ~~he was not always treated with respect~~ he was in the way - ~~then~~ the thought of being in the employ of Captain Barfoot ~~was grateful to him.~~ supported him. ~~M$^{rs.}$ Barfoot~~

He liked to think that while he chatted with M$^{rs.}$ Barfoot in the ~~front~~, ~~Ca~~ the Captain was on his way to M$^{rs.}$ Flanders. Poor M$^{rs.}$ Barfoot! Turning, he saw ~~her~~ that she was in conversation with M$^{rs.}$ Rogers; turning again he saw that M$^{rs.}$ Rogers had moved on; so he came back to the bathchair, & M$^{rs.}$ Barfoot ~~told him~~ asked him the time, & ~~as~~ he told her the time. ~~he~~ as if he knew a great deal more about everything than she did; ~~& pitied her. Which~~ But M$^{rs.}$ Barfoot knew ~~that Captain Barfoot was with M$^{rs.}$ Flanders.~~ ~~where~~ that Captain Barfoot was ~~;~~- with ~~this thought that it was a matter of indifference to her~~.

Mrs. Flanders.

Indeed he was well on the way there, having left the tram, & seeing Dodds Hill to the south east, green against a blue sky suffused with dust colour on the horizon. He was marching up the hill ~~to her~~ In spite of his lameness, ~~he~~ there was something military in his ~~progress~~, approach. ~~His~~ M$^{rs.}$ Jarvis, as she came out of the rectory, saw him coming, & her newfoundland dog, Nero, slowly swept his tail from side to side.

"Oh Captain Barfoot!" M$^{rs.}$ Jarvis exclaimed;

"Good day M$^{rs.}$ Jarvis" said the Captain.

They walked on together, & when they reached M$^{rs.}$ Flander's gate ~~he~~ Captain Barfoot took off his ~~his~~ straw hat & said

"~~I will bid you~~ good day to you M$^{rs.}$ Jarvis." ~~& turned~~

M$^{rs.}$ Jarvis walked on alone. She was going on to the moor. ~~to give her big dog exercise~~. Had she again been pacing her garden ~~late at~~ ~~after dinner~~ late at night? Had she again tapped on the study window & said "There's such a lovely moon Evan." Had Evan ~~replied~~ "looked up, & then looked down again at the ~~paper~~ ~~under~~ letter he was writing? M$^{rs.}$ Jarvis walked on the moor when she was unhappy;

She ~~went as far as a certain saucer-shaped hollow~~.
going as far as a certain saucer-shaped hollow, there sitting down, &
reading the ~~works of~~ Shelley, or Stephen Phillips, or Canon Baldwin:
but not for long. She was not as yet very unhappy; & seeing
would
that she was forty five, perhaps she ~~would~~ never / be very unhappy.
~~Yet how dangerous for a clergyman's wife to walk upon the moors!~~
But There is no need to say what risks a clergyman's wife runs when
sallow,
she walks upon the moors~~. Her~~ Short, dark, upright, with brown
dressed in a
kindling, eyes, ~~that wearing a~~ black cloak, ~~& a~~ with a feather in her
hat, M^rs. Jarvis, though she had two children, was the sort of
woman to lose her faith, or what is perhaps worse, ~~to be~~ not
to lose her faith, ~~but~~ not to leave her husband, not to read
any book through, & yet to go on walking alone, looking at
the moon, & feeling, as she lay on the short turf high above
Scarborough, that ~~there is a spirit of the universe—that~~
~~a universal spirit~~. ~~She had lent Jacob Flanders books.~~
~~There is something in the world~~ —. ~~She lent Jacob Flanders books~~.
Yes, Yes, When the lark soars above my head, when the
~~they~~ sheep, moving a step or two onward, crop the turf, & at
set
the same time, ~~set~~ their bells tinkling; when the breeze
~~comes comes~~ first blows, then dies down, when the ships in
down below seem ~~not~~ t to ~~come~~ cross each other & pass
on as if ~~invisibly moved.~~ drawn by a ~~hand, when, if~~
an invisible hand, when there are distant concussions in the
air, & sounds of phantom horsemen, when at my feet the
rocks
cowslip ~~swings~~ ~~to & fro~~ under the attack of a bee then,
~~of course~~ when the horizon swims blue ; green, emotional
then M^rs. Jarvis heaving a deep sigh ~~feels that she if~~
thinks ~~someone could give it~~ "if only someone could give it to me!"
but she does not know what ~~there~~ she wants to be given, or who
her
could give it./ Only she is discontented. For she cannot go on
feeling this for long.

If I could share it with someone!.

"Mrs. Flanders stepped out only five minutes ago" said Rebecca.
Captain ~~Bar~~ Barfoot sat him down in the arm chair to wait.
Resting his elbows on the arms, clasping his hands. The lame leg
with the rubbers ferrule
stretched straight out, the ~~oak~~ stick / laid beside it He looked -
there is only one word to use of him, & that is oak. And the
truth of that depends upon knowing that "quercus" is the Latin
for an oak tree; & somehow thinking at one blow of yellow, curled,
crinkled, leaves, bark, acorns - ~~things that~~ hardness; ~~&~~— Set your
oak tree on top of a heath; it is september; the sky is blue windy
curled
between the ~~crisp~~ leaves;— the sand gully at the roots.
Captain Barfoot did nothing. He merely waited for Mrs.
Flanders. Nothing was more clear than that he did not read.
again & again
But did he think? Probably the same thoughts. Were they
'nice' thoughts? What is clear enough is that he was a man
with a temper. Tenacious. Faithful. Women would have felt
Here is law - here is order - ~~here~~, therefore we must ~~sh~~ cherish this
man. He is on the Bridge at night. That at least is what
Mrs. Flanders felt; though as for running on into visions of
shipwreck & destruction, in which all the women come
running from the cabin, & ~~som~~ there is the Captain
matched by the storm - vanquished by it & by none other —
yet ~~no~~ I have a soul, & after all, the man's damned
& the cause of it
stupidity ~~is the~~ has run ~~out~~ us into this - still ~~I own~~ he
stands very firmly.& so forth - of course she thought none
of this:~~&~~

"~~I told~~ Oh!" said Mrs. Flanders, opening the door.
I hope Rebecca - I hope Jacob - I had to run after
Barkers man.

She was a little out of breath, yet not ~~in~~ at all
upset, & she put down her paper parcel & said,
"I' do so want to hear what Mrs. Rickets said,' &
yet she flung the window open & straightened
a cover & picked up a book & put it on the table,
as if she were very fond of the Captain, & a great many
years younger than he was. Indeed, in her blue apron, she
did not look more than 35. He was over 50.

all this
~~Her~~? She made arrangements about tea - & ~~during this~~ time
the Captain moved his head as she walked about, & made sounds, -
though
at his ease too actually saying nothing - for after twenty years –
at length
"Well, he said ~~suddenly~~, I've heard from ~~Polegate."~~ ~~my~~ Mr.
Polegate."
he could advise nothing better than to
He had heard from Mr. Polegate that ~~if a boy is good at his books~~ you
send a boy
~~had better send him~~ to Cambridge University.
"Mr. Floyd was at Cambridge; no, at Oxford - well at one or the
other." said Mrs. Flanders.
put her cup down opened or
As she said this she la~~y back~~ in her chair & ~~opened~~ her eyes - for
that was the effect of looking out of the window
~~her mind~~ she seemed to consider something; & the green light from
the ~~leaves~~ garden was reflected in her eyes.

"Archer is doing very well" she said

"I will l~~eave you~~ the letter to show Jacob," said ~~the~~ Captain
Barfoot, putting it ~~on the table.~~ back in its envelope.

cricket begins
"Johnny - "she began, but interrupted herself, ~~Its~~ the
this week
Cricket ~~beginning~~ of course

is
"There ~~was~~ that matter ~~about the power pump~~
~~about the pump. I enquired~~ about the water - said Captain
Barfoot –

But Mrs. Flanders
"~~Are~~ you going to stand for the Council Captain she
suddenly looking at Captain Barfoot with great interest
asked inconsequently, with a sudden rush of interest in her eyes

The Captain stirred his tea.

x III x x x x

The third class railway carriage contained two people, an elderly lady with grey hair, & a young man ~~between~~ of about eighteen or ~~n~~ twenty. ~~Open~~ Touching the spring of her dispatch box, the lady seemed to ~~inspect the~~ search for ~~a~~ something, though as a matter of fact she was only deciding ~~which of her possessi.~~ whether her French dictionary or her scent bottle would serve her best in case of attack by the young man in the corner. If he moved, with her right hand she would throw the ~~w~~ case itself at him, while with her left she would tug the communication cord. ~~Few women travel alone without deciding how m~~ Most women, ~~finding themselves alone in a carriage with a young man, decide all this before they settle down. how they will defend themselves before they settle down to travel~~ when they find themselves alone in a carriage with a man decide ~~all this~~ this point ~~before of defence & attack. before they settle down.~~ ~~find~~ what they will throw at him before they settle down. This lady was neither timid nor foolish.. It is a fact that men are dangerous. A very strange one, when you come to think of it. ~~After~~ She ~~then~~ read half a column of her newspaper &, then, stealthily looked over the edge to decide ~~whether~~ the question of safety ~~by the~~ by the infallible test of appearance. . . . She would like to offer him her paper. But do young men read the Daily Chronicle? She looked to see what he was reading - the Daily Telegraph.

Thus, in three seconds, the whole business was settled; irrevocably: the current of feeling flowed ~~of its own accord~~ - ~~this strange a woman's feeling about a man.~~ a woman's feeling ~~about~~ for a man.

Taking note of his socks trousers & tie - she ~~had~~ reached his face — ~~in particular his mouth, which~~ dwelt on his mouth; the lips were shut; eyes bent down, since he was reading; - all ~~wer~~ firm yet youthful; indifferent, determined - as for knocking one down! She looked out of the window; then came back again; smiling slightly now; for his grave, uncurious expression — now he looked up - past her - seeming so out of place somehow alone with a lady — then fixed his eyes - He had not realized her presence ~~existence~~ she thought. Yet it was none of her fault that this was not a smoking carriage, if that was what he meant;

Thus, it is quite impossible for an elderly woman to describe even the outward appearance of a young man. All that we can gather ~~from her description of Jacob Flanders~~ is that this ~~young~~ man ~~he~~ was ~~is~~ young, large, a gentleman, - rather abstracted. But since, even at her age, she ~~was ca~~ noticed his indifference, ~~there must have been some masculine quality in him which~~ presumably he was in some way or other ~~n~~ nice? handsome? interesting? charming? well built? - One must do the best one can with her report. Anyhow, this was Jacob Flanders. It is no use trying to sum people once & for all ~~up~~ in a phrase. One must follow up hints - for instance, when the train drew in to the station ~~up~~, Mr. Flanders burst open the door, ~~first took~~ put ~~his~~ own and put the ladies dressing case out for her — saying ‘Let me’ very shyly: indeed he was rather clumsy about it. “Who -” said the lady, meeting her son; ~~for the~~ but there being a great crowd on ~~hand~~ the platform, she did not finish her sentence - As this was Cambridge, as she was staying there for the weekend, as she saw nothing but young men ~~the~~ all day long,this sight of her fellow traveller was as completely lost in her mind as the as the crooked pin dropped by a child into a wishing well.

. <u>IV</u> .

They say the sky is the same everywhere. Travellers, the shipwrecked,
~~exi~~ exiles, draw comfort from the thought, & no doubt ~~in~~ if you are of a
mystical tendency, consolation. Even explanation showers down from the
unbroken surface. But above Cambridge - anyhow above the
roof of King's College Chapel - there is a difference. ~~Lo~~ t
Out at sea ~~the~~ a great city will cast a brightness up into the
~~ar.~~ air. Is it fanciful to suppose the sky washed into the
crevices of Kings College ~~Cape~~ Chapel lighter thinner more
Cambridge burn in the sky?
sparkling than the sky elsewhere? Does ~~it burn~~ upwards
Look
~~See~~, as they ~~cross~~ pass into service, how airily the
gowns blow out, as though ~~they~~ nothing dense & corporeal were within
Then - ~~& then~~, ~~&, yet~~ ~~Once within the great cave, hollow~~
authority
~~cave~~. What sculptured faces, what ~~an air of~~ certainty, ~~piety~~, –
there ~~march~~ tramp
although ~~there~~ are great boots / under the gowns. In what
orderly procession they enter; Thick wax candles stand straight;
& rise ~~golden~~
~~what~~ young men in white gowns, while the subservient eagle
bears up for inspection the great white book. ~~Wint~~ ~~Winter~~ &
~~In broad~~ ~~The light, which comes~~. An inclined plane of
light comes accurately through each window. & ~~as these~~
~~windows~~ purple, & yellow even its most diffused positions, while,
where it breaks upon stone, that stone is ~~softly yet~~ ~~distinctly~~
has
painted. Neither snow nor greenery, ~~outside change~~ ~~hav~~ the
heart ~~power over the glass as as old as this~~. ~~influence~~ over old
glass. Winter nor summer, has power over the old glass.
~~Indeed it has shut out a great deal, though~~
Yet, as the sides of the lantern protect the flame so that it
burns steady even in the wildest night - burns steady &
gravely illumines ~~little bits~~ of trees trunks, ~~so that ev~~ ~~for the~~
~~moment even this great forest, where the branches are~~
~~single trees appear distinct~~, so inside the chapel all was
orderly, gravely ~~so~~ sounded the voices; t ~~the organ~~ wisely the
organ replied, as if buttressing the human voice with
the support of the elementals. The white-robed figures
sometimes mounting steps - then descending
moved from side to side. ~~A giant grasshopper will often~~
And
~~come~~, if you stand a light under a tree.- every insect in
the forest ~~seems to know that it is there~~. creeps up to it.

Would you see a haze from out at sea?

controlled by piety,

softly chalked red blue & yell

beetles, grass hoppers, lady-birds; a giant grasshopper - a curious
assembly, since, though they scramble & swing & knock their
heads against the glass they seem to have no purpose - no object -
something senseless inspires them - one gets tired of watching
them, as they amble around the lantern, & blindly knock as if for
th of
admittance - Whats ~~is~~ that? A terrifying volley - pistol
~~shots~~ shots ringing out - spreading through the air? ~~A tree~~ - a
~~tree has fallen~~. merging into each other, dying away-? A tree -
far in the forest - a tree has fallen. ~~Thus,~~ the
~~Melancholy———But the reason why~~ A ~~sort~~ of death -
after that, the wind high in the trees sounds melancholy -
But this service in King's College Chapel - why allow
women to take part in it? Surely if the mind wanders,
upon
it is because ~~seveal~~ several hat shops, & cupboards ~~up &~~ cupboards
of coloured dresses are ~~sprinkled about.~~ ~~Scattered~~ displayed -
may be
so that, though ~~undoubtedly th~~e heads & bodies ~~are~~ devout
enough, one has a sense of individuals - some like blue,
others brown; ~~so~~ some feathers, others pansies & forget me nots -
No one would think of bringing a dog into church. For ~~a~~ though
a dog is all very well on a gravel path, & shows no
disrespect to flowers, the way ~~we~~ he wanders down an aisle,
looking, lifting a paw, & approaching a pillar with a
purpose that makes the ~~th~~ blood run cold with horror –
~~all this~~, ~~if seen by full congregation is so~~ destroys the
service entirely. So do these women - though [upstanding?]
devout, distinguished, & vouched for by the Theology,
Mathematics & Latin & Greek of their respective
yes
husbands - ~~Even~~ Mrs. Plumer ~~does aff affect~~ seems to me
like a dog in church. Heaven knows why it is.

280
 27
—
1960
560
——
7,560

. V .

"Waverley" the villa on the Road to Girton was called, not that
Mr. Plumer admired Scott. [But there are more complete
the
sets of classics in the suburbs of Cambridge than in the whole of
~~Europe put together.~~] ~~They left the name where it was~~. or would
any
have chosen ~~a~~ name at all; but names are useful when you have
to entertain undergraduates; & as they sat waiting for the
fourth undergraduate to appear, ~~the~~ there was talk about names on
gates.

"How tiresome — Mrs. Plumer broke in impulsively -

"Does anybody know Mr. Flanders?"

M~~r.~~ Durrant knew him; & therefore ~~felt~~ ~~it incumbent on him~~
to ~~say. that~~ ~~suggest that~~ blushed slightly & said something
about not waiting, looking at Mr. Plumer. Mr. Plumer got
up & stood in front of the fireplace. Mrs. Plumer laughed
like a straightforward friendly fellow. In short
anything more horrible than the scene, the setting, the
prospect. ~~The~~ & Even the May garden being afflicted with
[intended?] meaningful form of a conversation
chill sterility; ~~& or~~ cannot be imagined. There was the
garden of course. Everyone at the same moment looked at it.
The sun was covered by a passing cloud, ~~&~~ the little leaves
ruffled grey & the sparrows - ~~they merely hopped~~. there were 2 sparrows

"I think -" said Mrs. Plumer, taking advantage of the
at
momentary respite to look her husband - & he not accepting
responsibility for the ~~at~~ act, touched the bell.

There can be no excuse for ~~giving these parties~~. this outrage upon
an hour of human life save the reflection that if ~~there were~~
eon
no Don ever gave a lunch party ~~to undergraduates~~
if Sunday after Sunday passed ~~if you~~ if men went down -
Don ever gave a luncheon party
if as I say, no lunch parties were ever given -
At this moment ~~in (they were~~ in came Mr. Flanders.
He had mistaken the time.

Now, though ~~Mrs. Plumer had~~ they had finished their
meat, Mrs. Plumer took a second helping of cabbage & ~~was~~

Jacob determined of course that he would eat his meat in the time it took her to finish her cabbage - only he was infernally hungry. ~~Seeing this~~ Guessing all, M^rs. Plumer said ~~that~~ she was sure that M^r. Flanders would not mind - & the tart was ~~cut~~. brought in. Creditable though her action was, implying thought kindliness & breezy good nature, ~~we cannot~~ it is impossible to ~~gloss over~~ acquit her ~~of the~~ - No, no, no, M^rs. Plumer was not a nice woman - It was not her fault - since how could she control her father begetting her in ~~West~~ South Kensington forty years ago? ~~or any of the things that had happened to her since? But if we accept~~ & ~~that~~ act committed the rest followed ~~naturally. without fault on her part. Nonsense. She need not have been brisk jaunty & matter of fact poverty, she was a sharp little~~ & once begotten,.

how could she do other than grow up ~~the~~ bright, cheese paring, industrious commonplace, girl, wife, mother that she became - punctual ~~in her duties~~, ambitious, hard-headed & prosaic, with an instinctively perfectly accurate notion of the rungs of the ladder & an ant like assiduity in climbing ~~to the top~~ ~~pushing~~ & shoving & pushing George Plumer ahead of her? ~~To the activity of the ant, she added that nimble creature's basic brainlessness persistent conviction, that~~ What was at the top of the ladder? A sense that all the rungs were beneath one presumably; since by the time George Plumer became professor of physics or whatever it might be, M^rs. Plumer ~~would be~~ could only / be in a condition to cling tight to her eminence, look down at the ground ~~scold her two plain daughters~~ & schoo~~l~~ld her two plain daughters them into the same arduous process of climbing tht ladders ~~& pushing husband~~

—~~Yes~~ I was down at the Races yesterday" she said ~~brightly~~; brightly, with my two little girls

It was none of their fault either. In they came ~~in~~ to the drawing room~~;~~ white frocks & blue sashes. They handed the cigarettes.

But Rhoda had inherited her fathers cold grey eyes.

Cold grey eyes George Plumer had, but in~~to~~ them was an abstract light. He could ~~hold~~ talk about Persia & the

trade winds ~~& about~~ the Reform Bill ~~of~~ & ~~R~~ the cycle of the
harvest. Books were on his shelves by Wells & Shaw; on the
table ~~six~~ serious sixpennies written by pale men in
muddy boots, the Nation, the New Statesman, - ~~in which~~
the weekly
~~the screech & creek of brains wrung dry weekly~~
ch ~~of the brain~~
~~are heard the brain sere~~ creak & screech / ~~as it was~~
~~wrung dry.~~ of brains ~~wrung dry~~, & rinsed in cold water -
wrung dry ~~once a week~~ - melancholy papers.

"I don't feel that I know ~~my own~~ the truth about
anything until I've read them through" said M$^{rs.}$ Plumer
brightly.

"Oh God! Oh God, oh God!" exclaimed Jacob
as the four undergraduates left the house. 'Oh my God!'
~~He cried~~ my God!"
"

VI

"Bloody-beastly" he said, or words to that effect. He summed
up not in these words exactly, but ~~also~~ in a little jerking back
of his head, as he looked round him, ~~as if~~ searching for
other sights his discomfort, ~~his~~ ~~had as he sat at lunch~~
at the world that -, at lunch
The Plumers had shown him a ~~world~~ capable of existing —
~~but it was a bloody beastly world.~~ ~~indeed highly organized &~~ -
~~efficient.~~ ~~that affronted his conception him.~~ ~~Yet~~
that
there was no doubt about ~~yet~~, ~~Yet, o Lord, how~~
unnecessary
but so ~~impossible an & hideous, & a version~~ such an
absurd concoction, ~~compared,~~ ~~that is to say,~~ ~~such a~~
~~with~~ - such a thing to believe in - Shaw & Wells &
serious sixpenny-weeklies, earnest, avid, - what were
they after, scrubbing & demolishing, ~~when el~~ those
elderly people - ~~poor little girls~~, - a most distasteful world.
~~compared that is~~
~~In youth~~, & he saw it, ~~in its~~ as something
clearly outlined, against ~~another~~ all the feeling he
drew from youth & natural inclination; which would
overcome the Plumers world; but oh dear that this
elderly object should exist! ~~Against~~ The poor devil,

had rigged up this meagre object. Something of pity was in ~~his~~ him. ~~mind~~. Moreover this wretched contrivance, ~~for all its efficiency~~, would ~~giv~~ go down; for it was It ~~would have to be demolished~~. Those wretched little girls -
The extent to which he was disturbed certainly points to the fact that he was already agog. Indolent he was, & inexperienced; for who could not have told him that the flaming tide of youth, the deep fountains of the classics, breezes, & moors, & ~~sec~~ seas that fill the bays, all these elements of but sure enough, the meagre cities which the elderly of the race have cast upon the skyline showed like ~~skell~~ brick ~~skeleton~~ suburbs ~~upon~~ t against ~~the~~ a red & yellow flame. He was impressionable, but as we choose ~~write~~ the word, it is contradicted by the ~~quiet~~ composure with which he hollowed his hands to screen ~~round~~ a match. Then his walked on.

And, of course, ~~for~~ in any case, whether undergraduate or shop boy, man or woman, it must come as a shock about the age of twenty, - ~~this~~ the world of the elderly; ~~The~~ In our ~~hearts then there is amazement at the sight, & incredulity i the next year or two deciding whether~~ Thrown up ~~upon such a background of~~ in such black outline upon what we are; ~~at that age,~~ upon the reality/. ~~For~~ upon the moors & Byron; upon the sea ~~beach~~ ~~with the sea sweeping with~~ &. the lighthouse; the jaw bone with the teeth in it; upon ~~a~~ that ~~which~~ irrepressible feeling. 'I am - I am. ~~love. I hate.~~ for which there will be no form in this world unless he ~~Jacob~~ makes it; him ~~for himself.~~" The Plumers will try to prevent him making it. Every time he lunches out on Sunday - at dinners & tea parties - there will be this same shock; - recall ~~& The event can only be dreaded by Jacob himself~~; distinct horror; Then pleasure; ~~amazement~~; for he draws into him at every step, as he walks ~~along the bank~~ of the river such ~~a deep~~ steady certainty, such power; & ~~the the Plumers world, even~~ was it not M[rs.] Plumer who wished that the willow was pollarded

wh. a little boy has as he runs in the dark crying N N

Here they got into a boat, Jacob Flanders, & Tim Durrant, & rowed down the river, past the mill.

28th May 6 weeks ~~40~~

280
40

11,200

7

11,000 in six weeks

60

soft
the trees bowing, the grey spires ~~high~~ in the air, ~~or~~ voices howling
down the wind, in the ~~soft~~ springy air of May, the elastic air,
with its particles - chestnut blossom, pollen, I know not what it
in the nostrils
is that gives to the May air its potency, as of mead, to the
of Young ~~hoses~~ horses on the plains - & so the river, that, too,
~~runs~~ runs past, not at flood nor swiftly, but brimming, cloying
slowly dipping from
the oar that dips in it, & swimming green & deep ~~as if~~
over the bent rushes as if ~~in some~~ lavishly caressing. Then
the trees. Where they moored their boat, the trees
~~slow~~ showered down; ~~& trailing & the topmost~~ so that their
in the ripples;
topmost leaves trailed ~~down stream, &~~ on the surface of the
water; & the green wedge that lay in the water, ~~as it was~~
being made of leaves, shifted as the real leaves shifted. An edge of
sky, a shiver of wind - & as Durrant ate cherries he
dropped the ~~withered~~ stunted yellow cherries through the green ~~reflection.~~
twinkling in & out
~~le~~ wedge of leaves; their stalks ~~twinkling~~ as they wriggled ~~down~~
cherry
& sometimes, one, half bitten,/ would be red. ~~And on the bank~~
~~meadow~~ The meadow was on a level with Jacob's eyes
the trees not or the
gilt; but the grass ran like green water; like the grass in
grass
graveyards, about to overflow the tombstones; but more
white
juicy, & thick, ~~To him~~ looking backward the legs of children -
the white legs of
~~pink frocks~~ - ~~white~~ cows, ~~&~~ : ~~m~~ munch munch they went;
then a step through the grass; then munch munch -
Oh & that white butterfly circling higher & higher round
the top of the elm tree -
dropping off
"Jacobs ~~asleep~~" thought Durrant, looking up
from his novel, as he heard a sigh. ~~Then h~~ He kept
reading a few pages & then looking up in a
curiously methodical manner; & he went on
taking cherries out of the bag, methodically too.
Now Jacob was fast asleep. Meanwhile their boats

& each time he looked up he took a few cherries out of the bag. ~~Meanwhile~~, Other boats passed them, crossing the backwater from side to side ~~in~~ to avoid each other, for many were now moored & there were white dresses on the little island; white dresses & a flaw in the / [column of] air ~~above the [?] fire~~; between two trees~~;~~ Still more boats kept coming, & Durrant moved their boat to lie close to the bank - "Oh - h - h". went Jacob, as the boat rocked, & the trees rocked & the white dress, the white flannel trousers were so long, drawn out, up the bank....

"Oh dear!" He sat up. & rubbed his eyes.

as if some piece of elastic had snapped in his face.

. VII .

"..... ~~Oh~~ They're friends of my people's, said Durrant. So he took no end of trouble about the boat." And this boat had gone from Falmouth to St Ives bay, all round the coast. Therefore a larger boat, ... the twentieth of June - tides - primus stoves - the cash difficulty - my people - "Mother [said] ~~will go to Leeds~~ something about Leeds in her last letter" Jacob thought, & [felt his pocket for the letter] ~~wondered what he had done with the~~ letter. [feeling the pocket where he kept his letter]

~~"Hadn't you an Uncle?" said~~

~~"What about your Uncle, Jacob?"~~ Is it true that your uncle was last seen loading rice in Penang harbour?" asked Durrant.

Jacob had told the story of ~~his~~ Uncle / [Eliot] ~~the night before~~. in Durrants rooms the night before.

'~~Oh yes, it was all true' said Jacob~~['s].

'~~And how he~~ [Did] became a Mohammedan?'

'I say there's none left!" Jacob exclaimed. crumpling the bag ~~together &~~ - which had held cherries. ~~&~~ "Well, I expect [~~poor old Eliots~~] he's feeding the sharks [if the truth were known] by this time.... when you say there's ~~the Gulf~~ [a neap tide] stream / [Durrant] do you mean..."

Timmy Durrant, though only nineteen, knew all about tides; no woman, since the world began, has ever known what he knew at the age of nineteen. And the

matching one they often
way he did it was not exactly by reading, but by putting out a tentacle,
~~to which, so it~~ seemed, the things he wanted to know stuck. ~~Now he~~
another; ~~& keeping it safe.~~ locking it up; keeping it bright.
told the
Now he ~~explained~~ to Jacob, about the tides on South coast of
Cornwall, & there can be no possible doubt that what he said was
true: The two young men discussed what are known to be facts.
'But look here; said Jacob, & he went back through the argument,
step by step, until he came to the point which he thought
did not follow from what Durrant had said; but as he
began to state it, he understood what Durrant meant.

"Oh I see; I see" he said nodding his head. ~~Now~~ He was
satisfied. & keeping his eyes on the river, he went over ~~& over~~
the
~~this~~ thing that was undoubtedly true.
"Shall we move on' ~~said Durrant~~. "This beastly crowd'.
So up they went, past the island.

VIII

The feathery white moon never let the sky grow dark, & ~~the~~
all night long the chestnut blossoms were white on the trees.
The waiters must have been shuffling china plates like
cards ~~to~~ from the clatter that could be heard in the Great
Court. Jacob's rooms, however, were in Neville's Court; at the
top: so that reaching his door one went in a little out of
breath: but he wasn't there. Dining in hall presumably.
But it will be quite dark in Neville's Court long before
midnight; only the ~~stone will always be white.~~ pillars opposite will
always ~~be~~ white, & the fountain,- & A curious effect the gate has,
like lace. Even here, you hear the plates; a hum of talk too,
from the diners. ~~sitting~~ ~~lights showing~~; the hall lit up. & the
swing doors opening & shutting. ~~Well, what about the room?~~
~~That's Betty Flanders~~; & Some are late.
Jacob's room ~~is like most undergraduate's rooms. It~~ has
~~the~~ round table & ~~the~~ two low chairs. book cases.
There are yellow/ flags in a jar, & a photograph of his
mother; cards from societies, ~~&~~ notes, & pipes; an
essay, perhaps, on the table. The books are, after all,
possibly . . . ~~a~~ precious few French books, but you know

how anyone reads who's worth anything, just what he likes, with such extravagant enthusiasm. The Duke of Wellington - Spinoza - works of Dickens - oh I give it up! - ~~But~~ What I retrieve - ~~oh~~, the
Faery Queen - a Greek dictionary, & the petals of poppies pressed between the leaves - is, on the whole, ~~an not much~~
~~shape to him yet; & ther~~ vague, - poetical? His
slippers are incredibly shabby. Then these photographs
from the Greek - how tremendously English! And all
Jane Austen, in deference, I suppose to somebody's
elses standard. ~~Then there~~ Books upon Italian ~~painting~~.
painters of the Renaissance. A manual of the diseases of the Horse.
and all the usual note books.

~~IX~~

~~Professor Headicar~~

~~The air goes through an~~ empty ~~room when~~

Listless is the air in an empty room: just swelling the curtains;
~~&~~ the flowers in the jar shift~~ing~~ one fibre in the wicker
arm chair cracks.

IX.

Coming down the steps ~~the old~~ a little sideways the old man,
with his hands locked behind ~~his back~~ him & ~~his~~ his gown the floating; ~~out~~ ~~gown~~ black
lurched ~~under the~~ ~~along~~ under the ~~coll~~ colonnade.
~~Unsteadily; near the wall, until he reached~~ turned up ~~the staircase~~
~~a crab-like progress~~ unsteadily, near the wall, then up the stairs he went, into his room.
~~Why could he not walk straight? Learning, learning~~.
Then, another who raised his hand & praised the columns, the
gate, the ~~green~~ sky; another tripping & smug. Each went
in at a staircase: ~~& three lights now~~ three lights were
lit. ~~half way~~ ~~among t~~ in the dark windows.

If any light burns above Cambridge, it must be from
three such rooms; Greek burns here; science there; &
~~isn't~~ poor old Huxtable ~~a master of history?~~ master —
~~for in their rooms, at their tables~~, ~~has mastered his subject~~
though he can't walk straight. - ~~&~~ Sopwith too has praised the
sky any night these twenty years, - & Cowan still
chuckl~~ing~~es at the same stor~~y~~ies- ~~one~~ It is not simple
~~this~~ or pure, or wholly splendid, ~~this~~ the lamp of learning;
since if you see them there under its light (whether
Rossetti's on the wall or Van Goch~~)~~ whether there are
lilacs or only rusty pipes) how priestly they look!
[There must be something wrong with the oil.] How
like a suburb where you go to see a view, ~~where they~~ eat
~~make a~~ the cake; & ~~nowhere else do they make the same~~
~~cake~~. ~~That~~ "We are the sole purveyors of this cake".
Back you go to London; ~~& life begins again~~. for the
treat is over.

Old Professor Huxtable, performing with the ~~meth~~
method of a clock his change of dress ~~n~~ took his
seat in his chair, & his paper & his pipe; crossed his
feet with a grunt; extracted his glasses; the whole
flesh of the face then fell ~~into lines which as at~~
th~~e touch of a button~~. like a scene jerked by strings
into folds. Yet ~~how many dozen~~ rip a whole seat

of an underground carriage of its heads & old Huxtable's head will hold them all. Now, as his eye goes down the print, what a procession ~~goes~~ tramp~~ing~~s ~~down~~ through the corridors of ~~that old man's~~ his brain; orderly; firmly stepping; richly lit; knowledge; ideas.

Sopwith meanwhile, advancing with a curious trip from his fireplace cut the chocolate cake into segments. Until after midnight there would ~~always~~ be undergraduates in his rooms, sometimes as many as twelve, sometimes three or four; ~~it~~ but nobody got up when they went or when they came; Sopwith went on talking. Talking, talking, talking, - ~~the~~ as if everything could be talked - the soul itself sent slipping through the lips in thin silver disks which dissolved in the young men's minds, like silver, like moon~~shine~~. light - Oh, far away they'd remember it, & deep in dulness gaze back on it, come to refresh themselves ~~in it~~ again -

"Well I never - Thats old Chucky - my dear boy, how's the world treating you?"

& in came ~~poor~~ little Chucky. The ~~dull~~ unsuccessful provincial. Stenhouse his real name, but of course Sopwith, brought back, by using the other, everything everything, 'all I could never be, ~~all men ignored in me~~', - yes, though next day, buying his newspaper & catching the early train, it all seemed to him childish, absurd; ~~for the time~~ (the chocolate cake. The young men. ~~bring &~~ no, not all; he would send his son there; Sopwith went on talking; & twining ~~t~~ stiff fibres ~~into his own~~ silver ~~garland~~. ~~For~~ of awkward speech - things young men blurted out - ~~wrapping~~ plaiting them round in his own garland - making the bright side show - the vivid greens - the sharp thorns - manliness. Indeed to Sopwith a man could say ~~everything~~, anything, until perhaps he'd grown old, or gone under, gone deep, ~~plunged into~~ when the silver discs would twinkle, & the old stamp as they would ~~prove~~ look ~~to be~~ too pure, ~~too~~ & the outline always the same - the Greek boy's head. ~~For women, always a priest~~;
But he would respect still. A woman, divining the priest, would despise.

Cowan, Erasmus Cowan, sipped his port alone, or with one rosy
little man, whose memory held precisely the same span of
time; sipped his port & told his stories, & without book before him,
intoned Latin ~~verses~~, Catullus,& Virgil, as ~~unbid~~ if ~~langua~~ language
~~Latin~~ were wine upon his lips. Only — sometimes it
will come over one - What if the poet strode in? 'This my
image?' he might say, pointing to the ~~round~~ chubby man,
whose brain is, after all, Virgils representative among us,
though the body gluttonises, & as for love, bees, or even the
plough, Cowan takes his trips abroad with a French novel in
his pocket, a rug about his knees, & is thankful to be
home again ~~in Cambridge, nay in Trinity, where people~~
~~where people talk the language of educated men, Yes, he~~
~~has some complaint, incidental to people who drink~~
~~wine, comfortable, cosseted, understood~~ in his corner.
in his place, in his line, holding up ~~his round~~ in his snug little mirror
the image of ~~in which~~ Virgil ~~is~~ all rayed round with good stories of the
dons ~~of~~ Trinity, ~~&~~ red beams of port. ~~For I one~~
~~can't~~ see ~~cut Virgil clear anymore~~ - ~~& the cosy~~
~~bachelor ways -~~ But language is wine upon his lips.
Nowhere else would Virgil hear the like. And
though as she goes sauntering along the backs, old
Miss Umpheby sings him melodiously enough,
accurately too, she is always brought up by this
question, as she reaches Clare Bridge "But if I met him,
what should I wear?" - & then, ~~str~~ taking her way up
the avenue towards Newnham, she lets her fancy play
upon ~~with~~ other details of men's meeting with women ~~the intercourse of men & women~~
which have never got into her notes. Her lectures,
therefore, are not half so well attended as those of
Cowan, ~~since~~ & the thing she might have said,
in elucidation of the text, for ever left out. In
short, if ~~disaster~~ if face ~~ever you confront~~ a teacher ~~is faced~~ with the image of
him they ~~who is~~ taught, ~~disaster results. is the result.~~
~~&~~ the mirror breaks. But Cowan sipped his port.

His exaltation ~~is~~ was over. No longer the representative of Virgil.
No. The builder, assessor, surveyor, rather; ruling lines between
~~yo~~ names, ~~t~~ hanging lists upon doors;   Such is the fabric;
through which the light must shine, if shine it can.
The light of all these languages, ~~of~~ Chinese & Russian, Persian,
Arabic -of symbols, & figures, of history, ~~yes~~, the known things,
~~here~~ & things about to be known ~~burns~~;   So that if at
night far out at sea ~~one~~ over the tumbling waves one saw
all lit up - like a ship - a great three-decker - ~~all~~ its sails set -
~~for as one~~ one saw a a haze in the waters, a city
illuminated, - a whiteness even in the sky, ~~that would be~~
such as that now over the Hall of Trinity where they're
still dining, or washing up plates - yes, yes, this is the
light of Cambridge, all the lights coming out round the
court, & falling on the cobbles, picking out dark patches of grass single daisies,..
The young men are now back in their rooms. Heaven
knows what they're doing. What can <u>drop</u> like that?
And leaning down over a window box~~es~~ one ~~shouts to another~~
stops another, hurrying past, & up stairs they go & down
they go; - until ~~the bin blinds are drawn: but windows are~~
~~still open~~; a sort of ~~si~~ fulness settles ~~on the dorms, in~~
on the court, the hive ~~now~~ being full of bees; &
the bees humming, drowsy; ~~The Moonlight sonata~~
~~on a pianola.~~ suddenly vocal. Thats the Moonlight
sonata on a pianola: met by a ~~rapid~~ rapid walz.

The moonlight sonata tinkled away; the walz ~~came to a~~
~~crash~~. crashed. Although young men still went in & out
they walked as if keeping engagements. Now & then
there was a thud, as if some heavy piece of furniture had
again fallen, but unexpectedly, of its own accord, not
in the general ~~vibra~~ stir of life after dinner. One supposed
that young men raised their eyes from their books as the
furniture fell. Were they reading? ~~Was~~ Certainly
there was a sense of concentration in the air, ~~There~~
~~were so many young men sitting~~ behind the windows
sat so many young men; some undoubtedly reading, legs

perhaps over the arms of chairs; smoking; sprawling over the tables &
writing while their heads circled as the pen moved — simple
there is no need
young men these, who would - but ~~it is not necessary to~~
think ~~of them as people~~ of the future; others eating sweets;
here they boxed; and — and — well, Mr. Hawkins must have
[loved?] to throw up his window & bawl Jo-seph — Jo-seph -
& then he ran as hard as ever he could across the court -
~~why?~~ while an elderly man in an apron carried an
hesitated balanced & went on.
immense pile of plates; ~~But~~ But this was a diversion.
There were young men who read ~~their books~~, lying in
shallow arm chairs, holding their books as if they had
hold ~~of~~ in their very hands, of something that ~~was solid;~~
would see them through; they being ~~bewildered perhaps; at any rate~~
~~doubtful~~. in a torment; coming from ~~the seaside towns~~,
~~doctor's families, &~~ midland towns, clergymen's
families. Others read ~~Shakespeare~~ — Keats, ~~&~~ And
those long histories in many volumes, surely someone was
now beginning at the beginning in order to understand
the Holy Roman Empire, as one must. That was part of the
concentration, though it would be dangerous on a hot
spring night - dangerous I think to concentrate too much
upn single books, solitary pages. ~~Since~~ ~~They weren't~~
might &
~~reading~~ when, at any moment, the door opene~~d~~, Dijon
Keats wd
appeare~~d~~, or reading / no longer, Richard Seton, began
making long pink spills from an old paper, &
being alone, looked no more eager & contented but
almost fierce. Why? Only, perhaps, that Keats—
one wants to write poetry too; & to love; Keats died young-
Oh the brutes! - its ~~so difficult~~ damnably difficult;
Yet his melancholy, though as deep as any, could be
shared; ~~for he~~ his rage, that is [for though poetry is read to
the verge of the grave, brutality is tolerated, palliated -
c ~~C~~ompromise, sympathy, call it what you will;
a kind ~~of a~~ of pity, not for the wronged only - for the
wrong doers ~~do~~ too - an odious suspension - sharp
edges blurred - bright surfaces breathed upon until
whether its depth or darkness, we know not, only tha~~t~~ ~~to~~

its dim
~~grows old] dark & difficult~~] ~~horribly mixed~~] Brutality & rage -
clear
~~there~~ These were still ~~sharp~~ enough in the large room, where
some sort of meeting was being held, There was a
sofa, chairs, square table; & numbers of young men - six or
seven at least; Talking? One at a time.

But after all not so difficult if you ~~can be sure~~, on the next
staircase, ~~of one, two, three, actually five people~~ in the
large room, there are two, three, five, young men all
of
convinced of this - ~~about~~ brutality that is, ~~&~~ the clear
one way & another
division between right & wrong. There was a sofa,
chairs, a square table, & the window being open one
could see ~~one sitting~~. how they sat - legs issuing here,
there
one / crumpled in a corner of the sofa; & presumably.
him
for ~~him~~ you could not see, ~~one~~ somebody ~~must have been~~
stood by the ~~fire pl~~ fender, talking. Anyhow, Jacob
who sat astride a chair & ~~en~~ ate dates from a long
box, burst out laughing. The answer came from
the sofa corner; for his ~~legs dropped on the floor, &~~
pipe ~~waved in the air~~ was held in the air, then replaced.
Jacob wheeled round. He had something to say to that.
~~Whereupon the~~ Though the sturdy ~~boy~~, red haired boy
seemed to deny it, ~~wagging~~ his head slowly from side to side;
~~but saying nothing~~. then taking his pen knife to
clean his pipe he dug it again & again into the table,
as if the now the ~~man~~ voice from the fender ~~mark~~
the
spoke truth - ~~which~~ Jacob could not deny. Possibly when he
had done arranging the date stones he might find
something to say to it - indeed his lips opened - only,
then there was a roar of laughter -

The laughter died in the air. The sound of it could scarcely have reached anyone standing by the Chapel. The roof of the chapel ~~That~~ stretched across ~~the sky~~. Yet though only the gestures could be seen in the room, an ~~any~~ & swooping, which stretched along the opposite side of the court. The laughter died out; & only ~~arms~~ gestures with arms, movements of bodies, could be seen; ~~as, in Dorms the room the argument was shaped. Or perhaps it was not an argument. perhaps it was only talk~~ shaping something in the room. ~~an argument~~ Was it an argument? Was it nothing of the sort? ~~but merely what is talked only gossip, or~~ What was shaped? by the arms ~~that swop swooped, & the movements of bodies?~~ - & the bodies - ~~something in its way as enduring as the~~ moving in the dark air? ~~A spiritual shape~~; At ~~any rate,~~

Here, a step or two further on, there was nothing at all, except the enclosing buildings ~~-~~; chimneys upright, roofs horizontal; too much brick & building for a May night perhaps. And somehow before one's eyes would come the bare hills of Turkey - sharp lines, dry earth, coloured flowers, & colour in the shoulders of the women, ~~who, beat their linen on the stones, & stand~~ standing naked legged in the stream to ~~&~~ beat~~ing~~ linen on the stones - ~~in Soft, rich England, ancient The [Autrat~~?] The stream made loops of water round their ankles. But none of that could show clearly ~~shine~~ through the swaddlings - blanketing of the Cambridge night. ~~Th~~ The stroke of the clock even was muffled; as if intoned by somebody reverent from a pulpit; ~~&~~ as if ~~all~~ generations of learned men, ~~stretching back into the ages~~, heard the ~~hour~~ last hour go rolling through their ranks, ~~until~~ & issued it, already smooth & time worn, for the use of the living.

~~The last stroke purring through the air~~ was it to recei
Was it to receive this gift from the past that the young man
came to the window & stood there, looking out across the
court? It was Jacob. He stood smoking his pipe while
~~this gift~~ the ~~stroke of~~ last stroke of the clock purred softly
round him. Perhaps there had been an argument.
He looked satisfied; indeed masterly; which expression changed
slightly as he stood there; The sound of the clock conveying
to him (it may be) a sense of old buildings, & time, & himself the
inheritor; & then tomorrow; & friends; ~~in the room~~
~~behind~~; at the thought of whom, in sheer confidence &
pleasure, ~~it may be~~, he yawned & stretched himself.
after all these movements of young men
At any rate, whether argument or not, the shape was
there in the room,- as of glass ~~lines~~, compared with the
stone of the chapel opposite. hard, yet spiritual. Come
again to those rooms ~~in~~ in three years time & you will
find nothing. ~~It is Only that tonight the bubble had been~~
~~blown again which~~
~~But the building.~~ On~~ly arguments, five young men moving~~
~~in a room, undoubtedly.~~ left; & all these young men
Meanwhile, behind him, this shape they had made, whether
by argument or not, this spiritual shape, hard yet
~~transpare~~ ephemeral, as of glass compared with the dark
~~the~~ stone of the chapel, ~~of~~ was dashed to splinters, young
men rising from chairs & sofa corners, buzzing &
barging about the room ~~a~~ one driving another against
the bedroom door which giving way in they fell -
Then Jacob was left there, in the shallow arm chair, alone.
with Masham? Anderson? Headicar? Oh, it was
Headicar; The others had all gone.

"Julian the Apostate" ~~said Jacob~~
~~one or the other sai~~ which of them said that, & what were
the other words? ~~About midnight a~~ You know about
midnight there sometimes rises, - like a veiled figure
suddenly woken - a ~~wind~~, heavy, ~~&~~ wind; & this now
flapping through Trinity lifted unseen leaves, &

blurred everything. 'Julian the Apostate' .. & then the wind.
~~But the~~ The wind ~~what~~ Why does it always ~~come to~~
out - away
flaunt ones mind like a flag ~~out, away, as if as if .~~
up go the elm branches - out blow the sails - the ~~ol~~ old
schooners ~~plunge~~ ~~rise & sink~~ - ~~plunge &~~ rear & plunge——
~~tumb~~
the grey waves in the hot Indian ocean tumbling
sultrily, - ~~but~~ & then all falling flat again.
So, if the veiled lady stepped through the Courts of Trinity
she now drowsed once more, all her draperies about her, ~~&~~
her head ~~resting~~ against a pillar.

"Somehow it seems to matter."

~~That~~ The low voice was Simeon's.
The voice was even lower that answered him.
The sharp tap of a pipe on the mantelpiece ~~drowned~~
concealed the words. And perhaps Jacob only said
'hum', ~~He~~ or said nothing at all. ~~He~~ After a
few moments he spoke quite rapidly; & got up; & stood
with his back to the grate, & delivered himself of a ~~long~~
speech, — something enthusiastic, & a little absurd, since
at a word of the others, he flopped suddenly in to his
chair ~~;~~ grasping his ankles. True, the words were
inaudible~~;~~ ~~but~~ ~~There is no mistaking intimacy~~
~~though~~. It was the intimacy of it - ~~That no~~
~~wind blows away~~. ~~The soft wind might blow over~~
~~the~~ a
~~Intimacy~~ -~~a sort of~~ ~~spiritual suppleness, when minds~~
~~print upon each other indelibly - when~~ ~~warmed by~~
~~bubbling warm, & taking for indeli indelible~~
~~when minds print upon each other indelibly, no~~
~~wind blows~~ ~~that out; &~~ ~~no wind~~ blows out; ~~since in~~
~~indeed almost protects~~;
~~Indeed~~ intimacy ~~is quite visible through a pane of glass,~~
~~& as for being blown out by a storm of wind, that~~
a sort of spiritual suppleness, when minds print upon
each other indelibly.

280	
45	6
1400	
1120	36
12,600	

45 “You seem to have made the subject your special study”
said Jacob, rising & standing over Simeons chair;
He balanced himself; swaying a little. He appeared
extraordinarily happy, as if in a moment ~~he would begin~~
~~to laugh - should Simeon stir slightly the full brimming~~
~~surface of his mind~~; his mind would brim over in
laughter - if Simeon spoke.

Simeon said nothing. Jacob remained standing.
of it
But intimacy - ~~the room was~~ the room was full - still,
deep, like a dark pool. Without moving or speaking,
washed
it rose softly & ~~ebbe washed~~ over everything - mollifying
kindling
~~soothing~~, & coating the mind with the lustre of
pearl, so that if you talk of a light, of Cambridge
burning, its not languages only; its ~~the~~ —
But Jacob moved. He murmured good night.
He went out into the court. He buttoned his jacket
across. ~~He strode~~ his chest. He ~~strode along the~~
went back to his rooms, & being the only man,
~~as it happened,~~ who walked at that moment back
to his rooms, his footsteps rang out, his figure
seemed large. Back from the chapel, back from
the hall, back from the library ~~& the cleg~~
sound
~~pillars~~. came the ~~echo~~ of his footsteps; as if
~~authority echoed back~~ all the old stone echoed
~~the y~~ ~~back~~ The young man — the young man — the
young man———”

. X .

The feathery white moon never let the sky grow dark; all
night the chestnut blossoms were white, & dim was the
cow parsley in the meadows. Neither to Tartary nor to
Arabia went the wind of the Cambridge courts, but lapped
dreamily in the midst of ~~pale~~ grey blue ~~gauze~~ clouds over the roofs of
Newnham. There, ~~if~~ in the garden, if she needed space to
wander she might find it among the trees; & as none
but women's faces could meet her, face she might unveil it,
blank, featureless, -~~a flower hooded with~~ ~~white~~ ~~green~~ ~~purple~~ ;
~~like~~ a mark of womanhood, such as at / that hour one might
figure all the faces of women, laid upon pillows, eyes . white pigtails
extended, ringless hands outside the sheets - if it weren't
that there ~~are~~ were still lights in many bedrooms.

Angela Edwards - was that her name? ~~The~~
Her square looking glass ~~absorbed~~ concentrated into itself all
the light that came from the drop above it. The little
creature in white & gold~~en~~ ~~wrapper~~ was therefore
perfectly delineated; her crimson toes; ~~&~~ her
pale hair ~~bound~~ with the blue stones in it;
the whole of her indeed, perhaps the soul. Her
glass sucked it out of her & ~~gave~~ held it ~~back~~ up to her, untrembling,
for her inspection; ~~Such~~ for as she gazed steadily
face & reflection fitted like a finger glove, & nothing ~~of the~~
~~tremb tremulous fitful as of flickering like the~~ trembled or flickered
~~souls, marred the smooth surface. no rippled the~~
~~surface & no shadow~~ She was ~~pleased~~ glad to be herself.
~~glad when evening came to find~~ A sort of
glow worm ~~in the night~~, whose life spends itself in ~~its the~~ its
glow; whose duty is done: shine then, proof against
damp & dark; until..

in the brilliant corridor;

"Well, said Angela, addressing her own
image, it's time my dear; - " &

whereupon the image in the looking glass turned its back upon itself, & the glow was dissipated, for either the shadow of the wardrobe fell upon her face, or after the act of adoration worldly cares asserted themselves.

~~& her~~ I gaze ~~into~~ windows, where at that hour ~~were~~ laid upon pillows ~~marks~~ of womanhood, ~~eyelids~~ white upon eyes, pigtails straight, ringless hands ~~outside~~ upon the sheets; &

& gaze into rooms, where at that hour, blank, featureless, eyelids white over eyes, ringless hands extended upon sheets, there slept innumerable women. But here & there a light ~~still~~ burnt.

A double light one might figure in Angela's room seeing how bright she was, & how bright came back the reflection of herself from the square glass. The whole of her was perfectly delineated; perhaps the soul. For the the glass held up an untrembling image - white - gold, red slippers, pale hair with blue stones in it - & never a ripple of shadow to break the smooth kiss of Angela & ~~the~~ her reflection, as if she were glad to be Angela. Anyhow the moment was glad - ~~this~~ the picture in the heart of night, ~~the~~ the golden shrine in the dark Cathedral - Strange indeed to have this visible proof ~~about one~~, available at any moment ~~given & one chose to shut the door & seize the mirror,~~ granted glass & light, of the rightness of things; this this lily floating flawless upon ~~the~~ the times ~~roar~~ - ~~that one could~~ pool, fearless; as if this were sufficient - this reflection. Which meditation she destroyed by turning; ~~w wh~~ & the ~~the~~ mirror held nothing at all, or only a brass bedstead; & she, turning here & there, halting & darting, became like a ~~women~~ woman in a house, - & changed again, pursing her lips

& marking with her finger what surely could not be a
the
firm grasp of ~~some~~ professors logic? Only Angela Williams
was at Newnham for the purpose of earning her living, &
could not forget, even in moments of impassioned adoration
the cheques of her father at Swansea, - token that ~~the~~ even the
lily no longer floats altogether flawless upon the pool, -
~~indeed that these metaphors,~~ ~~sound now as~~ serve
not
~~but is supported~~ ~~on a black waters,~~ but ~~is~~
~~Unfortunately,~~ but has a name on a card, like any other;
Williams, A. one may read it in the moonlight, &
From all the rooms ~~this~~ where the women slept
this vapour blew ~~freely~~ attaching itself to limbs ~~as~~
~~then~~ like white mist, & then blowing freely out into the
was
open. That at least ~~is~~ the feeling of the dawn in the
garden. Elderly women slept, who would on waking
ivory
clasp immediately the / rod of office. Now smooth &
surrounded
colourless, reposing deeply they lay / supported, by
bodies of
~~the youth~~, the ~~sense of~~ youth, ~~sleeping round them~~,
~~which slept round them~~, recumbent, or grouped at
the window; pouring forth into the garden this
bubbling laughter. Irresponsible laughter.
Laughter of mind & body; life itself; floating ~~off~~ away
&
rules discipline, ~~firm~~ immensely fertilising; yet
formless, & chaotic, trailing & straying, & tufting the
rose bushes with ~~white shreds~~. shreds of vapour.
~~'Beautiful, beautiful~~' ~~so~~ Miranda breathed,
in her white night gown, sipping her ~~cup of~~ cocoa.
'Oh!' ~~Her exclamation was~~ Pain was in her voice.
She ~~drew the~~ leant her head out. The mist
was pierced by her cry. The facts were there.
She had been talking to Hilda Johnson, ~~for about~~ ———
& Hilda had described ~~the Isle of Man~~. ~~Norfolk~~
Bamborough Castle.

about Bamborough Castle; about the colour of the sands at
evening; about ' my father' 'my mother'; Dick; Midget.
Then simply this - 'I shall write & settle the day -'
kissing her
upon which Alice Avery / had gone to bed, & Miranda
positively unable to sit still, feeling like one possessed of a
wind-lashed sea in her heart, had stormed up & down
her room, throwing her arms out to relieve this excitement, -
-this agitation, this t incredible stooping of the miraculous
tree with the golden fruit at its summit - hadn't it
dropped into her arms? She held it glowing to her
breast. A thing not to be thought of yet, but left to glow
there. And then, slowly undressing, putting here her
stockings, there her stays, & folding her petticoat neatly on
top, Miranda - her other name being Gilham -
realised - how shall we express it? - that after a
a dark churning of myriad ages here was the light at the
end of the tunnel - life, the world. Beneath her it lay.
It was
~~That the world~~ ~~should~~ ~~be~~ ~~entirely~~ good; ~~&~~ all ~~human beings~~
men & women lovable; such was her discovery.
Indeed, how could one then feel surprise if, lying in bed,
she could not close her eyes? if, barely open in the shallow
looked
darkness, chair & chest of drawers ~~seemed~~ stately -&
the looking glass precious, with its ashen hint of day?
Sucking her thumb, like a child (her age 19) she lay ;
in this good world; this new world; the world at the
end of the tunnel; until ~~as~~ a desire to see it, or forestall it,
&
~~drove her to the window~~ drove her, tossing her blankets,
to guide herself to the window; & there, looking out
~~Miranda~~, upon the garden, ~~Mir~~ ~~white with mist,~~
one
where the mist lay, ~~&~~ all the windows open,
~~faintly~~ bluish, something ~~stirring~~ murmuring in
the distance, the ~~wind~~ world of course, & the
& the morning coming, Oh she cried, as if in pain

. XI .

July 19th Innumerable are the sentences with which this chapter might begin, & to tell the truth some of them are rejected for no better reason than that they ~~are~~ display an ignorance discreditable, indeed disgraceful; ~~but~~ inevitable, however, considering the present state of things. ~~The rest~~
As for the rest each one of them ends with a plain note of interrogation. Of course that is a cottage ~~plainly enough~~, & those / [on the bench] are pans in which M[rs.] Pascoe has / [presumably] boiled her cream; & the cottage is whitewashed; & the cabbage garden enclosed by a stone wall; & the hill slopes to a cliff & the cliff falls to the sea, which one hears sounding & dashing
on the rocks beneath; [&] ~~as one~~ sees ~~it~~ spread ~~blue~~ to the horizon. Seats have been [hollowed] ~~shaped~~ in the granite by long rain, & the grey lichen fills them, ~~as with~~ & there sitting, ~~time~~ now its the sailing ship you ~~see~~ watch, now the
or in the hedge bumble bee swinging on the foxglove.

July 28th

Rodmell
July 28th

. XI .

~~Many~~

Although it would be possible to knock at the cottage door, & ask for a ~~cup~~ glass of ~~water~~ milk; ~~one~~ it is only thirst that would compell ~~one thus to intrude. For~~ the intrusion. . Yet perhaps Mrs. Pascoe would welcome it. .. The ~~sume~~ summer's day may, ~~who knows~~?, ~~tick itself out lengthily~~ be long, ~~to her~~ Washing in her little scullery, she may hear the cheap clock tick, tick, tick,... She is alone in the house. Her husband - ~~but he is dead~~ ~~will~~ be yet at the harvest. Her daughter married: ~~went~~ gone to America. Her / elder son married, ~~&~~ too but she does not agree with his wife. ~~The younger boy went with the Salvation army. is a sailor. No matter,~~ - ~~Even So be it. No doubt she would In short, she is alone, in the house, &~~ ~~so the~~ Perhaps - But since the first sentence holds good, this is ~~in~~ guess work, & the only ~~truth~~ statement which can be reached for is that a steamer, probably bound for Cardiff, ~~is now~~ is crossing the horizon, while near at hand, a fox glove swings like a cathedral bell with a bumble bee for clapper.

The Wesleyan minister came along - took the young boy -

~~For There~~

~~For~~ There little white cottages are built almost on the edge of the cliff; ~~in~~ the garden ~~grows~~ grows gorse more early than cabbages; & ~~the granite~~ for hedge, some primeval man has piled granite boulders. In one of these, to hold / as some historians conjecture, the victim's blood, a basin has been hollowed, but ~~& now serves as a seat from the humbler purpose of a~~ in our time, ~~when~~ it serves more tamely to ~~as a seat~~, ~~for from which the tourist can~~ to seat ~~those~~ those tourists~~;~~ ~~desiring an uninterrupted view of the Gurnard's Head~~. who ~~wish to look at the Atlantic~~, who wish for an uninterrupted view of Gurnards Head. No one objects to a blue print dress, & white apron in the cottage garden.

- She has to draw her water from a well in the garden. -

- Very lonely it must be in winter, with the wind sweeping over these hills, & the waves dashing on the rocks.

~~Is~~ Having drawn her water, Mrs. Pascoe went in again, ~~just turning her head in the direction of the tourists. who were~~

the tourists ~~They~~ regretted having brought no glasses, so that they might have read the name on the tramp steamer. ~~Then there came up this matter of asking for milk~~, & Indeed, it was such a fine ~~clear~~ day that there was no saying what a pair of field glasses might not / have ~~br~~ fetched in to view - Two fishing luggers, probably from St Ives bay, ~~had now sai~~ were now sailing in an opposite direction from the steamer, & the floor of the sea became alternately clear ~~thin~~ & opaque, ~~as though~~ ~~The~~ As for the bee, having sucked its fill of honey it visited the teasle, & thence made a straight line into Mrs. Pascoe's patch, ~~& thus~~ once more ~~directed the~~ directing the visitors gaze to the old woman's print dress & white apron, for she had come to the door of the cottage & was standing there.

There she stood, shading her eyes & looking out to sea. Centuries have passed, & yet as for saying ~~what she saw~~ or thought ~~as she~~ stood ~~there~~, we are

X X X X X X

Yes, it is much easier to note ~~follow~~ the flight of the bee, or ~~the~~ note colour of the waves, than to conjecture ~~what she thinks~~. the thought in her brain, or the light in her eyes, or what it is that remains constant, ~~throug~~ behind everything. For the millionth time she looks at the sea. Probably this last look ~~is~~ confirms or alters something ~~she feels about life~~. ~~itself.~~ ~~Four rooms her cottage has; &~~ ~~There are four rooms in her cottage~~. always growing in her. It is part of the rinsings, scourings, copulations, births, & ~~violent~~ deep glooms & scoldings, which have gone in ~~on perhaps~~ for sixty years perhaps in the four rooms of the cottage. But nobody knows. The talkative

& anaylytic people have taken themselves ~~inland~~, to cities. Like a miser she has hoarded her feelings within her own breast. Not a penny piece has she changed all these years, &, ~~now~~, ~~env~~ watching her enviously it seems as if all within must be pure gold. The wise old woman, having fixed her eyes upon the sea, once more withdrew.

A peacock butterfly now ~~now~~ occupied ~~almost~~ the ~~entire~~ teasle; ~~a~~ fresh, newly emerged, as the blue & chocolate down on his wings testified. Yet no butterfly does much more than stain a patch on ~~one's~~ the retina; ~~or ... Mrs. Mrs.~~ ~~There is the Gurnard Head, too,~~ was ~~'I love to see the look'~~, ~~in words. The poet wrote something about 'cased~~ in ~~the unfeeling armour~~ of As for The black rocks in the sea testified. to the ~~way in which~~ endurance of this solitary crag of human life, fronting its waves - .Meanwhile Mrs. Pascoe had taken down the gaudy box placed askew upon her mantelpiece had made the tea, & was about to sip her first cup. ~~w~~

What with ~~the~~ buzzing of ~~a~~ blue bottle & the ticking of the clock the little room was noisy; & ~~a rich~~ geranium in the window gave ~~forth~~ a rich musty smell. She drank deeply & comfortably, cut herself a piece of bread, spread the butter thick, & in doing so ~~revealed~~ showed hands knobbed with labour & grimed with dirt. ~~The Perhap Perhaps~~ owing perhaps / to the small size ~~heat~~ of the room, & the rich musty smell of the geranium in the window, the presence of the body became very emphatic ~~important~~. ~~Two bodies would~~ Mrs. Pascoe She wore a dirty white ~~k~~ cloth of some kind round her neck, & the creases ~~of~~ in her skin were marked by black grains. ~~w When her husband came in, the~~ Two <u>bodies</u> together would ~~create an intolerable sense of be~~ make it impossible to think of anything except the body. One might go into the scullery; the other stumble up the stairs to the bedroom; but ~~in this four roomed cottage an~~ there would be no escaping the body. ~~Its functions are detestable~~. An earth closet out in the rain - sickness - a woman's period - ~~coput~~ copulation upstairs in the double bed, ~~or here before the fire perhaps~~ - childbirth ~~the~~ birth - ~~all all that veils & places in the shadow these natural functions of the body are all bodies~~ as the room filled with bodies, ~~these functions & desires would assert themselves. all these functions and desires would press~~ <u>become prominent</u>, it would be impossible not to think solely of these functions & desires. ~~& Whether The small room is altogether filled with the body~~. Yet the room was scrupulously clean. Her face ~~showed no~~ was assuredly not soft, sensual, or lecherous; but hard, wise, wholesome rather, ~~sn~~..signifying in a room full of sophisticated people, ~~the a sav~~ the flesh & blood of life; yet wistfully, for she too ~~might could h~~ would have liked to ~~a~~ ride in a carriage with springs. ~~& &~~ The soft swift syllables of educated speech often shamed her, few rude one. ~~plain ones~~. And then all night to hear the grinding of the Atlantic upon the rocks, instead of hansom cabs & footmen whistling for ~~mo~~ motor cars. So she may have dreamed, holding the picture paper close to her eyes;: though in what guise ~~shape~~ Lady Cynthia ~~Mosley~~ in her wedding dress appeared ~~to~~ against seventy years of sea, sky, & cliff side, ~~none~~ none can tell. ~~A~~ Awkward to both would have been the encounter; for undoubtedly old cottage women say disconcerting things at weddings.

Shut up in the room next door she prized mats & china & photographs, & by virtue of these & a picture of the king took her place in the machine, & proved herself no outlaw; ~~but a~~ though the mouldy little room was only saved from the salt breeze by the depth of a brick, & you saw the gannet drop like a stone from the windows, & ~~on the gulls were~~ on stormy nights the gulls came shuddering ~~down the gale - &~~ through the air, & now the steamers' light was deep, ~~in the~~ now high - but who sees & feels all this? Mrs. Pascoe ~~put down her cup~~, washed the tea round her cup to collect the last grains of sweetness, & wiped her lips with the back of her hand.

She was moving the kettle on the hob when ~~at~~ some distant unfamiliar sound caused her, like a wary animal, to stand alert. She listened. Three seconds later ~~a rap~~ there was a rap at the door.

"Mrs. Pascoe?" ~~A~~ The words were clear cut; ~~&~~ authority underlay the cheerful interrogation. ~~And When~~ Certainly Mrs. Durrant was a lady. Straight, spare, severe for all her gaiety there she stood on the cobbled path, ~~directing~~ pointing the the parasol with which she had ~~t~~rapped on the door to a clump of St. John's Wart.

"I envy you ~~your~~ that bush, Mrs. Pascoe" she said. Mrs. Pascoe looked at the bush ~~as though~~ deprecatingly, as if being hers it must needs be humble, & ~~yet having must have merit to have found favour with Mrs. Durrant~~. & yet was well enough since it had pleased the lady.

"I expect my son in a day or two" said Mrs. Durrant looking at the sea; "Sailing" from Falmouth with a friend in a little boat". ~~But I came to~~ But I came to ~~hear~~ ask — Any news of Lizzie yet, Mrs. Pascoe?" ~~For~~ For She had stopped her ponies & stepped down the muddy lane ~~not solely~~ ~~with a~~ from an undoubting simply from a desire to talk; ~~combined it is true with~~ ~~besides~~ Into the bargain, of course, she held unquestioned the instincts of her era — Free as a hawk she was to visit ~~to visit~~ any nook or crag she chose to perch upon. She came of an ancient Highland race.

The long tailed ponies stood ~~shifting~~ twitching their ears; ~~While~~. the boy Curnow flicked flies off them occasionally; ~~watching The two~~ He ~~watched~~ saw his mistress go into the cottage; come out again; & pass talking energetically, to judge from the motions of her hands, ~~round~~ to the ~~far side~~, vegetable patch on the far side.

Side by side the two women stood looking at the sea; Mrs. Durrant looked at it like one born to sail over it victoriously; Mrs. Pascoe judged it, questioned it, & kept her ~~own~~ opinion of it to herself.

"I'm sure Lizzie is grateful to you for all ~~your goodness~~ you've done for her ma'am", she said. ~~having gone with Mrs.~~

~~Durrant to the~~ making as if to ~~escort~~ go with Mrs. Durrant to her carriage. But M$^{rs.}$ Durrant would have none of it.

"Take care of that leg M$^{rs.}$ Pascoe, or I shall send the doctor to ~~see~~ you, she called back, laughingly, ~~&~~ having already walked some way down the lane, while M$^{rs.}$ Pascoe stood by the cottage door looking after her.

M$^{rs.}$ Durrant took the reins in her hands, & drove swiftly along the level. ~~When the~~ Soon the ~~p~~ long-tailed ponies ~~had to~~ attack$_{ed}$ the swelling moor road with ~~their~~ eager striving forelegs ~~& a M$^{rs.}$ D~~ The boy Curnow ~~dropped~~ jumped off behind, & M$^{rs.}$ Durrant let the reins fall slackly, ~~touching~~ & ~~leaning~~ leant backwards.

Her vivacity had left her. She gazed broodingly over the landscape as if the roofless cottages, ~~of the~~ long since deserted, the ~~futile heaps~~ mounds of slag ~~by the unworked mines~~, the ~~old~~
cottage gardens ~~gardens overrun now~~ overrun grown with brambles & fox gloves cast shade upon her mind. Her mind skimmed leagues while M$^{rs.}$ Pascoe's mind ~~adhered~~ kept close to its solitary patch. Forwards & backwards she cast her thoughts, as the ponies climbed the hill road, ~~in~~ being by reason of temperament, education, birth & fortune, the centre of so many ~~human~~ activities that she rarely ~~drove~~ climbed slowly up a hill without changing her mood many times. The top being reached, she stopped the carriage. The pale hills were round her, each set with its ancient cromlech; beneath was the sea;
varying ~~in~~ from green to purple like variable as a southern sea cameleon skies: she herself sat there looking from ~~one to the other~~ hill to sea, upright, aquiline, ~~capri capricious also~~. [She flicked the ponies so suddenly that] equally poised between tears & laughter. She flicked the ponies so suddenly that the boy Curnow had to swing himself ~~on board~~ up by the ~~heel~~ toe of his boot.

X X X X X

X X X X X X X X

rose
The rooks settled; the rooks ~~rise~~. The trees which they touched so
lodge
capriciously seemed insufficient to ~~accommodate~~ them.
the tree tops the trunks
Yet they sang ~~when~~ with the breeze in them, creaked audibly,
& dropped now & then, though the season was midsummer, husks,
or
leaves, twigs; Strange it is that the mind always
travels backwards, never forwards. ~~Here~~ Pacing here
must cross its mind
under the elm trees, it is the age of the earth we think of;
back through the eighteenth, seventeenth, sixteenth centuries
adventurers, smugglers.
we pass giving to each its dress & character, until we
reach the ~~first age~~, the lonely age, when Cornwall lay
naked; ~~himself~~: & indeed. She has disguised herself very little,
~~to find favour in the eye of man to We are ac~~
~~lights~~ lamps of such
~~the accidents~~; A few ships in the bay - a lighthouse
lights clustered
twinkling ~~its light eye, light;~~ ~~As for dreaming of the~~
~~future, when~~ There between the branches - that's ~~is all~~
As for the future, it is as if we were the last to live,
for all the thought we give it. ~~However this may be,~~
~~The moss was soft, & between the tree trunks~~
~~Perhaps there will be no moss in the future~~; Up went
the rooks & down again; ~~some com~~ rising in lesser numbers
each time, & making ready to settle ~~in for the night.~~
since the ~~sky was already~~ evening was already spent enough
to make the ~~Th~~ air inside the wood almost dark. The
moss was soft; the tree trunks spectral. Beyond them lay
a silvery meadow. ~~& beneath Suddenly came the~~
~~blare of a gong. Heavens! That's a house!~~
~~through the trees came a tremulous, melancholy sound,~~
Never, never, shall we go back ~~to life~~ again, but here
dissipate ourselves, ~~relinquishing~~ saying to the earth that
once more she has vanquished - when, far off, ~~tremulously~~
~~sun begins to shake & tremble~~ a familiar sound -
begins to shake & tremble - increases, fairly dins in our
~~bel~~
ears, - scares a sleepy family up into the air again:-
The dinner bell at the house.

move a house
or two, strip
one of its rails:
the railway,
she is
-,naked still,

XXXXXX

After three weeks of salt wind, rain & sun, Jacob Flanders had put
on ~~the dinner jacket~~ a dinner jacket ~~civilized clothes~~, & sat at table ~~feeling~~ in a
state of profound discomfort. This discreet black object
~~flat with paper upon it~~ ~~had seemed~~ had ~~appeared~~ made
its appearance now & then in the boat, ~~in the midst of~~ among
tins & ~~jars~~, preserves, & as the voyage went on had become
more & more irrelevant. ~~Nevertheless, Jacob maintained~~
~~that kept~~ ~~The state of things~~ ~~which its existence implied became~~
more & more remote. Yet Jacob, in defiance of laughter,
kept up ~~went through the~~ ceremony of preserving it ~~al~~ folded
at the bottom of his box, ~~though~~ And now, in a second,
~~this~~ the dinner jacket ~~had~~ ~~rewarded him~~, ~~asserted Th~~ preserved
him. He could not be sufficiently thankful for it.
Even so, his neck & wrists & face were exposed without
cover, &, ~~what with their stinging~~ his whole person, whether
exposed or not, ~~seemed~~ tingled & glowed so as to make / even black
cloth an imperfect screen. He withdrew ~~his~~ the great
red hand. that lay upon the tablecloth. Slim glasses,
smooth rolls. & ~~silver~~ bright silver ~~t~~ were offered him.
the bones of cutlets were decorated with pink frills
Opposite him were ~~women's~~ hazy shapes ~~in~~ ~~hazy in~~ of yellow gauze &
blue mist "He doesn't have to come down -" said one of them
~~vivacious~~ voice.

"It seems to me that ~~This~~ you behaved abominably'
said M[rs] Durrant.

"Well, mother, ~~it was his own fault~~ but. We didn't
ask him to play."

~~The~~ Behind them again was the garden, & ~~through~~ among the ~~tree~~
branches of the elm trees fishing boats seemed to be
suspended. ~~A~~ sailing ship slowly ~~crossed~~ passed
behind the ~~the~~ women's backs. ~~All flowed~~
& ~~moved~~ ~~Some~~ Two or three figures passed
along the terrace; & ~~took~~ coming into the room made Jacob feel that everything

was flowing round him. To this impression the conversation added, for ~~though~~ there was never a moment's silence, ~~the~~ & yet had he been asked to say what ~~it was about~~ was said, he would have shaken his head.

'O Clara! Clara!' said Mrs. Durrant, &
Timothy Durrant adding 'Clara, Clara.' Jacob found himself ~~think decid~~ calling the shape in the yellow gauze Clara~~;~~ ~~a~~
The girl sat ~~flushed & laug~~ smiling & flushed.
When the laugh had died down she said, "But mother, it was true. We shouldn't have asked him if he hadn't said so, should we ∈ Betty? Miss Eliot agreed with us,
~~didn't you, Miss Eliot?~~ '
And Miss Eliot was ~~talking to~~ making room beside her for the old man who had come in from the terrace.
The dinner would never end, Jacob thought, & he did not want it to end, though the ship had sailed right across the window, & a light marked the end of the pier. He saw Mrs. Durrant gaze at the light, ~~&~~ She turned to him.

"Was it you who ~~steered the took command~~ steered the boat, or Timothy?" she said. "Forgive me if I call you Jacob. I've heard so much of you," she added. Then her eyes went back ~~again~~ to the sea. "A ~~fishing~~ little village once, she said, & now grown —" she rose, taking her napkin with her & stood by the window.

"Did you quarrel?" Clara asked him.

"I should have."

Mrs. Durrant came back from the window.

"We get later & later" she said, gazing down the dinner table. "~~Its disgraceful~~. You ought to be ashamed of yourselves."

"Oh Mrs. Durrant!" one of the ladies cried.
The old man with a beard shook his head, ~~ate his~~ took a spoonfull of plum tart & was seized with an attack of sneezing. Mrs. Durrant passed down the room the ladies following her.

M[rs.] Durrant laughed, & leant back in her chair as if indulging him.

She owes me Miss Wilding owes me a sovereign. a sovereign.

"We put it to you, M[rs.] Durrant; I say the conditions were fulfilled ~~as laid down~~".

"~~He ate the bigonias~~ before ~~the fish~~: ~~not with it~~" ~~said~~ ~~cried~~ ~~Charlotte~~ - Charlotte Wilding.

~~"Oh what children:~~ Not ~~with~~ before the fish — with it" said M[rs.] Durrant said Charlotte Wilding.

That was the bet; with the fish" said Clara seriously. "Bigonias mother."

"Oh dear me," said M[rs.] Durrant.

"Charlotte wont pay ~~anyhow~~" said Timothy.

"How dare you — said Charlotte -

"That privilege will be mine" said the courtly M[r.] F ~~Felbrig~~ Wortley, producing ~~a silver case primed with~~ with a ~~wave of his hand & slipping~~ out a sovereigns.

Capricornus Bootes Algol Pegasus Corona

Then M[rs.] Durrant got up & passed down the room, holding herself very straight, & the ~~yellow &~~ girls in yellow & blue & silver gauze followed her, & elderly Miss Eliot in her ~~velvet dress~~. velvet; & a little woman, hesitating behind, scrupulous, probably a governess. All passed out at the open door.

"When you are as old as I am, Charlotte -" said M[rs.] Durrant, ~~taking~~ drawing the girls ~~han~~ arm within hers, as they paced up & down the terrace.

Libra Cygnus Altair Vega. Arcturus Cassiopeia Andromeda Lyra Laivita Sagittarius

"Why are you so sad?" Charlotte asked impulsively.

"Do I seem to you sad? I hope not" said M[rs.] Durrant.

"Well, just this When you said that. You're not old."

"Old enough to be Timothys mother."

Miss Eliot was looking through ~~the t~~ M[r.] Clutterbucks telescope at the edge of the terrace. The old ~~g~~ man stood beside her, fondling his beard, & ~~reading~~ reciting the constellations. Aldeberan. Gemini, /. . . . . .

"Aldebaran" murmured Miss Eliot, shifting the telescope slightly

"What ~~beautif~~ lovely names, they have - the stars" said Charlotte, pausing.

280	20
6	20
16,800	20

Mrs. Durrant. Charlotte looked along the black barrel of the instrument pointed at the skies.

"There are <u>millions</u> of stars" said Charlotte with conviction.

Miss Eliot withdrew from the telescope. The young men were laughing in the dining room.

"Let me look" said Charlotte eagerly.

"He has not spoken a word this evening" murmured Mrs. Durrant. as she moved away with ~~Miss~~ Julia Eliot. "It may be a letter — it may be —" she paused.

"I think not" said Miss Eliot. "Poor old man!" And she laughed, for there was something whimsical in the ~~notion~~ then got that Mr. Clutterbuck took ~~opium~~. drugs.

wordless
~~Surely that is one of the more important objects we have in view,~~ That is another way of saying the same thing Wortley".

"I hope Timothy is not ~~go~~ losing his temper ~~with Mr Wortley,~~" said Mrs. Durrant, hearing her son speak as they passed the dining room window.

"The stars make me melancholy" said Mrs. Durrant, walking down the terrace with Julia Eliot. I read a book once about the stars ~~once~~ — What are they saying?" She stopped in front of the dining room window. ."Timothy's laugh —"

"That silent young man, ~~his friend~~ — said Miss Eliot -

"Mother!" I didn't recognize you" exclaimed Clara Durrant coming ~~fr~~ in the opposite direction. with Elsbeth. "How delicious —" she breathed, drawing in the scented air. ~~The four women stood looking at the sea~~

~~"Jacob Flanders" said Mrs. Durrant.~~

Mrs. Durrant turned & walked away by herself.

"Clara" she called. Clara ~~followed her~~. went to her.

"How unlike they are!" said Miss Eliot.

Mr. Wortley passed them smoking a cigar; ~~&~~ more ~~"More & more as time passes~~ I find myself agreeing — he said ~~was saying~~ as he passed them.

"When we first came out we could see the flowers in that bed" said Elsbeth.

~~"Its getting dark." Oh look,~~

"Friends of mine, in the Hebrides — ~~said Miss Eliot.~~ Oh Mr. Flanders, have you ever sailed in the Hebrides?"

They went in.

"She must have been so beautiful, & everybody loved her, of course", said Charlotte. "I suppose Mrs. Wortley —" she ~~hesi~~ paused.

"Edward's death was a great ~~great~~ tragedy" said Miss Eliot.

Here Mr. Erskine joined them.

"There is no such thing as silence" he said. "I can name twenty different sounds, not counting your voices."

"Shall we bet? ~~"Done"~~ said Charlotte. "Done" said Mr. Erskine. a sound -

"one ~~First~~ the sea; two ~~then~~ the wind in the trees: ~~then~~, three: ~~something~~ bird ~~between a baby~~ & a dog:" —not a child, a bird -

listen — the others passed on ~~Here they passed~~ in -

"Poor Timothy, said Elsbeth, ~~When he saw them together he went in~~ -

"A / very fine night" shouted ~~Miss Eliot~~ ~~said~~ Miss Eliot into Mr. Clutterbucks ear.

~~"No, no thats~~ doesn't count ~~ruled out!" cried Charlotte~~."

Like to look at the stars?" said the old man, presenting the telescope to Elsbeth.

Doesn't it make you melancholy - looking at the stars?" shouted Miss Eliot

"Dear me, no, dear no" ~~the~~ Mr. Clutterbuck chuckled, when he understood her. Why should it make me melancholy "The idea nev~~er struck~~ me - not for a moment ~~oh~~ dear me no -"

"Thank you, Timothy, but I'm coming in" said Miss Eliot. Elsbeth — here's a shawl —"

"I'm coming in" too ~~said~~ Elsbeth murmured with her eye to the telescope. "Cassiopeia" she murmured.

~~They all went in.~~

"Where are you all?" ~~t~~ she asked, looking around her.

"How dark it is!"

In the drawing room Mrs. Durrant wound ~~wool~~ balls of wool; ~~from~~ Elsbeth played on the piano; &

~~Mr. Clutterbuck read the paper.~~ They all went in:
Mrs. Durrant sat ~~in the drawingroom~~ / by ~~the~~ a lamp winding a ball of wool.
Mr. Clutterbuck read the Times. In the distance was a
second lamp, & round it sat the young ~~wo~~ ladies cutting out
silver- spangled stuff for private theatricals.
"Lord Lansdowne is perfectly right" said Mrs. Durrant, drawing
herself up & ceasing to wind her wool. ~~"And so we shall find out
to our cost one of these days", she added a beginning to wind
again~~ And while Mr. Clutterbuck read the rest of the letter she
sat upright, without touching her ball.
"Ah Mr. Flanders, she said, speaking proudly as if to Lord
Lansdowne himself, — Then she sighed profoundly & began to
wind her wool again. "Sit here" she said.
~~Jacob~~ Jacob disliked her autocratic manner & ~~but~~ settled
~~stiffly~~ into the chair beside her. The lamplight fell full on his
face: he ~~looked out into the garden~~. The light poured over him ~~but~~

illuminating every cranny of his skin: but he sat quite still. looking out into the garden

"I want to hear about your voyage" said Mrs.
Durrant. "~~Twenty years ago we did the same thing.~~"
"Yes" he said.
"Twenty years ago we did the same thing."
"Yes." he said. She looked at him sharply.
He is extraordinarily awkward" "You ~~are horribly~~ shy" she thought, ~~see~~ seeing how he fingered touched
his socks: "& yet so distinguished looking ." ."
"In those days...." she ~~told him~~ resumed, taking him & told him how they had sailed; -
twenty years ago, ~~how~~" my husband, who knew a good deal
about sailing, for he kept a yacht before he married ___"
this she said as if she shared his tastes - & how rashly they
had defied the fishermen - 'almost paid for it with our
lives,' ~~she said~~ but so proud ~~we~~ of ourselves —' She
flung ~~her~~ the hands out that held the ~~yellow~~ ball of wool.
"Would it be any use if I held your wool?" Jacob asked. gruffly.
"You do that for your mother" said Mrs. Durrant,
looking at him again, keenly, as she transferred the
skein: "Yes, it goes much better."
He felt himself become a man of the world. His
enjoyment increased marvellously, & yet he preserved his
cynical detachment.

~~"F~~ Elsbeth Siddons hovered behind them, with

something silver on her arm.

"We want - she said - I've come -" she paused.

quietly
"Poor Jacob" said M$^{rs.}$ Durrant as if she had known him

the
all his life, "They're going to make you act in ~~their~~ play —

"If you <u>would</u>, said Elsbeth, kneeling beside M$^{rs.}$
Durrant's chair -

"Give me the wool" said M$^{rs.}$ Durrant.

"He's come - he's come!" cried Charlotte. "I've won
my bet!"

a lovely
"There's ~~another~~ bunch, right at the top,' said Clara Durrant
mounting ~~further~~ another step of the ladder." Jacob
held the ladder, as she ~~pi.~~ ~~picked the grapes from the roof~~
~~of the greenhouse.~~ ~~the~~ stretched out to reach the grapes
high up on the vine.

"There!" she said cutting through the stalk.

dappled with sun & ~~gr~~ shade
She looked ~~most~~ lovely, Jacob thought, up there among the
vine leaves & the purple bunches.

'The leaves want thinning' she said, & one green

spread like the
palm of a hand

one floated ~~down~~ to the ground.

"I have more than I can eat already" said Jacob. looking up

said
"It does seem absurd - " Clara ~~began~~, ~~looking down~~
~~on him~~. snipping her gardening scissors. To go back ~~to~~

"~~Don't rub it in Miss Durrant.~~

on a day like this "~~London" - or wherever it is.~~"

"I don't want to go back' said Jacob.

"Then, -" said Clara. "But you'll come
again" she said, snipping another leaf, rather carelessly

"If - if -

child ran past the greenhouse door
A ~~little boy was shouting in the garden~~. shouting.
Clara slowly descended the ladder with her basket of
grapes.

"One ~~w~~ bunch of white & two purple" she said,
& she placed two great leaves over them, where they

warm
lay curled / in the basket.

have enjoyed myself.
"~~Ive never enjoyed anything so much~~"

said Jacob.

"Yes its been quite delightful" she said vaguely, ~~& gave~~ him ~~the basket~~.

'Oh. he said, taking the basket of grapes; but she walked past him towards the door of the greenhouse.

"No, no, you're much too good ~~for me~~ [much too good] she said to herself -

The children where whirling past the door ~~of the~~ throwing things into the air.

"Little demons!" she cried.

"~~I haven't said it~~" Jacob thought to himself.

~~I want to say~~ it I ~~can't say it. Clara! Clara!~~

~~Clara~~!" They're throwing the onions." said Jacob.

'You will come next year, Jacob' said M$^{rs.}$ Durrant shaking hands with him, ~~&~~ while a humming bird moth sucked at a fuchsia which hung, like a scarlet ear ring, behind her head~~;~~ M$^{r.}$ Wortley came out of the window, carrying the Times, & holding out his hand.

~~God~~ Good bye, good bye, good bye, Jacob said to them all, & Charlotte Wilding flung up her bedroom x window & cried Good bye, M$^{r.}$Jacob! -
"Why did nobody tell me that M$^{r.}$ Flanders was going?" said M$^{r.}$ Clutterbuck at luncheon. "I should have liked to say good bye."

Aug 15th

XII

"I think, said Jacob, taking his pipe from his mouth, "its in Virgil;" & pushing back his chair, he went to the bookcase.
The rashest drivers in the world are, certainly, the drivers of Post office vans. It is perhaps the effect of wearing uniform - Swinging down ~~Gr~~ Lamb's Conduit Street, the scarlet van rounded the corner by the pillar box in such a way as to graze the kerb, & make the little girl who was standing on tip toe to post a letter look up, half-frightened, half-~~indignant~~ curious. ~~too~~ She paused with her hand in the mouth of the box; then dropped her letter & ran away - It is ~~only~~ seldom ~~only~~ that we see the child on tiptoe with any pity - more often a dim discomfort, a grain of sand in the shoe which its scarcely worth while to remove - thats our feeling - & so we turn the corner. Long ago great people lived here, & coming back from court, stood under the carved door post, while the footman roused himself, & the bitter rain rushed ~~by in~~ down the ~~gutter~~. kennel. Southampton Row, however, is chiefly remarkable for the ~~curious~~ fact that you will always find a man trying to sell a tortoise to a tailor.
There's a ~~sort~~ of fantastic imagination sometimes ~~in the~~ among street hawkers - the imagination of mimicry, perhaps; yet, after all, what fun! ~~to~~ about midnight, in one's basement or attic to ~~start~~ plan ~~one's~~ the days campaign, with the tortoises in a tray "showing off the tweeds, sir' I assure ~~gen~~. "What the gentry wants is something to catch the eye."- only that between you & starvation! - In Oxford Street, as usual, by Mudie's Corner, the omnibuses have ~~all~~ arrived run together like beads on a string.

The motor omnibuses ~~are at a standstill~~ are locked Mr. Spalding going to the city looked at Mr. Charles [~~Ar~~——?] Budgeon bound for Shepherds Bush. ~~The outside passengers~~ for ~~the omnibuses bound~~ The proximity of the omnibuses gave the outside passengers an opportunity to stare into each other's faces. Yet few took advantage of it.

Each had his own business to think of. Each had all his past
furled in him like the leaves of a book known to him by heart;
~~Yet~~ though his friends could only read the title James Spalding, or
Charles Budgeon~~;~~ ~~or~~ ~~as the case might be~~. & the passengers going
the opposite way ~~not even this~~ . nothing at all. The October
sunlight rested upon all these men & women; & little
Johnnie ~~Ap~~ Sturgeon took the ~~o~~ ~~oppor~~tunity to swing ~~off~~
~~the~~ down the staircase, carrying his large ~~la~~ mysterious
parcel, & so ~~by~~ dodging a zigzag course across the
street he reached [~~miss~~?] the pavement, started ~~a tune~~
to whistle a tune, & was soon out of sight - for ever.
The omnibuses jerked on, & every single person felt ~~a~~
~~momentary~~ relief at being a little nearer to his destination,
though some cajoled themselves past the immediate
engagement by the ~~thought of~~ promise of ~~some~~
indulgence beyond - dinner, drink, or a game of dominoes in
~~the smoky~~ corner of the dining room. ~~At any rate~~,
Oh yes, human life is very tolerable on top of an omnibus in
Fleet Street, & if there is such a thing as a shell secreted
to fit man, ~~as a~~ by man himself, here we find it, on the
banks of the Thames, where ~~Ludgate Circus~~ the great streets
join, & St Pauls Cathedral, ~~like the twisted curve of the~~
like the ~~curve~~ volute in the top of the shell —— St. Pauls
Cathedral — some ~~of of~~ people, getting ~~d~~ off their
omnibuses ~~actu~~ loiter up the steps, consult their
watches & ~~then~~ finally make up their minds ~~that they~~ to
~~will~~ go in — Does it need an effort? Yes,
~~for~~ these changes of mood wear us out.
Dim it is, haunted by ghosts of white marble, ~~chaunted~~
~~to~~ / to whom the organ for ever chants~~;~~ - If a boot
creaks, its awful; ~~&~~ then the order; the discipline.
The verger with his rod ~~has a smoothed~~ has ~~ironed out~~
life ironed out beneath him. ~~Simple~~ Sweet & holy are the
angelic choristers. And for ever round the marble
shoulders & in & out of the folded fingers go these
thin high sounds of voice & organ. For ever
requiem - repose.

This business ~~of p~~rayer - the black women & some ~~old~~ elderly men too being on their knees, - or shading their eyes, that the solemn mystery - ~~for Back~~ The leathern curtain of the heart flaps aside; ~~in~~ we stand in the shadow. And glory - those red & golden banners, ~~&~~
~~Men & women pray~~. The ~~leathern curtain of the heart is fa l~~ flaps open; ~~in we enter~~; & ~~flaps open~~; ~~withdraws flaps open~~. ~~Yet~~ - ~~yet~~ -
Tired with scrubbing the steps of the Prudential societies' office, which she did year in, year out, M^rs.^ ~~Pa Perrolt~~ Pidgett took her ~~seat near~~ seat beneath the great Duke's tomb, ~~&~~ ~~if the she saw anything in the arches~~ though had you asked her who ~~he~~ was buried there, or what happened on the field of Waterloo, ~~her~~ her hand would have shaken - ~~signifying quite a different field of vision~~ - for she saw ~~the steps &~~
folded her hands, ~~on~~ & closed her eyes. ~~The great Duke slept beside her~~. A magnificent place ~~to dream in~~ for an old woman to sit in, by the very side of the great Duke, whose victories mean nothing to her; whose name she knows not, though she never fails to greet the little angels opposite, ~~as~~ she passes out, wishing the like on her own tomb, ~~- but~~ for the leathern curtain of the heart was flapped ~~w~~ wide open, & out steal on tiptoe thoughts of ~~a~~ rest, sweet melodies;. . ~~angelic praise; or~~ Old Spicer ~~thinks~~ nothing of the kind. Strangely enough he'd never been in St Pauls all these years, though his office windows looked on the churchyard. So thats.. all? - Well, business pressures .... a gloomy old place - Where's Nelson's tomb? No time now - come again - always leave something in the box - going to rain? - Idly the children stray in - the verger dissuades them - & another & another & another casting their eyes up, the same shadow brushing the same faces; ~~as the flap, the organ, the~~ the leathern curtain of the heart ~~fl~~ flaps wide - . .

man
woman -
man
woman
boy -

Nothing could appear more certain, from the steps of St Pauls,
than that each person is ~~provided with an aim~~, miraculously
provided with coat, skirt & boots; an income; & an object -
So that if we descend among them we alone lack the
proper outfit, since indubitably in my hand, I carry a bag
in that bag ~~is~~ a book, which book I shall at ~~five~~ [?] nine thirty precisely
open under a shaded lamp & proceed to study ~~which~~ as no one
else will do of all these multitudes - ~~And~~ ~~Since~~ They are
not housed. No, the streets belong to them: ~~the streets~~, the
shops; the churches; theirs the innumerable desks; the
~~rows of lights;~~ the pendant lights; the vans are theirs; & the
~~trains~~ railway hung slung ~~across~~ a above the street. Why, if you look
closer you will see that three old men ~~at a~~ at a
little distance from each other run spiders, ~~m~~ along the
pavement. ~~mak~~ ~~making their perch on the kerb stone~~,
as if the street were all their dwelling ~~they~~ ~~need~~ed & here
against the wall a woman stares out at no one, bootlaces
in her hand, which she ~~forgets to~~ does not ask you to buy.
The posters are theirs too, & the news in them. A town
destroyed. A race won. They buy the vast rolls of brown
cloth in the window; & the sausages in shallow trays; &
the steel cylinders, ~~which~~ ~~& the~~ turn ~~behind the~~ in the basement
~~do~~ by their will. ~~They have no houses.~~ A homeless
race, circling beneath the sky ~~which is s over~~ ~~history~~ -whose blue or black held ~~off them~~ by a
~~stretched cov~~ ceiling ~~of~~ cloth of steel filings & horse dung
shredded to dust.

There, under the green shade with his head bent over
white paper M[r.] Sibley, t transferred figures from folios;
& upon each desk you observe, like provender, a
~~st~~ bunch of papers, the day's nutriment; slowly
destroyed by the industrious pen. Innumerable
overcoats of the quality prescribed hung empty all day in the corridors
but as the clock struck six each of these ~~were a~~ was
exactly filled, & the little figures split apart into
trousers or moulded into a single thickness ~~angel~~ jerked
rapidly with angular forward motion ~~into the~~ along

the pavement, they disappeared; dropped into darkness.
Beneath the pavement ~~the~~ such ~~far down in the~~ sunk in the earth
hollow drains, lined charged with yellow light, forever conveyed them,
& large letters upon enamel plates stood ~~for ever~~
eternally for the parks, squares, & circuses; ~~which wer~~ of stood
~~marked~~ upon the upper earth. 'Marble Arch'
'Shepherd's Bush' — to the majority ~~of us~~ these are white
letters upon a blue ground; Only at one ~~po~~ point,
~~are their~~ named Acton, perhaps, or Caledonian Road,
does the name mean shops & houses, in one of which,
down to the ~~left~~ right, where the pollard elm trees
grow out of the paving stones, there's a square curtained window,
& a bedroom —

Never silent, never empty, past midnight the streets are
grey white in the unchanging brightness of electric light.
With her back to the Union of London & Smiths Bank
a blind ~~an~~ old woman sat on a camp stool,clasping a brown
mongrel in her arms, & ~~si~~ & piping ~~singing straight~~ out into
the ~~the night~~ her ~~gay~~ defiant song, not for coppers;
~~defiantly~~; Three ~~girls walked with their sailors down the~~
~~Waterloo Road. Lurching like~~ sailors the women police
walked their beat. ~~The /~~ slow ~~market~~ carts, ~~coming up from~~
~~the coast~~ ~~impeded the traffic from motor cars.~~
~~Rosy silk & white shirt fronts~~ from a sinful wild
heart ~~for~~ Change this for green fields? Oh no, no, no.
the child ~~man~~ who fetches her is, ~~alas, no doubt~~, the fruit of sin, &
should have been in bed, - ~~instead of~~ curtained, asleep, instead
of hearing in the lamp light her mother's wild song,
~~&~~ where she sits against the Bank singing not for coppers
with her dog against her breast.

Home they went. The grey church spires received them;
the ~~old~~ ~~great~~ ~~grey~~ hoary city, ~~so~~ old, sinful & majestic;
~~compassionate~~. ~~sublime~~ ~~loved with its~~ One behind
another, round, or pointed, piercing the sky or massing
themselves ~~as if for p~~ like ships at anchor the
~~city~~ spires & offices, wharves & factories, crowd the bank,

~~Pilgrims, Defoe~~, e~~E~~ternally ~~the~~ the pilgrims trudge; ~~& dun coloured~~, ~~Chaucer, Dryden;~~ barges rest in midstream, heavy laden: as I believe, the city loves her prostitutes.

But few, alas are admitted to that degree. of all the carriages that leave the arch of the opera house, not one turns eastward, & when the little thief is caught in the empty market place, no one in black & white or rose-coloured evening dress can block the way by pausing with a hand on the carriage door to wish - to hope - to condemn. Though Lady Charles, to do her justice, sighs sadly as she ascends her staircase, takes down her Thomas a Kempis, & does not sleep ~~half so soundly as some who lie in prison~~ Till ~~th~~ her mind has lost itself tunnelling into the ~~diffi~~ complexity of things. ~~No, the~~ On the whole, its best to walk back from the opera, ~~so that~~ ~~The aut~~

fatigue is the ~~best~~ only ~~sedative~~ sleeping draught

The autumn season was in full swing. ~~Somebody~~ Tristan was twitching his rug up under his armpits ~~while the shepherd piped his melancholy tune~~ twice a week; & Isolde now waved her ~~k~~ scarf in miraculous sympathy ~~perfect time~~ with the conductor's baton. In all parts of the house were to be found stout hearts, & keen ears. When a royal hand ~~slipped out~~ & withdrew the red & white bouquet reposing on the scarlet ledge, ~~they let a~~ ~~to be~~ Queen of England seemed ~~&~~ some one ~~thing~~ to die for. Beauty, ~~though we know it to be no respecter of persons, is has, it must be~~ admitted, ~~one~~ in its hot-house ~~fo form~~ variety, which is none of its ~~commoness~~ worst, flowers in box after box~~;~~ & though nothing was said of profound importance, & though it is generally agreed that wit deserted beautiful lips about the time that Walpole died - at any rate when Victoria ascended the throne, the lips ~~ch~~ remained adorable, divine. ~~The Little~~ bald men, with gold headed canes, ~~to~~ strolled down the ~~av~~ crimson avenues between the acts, & ~~were~~ only ~~inter~~ tore themselves from their intercourse with the boxes when ~~by~~ the lights going down & the bows were raised.

depending from an invisible body

through an opera glass

Then two thousand hearts, in the semi darkness, remembered, anticipated, travelled dark ~~lay~~ labyrinths; & Clara Durrant, said farewell to Jacob Flanders, & tasted the sweetness of life in effigy; & M^rs. Durrant sat very ~~drew herself~~ upright at the the ~~back of the box, & dark~~ behind her, & Mr. Wortley, ~~directly the curtain went down said something courtly & witty to the wif wife of the Italian ambassador~~ — & shifting his position thought that ~~they were not singing~~ so ~~well this year~~. Brangaena was a trifle hoarse, & suspended ~~on~~ in the gallery many feet above their heads Edward Whittaker surreptitiously held a torch to his miniature score and -and - and —

in the dark
ness
back of the
box

In short, the observer is ~~soon~~ choked ~~himself from~~ with observations. They ~~Only to simplify matters &~~ prevent us from being submerged by chaos, nature & society between them have arranged ~~that~~ a system of classification which is simplicity itself:- ~~That there should~~ are ~~be~~ stalls, boxes, amphitheater & gallery. The moulds are filled nightly. There is no need to ~~divide~~ distinguish details. ~~But, while dif~~ The difficulty remains ~~is~~ to choose. For though I have no wish to be Queen of England, ~~to sit beside her~~; I would willingly sit beside her: ~~there~~ I would hear the Prime Minister gossip: a ~~Countess could tell me much~~; the massive fronts of the respectable have after all their ~~see~~ secret code; ~~& or w~~ why so impermeable ~~or~~ what do they believe?; & then ~~to sink down by~~ Doffing one's own headpiece to assume for a moment ~~that if the a~~ some one's, anyone's - to be a man who has passed examinations: to refer, while Brangaena sings her ~~song~~ to the lurid cities of ~~and~~ Asia Minor or ~~check some~~ abstract to angle angle in the higher mathematics ~~no exclaiming as noble~~ which see, as the shepherd sounds takes his pipe, the falsity ~~fallacy~~ of ~~Berkeleys the of the~~ fallacy of the syllogism - ~~To~~ be ~~Both~~ nobody, if by so being ~~I might~~ be everybody would suit me but: ~~but~~ But no. We must choose; ~~or happier submit to the choice made for us~~. Never was - there a ~~more~~ harsher necessity!

But the

the Countess
whisper;

(2)

was made with the Professorial title, & Leeds, ~~where the Professor taught, was~~ as a seat of learning was laughed to scorn. And the extraordinary thing was that these young men were perfectly right - extraordinary because, ~~when~~ even as Jacob copied his pages he knew that no one would ever print them; & sure enough back they came from the Fortnightly, the Contemporary, The Nineteenth Century - ~~though Jacob was perfectly right~~. When Jacob threw put them in ~~the fire~~ - to the black wooden box where he kept his mother's letters, his ~~flann~~ old flannel trousers, & a great many photographs of ~~young men~~. ~~He was disappointed~~, with a sense of its even disappointed ment but on the whole ~~he was~~ more puzzled than disappointed.

Anyhow The lid shut upon truth.

This black wooden box,/ upon which his name was still legible in white paint, stood between the two long windows ~~looking~~, ~~down upon Lamb's Conduit Street~~. and the sitting room.

3 wicker chairs & a gate-legged table No doubt the bedroom was behind. The furniture probably came from Cambridge. The carpet had been singed ~~burnt~~ by a kettle. ~~It is safe to~~ These houses, which are now for the most part let out in rooms, were built, say a hundred & fifty years ago, - ~~&~~ The rooms are shapely; the ceilings high; & over the door ways, a rose, or a ram's skull, carved in wood, ~~by a soothe somehow~~ in short, the eighteenth century has its distinction. 'Distinction.' Mrs. Durrant said that Jacob was 'distinguished looking.' "Extremely awkward" she said, but so distinguished looking'. Well, seeing him for the first time that is no doubt the right word for him. ~~Then he was sunburnt, now pale like a Londoner~~: Lying back in his chair, in front of the fire, smoking a pipe, & saying to Arthur Raisley, "About this opera now - (for they had ~~finished~~ ~~fin~~ done with indecency -) this fellow Wagner —"

~~as he~~ seemed not ~~thoug~~h awkward~~ness~~ is ~~in for the time in abeyance, one sees what Mrs. Durrant meant.~~ f but ~~the~~ distinction was one of the words to naturally perceptible; though the awkwardness had merged itself into a general appearance of vigour - as yet unexercised; & from looking at him, one would have found it difficult to say whether ~~as~~ he proposed to be this that or the other -

A writer? [I doubt it.] He lacked self-consciousness. A
painter? There was something in the shape of his hands -
(~~or~~ if its any help, ~~his~~ he was descended on his mother's side from
a family ~~which has lived at~~ of the greatest antiquity -
deepest obscurity) ~~testifying~~ which indicated sensibility -
Then his mouth ~~though~~ but surely of all futile occupations
this ~~one~~ of cataloguing features is the worst; ~~& merely~~
~~proves that the~~ one word is sufficient. But if one
cannot find it?

"I like Jacob Flanders' wrote Clara Durrant in her diary;
~~the day he left;~~ 'He is so unworldly; ~~at least~~, I mean he
gives himself no airs & one can say what one likes to him
though he's ~~is rather~~ ~~alarming~~ frightening because he'
but Mr. Letts allows little space in his shilling diaries; &
Clara did not like to encroach upon Wednesday. ~~or to~~
or memorandum Jacob
though a more modest sweeter natural creature
never lived, - 'No, no, no,' she said in the
greenhouse; feeling that [~~though~~?] it ~~would be~~ was too easy too
~~simple~~, to make Jacob love her –

or one which entails greater pain, or more certain disaster; for where ever I ~~lodge~~ rest myself, I shall die in exile. Whittaker in his ~~lodging~~ house; Lady Charles ~~d~~ at ~~the~~ the Manor.

Great Russell Street,

~~Now~~ A young man who had occupied a seven-and-sixpenny seat made his way down the stone stairs when the opera ended ~~slowly~~, as if he were still ~~set a little~~ set / a little apart from his fellows by the influence of the music.

Jacob Flanders hear~~ing~~d a rap ~~upon~~ at his door:

"~~You're the~~ By Jove!" he exclaimed. "~~You can tell~~ me ~~where to it comes find it~~ to it comes"; ~~for though it was now close upon twelve, he had not yet~~ & ~~taking~~ without ~~more ado they~~ 'You're the very man I want!' & without more ado they discovered the ~~very~~ lines which he had been seeking all day long; only ~~they come not in Virgil~~, ~~for~~ only they come not in Virgil but in Lucretius.

X X X X X

"I think that ~~will~~ should make him uncomfortable" sit up." said Borwick. as Jacob ~~I~~ stopped reading; ~~& laid aside his~~ Jacob was excited. ~~He had read his essay aloud~~ It was the first time he had read his ~~writing~~ essay aloud.

"~~I~~" "Damned swine!" he said. ~~Borwick had conveyed~~ Borwick was excited too. ~~A discussion followed upon the ethics of indecency~~. ~~He thought that~~ A discussion followed upon the ethics of indecency. Professor ~~Butlel~~ Bulteel had issued an edition of Wycherley without ~~adm~~ stating that he had left out, or ~~only~~ indicated / only by asterisks, some indecent phrases. ~~Jacobs essay~~ ~~Roused to fury~~, ~~Jacob had written twenty pages~~ ~~Now~~ An outrage, Jacob said this was - a breach of ~~hones~~ faith - sheer prudery - token of a lewd ~~& disgusting~~ mind - & a disgusting nature - ~~Indecency literature was~~ ~~The~~ Aristophanes & Shakespeare were cited. The effeminacy Modern life was repudiated. Great play

~~As for filling the space called 'Memo'~~, with ~~descriptions of talk of this~~
Humblest, most candid of women,! ~~to' fill~~ ~~to~~ ~~To~~ 'No, no, no'
she said, standing by the greenhouse door; 'dont break, dont
spoil' — 'What? Something wonderful ~~wonderful~~ ~~she wanted~~;
~~Yet she Jacob was simple~~ ~~It behooved her to protect him~~.
But what a word to use! ~~go~~ What is there 'wonderful' about
Jacob Flanders, - or Arthur Raisley for the matter of that - as they
sip whiskey, & talk ~~rather~~ about something quite dull : ——
~~it weren't that in young man's talk there is~~ always
trying to remember ~~the~~ the names of a landlady who ~~keeps an inn had escaped them~~;
~~&~~ or, of an inn ~~A~~ ~~The simplest jokes make them laugh~~
But then this is only a young woman's opinion, & she
loved, or ~~almost~~ refrained from loving; — ~~it matters not which~~.
She wished the moment to continue for ever, precisely as it was
that August morning. And moments don't. [Now, for
example, Jacob was telling a longwinded story about some
walking tour he'd taken, & the Inn had an odd name] -
he'd forgotten what ——] 'Wonderful' for ~~a~~ altogether young
woman's word, How can one accept & what ~~she says~~ about ~~her vision of a~~
~~a young man~~? Jacob Flanders?
Then, said Julia Eliot, 'the silent young man'; ~~as~~.
& she had more knowledge of the world than Clara.
'If he is going to get on in the world, she may have meant,
'he will have to find his tongue!
Timothy Durrant made ~~framed~~ no comment at all.
The housemaid found herself rather liberally
rewarded.
Mr. Sopwith's ~~op~~ opinion was as sentimental as Clara's,
though more skilfully ~~t~~ ~~phrased~~. expressed
~~Mrs.~~ Betty Flanders was romantic about Archer &
tender about John; ~~her~~ she was unreasonably irritated by
Jacob's clumsiness in the house.
Captain Barfoot liked him the best of the boys; but
as for giving a reason ——
~~Here~~ It seems then that men & women are both
equally at fault. It seems that a profound

impartial & absolutely just opinion of our fellow creatures, is
impossible beyond us. men
utterly ~~unknown~~known. ~~It seems that we must be either male~~
~~or female women. We~~ Either we are men, or we are women.
Either we are cold, or we are sentimental. ~~If we~~ Either we
are young or old. ~~But everyone is agreed that~~
In any case, ~~the whole~~ life is but a procession of
shadows, & God knows why it is that we embrace them so
depart being
eagerly & see them go from us with such anguish, ~~as if~~
it is
shadows — And why, ~~this being true, are we sometimes~~
~~surprised~~. This & much more than this being true -
are we yet surprised in the window corner by a
or a young man in a chair! sudden vision of truth? ~~It sinks again~~: ~~but momentarily~~
~~we know each other~~. That's Jacob Flanders: ~~oh yes~~:
And now I see nothing at all.
That the young man in the chair is of all things in the whole
world most real, most adorable, best known to us ~~,~~ why why
why? For the moment after, ~~the vision is gone~~.
We know nothing about him.

~~most manly, indolent, tenderhearted, confused, selfish,~~
~~It is upon us as he~~
[better known to us than ourselves - 'don't move, don't speak,
we say, only let me feast on your heart,' & drawing near,
crouching beside him on ~~the~~ hearthrug, it seems as if]
That is our

Such is our manner of seeing. ~~By~~ such ~~closed are~~
love;
we ~~enveloped. And yet~~, the condition of our ~~knowledge~~.

x x x x x x x X X

"I am twenty two ~~four~~. It is nearly ~~past~~ the end of October. Life is thoroughly
pleasant, although unfortunately there are a great many fools about.
~~The~~ One must apply oneself to something or other — God knows what —
Nothing is much worth doing except ~~what~~ talking to people one likes -
Still I rather suspect there's some humbug in that too.

'I say ~~sa~~ Bonamy, what about Beethoven?' -
Bonamy's an amazing ~~is amazing~~ - ~~how he finds time to character~~. He
knows practically everything, not so much about English literature as
do. But ~~he's read~~ all these Frogs - ~~Mallarme~~ Baudelaire, Mallarme

'~~You must~~ I rather suspect you're talking rot,
Bonamy. ~~Tennyson~~, in spite of what you say, Tennyson - '
The truth is, ~~I was~~ one has to be brought with people who read -
Now I suppose Barfoot is talking to mother. Thats an odd
affair to be sure, But I can't see Bonamy down there -
~~There's not much to be said for London after all~~. Damn London!
~~I wish I were down there~~ - [for the market carts were rattling down
~~but~~ then the ~~thought~~ thought ~~of~~ Clara Durrant, the street ~~had just come back~~-
occurred to him. He became restless.

'~~I say B~~ What about a walk on Saturday - —
~~And then the~~ Whats ~~the~~ happening on Saturday? ~~&~~
Then taking out his pocket book he assured himself that
the Durrants would be back next week.

~~Now~~

~~It is difficult impossible to say~~ But though all this may very well
be true - so Jacob thought & spoke - so he crossed his legs,
filled his pipe - sipped his whiskey, & once looked at his
pocket book, rumpling his hair as he did so, - there remains
over something which can never be conveyed to a second person
save by Jacob himself. Moreover, part of this is not Jacob, but
Arthur Bonamy; the room; the market carts; the hour; the
very moment of history. Then consider the effect of sex.

body
~~And here let everyone use the pen for himself or herself.~~
how between man & woman it hangs, wary, tremulous, ~~so that~~
so that here's a valley, here's a peak, where in truth all's as flat as
my hand;— Even the exact words get the wrong accent on them.
hum
And something is always impelling one, to ~~hang~~, like that moth,
vibrating at the mouth ~~of what~~ of the cavern of mystery -
~~en~~dowing Jacob Flanders with all sorts of qualities he had not at
all, - for though he certainly sat talking to Bonamy,
half of what he said ~~about the~~ ~~has been left out because it~~
was too dull to repeat: ~~half unin~~ much unintelligible:
what remains is ~~much a~~ matter of guesswork. And yet
over him we hang vibrating.

XIII

The flames had fairly caught.

'There's St Pauls!" some one cried; ~~as the~~

As the wood caught the city of London was lit up: for a second.

~~But on the~~ On other sides of the . ~~there were~~ fire there were trees.

of the faces which came out fresh & vivid, as if painted in yellow & red the most singular was a girls face. By a trick of the firelight, she seemed to have no body. The oval of face & hair ~~came out~~ hung beside the fire with ~~trees~~ dark ~~night~~ vacuum. for background.

As if dazed by the glare her green-blue eyes stared at the flames. Every muscle of her face was taut. There was something painful in the sight of her: she was thus staring faced between twentyfive & thirty.

A hand descending from ~~behi~~ the chequered darkness thrust on her head the conical white hat of a pierrot. Shaking her head, she still stared. A whiskered face appeared above her.

They dropped two legs of a table upon the fire, & an armful of twigs & leaves. All this blazed up & showed ~~a~~ faces far back - round, white, smooth, beaked: all intent: showed, too, St Pauls floating on the white mist; & extinguished shaped churches.

The flames were struggling through the wood & roaring up when goodness knows where from, ~~a~~ pails ~~of wat.~~ flung water in ~~as~~ beautiful hollow shapes, as of polished tortoiseshell: flung again & again: until the hiss was like a swarm of bees: & all the faces went out.

Oh Jacob, said the girl as they pounded up the hill in
the dark, ‘I’m so frightfully unhappy!”

Oh Jacob’s your Christian name is it -

You’re not a Jew, are you? she said. “I do hate Jews”.....
And she told him how a Jew had played her a dirty
trick, leaving ~~all~~ his dirty clothes scattered over the room, &
she having to pawn her mothers watch to pay the rent.
Shouts of laughter came from the others.
~~These were the artists of England. A stags head in~~
~~plaster was~~ The hotel dining room was brightly lit.
A stags head in plaster was at one end of the table:
at the other ~~a~~ some Greek ~~stat~~ bust blackened & reddened
to represent ~~Gy~~ Guy Fawkes - whose night it was.
The diners were linked together by wreaths of paper roses
so that when it came to singing Auld Lang Syne ~~their~~
~~ha crossed hands~~ a pink & yellow line rose & fell

with crossed hands

all down the table. There was an enormous tapping of
wine glasses. ~~Some~~ A young man stood ~~got~~ up & ~~sat down~~
<u>again abruptly</u>. ~~&~~ Florinda ~~picking u~~ taking one of the
purplish globes that lay on the table, flung it straight at
his head.

green

“I’m so frightfully unhappy” she said turning to Jacob
who sat beside her.

The table ~~was~~ ran, as if by invisible legs, to the side
of the room, & a barrel organ decorated with a
red cloth & two pots of paper flowers ~~was~~ reeled out ~~the~~
walz music.

Jacob could not dance. He stood against the
wall, smoking his pipe.

“We think, said two of the dancers, breaking off from
the rest, that you are the most beautiful man we
have ever seen.

& bowing profoundly before ~~him~~

So they wreathed his shoulders with paper flowers.
~~Jacob never spoke a word~~.

Then somebody brought out a white & gilt chair & made him
sit on it. As they passed, people hung ~~grapes~~ glass grapes
on his shoulders; Then ~~Clara~~ Florinda got upon his knee,
& hid her face in his waistcoat.
'Now let us talk, said Jacob as he walked down ~~the~~
Haverstock Hill between four & five oclock on November
the sixth, ~~about something~~ arm in arm with
'the Greeks'
James Raisley 'about something sensible."

The Greeks — Yes, that was what they talked about — how,
~~after all~~ when all's said & done when one's rinsed one's
mouth with every literature in~~to~~ the world, including
~~Rus~~ Chinese & Russian - (but these Slav's aren't
civilised-) ~~still~~ its the flavour of Greek that remains -
one
~~like sharp & distinct on the tongue~~ Raisley quoted ~~Sophocles~~ -
Sophocles true
Aeschylus verse - Jacob ~~another~~. Its ~~my~~ ~~belief~~ that no Greek
could have understood, or Professor endured. Never mind.
shouted
What is Greek for if not to be ~~quoted~~ on Haverstock Hill in
the dawn? Moreover, Raisley never listened to
Sophocles, nor Jacob to Aeschylus. ~~If set to construe~~
~~the words no doubt each could have produced something~~
~~passable~~ - ~~They were boastful, triumphant; in~~
whole
dismissing ~~whole~~ civilizations; dashing ~~volumes~~ ages from
their lips; masterfully tipping out from the trough
waves of the past this shapely vase, ~~this of~~ ~~Moreover (&~~
this is ~~the main thing~~) They were boastful,
triumphant. It seemed to both ~~of them~~ that
they had read every book in the world: known
every sin, passion, & joy. Civilisation lay around
them like flowers ready for picking. Ages
fit for sailing
lapped at their feet like waves of the sea.
~~All was theirs for the asking~~. ~~And then~~
~~impelled by some masterful instinct,~~ ~~Why~~
Yet, able ~~to pick anything; to shove off anywhere, it was~~

~~the Greeks they chose~~, And surveying all this, the two young men decided in favour of Greece.

~~How it comes about that this ancient torch~~

~~That~~ The main thing was that each was at the same point of ignorance. ~~Neither had been able to pass examinations brilliantly~~. Each believed, & disbelieved about the same amount.

"We are, said Jacob, probably ~~int~~ the only people in the world who understand what the Greeks meant -"

Here they stopped & drank coffee at a stall where the ~~carters~~ carts stopped; the urns were burnished brass; & little lamps burnt along the counter.

The stall keeper told them about his boy at Gibraltar; taking Jacob for a military man.
And so on again down the hill, talking about the Greeks. A strange thing - when you come to think of it - this love of Greek - flourishing in such obscurity, ~~running~~ discouraged, ~~starved~~, ~~&~~ yet leaping out, all of a sudden, especially on leaving crowded rooms, or when the ~~pale~~ moon floats among the waves of the downs; at night; or in hollow, sallow, fruitless London days; ~~as if we could take off our undo our heavy clothes & step into clean water;~~ as if ~~stepp~~ letting this ~~cumbersome world hurtle~~ its ~~we could~~

as if it were a cordial near at hand

always a miracle. Jacob knew no more Greek than served him to stumble through a play with a dictionary. However, as he tramped into London, it seemed to him that he was making the flagstones ring on the road to the Acropolis ~~ring beneath him~~; anyhow that Socrates was a friendly old man, & ~~Aspasia~~ ~~The H~~ The queer thing is how free & friendly they show themselves; ~~& then~~ how ~~gent~~ kindly they ~~the~~ whole sentiment of the place entirely in harmony with his own - which was superbly high-spirited. ~~Not naked, no, not drunk, no; but free & fine; the~~ ~~She had called him Jacob without asking leave. She had sat upon his knee~~.

all good did in the days
& thus ~~all good~~ women ~~lived with men in~~ the ~~time~~ of the Greeks.

At this moment there shook out into the air a wavering, quavering, doleful lamentation, which seemed to lack strength to unfold itself; & yet flagged on: ~~the workmens whistles~~ at the sound of which. I suppose, doors in back streets burst open; the day had begun again.

Florinda had been sick.

x x x x x
~~For the story of Florinda~~

by the side of
M$^{rs.}$ Durrant, sleepless as usual, scored a mark ~~against~~ certain
buried in her
lines in ~~Dante~~; the Inferno. Clara slept ~~perfectly~~ pillows ~~soundly~~; on her dressing table ~~some~~ dishevelled roses & a pair of long white gloves.

~~\ \ \ \~~ \ \ \

Still

Still wearing the conical white hat of a Pierrot Florinda was sick.

No doubt there was a basin & the rest of it.

The bedroom seemed ~~used to~~ fit for these catastrophes - ~~cheap, mustard coloured obviously~~ ~~a an attic studio~~ cheap, mustard coloured, curiously ornamented with silver ~~stars,~~ paper stars, Dutch women's hats & rosaries pendent from the gas brackets - As for Florinda's history, her name was bestowed upon her by a ~~th~~ ~~celebrated painter,~~ ~~after~~ ~~upon an occasion~~ a painter, who wished to signify that the flower of / her maidenhood ~~had left his~~ [margin: was still ~~had been~~] ~~hands~~ unplucked. ~~As she had no Florinda was still~~ Be that as it may, ~~the fact remains that~~ she was without a surname; ~~& for all~~ ~~& though she~~ & for parents had only the photograph of a tombstone beneath which, she said, her father was buried. Sometimes she would dwell upon ~~her~~ ~~fathers height; sometimes on her mothers beauty~~. the size of it, & rumour had it that Florinda's father had died from the growth of his bones, which nothing could stop; just as her mother enjoyed the confidence of ~~the~~ a Royal [margin: master] ~~family;~~ & some~~how~~ now & again or other ~~had~~ Florinda herself was a Princess - ~~chiefly~~ ~~mostly~~ ~~though~~ but chiefly when drunk. Thus deserted, pretty into the bargain; with tragic eyes & the lips of a child, she talked more about virginity than women mostly do; & had lost it only the night before or cherished it beyond the heart in her breast according to the man she talked to. Did she always talk to men, then? No, she had her confidante,- Mother Stuart; Stuart, ~~as the~~ the lady would point out is ~~one of the~~ a Royal name - but what this signified, & what her ~~relationship~~ business was, no one knew; Postal orders always saved them ~~on~~ at the ~~very~~ last; ~~moment~~. M^rs. Stuart liked a compliment to her parrot;

kept a parrot; believed in the transmigration of souls; & could read the future in tea leaves-

~~only that Mrs. Stuart got postal orders every Monday morning, &~~
only that M[rs.] Stuart got postal orders every Monday
morning,— Dirty lodginghouse wall paper she was,
behind the chastity of Florinda.

For Florinda often ~~spent the day rambling the~~ wept, -
~~M[rs.] Stuart banged her on the head with the tea cosy~~ -
& spent the day ~~ramb~~ wandering the streets, stood at Chelsea
watching the river swim past, ~~exchanged hats with young men in~~
~~restaurants~~ ~~rambled off~~ [trailed], ~~am~~ along the shopping streets,
opened her bag & powdered her cheeks in omnibuses,
read love letters ~~which~~ at tea propping them against the
teapot in the A.B.C., ~~of~~ detected glass in the sugar;
~~called~~ [accused] the waitress ~~of~~ [for] wishing to poison her; [accused young men of staring at her;] got into
talk with young men, & found herself towards evening
slowly sauntering down Jacob's street, when it
occurred to her to her ~~to~~ that she liked him better than those dirty
Jews, & sitting at ~~the~~ [his] table she drew off her gloves &
told him how Mother Stuart had ~~pos~~ banged her on the
head with ~~the~~ [a] tea cosy.

Jacob took her word for it that she was chaste.
~~She needed his protection~~. She had read absolutely
nothing. She prattled, sitting by the fireside, about
famous painters. The tomb of her father was
mentioned. Wild & frail & beautiful she looked;
& thus the women of the Greeks were, Jacob thought;
& this was life; & himself grown up & Florinda
chaste. She left with one of Jane Austen's novels
beneath her arm. M[rs.] Stuart, she said, often talked of her.

As for Jacob, he paced his room. Ought he to ~~have~~ gone with her to
the station? ~~So~~ so young a creature, out alone, ~~in the~~
late in the evening - ~~or~~ asked her to dine? But then where?
At ten o'clock he left the house.

x x x x x

Beautiful are the innocent. ~~To believe even as lies are~~
~~told you that there is that in the speaker which transcends all~~
~~lies~~; To believe that the girl herself transcends all lies; ~~but~~
(for as she spoke Jacob was not so foolish as to ~~believe the~~ [?] illusion implicitly
~~letter of what she said~~) to marvel, curiously ~~almost,~~ at the
unanchored life - his own seeming petted & [~~rus~~?] cloistered in
comparison - 'That was in Paris' when we were in
Rome' Florinda had said, — to have at hand such
sovereign specifics for all disorders of the soul as Gryll Grange, &
the plays of Shakespeare - ~~this innocence,~~ to figure out
a comradeship 'like that of the Greeks (how they ran in his
head!) all spirited on her side, protective on his, yet
equal on both, for if there's one thing damnable its
condescension from man to woman, — innocence such as
this is beautiful, ~~as the rose~~ & perhaps not so foolish
after all.

For when Florinda got home that night, she first
washed her head, then ate a chocolate cream & then
opened ~~Jaco Jacobs~~ Peacock. True, she was horribly bored.
What on earth was it about? She had to wager with
herself that ~~no more~~ she would turn the page before she
ate another ~~cream~~ - ~~Her~~ In fact she slept. But
then her day had been a very long one - mother Stuart
had thrown the tea cosy ~~across the room at breakfast~~ -
~~that morning~~ - at breakfast - there are formidable things in the
streets, - & though Florinda was as ~~st~~ ignorant as an
owl, & would ~~perhaps~~ never learn ~~to~~ to ~~spell~~ ~~read with~~ read even her
love letters correctly, still as ~~as his her history proves~~
she had her feelings, liked some men better than others,
& was entirely at the beck & call of life. Whether or

Unless indeed, it is the only thing that does matter.
Jacob was restless when she left him.
All night men & women seethed up & down the well known beats.
Late home comers would see shadows against the blinds even in the most respectable suburbs. Not a square even in ~~To say that there is nothing more in it than~~ winter lacked its amorous shadowy couple; ~~loitering~~ ~~The cabs~~ All plays (~~winter drifting~~ turned on the same matter. Bullets went through heads in hotel bedrooms almost nightly on that account; ~~alone~~. ~~&~~ When the body escaped mutilation seldom did the heart go to the grave unscarred. Little else was talked of in theatres & popular novels. Yet we say it is a matter of no importance whatever.

What with Shakespeare & Gryll Grange, Mozart, Bishop Berkeley - choose whom you like - the fact is concealed, & the evenings for most of us pass reputably, or only with the sort of tremor that a snake makes passing through the grass.
But then concealment by itself distracts the mind from the print & the sound - If Florinda had had a mind she might have read with clearer eyes than we can.
She & her sort have solved the question by turning it into a matter of washing the hands nightly before going to bed — The only ~~difficult~~ question ~~matter~~ ~~of dispute~~ being whether you prefer ~~like~~ your water hot or cold - ~~only~~ — after which being settled, the mind can go about its business unassailed. ~~Only~~, ~~in~~
if the mind survives
~~For~~ But it did occur to Jacob, halfway through dinner, to wonder whether she had a ~~any~~ mind. ~~at all~~.

x x x x

x x x x x x x

They sat at a little table in the restaurant.
Florinda leant the points of her elbows on the table & held her chin
in the cup of her hands. Her black cloak had slipped down.
~~Coloured &~~ ~~She was coloured~~ &
~~back~~. ~~from her shou~~lders. ~~She emerged~~, ~~as if~~ Gold &
white, with bright beads on her, she emerged; her face with the
yellow hair on top, ~~almost literally~~ flowering from her body;
innocent, scarcely tinted; ~~in~~ the eyes ~~in~~ frankly gazing
slowly
about her, or ~~slowly~~ f resting on Jacob~~s face~~. as he talked.
Then she talked; not consecutively.

"You know that big black box the Australian left in
They say
my room ever so long ago? — I do think furs make a
woman look old. Thats Bechstein come in now -
I was wondering what you looked like when you were a tiny
Nibbling the roll she looked at
little boy. ~~We had~~ Jacob. She nibbled her roll. him.
Jacob, you're like one of those statues." I think ~~theyre a~~
there are lovely things in the British Museum, dont
you? Lots of lovely things ___"

The room was filling. The heat increasing.
dazed
Talk in a restaurant is like sleep-walkers talk, - so
many things to look at - ~~of [purs~~?] so much noise - other
people talking - can one overhear? Oh but then they mustn't
over hear us - ~~Jacob himself felt it.~~ And the
~~excitement~~

'thats Ellen Nagle ~~over t~~ - that girl -'
~~& so on~~. '~~I took my lunch with me ' she said~~.
"I'm awfully happy since I've known you, Jacob
~~she said~~. 'You're such a good man'.
And sitting up she suddenly ~~poured forth She~~
told him a story -

It was like a child's story. ~~Yet fam~~ous names

Jacob may have been sentimental. It seemed to him extraordinarily pathetic. ~~She~~ had ~~forgotten everything else.~~

But But ~~her eyes~~ she was staring. Everyone was staring.
The woman ~~spoke loud~~ - was speaking loudly. It was intended.
~~She swept the plates off the table & strode out~~. Everyone was ~~silent~~ listened; waited; She swept the plates off the table.
The man half jumped up. Out she strode.
And Florinda's eyes filled with admiration.

The room got fuller & fuller, talk louder; knives more clattering.
"Well you see what makes her say things like that—"
She stopped. So did everyone.

'Tomorrow - Sunday - a beastly - tell you to go -'

Crash

[quicker & quicker higher & higher - all the plates swept from the table - crash!] And out she swept.

It was ~~the~~ at the table next them that ~~this~~

the voice spun higher & higher Suddenly the woman dashed plates the floor. The man was left there

[the woman spoke louder, faster, suddenly dashed the plates ~~off on~~ to the floor. & The man sat ~~staring~~ they were down again
Everybody stared Then — "well, poor ~~p~~ chap we mustn't sit staring - what a go - did you hear what she said then? By God he looks uncomfortable' -
~~The waiters are laughing No wonder~~ - ~~Only the~~ two ~~plates broken What a~~ He didn't come up to the scratch I suppose - 'All the mustard on the floor -
The waiters laughing
Theyre wiping it up - '

"~~I say Florinda~~ —

~~Florinda was sat~~ ~~Now~~ Jacob observed ~~t~~ Florinda; ~~&~~ in her face there seemed to him something horribly brainless: ~~she was excited~~ ~~She was triumphant. as if she too might have done that.~~ ~~as~~ if it were a very good scene] as she sat staring, ~~exulting~~.

x x x x x x

Out she swept, this little black woman with the dancing

feather in her hat; ~~the~~ & ~~had her~~
Yet she had to go somewhere. The night is not a

in to wh. you

~~which one sails.~~ tumultuous black ocean, sprinkled with fires. sink or leave

wh. swallows a entirely & leaves only a dancing star &

only a . . . star -

~~There~~ As a matter of fact it was a wet November night

The lamps of Soho made large greasy circles of light upon the pavement. The bye streets were dark enough to shelter ~~a~~ man or woman leaning against the doorway - ~~which in this region~~, One detached herself as Jacob & Florinda approached: ~~walked in~~

'She's dropped her glove' said ~~Jacob~~. Florinda.

Jacob pressing forward, raising his hat, gave it her.

Effusively she thanked him:

~~"Oh" she mur~~mured; retraced her steps; dropped her glove again; - And why? For whom?

~~What does it all mean?~~ She

Meanwhile, where had the other woman got to? And. the man? ~~What is happening~~?

(Sept. 10th 1920) x x x x x

These narrow strips of pavement hanging above ~~dark charms~~
are ~~dangerous walking;~~ &
The street lamps ~~never~~ do not carry far enough. On either
side of the way from Soho to Bloomsbury the forest, ~~into~~ is
~~which these wild animals slip~~, is impenetrable. ~~The~~
~~herds are hide behind the trees, but watch us, unseen~~
~~nor would lamplight illumine what we~~ ~~Figures~~
to tell us that. The voices, angry, lustful, despairing,
passionate, ~~never~~ scarcely tell us more than the ~~v~~ voices of caged beasts
at night. Only . They are not caged; not beasts. ~~No~~.
Stop a man; Ask ~~them~~ him the way. ~~They'll~~ he'll tell it you. ~~only~~ but ~~The truth is~~
one's afraid to ask ~~them~~ him the way.— ~~The truth is they~~
afraid, somehow, of what they know & we either dare not
~~know~~ or cannot know.. ~~For instance, this tailors shop~~,
~~now~~? And its that ~~that~~ lures us; as if the
road from Soho to Bloomsbury were a forest track,
on on each side you heard the wild horns & ~~the cries of~~
a ~~disn~~ ~~distant hunt.~~__ ~~For~~ ~~& the beautiful~~
Then, right in the middle of the street blatantly advertising its
meritorious solidity a boarding house exhibits behind
uncurtained window its testimony to the soundness of
London - ~~rather~~ as ~~of a section of~~ There they sit dressed
like ladies & gentlemen in bamboo chairs. ~~And~~ The
widows of ~~off~~ business men ~~pleasantly~~ ~~recall~~ ~~endevaour to~~
prove ~~assert~~ ~~the fact~~ laboriously that they ~~are~~ ~~have relatives~~ ~~who~~ ~~&~~
~~in the~~ are related to judges. ~~And~~ The wives of coal merchants,
~~are busy~~ ~~produce~~ ~~Eagerly~~ instantly reply that ~~this is the~~
their fathers kept coachmen ~~very first time they've stayed in a boarding house.~~
~~& Young bank clerks~~, ~~Bank clerks make love because~~
~~other bank clerks~~

On the whole, these appeared more repulsive to
Jacob than the others.

What does one fear? Partly that he may tell us what we refuse to know - how few we are, the sober ones, how narrow ~~The strips~~ of pavement ~~from Soho to Bloomsbury~~, . how deep the chasm. There! They've melted into it - both man & woman. ~~Then~~ Further on, blatantly advertising its meritorious ~~solidit~~ respectability.

/A servant brings coffee: & the crotchet basket has to be moved. /And so in again, down the street, passing a girl here for_sale, or there an old woman with only matches to offer , ~~the~~ passing the crowd ~~with~~ from the Tube station, ~~met~~ the women with veiled hair, passing ~~shuttered shops, flats that open to latch keys &~~ but shut doors, at length no one at all but a solitary policeman Jacob with Florinda on his arm, reached his room, & ~~litt~~ lighting the ~~gas~~ lamp said nothing at all.

"I don't like you when you look like that. Jacob,' Florinda said.

The problem ~~is~~ ~~was~~ is insoluble. [The body is harnessed to a brain. A defence of indecency indeed.] - The ~~body is harnessed to a brain~~: ~~Must he then~~ ~~The Such That such stupidity should go with~~ ~~Beauty & stupidity~~; [Simplicity was ~~veined with~~ had become complexity.] Beauty ~~went~~ goes hand in hand with stupidity. ~~Love itself was a revolting mixture:~~ & ~~There~~ Florinda sat on the hearthrug, ~~unconscious~~; ~~of every thing~~; ~~unheeding a single word he'd said to her; since when~~ the staring at the fire; staring at the broken mustard pot — Love, civilisation.] Its all very well to defend indecency on paper, but when it comes to Beautiful women ~~will~~ ~~rejoice~~ exult when mustard pots are broken - ~~Stupidity is brutal~~. The body is harnessed to a brain. Stupidity - ~~There she sat staring at the fire~~ — is damnable. And as for having taught Florinda Florinda had

The problem is insoluble. The body is harnessed to a brain. Beauty goes hand in hand with stupidity. There she sat staring at the fire as she had stared at the broken mustard pot. A common housefly showed more vivacity, & ~~as for simplicity~~, in spite of defending indecency; Jacob doubted very much whether it ~~w~~ gave him the pleasure ~~Probably she had never understood a word he had said to her, &~~ In spite of defending indecency, Jacob doubted whether he liked it in the raw. In short, he had a violent reversion towards male society & the works of the classics; ~~&~~ & was ready to ~~pour des~~ turn ~~with indignation~~ in wrath. upon whoever it was who fashioned life thus. ~~But then~~ — ~~His gloom was profound~~.

~~But~~ Then Florinda laid her hand upon his knee. ~~Perhaps she~~ After all it was none of her fault. ~~Yet~~ But the thought saddened him. Its not catastrophes, murders, deaths, diseases, that age & kill: its the way people look, & laugh, ~~go their ways~~. & run up the steps of omnibuses. ~~She went home submissively;~~

~~'Good night' he said; & perhaps envied her. More probably, it was on her account that he sat up till the da dawn seeking something in books to~~ He went home & read Milton: ~~Milton bored him. At least Milton was not~~

~~He took down his Milton after she had gone: but~~ Any ~~thing~~ excuse serves a stupid woman. He told her his head ached.

~~But~~ But oh dear, when she looked at him, half guessing, ~~und~~ half understanding, apologising perhaps, anyhow saying as he had, its ~~not~~ none of my fault, ~~&~~ beautiful in body, her face ~~strange & wild in face, her close fur cap, her half~~ while, like a ~~wil~~ wild rose, wild & innocent of countenance, he ~~was left~~ found no comfort in the classics.

Branden

. XIV .

a firm of.
About this time,/ merchants having dealings with the East put on
the market little paper flowers which opened on touching water.
~~The finger bowls which~~ ~~then invar~~ As it was the custom
also to ~~dip~~ ~~set before~~ use finger bowls at the end of dinner
~~these a~~ ~~it was~~ ~~it was usual to produce~~ the new discovery
was ~~to put a~~ found of excellent service. In these sheltered
lakes - ~~these~~ the little coloured flowers swam & slided;
surmounted smooth slippery waves, & sometimes foundered
~~beneath the~~ & lay like pebbles on the glass floor. Their
fortunes ~~adventures~~ were watched by eyes intent & lovely. It is
surely a great discovery that leads to the union of hearts &
the foundation of homes. The paper flowers ~~often~~
did no less.

~~though~~
It must not be thought / that they ousted real flowers.
Roses, lilies, carnations in particular, looked over the rims of
~~their~~ vases & ~~pitied the~~ surveyed the bright lives & swift
dooms of their artificial relations. ~~Mr.~~ M^r. ~~Ormond~~
Stuart Ormond ~~said very ni~~ made ~~this~~ this very observation;
& charming it was thought; & Kitty Craster married him six
months later.— But Real flowers can never be dispensed
with. If they could be, ~~if that is to say the long table~~
~~could be left bare & the drawing room too, then tables too,~~
~~then — well then Kitty Craster would there wou hum~~
human life would be a different affair. For Flowers fade;-
really
Chrysanthemums are ~~perfectly~~ awful: ~~in the~~ perfect over
night, & yellow & jaded next morning - not fit to be seen.
On the whole, though the price is sinful, carnations
pay best;- it's a question, however, whether its wise
to have them wired. Some shops advise it. ~~Of course,~~
no doubt, ~~Its~~ the only way to keep them at a dance; but ~~at~~
~~dinner parties — the~~ whether it is necessary at
dinner parties, unless the rooms are very hot, ~~has not is~~
~~still~~ remains in dispute. Old M^rs. Temple used

to ~~say that a~~ recommend an ivy leaf - just one, dropped into the bowl. She ~~used~~ said it kept the water pure for days — ~~but her there is is reason to think that she without being changed.~~ ~~That would be a discovery indeed~~ But there is some reason to think that she referred to wall flowers only. or that the problem of ivy in London is insurmountable.

At any rate, what with visits to the florist, to the French baker who cannot be depended on to send sweets in time, above all to the dressmaker, the morning passed, & the afternoon was here, with its problem of scattering cards, its reprieves, anxieties, calamities - alas, M^rs. Bonhamy was in; ~~& the call~~ & dreadful M^r. Grice was there & ~~the visit~~ one ~~had to stay half an hour~~ — couldn't go just as tea came in — so the day fluttered swiftly to its end, & there! ~~was~~ the dinner bell rang / in the middle of dressing.

It is universally agreed that devotion to a typewriter is far more meritorious; that to have made ten pounds is a greater benefaction; & that

But we are forgetting the poor. If you liken the frivolous days to scarlet flamingoes, ~~one in the week was seven black.~~ There was one coloured soot black, Innumerable old women displayed their bad legs. Innumerable facts were entered in books; & elastic stockings were granted ~~applied for~~ Then, ~~In~~ Signor Panizzi came on Tuesdays: the piano tuners h wife had consumption.

But perhaps ~~there are~~ the Then ~~there~~ small cards with names engraved on them — were more serious than the flowers of a problem

for In the delivery of them more horses have been worn out, than ~~would have~~ served to win in the battle of Waterloo. ~~Mrs. Page~~ Mercifully the parlourmaid nine times out of ten replied ~~Not at Home;~~ but each afternoon had its reprieves, anxieties & calamities. Then the battle itself & were the source of more

but ~~&, what was worse,~~ sometimes ~~Mrs. Bonham~~ ladies ~~was~~ ~~were~~ at home - Then, of course, the poor, with their bad legs, could only get elastic stockings if ~~the~~ sufficient signatures were obtained Signor Panizzi came on Tuesday, The piano tuners wife was threatened with consumption.

~~Then, of course,~~ Still, even if the cards had been superseded,
no power on earth can compell confectioners to be punctual,
~~or~~ dressmakers ~~&~~ to keep their promises. There were
unruly powers at work blowing life into storms,
utterly disordering the sedulous morning, & ~~the~~ uprooting
the stability of the afternoon — dressmakers & confectioners
that is to say. Six yards of silk will cover one body: ~~have~~;
but if you have ^to devise six hundred different colours, & twice as
many shapes ~~?~~ in the middle of which problem, there is
~~faith fickle man has forgotten to send the sweets, &~~
~~then~~ the ~~pres~~ urgent question of ~~the sweet for dinner~~ -
the ~~pudd ice~~ pudding crested with tufts of green ~~fo~~ cream &
fortifications of almond — ^not arrived [~~Flamingo hours~~
fluttering softly through the sky] — It has not
arrived.

~~Eviden Unmistakably, some sort of invention was needed,~~

The flamingo hours fluttered softly through the
sky — ~~here Sometimes~~ a But occasionally they dipped
their wings in pitch black: Notting Hill, for instance, on the
purlieus of Clerkenwell. No wonder that Italian
remained a hidden art, & the piano always played the
same t ~~fragments~~ of sonatas. ~~Here win~~
In order to buy one pair of elastic stockings, for Mrs. Page,
widow, aged 63, in receipt of ~~no~~ 5/ from the guardians
~~but h~~ & help from son in dye works intermittent —
letters have to be procured, ~~from Governors~~ & forms filled up
~~by~~ ^in the same round simple hand that ~~already had~~
~~completed~~ entered into Mrs. Lett's diary the facts that
the weather was fine & Jacob Flanders unworldly.
~~This was~~ Clara Durrant's ~~life. kept a diary~~. got the
stockings, played the sonata, filled the vases, ~~kept~~
fetched the pudding, left the cards, ~~&~~ & when that
great invention of paper flowers took place, she was one

And read their doom in Chloe's eyes.

Those who most enjoyed their brief lives; ~~& what marvelled at the~~
~~wit of the clever young men~~ ~~though~~ ~~Some people were~~
~~wonderfully clever.~~
Nor were there wanting poets to celebrate the theme Edwin
~~cop~~ verses
Mallett, for example, ~~s~~ wrote his ~~sonnet~~, ending

And read their doom in Chloe's eyes

~~copied them & dropped them in the Durrant's letter box~~
~~at~~ which caused ~~so~~ Clara to blush at the first reading,
& to laugh at the second, saying that it was just like him
~~instead of~~
~~not~~ to call her ~~Clara~~ - Chloe ~~instead of Clara~~ — ~~when he~~
when her name was
~~meant~~ Clara. But when, between eleven & twelve
on a rainy morning, Edwin Mallett laid his life at her
feet, she ran out of the room & hid herself in her bedroom, —
Timothy could not get on with his dissertation on account
of her sobs. And that is

happens if you
"Which is what ~~comes of~~ ~~letting~~ yourself forget at
the moment", said Mrs. Durrant severely, surveying the
dance programme all scored with the same initials
R. B:
or rather they were different this time - ~~A. R.~~ instead of
Richard Bonamy
E.M.; ~~Arthur Raisley~~, it was now, the young man with
the Wellington nose.

'But I could never marry a man with a
nose like that' said Clara.

'Nonsense' said Mrs. Durrant. ~~She was~~
~~For this was ser serious~~.
~~not thinking of Mrs. Durrant's nose. she was thinking~~
~~of the whole of life all in a second~~.

'No wonder, she thought to herself, ' that everybody
wants to marry her' -
tore up
For Clara, losing all vivacity, ~~left~~ ~~threw away~~ the dance
programme, & threw it in the fender. [~~More than~~
~~any young man in the world, she loved her mother~~]

~~But young men are ridiculous, its quite true~~ - ~~For~~

Richard Bonamy was forever strumming Wagner; &
had written part of an opera which he wanted Clara to play
for him; & he knew nothing whatever of music - Still, he
wasn't a prig, like M^r. Parry; ~~who never said~~ ~~Mr. Parry~~
was ~~in the Civil private secretary to the postmaster general~~,
was talked like a book; or silly like little M^r. Hopkins; as for
M^r. Deniden he never forgot his profile for a second;
M^r. Strachan was a great mathematical genius; poor
~~thing~~ - &
Thus it cannot be denied that the paper flowers had very
serious consequences.

'Please, said Julia Eliot, taking up her position by the curtain
almost opposite the door, 'don't introduce me. I like to ~~wat~~
look on - I always think, she went on, addressing M$^{r.}$ Salvin
m
who, owing to his lameness was accom/odated with a chair,
that the amazing thing about a party is to watch the people -
coming - going - coming & going.

"Last time we met, said M$^{r.}$ Salvin, was at the
Farqhars - Poor lady! She has much to put up with.
"Doesn't she look lovely!" exclaimed Miss Eliot, as Clara Durrant
passed them, ~~with~~

And which of them will it be?" asked M$^{r.}$ Salvin in a
~~lou~~ quizzical voice.

"There are so many —" Miss Eliot replied, as three
young men appeared at the door looking for their hostess -
~~"Where's Judith Durrant?" Miss Eliot asked~~.

"You don't remember her as I do" said M$^{r.}$ Salvin.
Highland
years ago dancing ~~the Highland~~ reels at Banchorie –
Clara lacks her mother's spirit. Clara is like her father —'
What you meet here
~~"You meet very~~ different people at ~~this house don't you~~?"
said Miss Eliot; as two ~~elderly politicians greeted each
other~~. grizzled men nodded.
"Happily we are not governed by the evening papers' said
M$^{r.}$ Salvin.

"I didn't read them" said Miss Eliot. "I know nothing about
politics' she added. '~~They both look~~
well. business
"This fresh ~~question~~" said M$^{r.}$ Salvin
"~~Well~~, the piano's in tune, said Clara passing in front of
for us."
them, but we may have to get someone to move it out.

"Theyre going to dance?" asked M$^{r.}$ Salvin.

"Nobody is going to disturb you' said M$^{rs.}$
Durrant peremptorily as she passed.

"Julia Eliot; ~~I~~ it is Julia Eliot' said old

Lady Hibbert, raising her lorgnette. "And Mr. Salvin.
What is going to happen to us, Mr. Salvin? ~~I was down at the House last night & Sir John~~ —" In all my
experience of English politics - my dear, I was thinking of your
father last night; ~~when I heard~~ what would he have said?
If her father had been alive now, Mr. Salvin - one of my
oldest friends; the man I admired most. Yes. ~~He~~
I was too young to marry him; but never tell me that
girls of ten are incapable of love! ~~I'd read all~~
I had all Shakespeare by heart before I was in my
teens, Mr. Salvin.'

"You don't say so, said Mr. Salvin.

"~~And who is that? asked Lady Hibbert.~~

"But I do" said Lady Hibbert." ~~But~~ Sir John in the House {last night -,}

Oh Mr. Salvin ~~They want us to move" said Julia Eliot~~.

{said [?]} ~~I can easily~~ will remove myself, if you will kindly lend me
a hand" said Mr. Salvin -

"I'll find you a seat by my mother' said Clara."

"~~I want to know who that young man is, Clara" said Julia Eliot~~. Everybody seems to be in here."
Mr. Calthorp, she said, let me introduce you to Miss
Edwards."

"Are you going away for Christmas?" said Mr. Calthorp.

"~~That~~ We had thought of ~~went~~ St Moritz" said Miss Edwards.
But ~~we can~~ it depends on my brother. He may not get leave.'

"What regiment is he in?" asked Mr. Calthorp.

"The 20th Hussars" said Miss Edwards.

Then perhaps ~~Does he~~ {he} knows my brother?" asked Mr. Calthorp.

"~~I beg your pardon~~. I / {am afraid} did not catch your name"
~~said Miss Edwards.~~

"Calthorp" said M$^{r.}$ Calthorp.

"But what proof was there that the marriage service was actually performed?" asked ~~Mr Sir~~ M$^{r.}$ Crosby.

There is no reason to doubt that "Charles James Fox" M$^{r.}$ Burley began; but ~~was~~ here he was introduced to ~~Str~~ M$^{rs.}$ Stretton who knew his sister - in fact had stayed with her six weeks ~~not long~~ ago, & thought the house ~~v char~~ charming but bleak in winter.

"~~Yes: I think its a~~

"~~M$^{rs.}$~~ It may be true, said M$^{rs.}$ Forster, that girls are less well mannered nowadays.-.

M$^{r.}$ Graham looked round ~~to see if~~ him, & seeing Miss Rose Shaw ~~carrying a excused himself & said asked her whether she had~~ said 'Well?' in such a tone that she burst out laughing. & ~~made~~ him a curtsey

"~~This is pretty dull isn't it,~~ "There's not much to be said for this kind of thing is there?" "Jacob?" said Timothy.

"I say theyre they're not going to dance, are they?" asked Jacob.

"We slip off presently & have a pipe in my room" ~~said~~ Timothy.

"~~Now~~ What have you been doing with yourself since August M$^{r.}$ Flanders?" said Julia Eliot.

"~~Well?" she said laughing~~.

"Do ~~let us~~ get into a corner ~~somewhere" he & talk"~~ he said.

Well, what is the news? he asked.

I must ~~ask you what happened~~ know what ~~happened~~ what happen when "Now ~~Miss Shaw~~ come over here & tell me, he ~~began~~ said.

"~~Oh dear Mr. For~~ Graham there's nothing to tell" she said plaintively. ~~I can't think what~~ Nothing! Nothing! Nothing Yet ~~they~~ I left them alone the whole afternoon on purpose."

"Tut. tut. tut"

M~~rs.~~ Graham was ~~always~~ —said M~~r.~~ Graham ~~shook his head~~.

"~~I like the boy" he said.~~

"We must have patience" he said sententiously.

"Who could possibly visit her - or him for the matter of that!- Dearest Clara- ~~where did you get~~ we mustn't ask you to come & ~~sit with~~ talk to us?"

"You & Mr. Graham are ~~talking~~ gossiping" / I know said Clara.

"Its a brilliant success" said Mr. Graham.

'Its a very sad story: ~~really~~" said Timothy, taking Miss Judith Parsons into the next room to have tea. Poor old fellow', he lives on opium because his wife treats him so brutally - a little vixen of a woman - Welsh - I hate the Welsh." But dont go & say I told you. My mother would be furious - Thats why we have him to stay.

"~~Everybody has somet~~ Everybody has something awful if you know them" said Judith Parsons

"What makes you say that?" said Timothy sitting down & ~~cros~~ in the corner chair & crossing his legs.

She told him the history of her mothers life.

I say don't go & repeat ——

But

~~Why is life so~~ "Life is wicked & perverse" said Rose Shaw.

But Mr. Durrant, I dont know why I've told you - you won't repeat" she said -

The plays of Wycherley, said ~~Miss~~ Julia Eliot, acc~~epting~~ a cup of tea. "Wycherley." — ~~You should~~

"Life is wicked - life is detestable" said Rose Shaw.

"There's not much to be said for this sort of thing, is there?" said Timothy Durrant to Jacob~~; who stood in the door~~ -
'Women like it.'

Like what?" said Charlotte Wilding.
"Come ~~& eat~~ along" said Timothy; le leading her away. ~~There's food downstairs'~~ -
'Where have you come from? said Timothy.
'Dining somewhere, I suppose."
"~~Give me an ice" said Charlotte~~.
"I don't see why not" said ~~Cla~~ Charlotte.
"~~T Tea is downst~~ "~~Take Charlotte to have an ice" said~~ Clara passing - ~~Everybody Tell~~ People ~~to go~~ must go downstairs, Take Charlotte." How'd'you do, M^r. Flanders."
"How d'you do, M^r. Flanders," said Julia Eliot.
What's been happening to you?"

~~“~~Drink to me only with thine eyes,
And I will pledge with mine;

sang Elsbeth Siddons.

Everyone stood where they were, or sat down, if a chair was empty.
“Ah” sighed Clara, standing beside Jacob, halfway through.
~~“Ah” she exclaimed~~.

Since when it grows, & smells, I swear,
Not of itself but thee!”

“Ah” she exclaimed, out loud, ~~in common~~ & clapped
her gloved hands, as every one else did; & ~~she~~ moved forward &
directed ~~old ladies~~ people to ~~into corners~~ ~~to seats~~ ~~as~~ come in from the doorway.

“You ~~were~~ are living in London? asked ~~Miss~~ Julia
Eliot.

“Yes” said Jacob.

“In rooms?”

“Yes”

“There is Mr. Clutterbuck - you always see Mr.
Clutterbuck here. He is not very happy at home, I am afraid -
~~You know his wife.~~ They say that Mrs. Clutterbuck ~~do~~
~~not make things very~~ ~~treats him~~ - she finds him rather trying
~~You know~~ thats why he stays with the Durrants; ~~Edward~~
~~Durr~~ ~~Mrs. Durrant is very good to people always doing~~
~~things like that~~ ~~Its Opium~~ — I ~~suppose you've heard~~ —
~~Everyone knows~~. ~~They say you dream beautifully~~ -
~~He takes opium - in fact, at Trevenen last summer~~
Where you there when ~~we~~ they acted Mr. Wortley's play? Oh
no, ~~of course not~~. — ~~that was what made them so~~
~~cross~~. & ~~they couldn't~~ at the last moment -
~~but~~ you had to go - to meet your mother, I remember,
up at Harrogate - At the last moment, as I was
saying — Now, Elsbeth is going to sing again —
~~I~~ Clara is playing the accompaniment - or turning over
for Mr. Carter, I think -

"This is Bach, I think" she whispered, as Mr. Carter played the first bars.

"Are you fond of music?" said Mrs. Durrant. "~~Or~~
~~I~~ ~~So many people~~
~~N~~ Yes - I mean I like hearing it." said Jacob.
'~~You mean you~~ "I know nothing about it" he added.
"Very few people do that" said Mrs. Durrant.
[That gentleman over there is Sir Jasper Bigham. ~~If you~~
I must] ~~But~~ I daresay you were never]
taught. ~~Sir Jasper, you I believe~~ ~~Sir 'Why are~~
~~we not taught music~~ Sir Jasper? - ~~When we are~~
Why that
~~What is~~ ~~the reason of that~~ Sir Jasper? Sir Jasper Bigham -
Mr. Flanders - Why is nobody taught ~~what~~ anything
useful, Sir Jasper? "she left them, standing against the
wall.

Why is nobody taught anything useful" said Sir Jasper. For two minutes nothing ~~wa~~ more was said by either of them. Then Jacob crossed the room:

"~~Will you let me~~ Will ~~Wont~~ you come & have something to eat?" he said to Clara Durrant.

"Yes. ~~I want~~ an ice, she said. "Only quickly — ~~we must~~ go ~~at once or the music~~ - Now - "

Downstairs they went.

But halfway they met M^r.^ & Mrs. Gresham, Herbert Turner, Sylvia Rashleigh, & a friend whom they had
that
Mrs. Durrant dared to bring, from America - "~~We~~ "knowing ~~you~~
~~kind~~ wishing dear kind people, - ~~wish~~ if one does want visitors to
to show
Mr. Pilcher take away - Mr. Pilcher - from New York.
Mr. Pilcher from New York -

Miss Durrant - So Clara left him.

G .XV.

After toiling up the hill side, there ~~filling~~ filling up the gap between
the hills on the horizon is ~~the~~ undoubtedly, the sea.
The Sea! the Sea!
what
But ~~why~~ that cry ~~should~~ signifies, it ~~w~~ is hard to say.
~~Perhaps~~ - a certain ~~amount of~~ relief; a sense of freedom;
licence to indulge dreams.

Then the little boat sidles up to the pier,
standing up
John Stephens in ~~his~~ oilskins ~~sp~~ throws a rope
which Mathew Paynter finally catches & secures.
You jump a little too much to the right. Directly
afterwards the land is seen from the sea. The ~~spiri~~
As a face composed in sleep it looks, quiet, spiritual.
In particular the smoke from the houses is visible.
the shore
There hang over it the atmosphere of something left
behind, to which one has said farewell. But in
the boat itself ~~the~~ boots, hands, jerseys, are ~~lifesize~~
& near
~~as~~ large as life; the oars creak upon the rowlocks,
which are now spat upon, now moistened with sea water.

The sea about midday, is dull enough. For out at sea,
where the waves are not breaking but swelling &
sinking - ~~swelling & sinking~~ there is nothing to
expect; everywhere is the same material, agitated by the same
movement.
And that perhaps is a disillusionment.
Lying full length in his little cabin on deck, Jacob
~~came~~ concluded that ~~there is little~~ to be out of sight of
land is nothing in particular. ~~Inf Indeed, about~~
~~midday, it seemed to him that to catch sight of England~~
again ~~would be in was desirable.~~ ~~The~~ ~~Now was the~~
However, he would prove the matter, - he would read
Shakespeare. ~~He had~~ provided ~~Shakespeare to read out~~
~~of sight of land, & had for in order to~~
Only, if the sea is merely brown-purple water, there is

3+
2,400

Gissing
A. B X
Addison
Modern Fiction
Defoe
Sterne X
JA. X
~~C Pel~~ Evelyn

no reason to suppose that any miracle ~~would~~ will happen. He looked for ~~the~~ signs of the court of Devonshire; saw none; & opened King Lear.

~~B~~ The management of the Primus stoves had been entrusted to him. Happily ~~Jimmy Durrant~~ it was time to attend to them; for he could make nothing of King Lear. Yet everything had been propitious. Silence, sea, sky; dinner to get ready with one's own hands; & a Cornish sailor, chewing tobacco, ~~with~~ rings in his ears - Finding an old number of Punch Jacob fiercely stayed his mind with that. Didactically he had primed his box with this paper edition of all the great writers. It is a very serious thing on the second day of a voyage to ~~find no si~~gn to disbelieve in so much.

Nov:
24th 1920

XV

About half past nine ~~every morning~~ Jacob left the house,
his door slamming, other doors slamming, he buying
his paper, mounting his omnibus, or, weather permitting,
walking his ~~road~~, ~~street~~, road, as other people do.
books bound in green leather
Head bent down, ~~papers~~ a desk, a telephone, ~~papers~~,
~~correspondence~~, electric light - "~~Shall I~~ Fresh coals ~~wanted~~ Sir?"
"Your tea." - ~~the talk about Harlequins~~ the - talk about football-
six thirty Star brought in by the office boy; the rooks of
branches
Grays Inn passing overhead; ~~fog across the street~~ mist.
~~through which came the cries, t wh the roar of wheels,~~
~~roar, thus the~~ . &, through the roar of traffic now &
again a voice shouting, ~~something.~~ "Whats the verdict?
Who's won?" & so on, while ~~papers~~ letters catch the evening
post signed by his hand, are distributed over the globe,
& each evening finds him with ~~something new in his head~~ some.
muscle of the brain newly stretched.
Then — Sometimes a game of chess; or ~~the~~ an exhibition in Bond
Street, or a long way home to ~~look~~ take the air with
Bonamy on his arm, meditatively marching, the
early moon above the steeples coming in for praise —
and the seagulls ~~hi~~ flying high, flying high,
Nelson on his column ~~seeming to our~~ our figure head, & the
world ~~our~~ a ship.
Meanwhile, poor Betty Flanders letter ~~which had come~~
~~by the second post~~ lay on the hall table waiting.
Poor Betty Flanders, writing her son's name Jacob Alan
Flanders ~~esqu~~ Esq, as mothers do; ~~though no one~~
& the ink ~~was~~ pale, profuse, ~~& blotted~~.
suggesting how mothers down at Scarborough
~~think it t well~~, dream over the fire, when tea's
cleared away, & can never never say ~~what they w~~
whatever it may be -~~w~~ probably this, Don't go with

home
bad women, do wear your thick shirts, & come ~~to me~~ for ~~the~~
~~holidays~~. Christmas.
~~Only~~ Far from saying it this was what she said,
Miss
Do you remember old ~~Mrs.~~ Wargrave who used to be so kind
~~to you~~ when you were small? She's had at last poor
thing - it would be kind of you to write ~~Two days ago~~
~~Miss~~ Ellen came over ~~& spent the night~~. & we went
Old
shopping - ~~Poor~~ Mouse is very stiff - we walk him up
the smallest
~~every~~ hills - Rebecca, at last, after I dont know how
long went ~~to the dentist~~ - into Mr. Adamson's -
Three teeth he says, must come out. Such fine
with buds on the pear trees
weather for the time of year, ~~the gorse actually~~
~~in bud in the orchard.~~ And Mrs. Jarvis.– "—
(It must be explained that Mrs. Flanders liked Mrs. Jarvis.
always said of her that she was too good for such a ~~little~~ quiet
~~village, &~~ place, & though she never listened to
& told at the end of it
her discontent, ~~gave~~ her ~~good~~ advice at the end of it,
kept them ~~how nicely for~~ that a little peat wrapped round the
from the Iris roots - ~~oh but you should have taken yours~~ up
starts
frost, ~~weeks ago~~ - & Parrots great white sale ~~is the~~
next Tuesday, "do remember -" - ~~such was their~~
~~relationship, & so in the letters the story was told,~~
~~of Mrs. Jarvis having~~ ~~a~~ knew precisely how
Mrs. Jarvis felt & oh dear how interesting her letters
were, about Mrs. Jarvis, could one read them year in year
out - the ~~unwritten novels~~ unpublished works of women -
profusion
written by the fireside in pale ~~profus~~ ~~ink~~ dried
flame worn to holes
by the ~~fire~~, for the blotting paper's in ~~shreds~~, &
the pen, ~~why its clo~~ cleft & clotted. Then
Captain Barfoot. Him she called "The Captain",
spoke of frankly, yet never without reserve. The
for her
Captain was ~~man making~~ enquiring ~~for her~~ about
Garfits acre; advised chickens; & could promise

profit; or he had the sciatica, or Mrs. Barfoot had been indoors
for weeks; or the Captain says. ~~Ireland~~ things look bad,
politics that is, for, as Jacob knew the Captain would
sometimes talk, as the evening ~~wore on~~ waned, about the state
of India; & then Mrs. Flanders would fall a-musing about
Eliot her brother, lost all these years, had the Indians got him,
or his ship sunk, ~~in the~~ or ~~did the~~ ~~could~~ would the Admiralty
tell her? - - The Captain knocking his pipe out, as
Jacob knew - ~~Indeed~~ The chicken farm was uppermost
in Betty Flanders thoughts. A woman of character, ~~&~~
apt to spring hither & thither, yet practical, for all her
impulse; like Jacob in the blur of the outline; ~~soft;~~
~~ant~~ owl like; moth like; but powerful, as he was;
growing old though, haphazard, & apt to laugh things
off, or sigh them off; a melodious woman.

Nov. 26th 1920

Hogarth House

Richmond

26 Nov. 1920

the idea of the chicken farm came back & back, even at fifty,
~~&~~ the woman being impulsive, sketching ~~her plans~~ in the
cloudy future plans for owning Leghorns, Cochin Chinas, ~~&~~
Orpingtons; like Jacob in the blur of her outline,
owllike, mothlike; but powerful as he was; fresh &
vigorous, ~~apt to laugh things off, or sigh them off, &~~
with her tears & laughter, running about the house, scolding
Rebecca.

Poor Betty Flanders! ~~Hard~~ Poor mothers - poor women - poor
anyone indeed who lives in ignorance, & must ~~hide their~~
hint what they want to ask instead of asking it. This question
then say
she cd not ~~w~~ ask — of her son's chastity, - ~~& then, are you hiding anything,~~
~~the sense that ignorance of~~. how it mattered, ~~to her~~,
ed
as if — someone, or something interven~~ing~~, he becoming strange - indeed
she never knew him as she knew the others, ~~his~~ something
came between
~~estranging~~ them, the way he lounged or ~~smoked~~, though
of her lads,.....
she knew him for the finest, the most powerful - for
most like his father too, — which very reason, as she sat over the fire, she turned to him,
tried to figure him in London, planned to visit him,
thought of shops in Oxford Street, where she used to deal,
went back to old days, simple ~~pieties~~ children, tea at
Burzard's after the dentist, & then returned to Jacob, now
Could she question him? No, she ~~tried~~
grown a man with passions; ~~so she sighed & wrote on~~
~~tried to make him~~

The letter lay upon the hall table. Florinda
coming seven
~~came~~ in at ~~half past six~~ & ~~seeing it there~~ took it up, with her,
~~put it~~ put it on the table as she kissed Jacob,
& Jacob seeing the hand left it there under the lamp,
between the biscuit tin & the tobacco box.
They withdrew -

The room neither knew nor cared. Why, the door was
shut; ~~the lamp burnt; the~~ once the clock struck;
a coal shifted; but as lamp burnt evenly no
shadow danced, & the pale plump letter lay blue ~~in the~~
beneath the light. The ~~glass~~ cut glass bowl held a

& to suppose that wood when it creaks transmits anything save the
subterranean activities of rats or the ~~draught~~ inexplicable stir in
its own fibres is ~~ridiculous~~. childish - These old houses
are only brick & wood soaked in human sweat, grained with
human dirt. But if the pale blue envelope lying in the
lamplight had the feelings of a woman the heart was
ravaged ~~as it heard the sounds. knives~~ by the little
creak, the sudden ~~give~~. stir. Behind the door ~~knives~~ cut
~~human flesh from the bone, as death alights.~~
the
was ~~this~~ obscene ~~form~~ thing; ~~the~~ the alarming presence unveiled;
& terror would come over her, as at death mysteri~~ously~~ & having
the
descending, or ~~child~~ birth. of a child. Surgeons were there with their
knives. Something was visible that only austere men or
women in white capes might see; & having seen would
never speak of. Oh better perhaps to burst in & see for
oneself than to wait in the antechamber listening to the
~~sudd~~ little crack, the sudden stir; for her heart was
swollen & pain threaded it. My son, my son - such would
be her ~~cy~~ cry, - uttered to hide ~~the face~~ her vision
of him stretched with Florinda - Inexcusable, irrational, -
yet such ~~were~~ would be her feeling; poor elderly woman had
she come up from Scarborough; ~~though if the marriage had been~~
~~solemnised would she have felt anything of the kind?~~
had she waited, had she heard. And the fault lay with Florinda . . .
Indeed, when the door opened, & the couple came out, Mrs
Flanders would have have flounced upon her - only it
was Jacob who came first, in his dressing gown, amiable,
~~handsome~~, ~~looking rather~~ authoritative, ~~looking in~~
beautifully healthy like a baby after an airing, ~~&~~
an eye ~~clear as the bright as~~ clear as
with ~~the composure of a full grown man~~ water.
Florinda followed; lazily stretching; yawning a little,
arranging her hair at the looking glass while Jacob
read his mother's letter.

X X X X X

Let us consider letters,- how they ~~they~~ come at breakfast, at
teatime & at night, with their yellow stamps their green
stamps, ~~looking different when this~~ immortalized by the
postmark; for ~~letters~~ to see one's own envelope upon
another table is to realize ~~a strange fact, a mil~~
~~majestic fact~~ that ~~once~~ one's own deeds, ~~having left one~~,
become stern & alien. Then at last the power of the
mind to quit the body, ~~cleave the air, st take wing~~
& ~~through quiet rooms, & stir in t~~ is manifest; &
perhaps we fear or hate or ~~can't~~ wish ~~annhi~~ annihilated
imp
this little phantom of ourselves; ~~this changeling,~~
~~this imp~~; Still, there are letters that merely say
how dinner's at seven; others ordering coal; making
~~appointing~~ appointments - ~~letters written automatically~~
~~by a~~ The hand in them is scarcely perceptible, let
alone the voice or scowl. Ah, but when the post knocks
& the letter comes always the miracle seems repeated
attempted
speech attempting ~~by which~~ ~~in th~~is one person ~~speaks~~ to another. Venerable are
letters; infinitely brave, forlorn, & lost.

Life would split asunder ~~like a~~ without them.
Come to tea, come to dinner; what's the truth of the story?;
have you heard the news?; life in the capital is
gay; The Russian dancers - ... These are our
stays & props. These lace our days together and make of
Dinner at 8:
life a perfect globe. And yet & yet- the horse or
the train has conveyed you; hands are touched; the
evenings over. Try again; this time; gossip
tea & the
imparted; the evenings over. And of these ~~evenings~~
the number is only so many in the

When we go to tea, when we go to dinner, when pressing finger
tips we ~~suggest that~~ hope to meet somewhere soon,
a doubt insinuates itself: ~~a whether this can be all~~.
~~whether~~ ~~Never will I make another engagement considering that~~
~~life is issued in a limited number of days~~, & ~~there must~~
~~whether this can be~~
~~to~~ is this the way to spend our days? So the rare,
limited ~~days~~ of life, so soon dealt out to ~~us, & with everyone.~~
the pack diminishes, & we ~~know~~ see the rare, the limited,
so soon dealt out to us, - drinking tea, dining out? - ~~pressing~~
~~writing letters?~~ ~~fingertips~~? And the notes accumulate.
And the telephone rings. ~~Voices endeavouring before its too~~
~~late to~~ ~~For if~~ ~~as if~~ And every where we go wires &
tubes surround us, ~~imparting,~~ ~~pierced with~~ ~~the voices of~~
~~like arrows aimed at~~ us <u>endeavouring</u> to have speech
~~with us before the last card is dealt & the days~~ are over.
to carry the voices that ~~w~~ try to penetrate before the
last card is dealt & the days are over ~~A~~ Try to
penetrate - for ~~that~~ ~~even~~ as we lift the cup, ~~or~~
shake
~~take~~ the hand, ~~do we~~ express the hope, something whispers
Is this all? ~~Am I never to~~ Can I never know?
~~Never~~ share? Impart ~~nothing~~? Am I doomed
then all my days to write letters, send voices, which
fall upon the tea table, fade upon ~~the vapid~~
~~drawing room?~~ corridor, where the telephone hangs,
making an appointment to come to tea?
valiant
Venerable are letters; ~~humane~~ the telephone. for ~~nothing~~
~~never was there any attempt. more~~ after all.
The journey is a lonely one, risky, terrible; & if
~~by ringing a bell~~ or ~~reading~~ we could go in company
~~perhaps~~ - bound together by ~~telep~~ notes & telephones -
by
perhaps we might crack jokes, ~~on the way~~.
dance by the way. Withdrawing beneath the shelter of the
pine trees, one old man might hold forth to another; ~~upon~~

The good old women share the wisdom of centuries; &
loneliness
the young, both boys & girls ~~share~~ lose the ~~desperation~~ which is
the halo round their heads. Well, people have tried.
Byron wrote letters. So did Cowper, ~~poor Jane Carlyle, &~~
~~when Mrs. Carlyle~~ For centuries now the writing desk
has contained sheets fit precisely for the communications
of friends. Masters of language, poets of long ages
have turned from the sheet that endures to the sheet
that perishes, pushing aside the tea tray drawing up to
the fire (for all letters are written ~~between~~ in ~~the dusk~~ &
~~written the when~~ in winter when the dark presses
ed
round a bright red cave) & address~~ing~~ themselves to the
task of reaching, touching, penetrating the individual
heart. Were it possible! But I doubt it.
Words ~~already used;~~ have been used too often;
turned & mauled & left exposed to the dust of the street.
The words I seek hang close to the tree. ~~Unplucked~~
beneath
~~hitherto;~~ I come at dawn & find them sweet, ...
~~the leaf~~; beneath the leaf. ~~And~~
. . .

Mrs. Flanders wrote; Mrs. Jarvis wrote; Mrs.
Durrant wrote; Mother Stuart actually scented her
letters, thereby adding a touch which the English
fails
language ~~refuses~~ to provide. Jacob had written in his
day long letters about art morality & ~~polit~~
politics to young men at ~~Cambri~~ Cambridge;
Clara Durrant's letters were those of a child; ~~&~~
Florinda - the impediment between Florinda & her
pen was something impassable. Fancy a
butterfly, a gnat, or any other small insect, attached
to a twig, which, clogged with mud, it rolls
across a page.— Her spelling was abominable.
Her sentiments infantile. And for some reason when

she wrote she believed in God. Then there were crosses &
tear stains; & the hand itself crabbed, ugly, &
redeemed only by ~~its~~ the fact, which always did redeem
a fact ~~sincere~~
Florinda of being ~~sincere Not consciously &~~
~~meritoriously sincere; but sincere instinctively~~, -
~~so that~~
that she cared. Yes, whether it was for chocolate creams,
hot baths, the shape of her own face ~~in the lodging house~~
~~glass~~, Florinda could no more pretend a ~~feel~~. ~~taste~~
feeling than swallow whisky - ~~Stupidity forbade~~
Incontinent was her rejection; ~~gall the~~
~~Honest, humble, doglike, staring in the fire~~,
Great men are truthful; & these little prostitutes
staring in the fire, taking out a powder puff &
lips at
decorating ~~their face at by~~ an inch of looking
glass - ~~they too~~ have (so Jacob thought)
a perfect
~~an inviolable~~ fidelity.

And then he saw her ~~turn~~ turning up
upon another man's arm.
Greek Street; ~~with [But?] arm in arm with~~
~~Errington~~.

X X X X

X X X X

The light from the arc lamp drenched him from head to toe.
He stood for a moment ~~on the~~ motionless beneath it.
Shadows chequered the street. ~~The couple disappeared;~~
couples almost instantly
~~&~~ other~~s~~ crossing this way & that obliterated ~~them~~.
Florinda & the man.

As I say the light drenched Jacob from head to toe.
You could see ~~his~~ the pattern on his trousers; the ~~t~~ old
thorns on his stick; his shoelaces; bare hands; a face.
it was as if a stone was
~~You might~~ ~~imag~~ine some ~~pebble~~ ~~being~~ ground to dust ~~on the~~
~~pave~~ment. ~~Does that give the~~ feeling ~~of a grinding;-as of a~~
as if flew whet-
~~grinding - rust~~ - white sparks ~~flying~~ from the livid stone?
was his
which ~~is~~ ~~somehow~~ the man's spine ~~?~~ - And then it was as
if the switchback railway ~~instead of rising at the end~~ of the
dow fell fell fell
plunged went on ~~down- that~~ plunging down -
~~all this was in his face, for the moment~~. ~~That~~
~~grinding & plunging were in his face.~~ This was in
his face. Whether we ever know what happens to
another person is the question. Granted ten years seniority &
fear
a difference of sex ~~probably~~ ~~there~~ would probably ~~be~~ come
first ~~a fear; then~~ this would be swallowed by an
overwhelming desire to help - overwhelming sense
wd.
reason & the time of night; ~~rage~~ anger follow~~ing~~ close on
that;~~& finally~~ with Florinda, with destiny; & then
~~an equally irrational~~ up would bubble an
But
~~irrepressible~~ irresponsible optimism. ~~"Well,~~ my dear
Jacob, look at the lights & the theatres. I assure you
there's enough life in this street to drown all our
is
cares this very moment." Ah, but that~~'s~~ no good.
Even while I speak, destiny is chipping a little
dent in him; & as for following him back to his rooms,
no, no, no.

X X X X

Yet that ~~is~~ of course is precisely what one does. Poor young man!
He let himself in & shut the door, though it was only now
striking ten on one of the city clocks. ~~And one can't go to~~
~~bed at ten, or if one does,~~ [~~In this neighborhood,~~
~~the barrel organs are still playing in the ne mewses~~]
No one can go to bed at ten. Nobody was thinking of
going to bed. Indeed, what strikes one about ~~the~~
poor streets at night is that the ~~old convention~~ ~~about going to~~
~~bed~~ It was January & dismal, but Mrs. Wagg stood on her
doorstep; as if looking for something to happen: a
barrel organ played ~~an~~ like an obscene nightingale;
& ~~the~~ children ran across the road - Here & there
one could see brown pannelling inside the hall door.
The march that the mind keeps up & down beneath the
windows of others is queer enough. Now distracted by ~~t~~
brown pannelling; ~~then~~ now by a fern in a pot;
here improvising a few phrases to ~~run~~ dance with the barrel
organ; again snatching a detached gaiety ~~simply~~ from
a drunken man; & then altogether ~~controlled~~
absorbed by what the poor shout across the street -
~~one parting~~, two girls trailing arm in arm looking
back over their shoulder, while a young man & woman
stand by the pillar box engaged in repartee.
at each other - yet all the while, ~~composing this~~
having a centre for it - ~~poor Jacob alone in his rooms~~
~~a pi~~ a magnet for it - something that interprets the
~~entire world~~. ~~dis~~ poor street.
~~having the sense of some one~~ suffering organ, ferns, drunkards,
gaslight, puddles, blasphemy to one figure,
up there behind the blind, - ~~making the world into shape~~.

beneath
dripping
leaves

a young man alone in his room.
"Life is wicked - life is detestable!" ~~sa~~ cried
Rose Shaw.
The strange thing about life is that though the nature
of it must have been apparent to everyone for hundreds
of years no one has left any adequate account of it.
The streets of London have their map, but our passions are
uncharted. What am I going to meet if I turn this
corner? "Holborne is straight ahead of you" says the
policeman. ~~And yet I go~~ ~~But no~~ But ~~it takes~~
~~if, yielding to an impulse rising I know not whence,~~
[?] ~~Where shall I be if~~ Ah, but ~~suppose I~~
the ~~chain of events drawing me~~ where am I going, ~~we~~ if
~~I~~ instead of brushing past the old man with the white
beard & the ~~three~~ silver medal I let him go on with his
story, - which, ends in an invitation to step somewhere -
to his room presumably off Queen Square. ~~right~~
~~where, right at the top of the house, he has~~ & there
he shows me a collection of birds eggs, & this (skipping the
intermediate stages) brings me one winters day to the
Essex Coast, where the little boat makes off to the
ship; & the ship sails, & I behold, on the skyline, the
Azores; & the flamingoes ~~rising - &~~ rise, &
there I sit on the verge of the marsh drinking punch,
~~an~~ outcast from civilization, infected with yellow
fever as likely as not, & the witness of unnameable
vices in the brothels of California. And that is
a sketch - ~~cloudy &~~ a cloud. No one can foretell
~~what~~ the ~~real result of talking to an old man.~~
~~might be~~. truth. As ~~frequent corn~~ frequent as
~~corners~~ street corners in Holborn are these ~~deep~~
~~openings, vistas, chances; which~~. chasms in the continuity

of life.

Rose Shaw, talking in rather an emotional manner to Mr.
Bowley at Mrs. Durrant's evening party a few nights
back said that life was ~~det~~ wicked because a man
called Jimmy refused to marry ~~a woman wh called~~
Helen
a woman called (if memory serves) ~~Minny~~ Aitkin.
Both were beautiful. Both were inanimate. The
oval tea table invariably separated them, & the plate of
biscuits was all he ever gave her. He bowed ~~&~~ she
inclined her head. They danced. ~~Sitting out~~
He danced divinely. They sat in the alcove; ~~&~~
~~her fan rose & sank~~. ~~The pink plumes of her fan~~
~~rose & fell with her breathing.~~ Never a word was
spoken. Her pillow was wet with tears. Kind
Mr Bowley & dear Rose Shaw ~~divined~~ marvelled &
deplored. ~~These songs without words are those we~~
Songs without words are those we sing in solitude.
The sufferings of statues command our homage;
~~Helen~~. Jimmy never spoke, & Helen in my belief
But how put words into the mouths of statues,
~~But they could not put words into the mouths of~~
Stat~~ues, w & Helen was dumb~~. & But Helen,
in common with all ~~the~~ other daughters of judges,
had no command of language; & ~~indeed~~
~~to watch these stately ships, without rudder or pilot,~~
~~merely Nothing could be done, &~~
Bowley had rooms in the Albany. Rose ~~Shaw had~~
no ~~existence until eight in the evening when she~~
~~Heaped up in profane clusters all over London~~ -
preciseley as the clock struck
was re-born every evening at eight. All four were
~~equally~~ civilization's triumphs, & if you persist
that a command of the English language is ~~one of~~
is part of your inheritance, I can only reply that

beauty is almost always dumb. Male beauty in association
therefore
with female beauty ~~often~~ breeds in the onlooker~~s~~ a sense of
&
fear. Often have I seen them, Helen ~~here~~, Jimmy ~~there~~,
& likened them to ships adrift, & feared for my own little
~~boat~~ craft. ~~The world~~ Or again have you ever
watched fine collie dogs couchant at twenty yards
distance? As she gave him his tea, there was that
quiver in her flanks. Bowley saw ~~was~~ what was
up. Helen must have confided in Rose. For my own
interpret
part I find it exceedingly difficult to ~~sing these~~ songs
And
without words. ~~Yet~~ now ~~that~~ Jimmy ~~is~~ feeds
the crows in Flanders, & Rose visits hospitals - oh
life is damnable, life is wicked, as Rose Shaw said.

The lamps of London uphold the dark as upon the points
of burning bayonets, - ~~ov~~ The yellow canopy balloons
over the great four poster. So the passengers in the
mail coaches running into London in the Eighteenth
it
Century must have seen ~~it~~. flaring beneath them -
~~the lamps have never been put out. No one has ever~~
~~been to bed~~. The light burns behind yellow blinds
& pink blinds, & above fanlights, ~~which~~ & down in
basement windows. The street market in Soho is
fierce with light; Raw meat, china, & silk stockings
blaze in it. ~~Voices~~ Raw voices wrap themselves
round the flaring gas jets. Arms akimbo,
m
~~s~~ they stand on the pavement bawling - Messrs
Kettle & Wilkinson; their wives sitting in doors,
wrapped
fur~~s~~ round their necks, ~~watching, wi arms~~
arms folded, eyes contemptuous. Such
little man
faces as one sees. The ~~dwarf~~ fingering the meat,
before the fire
must have squatted in innumerable ~~lodging house~~
common lodging houses, & heard & seen & known
so much that now it seems to ~~come~~ utter itself even

volubly from dark eyes, loose lips, ~~& f~~ as he fingers the meat silently; his face ~~sd~~ sad as a poets; & never a song poem sung. Rude illustrations, pictures in a book whose pages we turn ~~& turn~~ over & over as if ~~looking for something~~. we should at last find ~~find something~~ - ~~but what? some explanation.~~ What we look for. Every face is a picture, & every shop, & the bedroom windows, & ~~the alleys~~ the public houses, & the dark squares, where the policeman walks, ~~&~~ From the house by the church issues the fiftieth voice ~~in~~ heard in ten minutes singing passionately some song without words. It is much the same with ~~the~~ books. We turn page after page looking for something: Not in this one? Well ~~then~~ in the next then - Still hopefully turning the pages — oh here is Jacob's room. ~~by the way~~.

―(――――――――)

He sat at the table reading the Globe. The pinkish sheet was spread flat before him. He ~~rested~~ propped his face in his hand, so that the skin of his ~~the~~ cheek was pressed up in deep wrinkles ~~wrinkled~~. Terribly severe he looked, set, & defiant. (What people go through in half an hour!)– But nothing could save him. These events are part of the landscape. A foreigner coming to London would ~~not be likely to~~ scarcely miss seeing St Pauls.) He judged life. These ~~pale~~ pinkish & greenish ~~&~~ newspapers ~~sheets~~ are like thin ~~layer~~ sheets of ~~gla~~ gelatin pressed nightly over the ~~human human brain~~. days work. They take the impression of ~~the whole~~. England from one end to the other. Jacob cast his eye over it. Up in the North was a strike; in the Midlands a murder. Several

games of football ~~had been played~~. ~~Single lines at the bottom of columns spoke to eels caught or bodies found.~~
A strike, a murder, football, eels caught & bodies found - poor world, what a wretched show you make in the eyes of youth! How miserable it is that you can

~~Give~~ Offer ~~Show~~ nothing better to Jacob Flanders! ~~W~~ Indeed, when a child begins to read history one wishes ~~feels inclined~~ to tear out whole ~~the~~ chapters, & assure him that they never existed. ~~Let us so write the past~~
~~Don't~~ ~~Let us not hand on this old whorehouse~~ - why should it be handed on?
~~doubts~~ ~~what~~ ~~doubts the/w~~ marvels, sorrowfully, to hear him spell out once more the old facts - Time they were obliterated.

Feeling in his pocket Jacob took out a pipe & proceeded to fill it. ~~There~~ ~~There were~~ The Prime Minister's speech was reported in something over five columns. Five minutes, ten~~;~~ minutes, fifteen minutes passed. Jacob took the paper over to the fire. What ~~are the conditions of the Home Rule Bill?~~ The Prime Minister proposed a measure for giving Home Rule to Ireland. Jacob knocked out his pipe. He was ~~certainly~~ thinking about Home Rule in Ireland. ~~He went~~ to ~~bed~~. The clock struck eleven. He raked out the fire. He went to bed.

X X X X X X X X X

The snow ~~covered the~~ which had been falling
all night lay at three o'clock in the afternoon ~~over~~
~~the snow of upon the hill~~, over the fields & the hill.
Clumps of grass stood out upon the hill top; ~~Particles of~~
~~frozen snow slithered over the surface.~~ ~~The~~
~~furze~~ bushes were black. ~~There was no sound but~~
~~the sound of the~~ ~~& the sound of the wind~~
the
~~now & that sound was the only sound.~~ ~~There~~ ~~were~~
were black
~~black~~ furze bushes; & now & then a black
shiver crossed the ~~fr~~ mow as the wind drove ~~a~~
flurry of frozen particles before it. The
~~left to itself~~
Earth was abandoned.

The stream crept along by the roadside,
unseen by anyone; sticks & straws caught in the
frozen grass. Nor was it beautiful.
The sky was sullen; & the trees of black iron.
~~This a painful world~~. ~~Pain~~ At four o'clock
the snow was again falling; ~~the~~ the day had gone
out. ~~Nor was there any change~~, ~~save that the~~
~~wind~~ ~~thi~~ ~~The stream~~

A window, tinged yellow, about ~~the size of a~~
two feet across, was the only force ~~in t~~ which
combated the white & the iron black.
At six o'clock a man's figure ~~went up the~~
~~crossed the field~~, carrying a lantern.
crossed the field. Sheep were heard bleating.
A raft of twigs suddenly detached itself &
floated towards the culvert. A load of
snow fell from the fir branches. Later

there was a mournful cry. A motor car came along the
road shoving the dark before it with its headlights.
The man's lantern was seen ~~crossing the~~ ~~going~~ crossing
~~across~~ the further field.   Nothing ceases.

Jacob raked out the fire, cut off the electric light
& went to bed.

Spaces of complete immobility separated each
~~movement.~~ ~~slight stir. of~~ of these movements.
~~was it now dead?~~ No the land lay dead.
~~Yet~~ ~~Yet nothing ceased~~: ~~the stiffly~~ the old
shepherd came stiffly ~~down t~~ across the field.
Stiffly, painfully, the frozen earth ~~like a wheel~~
~~trod~~. was trodden under. & ~~revolved, like a~~
gave beneath pressure like a treadmill.
~~The faint~~ ~~The clocks repeated all night through~~.
~~though the sound was worn to a ghost.~~
The worn voices of clocks repeated the fact of the hour
all night long.

Jacob, too heard them; & raked out the fire;
Nothing ceases.
& stretched himself, ~~& went to bed~~. ~~Nothing ceases.~~
~~& turned out the light & slept & dreamt &~~
~~woke & remembered~~ &

Rocksbier
Rookham
Rockseave
Rockhold
Rock.

123
280
984
246
34,440

16

The Countess
Hunting.
Bohemian party } Fanny
Paris

17.
Fanny
Greece.
18.
London
War.

———

Jan. 3rd. 1921

. XVI .

~~Old~~ The Countess ~~of Rockhand Redvers Rockhand Rocksway~~ Rocksbier ~~sat at the~~ sat at the head of the table. Fed upon Champagne & spices for ~~a~~ at least two centuries (eight, if you count the female line) the Countess Lucy looked well fed. A discriminating nose she had for scents; ~~& deli~~ the underlip protruded, bright red; small eyes; & sandy tufts for eyebrows. Behind her (the windows opened on Grosvenor Square) ~~stoo~~ on the pavement stood ~~Gla Amy Dish~~ Mol~~ly~~ Pratt offering violets for sale; & Mrs. Ellen Thomas, preparing to cross the road. One was from Walworth; the other from Surbiton. Both wore black stockings; ~~&~~ but Ellen had rolls of fur. ~~But for faces~~, However the ~~contrast~~ comparison was ~~t~~ much in Lady Rockbier's favour. Moll had more humour; but was violent. stupid too; Ellen Thomas was mealy-mouthed, ~~an~~ all ~~the~~ her ornaments in place, & the windows shut. Lady Rocksbier, ~~what ever~~ whatever the deficiencies of her profile, had been a great rider to hounds. She used her knife with authority, tore her chicken bones, asking Jacob's pardon, with her own hands.

prolonged in ~~search~~ quest of them

'Who is that driving by?' she asked Boxall, the butler.

"Lady Fittlemere's carriage". my lady."

which reminded her to send a card to ask after ~~somebodies health~~. A rude old lady, Jacob thought. ~~Yet~~ - The wine was excellent. She ~~was perpetually calling~~ called herself an 'old woman', which flattered him. She talked of 'Jo Chamberlain' whom she had known. She said that Jacob must come & meet - one of our celebrities. And then Lady Alice came in with three dogs on a leash.- Jackie her son. And Boxall brought in a telegram, & Jacob was given a

his lordships ~~h~~ health.

'So kind to lunch with an old woman'

ran
~~her son~~, who ~~was told~~ to kiss his grandmother; while
Boxall brought in a telegram, & Jacob was given a good
cigar.

~~The~~ A few moments before a horse jumps it ~~gathers itself~~
slows ~~slows~~
~~slackens~~, ~~slows~~, sidles, gathers itself together, goes up
like a monster wave, & pitches down on the other side.
Hedges & sky swoop ~~in the like~~ in a semi-circle ~~in the~~
~~riders eye.~~ Then, as if your own body ran into the
horses body & it was your own forelegs that sprang,
rushing through the air you go, a mass of muscle,
command
yet ~~eyes too, &~~ you have ~~stillness~~, too, ~~command~~,
~~eyes~~ upright stillness, eyes accurately judging.
Then ~~you draw rain~~ The curves ~~ce~~ cease, changing to
hammer of legs upon road.
downright beating of the hooves; & you draw up;
with a little jolt; sitting flushed & sparkling, tingling,
~~l~~ glazed with ice over pounding arteries, exchanging
~~those~~ words. "Ah! Ho! Hah!" the steam
going up from all the horses as they stand together
at the cross roads, ~~while Jackman the Huntsman,~~
~~wheels round, & the marker trots off by his side down~~
~~the road~~ - where the signpost is; & the ~~little~~ woman
es
~~stands~~ star~~ing~~ at the ~~cottage door~~. garden gate.

The labourer raises himself to stare.

So Jacob galloped over the fields of Essex,
He
~~Jacob~~ fell, ~~into ditches~~. flopped in the mud, lost the
by himself
hunt, & rode ~~alone~~ eating sandwiches on horseback,
~~o~~ looking over the hedges, ~~on either side~~; ~~or~~
newly
~~he~~ noticing the colours, as if they ~~had been~~ scraped ~~bare~~.
yet ~~wishing all the time~~; ~~to find the his ill . luck~~
cursing
~~his~~ luck.

He had tea at the Inn; & ~~they~~ there they
all were, slapping, stamping, saying 'After you,'

clipped, curt, jocose, red as the wattles of turkeys, eating ~~beef~~,
~~speak~~ using free speech, until Mrs. Hawkeslord & her friend Miss
Dudding appeared at the doorway, with their skirts
hitched ~~looped~~ up, & ~~stray~~ hair looping down ~~when The~~
Tom Dudding tapped at the window with his riding whip.
A motor car throbbed in the yard. Talk burst out
again; & Jacob went into the bar, with Brandy
Jones ~~Matthews~~ to smoke with the rustics. There
was ~~the~~ old Jevons with ~~his~~ ferrets~~; & his talk of~~
~~badgers~~, - & all this within thirty miles of London.
I hear from old Jevons about the badgers earths.
~~Old Jevons sat smoking his cutty & Jacob leant against~~
~~the in bar, a fine young man, they thought him,~~
old Jevons with one eye gone, & his clothes the colour of
mud earth, & his bag over his ~~bag~~ back, & his brains
~~all~~ laid in earth, ~~like a crafty~~ like a beast of the
fields; & ~~yet~~ this within thirty miles of London.

Mrs. Papworth, of Endell Street Covent Garden, did for Mr.
Bonamy in ~~Lincolns Inn~~ New Square Lincoln's Inn,
& as she washed up the dinner things in the scullery she
heard the ~~gen~~ young gentlemen talking in the
~~roo sitting room~~. room next door. Mr. Sanders was
there again; ~~for she never pinned a name down~~
~~accurately~~. Flanders, she meant; ~~but it~~ but where a
brisk old woman gets a name wrong, what chance
is there that she will faithfully report an argument?
As she ~~dealt the plates so~~ held the plates under
water & then dealt them on the pile beneath the
hissing ~~flaring~~ gas she listened; ~~but what could she make of~~
heard Sanders ~~say speaking I~~ speaking in a loud

rather overbearing tone of voice: 'good' he said, & 'absolute',
& 'justice' & 'punishment' & the will of the majority'
Then her gentleman piped up; she backed him against
Sanders. Yet Sanders ~~had the~~ was a fine young fellow.
(here all the scraps went swirling round the sink &
she ~~reached~~ ~~dried her hands on the towel~~ reached for
the towel) & her purple hands scoured ~~round~~)
after) Women - ~~but her gentleman was one of the~~
~~quiet ones~~ she thought, & what ~~why~~, ~~she~~ wondered ~~didn't~~
~~they talk about women?~~ - What Sanders & her gentleman
did in that line - one eyelid sinking perceptibly as she
mused, ~~as if used~~ for she was the mother of nine.
Putting the plates in the rack she heard once more
Sanders at it again. The gentry are the gentry -
Her Bonamy was a much better sort than Mr. Doggets
Robertson in the next stair. "Objective reality'
said Bonamy; & "common ground' & ~~evolution,~~
some other long word, - Book learning, she thought to
herself, - ~~&~~ considered what it could be, as she
reached for her jacket; & as she thrust her arms
into it, ~~w~~ she heard something - might be the little
table by the fire - fall; & then stamp, stamp, stamp,
as if they were having at each other - stamp, stamp,
stamp - round the room, making the plates jingle.
~~T~~ "~~Tomorrow's b~~ Tomorrow's breakfast..." she said,
~~st~~ opening the door, & there were Sanders & Bonamy
like two bulls of Bashan driving each other
up & down, making such a racket - they never
noticed her. "Your breakfast, Sir" she
said as they came near. ~~Bonamy~~ And
Bonamy, all his hair tousled & his tie flying,
broke off, & said he ~~was teaching~~ Mr. ~~/ Sanders~~
~~some long word or other~~. Mr. Sanders had
~~broken~~ smashed the coffee pot. & he was

teaching Mr. Sanders -

Sure enough the coffee pot was lying broken on the
hearth rug

this week
"Any day, except Thursday, wrote Miss Perry, would suit me,"- ~~Name~~
~~whatever time suits you~~." ~~your own time~~ & this was not
the first invitation by any means. Were all Miss Perry's
empty
weeks ~~completely blank~~ (with the exception of Thursdays) &
the only she desires see
was ~~the only passion in her life~~ ~~the~~ desire to ~~make the~~ ~~know~~
~~acquaintance~~ of Jacob, her old friend's son? Time is
issued to spinster ladies of wealth in long white ribbons
~~On Thursday they visit the workhouse~~. These they wind
round
round & round, & round, assisted by five female servants
Mudie's library
a butler, a fine Mexican parrot, regular meals, &
friends dropping in. A little hurt she was already that
Jacob had not been.

is oldest
"Your mother, she said, ~~was~~ one of my ~~greatest~~
friends."

Miss Rosseter, who was sitting by the fire
cheek
holding the Spectator between her the blaze refused
to have a fire screen, but finally accepted it.
The weather was then discussed. ~~Mr.~~
for in deference to Parker who was opening little tables,
graver matters were postponed. Miss Rosseter drew

Jacob's attention to the beauty of the ~~furn~~ ~~ta~~ ~~furniture~~.
cabinet. "So wonderfully clever in picking things up" she
said. Miss Perry had found it in Yorkshire. The
north of England was discussed. ~~"Mr. Benson"~~
~~was announced~~. ~~The ladies~~ ~~Jacob~~ When Jacob spoke
they both listened. ~~The d~~ The door opened &
Mr. Benson was announced. Now there were

four people sitting in that room. Miss Perry was 65; Miss Rosseter was 42; Mr. Benson ~~was~~ 38; & Jacob ~~was about~~ 25. ~~It is impossible to imagine them naked~~; ~~The chances that had brought them together~~,

~~A~~ ~~Our~~ My old friend looks in good health ' said Mr. Benson, referring to the parrot; ~~&~~ Miss Rosseter simultaneously praised the tea; - Jacob, of course, ~~had to~~ offered the wrong plate passed the rolls. & Miss Perry signified her desire to approach ~~him~~ more closely. ~~Tell me about~~. ~~That cha~~ "Your brothers, she began vaguely; then to her pleasure remembered Rebecca's name; & ~~recalled~~ how one day 'when you were three little boys ~~quite~~ small, ~~walking~~ playing in the "drawing room -"

"But ~~she is~~ Miss Perry has the ~~holding the~~ kettle holder" said Miss Rosseter, & indeed Miss Perry was clasping it to her breast as she spoke.

~~Mr. Benson had something annoying to tell her~~ The truth was she still cherished some feeling about Betty Flanders -

~~Mr. B~~ "So clever - ~~so clever~~ not so good as usual - most unfair ~~so clever~~ -

(Mr. Benson & Miss Rosseter was discussing the Saturday Westminster. ~~Had~~ Did they not compete regularly for prizes? Had they not ~~been~~ won there? ~~mentioned~~? Of course, Everard Benson was weakly - but still, to toady Miss Perry, to write acrostics, to ~~what if~~ remember parrots, to despise Miss Rosseter, & give tea parties in his rooms, (Which were in the style of Whistler - & he had first editions ~~of some of the Essayists~~ the Essays of Elia) - ~~T~~ all this, as Jacob felt without knowing it, made him a contemptible ass.

Miss Rosseter was the daughter of the vicar in the parish where Miss Perry's father, had been Squire. ~~She is excused~~. did water colours. Her father was intolerable. She is excused.

"Running away so soon?" said Miss
Perry, vaguely. "At home every afternoon, if you've nothing
better to do - except Thursdays" her

"I've never know ~~her~~ you desert the old ladies
~~yet~~." ~~said~~ Miss Rosseter was saying - smiling -
~~in~~ bowing to Jacob, for ~~their intimacy was not such as~~
~~to~~ you didn't shake hands after this kind of party -
gentlemen say nothing whatever.

The fire burnt [?] clear between two pillars of greenish
marble, & on the mantelpiece ~~a~~ there was a ~~green~~ green clock guarded by
Britannia ~~with~~ leaning on her spear. [Laurette & Jacob sat with
their toes in the fender, side by side in two large
chairs covered in green plush.] As for pictures - A maiden in a large
hat offered roses ~~to~~ over the garden gate to a / gentleman
on horseback. - ~~A~~ a mastiff lay extended ~~in front~~
against a battered door. The lower panes of the
windows were of ground glass, & the curtains, accurately
looped, were of plush, & green too.

Laurette & Jacob sat with their toes in the fender
side by side, in two large chairs covered in green
plush. ~~Fr~~ Laurette's skirts were short; ~~&~~ her legs
long, thin, ~~finely covered~~. ~~stockinged~~. transparently
covered. ~~The f~~ Her fingers, ~~fine white~~ stroked her ankles.

"Its not exactly that I don't understand them, she
was saying thoughtfully. "I don't know what it is.
I shall try to / go again."

"What time will you be there?" said Jacob.

She shrugged her shoulders.

"~~Why do they always take up the roads at this time~~
~~of year?" she asked.~~

"Tomorrow?" ~~no~~ No, she said, she couldn't go tomorrow.
long for
"This sort of weather makes me want to be in the country" she said.

~~Jacob told~~ her ~~how he had been to [Dunnow?~~]
"Oh you ought to have been with me on Saturday" said Jacob.

"I used to ride" she said. She got up, gracefully,
smiled at him.,
calmly. Jacob got up. She nodded & ~~left the room~~.
He put so many shillings on the mantelpiece; as she shut the
door
~~An old woman in~~ ~~Jacob had a little talk with an old lady before he left.~~ Altogether a most reasonable conversation; a most respectable room; an intelligent girl. [Only Madame herself, seeing Jacob out, ~~seemed like the old sink of~~] ~~was the very sink of iniquity; into~~ had about her that leer, that lewdness, that quake of the surface which threatens ~~to split & spil~~ spill the whole bage of ordure, with difficulty held together, over the pavement. In short, there was something wrong somewhere.

Every time the door opened & fresh people came in, those already in the room shifted slightly; ~~& some looked towards the doorway~~.
Those who were standing looked over their shoulders.
those who were sitting stopped in the middle of sentences.
What with the light, the wine, the strumming of a guitar,
~~it seemed that as if the excitement increased~~
something exciting happened ~~w~~ each time the door opened.
Who was coming in? "Well, he's rather tall & very young -
~~I d~~ I don't know him."...

Gibson
"That's ~~Hugh Gib~~ with him.

"The painter?"

you saying -
"But ~~lets~~ go on with what ~~we~~ were ~~talking about~~.
They were saying something that was far, far too serious

to be said, outright. But ~~when the~~ the noise of the voices served like a clapper in little Mrs. ~~Winder's Wiver's~~ Withers mind scaring into the air flocks of ~~little~~ small birds - & then they'd settle, & then she'd feel she'd ~~said too much~~ feel afraid - ~~& shiver, &~~ put ~~clasp her~~ one hand to her throat, & bind ~~them~~ both round her knees & look / up at Oliver Shiller & say Promise, promise, you tell no one." . . . So considerate he was, so tender, - ~~She was ready to risk everything~~. It was her husbands character she discussed. He was cold, she said.

Down upon them came the splendid Magdalen; brown, warm, voluminous, ~~yet~~ yet scarcely touching the ~~top of her~~ ~~m~~ ~~mo~~ top of her grass down with her sandalled feet - Her hair flew; & somehow pins seemed scarcely to attach the flying silks - An actress, of course. ~~the~~ a ~~row~~ line ~~of little~~ lights perpetually beneath her. ~~to M~~ It was only 'My dear' that she said, but her voice went yodelling between alpine passes. ~~That she should never be~~ And down she tumbled on the floor; & sang; since there was nothing to be said; ~~&~~ ~~They all came round her~~; ~~They~~ round ah's & oh's - Mangin, the poet, coming up to her, stood looking down at her, drawing at his pipe. The dancing began.

Mrs. Keymer, ~~said to~~ who was too old to dance, ~~said to~~ asked Dick Graves to tell her who Mangin was; & said she had seen too much of this sort of thing in Paris to be shocked. (Magdalen was sitting on his knee: now his pipe was in her mouth) Who is that? she said, staying her glasses when they came to Jacob; ~~he was~~ for indeed he looked quiet, not indifferent, but like someone on a beach, watching. Mrs. Keymer thought it a pity that he should be here. (She ~~had a~~ turned & looked at the pictures)

"Oh my dear, let me lean on you ~~while I tie up~~" ~~Miri~~ gasped Helen ~~Sel~~; ~~And~~ Askew, hopping on one foot, the silver cord round her ankle being loose. "Look at Jacob" she said - (~~They had~~ bound his eyes for some game)

What d'you think of Jacob? she asked. "I adore him" she added. ("

And Dick Graves, being a little drunk, & very faithful, very simple minded, told her that Jacob was the greatest man he had ever known.

~~Helen Askew wanted to know what he was going to~~ do.

~~And Dick Graves had~~ And then they both sat down on a pillow & talked about Jacob; ~~but~~ & Helen's voice trembled with emotion - ~~the~~ both of them seeming heroes to her, & the friendship between them ~~u~~ so much more beautiful than women's friendships. Anthony Pollet now asked her to dance. She had no illusions about him. (He was in love with her,) ~~poor young man~~. but she ~~went off with him~~ danced with him. And ~~Dick danced, & Jacob danced~~. When Dick & Jacob stood pouring out white wine at the supper table she looked over her shoulder at them.

Romance.

written to the tune of [a] street fiddle~~s~~.

This is Holborn Viaduct ~~&~~ . . . And theres a pale lawn~~.~~
~~all set with There are trees, & antelopes.~~ Antelopes
sun dappled, ~~draw~~ [withdrew] ~~disappear, among~~ [withdrew] ~~the~~ trees.
~~Thes the pale purple clematis~~ ~~Pale~~ [Purple] starry
flowers ~~h.~~ climb & hang. ~~A lawn softly undulating~~ [Alls nodding & waving] -
a ~~river forever a savannah~~. ~~The sweet breeze~~
floats ~~over the~~ the pale grass - Then why, wretched
little boy, do you run across the ~~corner~~ [street] with your
arm crooked against the wind?
But ~~An~~ [in] the basements of Gower Street tea is being
laid. ~~The cook sits with her arms on the table.~~
~~The fire is red between the bars~~
Still, still, ~~in the basements of Gower Street~~ [through the bars of the railings,] th~~e~~ cook is
drinking tea; the parlourmaid, with her feet against the
fireplace, t reads John Bull~~; & the~~ newspaper; &
a paper; The news; There are ~~yellow~~ caves of ~~yellow~~ -
~~red light~~. redness - Brad on the table. ~~The cook drinks~~, [tea]
~~& the~~ [The] bootboy tipping his concertina squeezes out
melody, & [[on the?]] The kitchen table, ~~with~~ its yellow loaf.
Stricken down to the heart of the world - Then why
is the blood smeared paper sucked to the ~~pill~~ railing?
~~Then why is~~ [But] blood smeard paper ~~sucked to the~~
~~tight to the corner railing~~! wraps itself round my
legs?
Oh upstairs, three steps at a time, past the
wafer the buns & the Chinese pot, into joss

drawing room ~~I rush~~ - ~~demanding safety, I fly~~ (the

~~number eighty.~~

Upstairs at ~~no~~ number fifty you sit ~~over the~~
under the ~~crysanthemums~~ - flowers. (the fiddles ~~in~~ "

upstairs three steps at a time, I rush: surely,
surely, since the fire light is red upon your
fox terrier, curved pictures in the cheeks of the
tea pot, & ~~oh~~ green dragons on the china,
<u>you</u> can't ~~know disillusionment?~~
be unhappy?
~~what life is?~~

<u>The telephone:</u>

London softly surges against the windowpanes. ~~Surrounds~~
Innumerable houses, points of light, [[? go ?]] ribbons of streets,
have sunk to the bottom or float sprinkled [in millions] - of particles
~~forever washed by~~ ~~in the brown brown vapour~~
~~& like~~ a tethered balloon ~~slowly it~~ ~~it~~ the
man floats ~~this way & that~~, a little this way,
& a little that. Suddenly the nerve ~~which~~
~~attaches us~~ - ~~the telephone~~ - ~~tingles~~ vibrates. The
telephone rings. ~~We are part of her, then.~~

But from what height or depth? ~~Which~~
Is there a spark burning in a tower, or [green] ~~from~~ the depths of the
sea? coming - coming - coming. But to whom?
What prowling him; what vociferating
~~Crowded yet confined the~~ Suddenly the telephone rings
from. ~~the~~ like a nerve twitched. ~~from~~

~~Coming coming coming. But to whom?~~
Suddenly [a] ~~the voice cries out from her~~. The telephone
rings. ~~The old balloon is tugging at us.~~
Ring - ~~ring - ring~~ ~~adventure~~. the bout starts
tomorrow. ring, "I ~~am~~ love" ring, "I ~~hope~~ -
~~command - entreat~~" ~~Try to~~ Londons voice

> I come; I come Only- no I will not answer the telephone.

is Ring - Ring. But ~~it is better not to answer~~.
don't answer the telephone.
how wonderful to be attached to this volume of
gold & marble. ~~th~~ & all these myriads of lives!
Ring Ring - Yes; But how can one thread

~~Fragment from a letter~~:

Written for a picture:

~~Th~~

A letter to a lady.

Old Mrs. Hutchings gave parties in South Kensington,
to which she asked all her late husbands friends
They came in numbers; old generals, stockbrokers. -
people of means. The violinists were set up on a
platform. The lights were turned on.
Then the most extraordinary things happened.
Of course the generals dreamt they were fairies, & the
stockbrokers had no doubt they were in heaven.
Miss Hutchins, however, took ~~a~~ the very opposite turn
& said that she was the newfoundland dog on the hearth.
Old Mrs. Hutchings.

A death in the Newspaper.

Humphry Hammond dead!.. How death has changed everything. the colours go out, the trees look thin as paper. The chill little breeze is perceptible, & the roar of traffic sounds across a gulf. ~~Then a moment later, distances are bridged, sounds merged~~; ~~Dea~~ ~~There are~~ ~~Everything~~ So from an express train I have seen a man with a scythe look up from the hedge as we pass, & lovers lying in the long grass stare at me without disguise as I stare at them without disguise. Wheels & cries sound now high now low in harmony. Humphry Hammond is dead. One bee hums through the air & out again. Where does it go to next? There's one on the Canterbury Bell, but finds no honey there, & so tries the yellow wall-flower. But ~~in these ancient London gardens what hope of honey?~~ Dead! Dead! Humph ~~Hammond?~~ But ~~my Hammond~~ ~~he~~ Humphry [~~Hammin~~?] spelt his with only one m. - Good God, are you ~~he's~~ still alive then?

Death how sweet you are! Yet - he spelt it with one M.
alive
Humphrey's you'~~re alive~~! Death what a fraud you are!

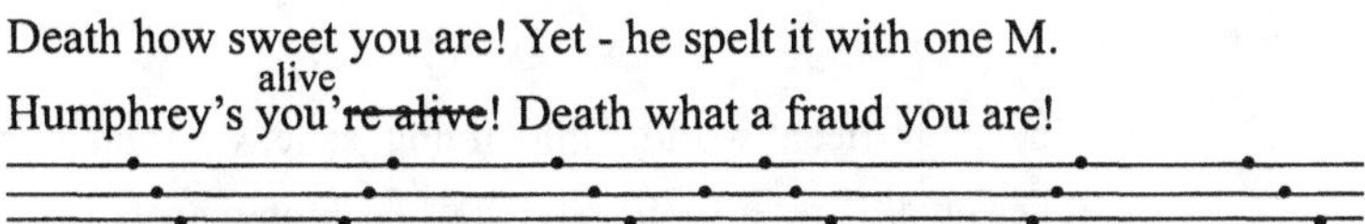

But this city, to which we travel, has neither stone nor
marble; hangs enduring; stands unshakable;
~~march, march~~; nor does a face, nor does a flag
greet or welcome. Leaves then to perish poor
hope; droop in the desert my joy; naked
advance; bare are the pillars; auspicious to none;
severe you only stone,[?]
So Casting no shade; resplendent; ~~august~~ ; ~~though~~ marble
~~Yet~~ back content languid pillars
~~For~~ ~~back~~ I fall , ~~languid~~, [deposed?] eager no more, arches
[ellini?]
~~consumed, content, oh deeply content,~~
desiring only to go, find the street, mark the
buildings, ~~surv~~ greet the applewoman, say
to the maid who opens the door A starry
night.

Goodnight. Good night. You go this way?
Alas; I go that.

Jan. 21st

X X X X X X X X

The magnificent world. . . the living, sane, vigorous world. . . These words refer to the stretch of London between Hammersmith ~~Chelsea~~ & Holborn, in ~~on a~~ January ~~night between two~~ between two & three in the morning. At least that was ~~Jacob's~~ the ground beneath Jacob's feet. ~~Strangely enough ht he was by a accompanied however by certain visions. He was exhilarated. amazed to find that People, besides being The feeling of health was caused by the tingling in his own brain.~~

It was healthy, & magnificent because one room contained perhaps fifty excited, talkative, friendly, people, And then to cover the ground quickly (there was scarcely a cab or a policeman in sight) is of itself exhilarating. Piccadilly shows to best advantage when it is empty. A young man has nothing to fear. On the contrary, though he may not ~~have distinguished himself by~~ have said. ~~saying~~ anything brilliant, he feels pretty confident that he can hold his own; (Here the things he said came to mind; ~~&~~ he was pleased to ~~think that~~ have met Mangin; he admired the young woman on the floor -) he liked them all: he liked that sort of thing. In short, all the drums & trumpets were sounding. The street scavengers were the only people about at the moment. ~~It is~~ scarcely necessary to say how well ~~Jacob disposed~~ Jacob felt / well disposed towards them, ~~how~~ & how it pleased him to let himself in with his latch key at his own door. & how ~~ten or eleven people appeared fairly vividly before him~~, he seemed to bring back with him into his sitting room about 10 or 11 new ~~p~~ people; whom he had not known went he out;when & how he looked about for something to read, & found it, & never read it, & fell asleep.

Indeed "drums & trumpets" is no phrase. Indeed, if Piccadilly -
Holborn & the empty sitting room, & the sitting room
with fifty people in it ~~were not at any moment~~
at any moment
are liable to blow such music into the air.
Women, perhaps are more excitable than men. At any rate,
no one ever says anything about it, & to see the
hordes crossing Waterloo Bridge to catch the non-stop to
~~t S~~ Surbiton one might think that reason impelled
the
them. No, no: it is drums & trumpets. ~~To be~~
~~candid~~, ~~T~~ ~~Only~~, Only, (should you turn aside into ~~th~~
the
one of ~~those~~ little bays on Waterloo Bridge to think
the matter over; should the tide be high, should ~~the~~
there be barges; & the big hotels lit up on one side &
~~the~~ St. Pauls be floating like a grey bubble on the other.
~~The maj beauty of it will so overcome you~~,
~~so many ideas will come into your head~~
it will probably seem to you ~~that~~ an inexplicable
mystery -
~~after a few minutes~~
probably
~~become~~ it will ~~soon~~ appear to you an inexplicable
mystery. They cross the Bridge ~~almost~~ incessantly.
Sometimes in the midst of carts and omnibuses a
lorry will appear with forest trees chained to it.
Then perhaps a mason's van with newly cut
some one loved someone also is ~~dead~~
tombstones, recording ~~how Mary was the beloved~~
~~wife of someone in Putney~~. ~~Meanwhile, on either side~~
~~people never stop hurrying both ways~~.
buried at Putney. Then, the ~~horse in~~ motor car in front
~~having moved, the~~ jerks; & the tombstones pass,
too quick for you to read more. All the time the stream of
people ~~fro~~ never ceases passing from the Surrey side to
the Strand; from the Strand to the Surrey side. It seems

as if the poor had gone raiding the city. ~~of riches~~ & now trapesed back to their own quarters, like beetles scurrying ~~under the back~~ into their holes - for that old woman fairly hobbles towards Waterloo, grasping a shiny bag, ~~like a as~~ as if she had been out into the light - ~~& how can one figure such as her in Mayfair~~. & now made off, with some scraped chicken bone, to her ~~own dark shelter~~. her hovel underground. She is ~~already~~ scarcely fit for daylight as it is, & soon her coat will be beyond the reach of pins. ~~Soon she will not be able~~ On the other hand, though the wind is rough & blowing in their faces, those girls there, striding hand in hand, shouting out a song, seem to feel neither cold nor shame, ~~& triumph over the force of the world~~, ~~which has done all it can do to~~ They are hatless. They triumph. It is windy So the water goes racing beneath us; & the men standing ~~at t~~ ~~up~~ on the barges, have to lean all their weight on the tiller; ~~as the tug~~

where ~~a few~~ a black tarpaulin is tied down over a load of golden straw.

As usual, painters are slung on planks across the great hotels on the bank, & the hotel windows ~~are already lit up~~. have already points of light in them ~~St Pauls~~ The city on the other side is white as if with age; all the ~~houses~~ build turning white round St Pauls, which, ~~as usual~~, ~~floats~~ swells ~~among~~ above them; [as usual the sun gilds the cross;] & somehow ~~though without~~ ~~stirs in us a deep, a un appears to be London; as the London that has always been & always will be~~ - ~~it being~~ But what century have we reached? This procession from the Surrey side to the Strand has gone on for ever? ~~T~~ That old man has been crossing the Bridge these six hundred years, with the rabble of little boys at his heels, for he is drunk; or ~~is he merely half~~blind with misery; & tied round with old clouts of clothing, such as pilgrims might have worn. He shuffles on. No one stands still. ~~&~~ If we stop, someone has to step ~~into~~ off the pavement; ~~or the. except that we may stop at a shop window~~ - ~~This book stall for instance,~~ where ~~We~~

St Pauls ~~swells~~ bubbles up among the hoary buildings
which press round it, pointed, & fretted, or oblong & smooth.
But what century have we reached? It seems as if this
procession had been passing across the Bridge for ~~centuries~~. Ever
~~Yet not in melancholy~~; for ~~whether it is the breeze, or~~
or ~~the river~~ It seems as if we marched to the sound of
music; ~~the~~ perhaps the wind & the river; perhaps
~~these same drums & trumpets, / Possibly~~
Has this procession from the Surrey side to the Strand gone on
forever? That old man has been crossing the Bridge
these six hundred years, with the rabble of little boys at
his heels, for he is drunk; or blind with misery, & tied
round with old clouts of clothing such as pilgrims
might have worn. He shuffles on. No one stands
still. It seems as if we marched to the sound of
music. perhaps the wind & the river; perhaps these
same drums & trumpets. ~~If~~ Why, even the unhappy
laugh, & the policeman far from judging the drunk man
surveys him humorously, & the little boys scamper
back again, & the clerk has nothing but tolerance for him,
& the ~~y~~ man who is reading half a page of Lothair at
the bookstall muses ~~his~~ charitably, & the girl
who ~~seems to have no particular~~ hesitates at the
crossing turns on him ~~her~~ ~~that~~ the bright yet vague glance
~~which~~ of the ~~very~~ young.

Bright yet vague; - She is perhaps twenty two;
She is ~~tall~~ shabby. She crosses the road & looks
at the flower shop window. She hesitates, &
makes off in the direction of Temple Bar ~~She~~
She ~~seems to~~ walks fast, yet anything distracts her.
~~She looks closely at~~ Now she seems to see, & now
to notice nothing.

XVII

There is a deserted graveyard in the parish of St Pancras,
& there Fanny Filmer often ~~stopp~~ ~~strolled~~ strayed, ~~reading the names~~
~~on the stones~~, ~~&~~ & notice read the names on the weather-beaten
stone, & noticed the bent yellow crocuses. Once a
catalogue of Madame Tussaud's show dropped from her
~~bag~~. hand. And once, when no one was looking,
she stepped across the ~~bi~~ turf ~~grass~~ & pushed aside the
grass & read ~~the~~ ~~name which~~ a date ~~that~~ which had been
overgrown. She started when the grave keeper in his
laced hat appeared. ~~She hurried through the gate~~.
She flushed & passed him with her eyes cast down.
At the gate she hesitated, & was for running back &
telling him that she meant to bring bulbs & plant
them; but she wavered.

Fanny Filmer was thus courageous ~~& sudden~~ &: thus
cast down. She was ~~at an~~ now violent & now as soft
as water. She had one hundred pounds a year & had come
to London to make her way upon the stage -

XVII

140 There is a ~~deserted~~ disused graveyard in the Parish of St Pancras.
280
1120 Fanny Filmer, having walked down Fleet Street, up Chancery Lane,
280 through Grays Inn, ~~& up along~~ now strayed, ~~through~~
39,200 through the graveyard, looking at this & that, ~~indeed~~
280 crossing the grass to read a name; ~~& has hastening when~~
140
1120 ~~the gravekeeper~~. & hurrying on when ~~the~~ a man in a
200
39,200 laced hat appeared - hurrying into the ~~road~~ street outside,
passing now by a ~~shop~~ window with blue china, now quickly
making up for lost time, ~~divin~~ abruptly entering a
bakers shop buying indiscriminately rolls & cakes;
~~on again she went~~, t ~~& either~~ going in again,
so that anyone wishing to follow must fairly trot.
Of course, ~~the its very~~ in this dusk, rapid movement,
quick glances, soaring hopes, come naturally. ~~Yet~~
~~Now Fanny, after having pulled up, looked this~~
~~Of course~~, ~~She turned in at the door, ran upstairs,~~
~~&, fitting her key, took the little jug~~ pewter ~~which stood t on the~~
~~floor.~~

~~X X X X X~~

She passed beneath Jacob's window

· X · ·X · · ··X ·X

The house was flat, dark, & silent. Jacob, however,
was at home, sitting in his back room. ~~&~~ Mrs.
Whitehorn had brought up his tea. Jacob had
~~lit his pipe~~, and was engaged in working out a ~~problem~~
chess problem, ~~with the board on a stool between~~ with his
~~legs~~ the board being on a stool between his legs.

Books, so people say, ~~are provide~~ are an infallible
guide to character. Thus we might be worse occupied ~~in~~
than in examining the works of Shakespeare, the plays of
Ben Jonson - Mrs Aphra Behn's Lyrics : ~~&, - reflecting~~
~~how~~, ~~We thus~~ ~~which last~~ ~~Youn young men~~

50
2
53
280
50
14,000

There is a great deal to be said for the tradition, & yet the tradition
280 / 31 / 280 / 40 / 8,680
is a severe one. With With Tono - Bungay & - Howards End, -
perhaps there we come nearer the mark there. perhaps,
For some reason his shoes, though, are more characteristic of him,
& the heather coloured dressing gown clumsily slung to the door -
The shaving brush, the Durer etching & the photograph from
the Greek, stood over the washing table

One hand was ~~at the back of his head~~. fingering the hair at
the back of his head. He slowly brought it forward &
~~rested the fingers on lif~~ raised the white queen from her
square; then ~~replaced her~~ put her down again on the
same spot. He filled his pipe; then advanced ~~&~~ the
black knight; ~~al~~ ~~When the clock struck.~~ The problem was solved. ~~The~~
~~Standing at the window he heard the boy calling the~~
6.30 papers; ~~went downstairs~~, Now Fanny Elmer
passed ~~by . . . .~~ under the window.

t moved 2 pawns. The ~~white~~ black Queen. advanced ~~All the pie~~ He swept the pieces off the board.

X X X XX XX

She sat ~~with~~ a in a tight black satin dress; ~~black lace shawl~~ over her shoulders,
~~a silver fan~~ in her hand a silver fan; & at her
breast ~~a~~ red carnations. ~~streaked with purple~~
one arm ~~h~~ hung over the arm of the chair, negligently.
"A little lower, a little looser, so -better -
that's right" mumbled ~~Bentley, who Bunt~~
~~Bunbury~~ who was drawing. her. & smoking at the
same time. But he was naturally inarticulate~~,~~
& his head might have been the work of a sculptor ~~potter in in~~
~~white apron~~, who, after squaring the forehead, ~~left~~ &
stretching the mouth left marks of his thumbs, &
streaks from his fingers in the clay. ~~His~~
~~thu~~ ~~The eyes were~~ But the eyes had never been
shut. They were rather prominent & rather bloodshot
as if from staring & staring; ~~And~~ ~~His Words~~
& when he spoke they paid no attention to ~~what~~ ~~stared without connection with~~
what he said. They still stared save to look. for a second disturbed

Burnham

An unshaded light above hung ~~over~~ Fanny's head.

As for the beauty of women, ~~it scarcely exists.~~ it is like the
light on the sea, never constant to a single wave. They
all have it, & lose it; ~~&~~ now she is dull as thick bacon;
now transparent as a hanging glass. The fixed
beauties are the dull ones. ~~There~~ Here comes Lady
Venice, displayed ~~set out~~ like a monument for admiration;
but carved in alabaster, to be set on the
mantelpiece, & ~~allowed~~ never dusted. ~~Pretty~~
~~women, tinted, frilled, tinkling & respen~~ A
~~sugar~~ dapper brunette, complete from head to foot
only serves as an illustration ~~in~~ to lie upon the
drawing room table. ~~Almost all day long women~~
~~are insignificant. They have the faces of playing~~
~~cards; smooth painted paste board; or mere~~
The women in the streets have the faces of
playing cards; ~~the inexpressive as inexpensive~~; the
outlines accurately ~~shaded filled with a~~ painted;
& the lines drawn tight. Then, at a top floor
window, leaning out & looking down on the street you see
beauty itself; or in the corner of the omnibus; or
squatted in a ditch __ Beauty glowing out, suddenly
expressive, withdrawn the moment after.
No one can count on it; or seize it. Nothing is to be
won from the shops; & Heaven knows it would be
better to sit at home than haunt the plate glass
windows in the hope of ~~sna~~. lifting the shining
green, the glowing ruby, ~~from them to you~~. out of them alive.
~~Sea~~ ~~The glass in the sea is no more preserved~~
Sea Glass in a saucer ~~taken from the sea~~ loses its lustre no sooner
than they do. Thus if you talk of a beautiful
woman you mean only ~~a moment~~, ~~or~~ something
flying fast which for a second ~~looks out of a face~~
~~not~~ uses the nose & the eyes & the cheeks of
Fanny Elmer, for example, like a master, to express it.

She was not beautiful; as she sat stiffly; her underlip
a little too prominent, her nose too large; her eyes too
near together; ~~&~~ a ~~sulky looking~~, thin girl, ~~immature~~,
will brilliant cheeks, & dark hair; ~~& now sulky, or~~
~~& sudden impulses~~. sulky, just now, or stiff with ~~too~~
~~long a sitting~~. sitting ~~A Immature & yet~~
~~formal;~~ When ~~Burnham~~ Maugham. snapped his stick of
charcoal, she started, Burnham was out of temper.
He squatted before the gas fire ~~l~~ warming his
hands. Meanwhile she looked at his drawing.
He grunted. Fanny then threw on a
~~shabby~~ dressing gown, & boiled something in a
60,000 saucepan.
280 "By God, its bad" said Bramham.~~without~~
230
840 Fanny dropped on the floor & ~~leant her head~~
& 560
64.40 ~~against his side~~ . clasped her hands round his knees.
& ~~She~~ looked at him as a child might look - her beautiful
eyes -

Yes, ~~the word insists upon~~ ~~comes naturally~~ ~~being used, not that~~
~~she was beautiful, but that~~ beauty flying through
the room ~~lit~~ shone there for a second Fanny's eyes
seeming to question, to commiserate, to be for a
second love itself - But she exaggerated.
Bramham noticed nothing. And when the kettle
boiled she scrambled up, more like a colt or a
puppy than a ~~passi~~ loving woman.

Now Jacob walked over to the window, & stood with
his hands in his pockets. ~~The~~ Mr. Springett opposite came
~~round~~ out & looked at his shop window & went ~~back~~ in
again. The children ~~stood looking at~~ eyed the pink
sticks of sweetstuff. ~~A~~ Pickford's van swung down
the street. ~~Here~~ Jacob ~~turned away~~ pulled down the blind, ~~&~~ Two minutes
later, he ~~came~~ opened the front door, walked off
in the direction of Holborn.

~~Fanny Elmer took her cloak from~~ the hook, & ~~Nick Bramham~~ & ~~she &~~ walked with Nick Bramham in the direction of Holborn.

They ascended the crimson stairs ~~at of~~ at the Empire & went up & up until they reached the promenade. & ~~had to stand~~ stood, leaning over the barrier. ~~as there were~~ ~~the house~~ ~~no seats to be had.~~ ~~was full.~~ ~~looking through the smoke~~.

Five minutes later, Jacob ~~pushed~~ ascended the crimson stairs at the Empire & ~~we~~ pushed through the swing doors, & leant over the barrier.

'Hullo Flanders - said Nick

"When'll this rot be over?" said Jacob.

"You know Miss Elmer?"

Then they sat on the velvet seats.

Fanny Elmer reached her cloak from a hook. Nick Bramham unpinned his drawing & rolled up it under his arm. ~~Fanny~~ They set off ~~down the~~ turned out the lights; street ~~together~~, holding on their way, through all the people, motor cars, omnibuses, carts, until they reached Leicester Square; through

~~Almost Five minutes later, Jacob reached it,~~
five minutes before Jacob reached it, for his way was slightly longer, & also he had been stopped by a block in Holborn; so that Nick & Fanny were already leaning over the barrier in the promenade at the Empire when Jacob pushed through the swing doors & took his place beside them.

"Hullo, never noticed you" said Nick five minutes later. "

"Bloody rot" said Jacob.

'Miss Elmer' said Nick.

Jacob at once looked very awkwardly. took his pipe out of his mouth -

Evelyn
Addison
G. Eliot
D. Wordsworth
~~Hardy~~
Modern novels
Defoe
C. Bronte

Very awkward he was. And when they sat upon a plush
sofa & let the smoke go up between them & the stage &
heard far off the ~~[salt?][te?]~~ high pitched voices & the
~~jolly timely~~ jolly orchestra breaking in opportunely
he was still awkward, only Fanny thought 'What a
beautiful voice!' She thought how little he said, yet
how firm it was. She thought how young men are
dignified & aloof, & how unconscious they are, & how
~~indifferent~~; ~~admirable~~ quietly, ~~quietly~~ one might sit
beside Jacob & look at him.

His beauty was no flying light, ~~his~~ It was a face
that surveyed the turmoil of human affairs; had somehow
~~survived~~ escaped humiliation; was prepared for the
attack; would yield nothing, & yet (so Fanny thought)
he will do foolish, simple minded things. He will
be overbearing. "And I wouldn't give way" she
added
~~thought to h~~erself. How childlike he would be, come in
tired of an evening; & how majestic. ~~For the
beauty of~~ He sat up & leant over the barrier.
The smoke hung about him.

~~The beauty of young men is~~ Beauty, indeed,
ought to be forbidden in a rational world. All the
~~things we can never have, what we~~ have learnt ~~to do
without~~, It leads one to rhapsodise. It
seemed that How he laughed! Indeed,
though ~~the ruin of general~~ no one nowadays
~~has~~ altogether escapes a hint of sternness,
And forever, the beauty of young men seems to be
set in smoke; ~~seems~~ however lustily they
chase footballs, or drive cricket balls, dance,
run, or stride along roads; Possibly they a
~~may~~ are soon to lose it; ~~possibly for a moment~~

it is they who look furthest, & see most; And they say so little: ~~They are a [light?] so firmly.~~ ~~n~~ Nothing possibly they look into the eyes of the faraway heroes;

& have little to say ~~about it~~; & take their station among us half contemptuously.

Or it may be that they ~~have as yet taken no sides;~~ hesitate, or that they are unhappy, or that, when it comes to sitting on a stool in an office they want to be out of doors, hunting, playing hockey on horseback on a long sea beach. Anyhow they love silence, & speak beautifully, each word falling like a disc new cut, not a hubble bubble of small smooth coins ~~as~~ such as girls use; & they move ~~like in~~ decidedly ~~never stopping~~ as if they knew ~~to a second~~ how long to stay, when to go, ~~& could not be persuaded having something to do; no doubts teasing them; & there being for them always a straight way~~ -

Oh but Jacob was only gone to get a programme. ~~He~~ The ~~juggler was~~ dancers came right at the end of the evening he said. ~~They sat down again on the sofa.~~

And isn't it pleasant, Fanny went on thinking, ~~When~~ how ~~how~~ young men bring out lots of silver coins ~~& look at~~ from their trouser pockets & look at them, instead of having just so many in a purse?

[There she stood staring at the stage, ~~&~~ Jacob separated from her by perhaps two feet.

Her ~~H~~ desire to be ~~at one~~ was melted with the music ~~overcame her. A carnal desire? Not in the least.~~ to be light & sound &] ~~Why; An~~ She saw herself dancing across the stage ~~in~~ merrily,

Already this horrible nonsense

And then, there she was herself whirling across the stage in
white flounces; & the music was the dance & ~~soft~~ fling of her
own soul, & the whole machinery & gear & rock of the world
soft eddies & ~~whirlpool~~ falls
was spun out into those soft swirls & ~~curvages~~ she felt
though She stood
~~So she felt~~ ~~standing~~ rigid leaning over the barrier, ~~two~~
~~feet from Jacob Flanders~~. two feet from Jacob Flanders.
~~Ind~~ ~~Indeed~~ It was as much as he could ~~mana~~ do to stand
perfectly still beside her. ~~But this she never guessed~~
~~She~~ Who, indeed, can measure the wild ~~fantastic~~ folly of
this ~~absurd passion;~~ kind of thinking, or how it seems to
break ~~upon the~~ the soul ~~upon~~ in spray upon rocks,
& sucks it back ~~into~~ & flings it out, & for ever
sweeps us ~~& tosses~~ hither thither in a flood? ~~against~~
wrung together
Her screwed up black grove dropped to the floor. When Jacob
gave it her she started ~~almost indignantly~~. ~~with almost~~
~~annoyance~~. angrily. For there never was a more
irrational passion; ~~a~~ And Jacob ~~saw that her feelings~~
~~were beyond her control~~. was afraid of her for a moment.
Surely a rational ~~world will find some means of~~
~~excluding all~~ this: ~~for~~ ~~What~~ So
is it
violent, so dangerous, ~~so~~ ~~it~~ is when young ~~men~~
women ~~begin~~ ~~let themselves flash~~, ~~w~~ ~~flin~~ ~~fling~~
~~& fly;~~ ~~whirl, across the stage,~~ ~~take to whirling~~
stand rigid; grasp the barrier; fall in love.
when dancing, whirling, ~~screw~~ wringing their gloves to
dish clouts, young women feel their hearts breaking
upon the world, ~~breaking with all~~ in millions of waves,
~~& each so~~ swirling round music [that sweeps?] in
~~w~~ volleying clouds; ~~stand so st~~ stand

X X X X X X

It was the middle of February.

~~Out of a tremulous haze~~ the roofs of Hampstead garden
suburb lay in a tremulous haze. It was too hot to
walk. A dog barked, barked; barked, down in the hollow.
In sheer weakness after ~~a long~~ illness ~~so one sits thus~~
up on the wood~~en seat;~~ bench; The body after long illness
is languid, passive, receptive of ~~too great~~ sweetness, ~~which~~ of
but
~~warmth of which~~ ~~Indeed~~ too weak to contain it; the
tears well & fall as the dog barks in the hollow, the
skim after hoops
children ~~run~~ ~~shout~~, the ~~clouds~~ country darkens &
It is sky
lightens. ~~As~~ beyond a veil it seems; & Ah but draw the
faint with this
curtains thicker, lest I perish ~~with of~~ pleasure!
~~But~~ So weak was Fanny Elmer.
~~B~~ 'My limbs shake. My eyes are full of tears.'
~~For the world is tender, & I am young~~ beaut
went barking
Yet the ~~barking~~ dog ~~rent the veil of~~ ~~Agitation~~
~~was at her heart~~. The motor cars hooted far off.
She could hear a far away rush & humming. Agitation
Up she got & walked. The grass was freshly green
No children
The sun hot. All round ~~Leg of mutton~~ pond / were
were
children stooping to launch little boats; or drawn away
screaming by their nurses.

The liquid shadows went over the ~~di~~ land.

veil before my eyes

was on her.

At midday young women ~~come~~ walk out into the
air. All the men are busy in the town. They stand
by the edge of the blue pond. The fresh wind scatters the
childrens voices all about. ~~"My children"~~
'My children,' thought Fanny Elmer The women
stand round the pond, beating off great prancing
shaggy dogs. Gently the baby is rocked in
the perambulator. And all their eyes are
absorbed as if they did ~~their business~~.

The eyes of all the nurses, mothers, & wandering women are a little glazed, absorbed; They gently nod instead of answering when the little boys tugs at their skirts begging them to move on.

And Fanny moved hearing ~~that~~ some cry - a workman's whistle perhaps - up in midair, ~~The~~ Now it was the thrush, ~~there on the~~ trilling out into the warm air, ~~with that~~ a flutter of jubilation - ~~save that~~ but ~~somewhere a~~ fear seemed to ~~urge~~ spur ~~his~~ him - Fanny thought: as if he too ~~were~~ were anxious, with such joy in his heart. - as if he were watched, as he sang, ~~by some~~ & ~~something~~ pressed ~~urged~~ on to sing - There! Restless, he ~~has~~ had ~~has~~ ~~flown~~ flew to the next tree.

She heard His song ~~was~~ ~~further away~~. more faintly - Beyond it was the ~~rushing~~ humming of the wheels & the ~~air~~ wind ~~ri~~. rushing.

The earth is a cradle, so they say; & ~~couched upon her grey green br~~ our mother rocks us, ~~where we lie so peacefully~~, ~~flat.~~ ~~the~~ Quiet is her heart, cool her grass, sweet her rivers Look how the ~~grass~~ reed. blows this way & that. ~~It~~ They cares nothing that ~~it~~ they is watched. And now the sun burns my cheek. The fontourell butterfly bathes his wings in its heat. Mournfully the cloud blows ~~over us~~ its purple over us. For as long as I care to watch it the granite boulder will lie ~~in the same~~ ~~there~~, unmoved. ~~strew me then with~~ ~~Oh, but cold hearted mother, cradle of stone.~~ ~~my~~ sun hold me, ~~still; but~~

~~So up got Fanny &~~ Strew me then with leaves. Time my heart by yours. ~~The~~ Then the birds ~~fly like grain~~ come flung by like grain a sower, one trails behind the next. Cries pee wit pee wit - So up got Fanny Elmer.

She ran down the green slope; the gold & purple crocuses
in the green &
burnt ~~like little candle flames~~, burnt some sense in
her with joy.

"Dear, miss, ~~she's left h~~ she's left her umbrella"
red
said the ~~pale~~ mottled woman in the glass box at the
Express dairy Company's ~~shh~~ shop.

"Perhaps I'll catch her" answered Molly Edwards,
the waitress, with the pale plait of hair; & she
dashed through the door.

"No good", she said, coming back a moment later
with Fanny's cheap umbrella. She tidied her
plait.

"Give it here" said the cashier. "Oh that door!"
Her hands were cased in black mittens & the
through the finger hole
finger tips ~~protrud~~ that drew in the paper slips
were swollen as sausages.

"~~Ham~~ Pie & greens - for one" "Large coffee &
", Tea
crumpets". "Eggs on toast ~~;~~ & madeira cakes."
~~So the hard~~ Thus the sharp voices of the waitresses
~~cried~~ snapped. The lunchers heard their orders
repeated with approval, saw the next table
Their eyes strayed ~~to theirs~~ served with anticipation. Their own
no more
at last satisfaction possessed them.
eggs on toast were delivered. & their eyes wandered no
more.

But oh, when stout suburban women
satisfy nature's needs how unnecessary it
appears! So equably could we let that fire
~~be extinguished~~. ~~die~~ be quenched. ~~To~~
~~watch~~ damp clods of ~~pastry taken~~ in ~~at~~ the
~~mouth & to reflect that thereby~~ the machine is
~~is stoked for more perambulation of the streets~~

~~is to commit blasphemy~~.
The mouth however is opened wide, & damp clods of pastry ~~des &~~ ~~And~~ No fire can come from damp clods of pastry. It is ~~prettier~~ better far to see lions with ~~their~~ bloody bones in their paws than these cheap lunching women.

"~~Which~~", ~~said~~ Could never tell you, said Mrs. Mary Parsons, how I lived through it. Still there's no saying what one can do till one tries." The doctor t said to me "We shall be having you ill next" Mrs. Parsons he said; & I said to him "I haven't time to be ill. Doctor. No more I have. ~~We mothers haven't time to be ill.~~"
And this was quite true. The plate of ~~cakes~~ pastry, glazed yellow white & pink was slowly scrutinized. Nelly Jenkins crumbled her cake indifferently enough. Everytime the door opened she looked up, but so vacantly that it was pitiful to see her. for she saw only phantoms & task masters in other human beings. The world was all a misty, ~~to her~~. ~~&~~ The coal merchants, the solicitors clerks, the young ~~women fr~~. business women & the ~~old moth~~ married women ~~were all of a piece to her~~ all shapes cut ~~of~~ out of grey brown stuff.

"Did you ever hear the like for impertinence?" Mrs. Parsons wound up.

"~~Large~~ Hot milk & scones for one" cried the waitress." "Pot of tea, roll & butter. Sausage rolls ~~& mashed~~ for two"

The truth is, the world must go on.

A great broom had swept the streets, Fanny thought. as she leant a little forward in the front seat of the motor omnibus. they were - so clean A broom had swept the sky — so clear the air was , & yet ~~so~~ so bare, It was the ~~milk~~ milky air of early spring. ~~Brilliantly~~ Crystal clear were the shop windows; with all their greens & reds & yellows displayed for a moment as the omnibus swung ~~to~~ down the hill. ~~Very few people were~~ ~~The tramlines gleamed silver~~. ~~Very few people were on the pavement.~~ Single figures flitted along the pavement. ~~The lamps~~ Points of pale yellow light ~~wer~~ ~~sprung here - there~~ - ~~were high & low & then were all the ground~~ pierced ~~through~~ ~~here~~ the fading ~~of~~ afternoon - ~~And~~ She thought the world transparent, spiritual. She thought that men & women had stars with in their breasts.

"I've lost my umbrella" she said to the conductor. ~~She~~ smiling at him. He smiled back at her. - so ~~He had sad honest eyes, & beautiful white teeth~~. He ~~held~~ pressed her arm, as she stepped onto the pavement. ~~And~~ A little boy was spinning his top ~~against~~ by the wall of school[bread?] shop; ~~&~~ he crooked his arm to protect it from the passers by, & hissed, as the ~~top spun~~, like a groom, ~~in~~ ~~with~~ engrossed. ~~The~~ in watching it. ~~He~~ Carefully she / stepped ~~the~~ out ~~round him; watched him tenderly~~. to avoid his top.

Friendly the world was.

~~Lover are charitable; they~~ So charitable are lovers. So tenderly they respect the private flames of others. So.

So plainly they perceive what keeps us

Down Jacob's street she passed. His windows were dark. She passed on. She came back. Now they were ~~alight~~ illuminated. Her heart crowded ~~the~~ its beats. ~~But~~ Hhow could she go in? How speak to him? And who was with him? ~~Now passion washed out all tenderness for others~~.

A woman selling violets pressed her

But ~~She was cruel as a balked horse~~ what now had

Emerson
Addisson.
Thoreau
G. Eliot
Ch. Brontë
D. Wordsworth
Modern Fiction
Defoe
Henry James
Evelyn.
Gissing.

she of violets? She hated women.

Poor Nick Bramham was mixing blue & white on his
&
palate. On a chair stood a blue pot, a bunch of
bananas, ~~she~~ Quickly, decidedly, he ~~glan~~ looked from
his palate to the chair & back again. He looked at
the window. ~~He lit the gas~~. He lit the gas.
Nothing could be done. He opened a large book of
Michael Angelo's drawings which lay, stuffed with
drawing
old envelopes & ~~sht~~ sheets of ~~paper~~, upon the
table. He had lunched there off sardines, olives
and bread. He ~~p~~ shuffled through the pages:
the plates were all loose. ~~He ran his fingers~~
~~through his hair~~. ~~And then His tears began to fall~~
~~one by one on the page.~~ ~~He pushed it away.~~
He a tumbler
~~The tumbler fell & w~~as knocked over, ~~& rolled on the~~
~~floor~~. which rolled upon the floor. He stooped -

Poor Nick Bramham! - ~~&~~ Utterly unable to
or
master tumblers, ~~clear a~~ clear a way for himself;
only
depending on Fanny Elmer, wishing to paint - but
easily down cast; lost like a child, now that
Fanny loved another; hurt; discontented; waiting
for Fanny to come - "but she's with Jacob
Flanders ; Somehow the tumbler ~~t~~ rolled
beneath his foot & he kicked it; ~~Then~~ So that it
wobbled foolishly away. And then he burst
out crying.

~~He~~ The papers slid out of the book & fluttered to the floor.
Suddenly ~~rolling~~ throwing himself over he pressed his face
in the sofa corner ~~in a cushion & burst into tears.~~ There he sobbed.
His thick soled boots kicked out — ~~he~~ pawed the pages, the
old letters -
~~And then, when the~~
tree
[~~Like some uneasy sea; like some storm tossed forest~~,]
[like sharp waves, ~~v~~ violent branches; ~~The the~~
like the thongs of whips, ~~or~~ the lashing of tails, -
~~like always like something jerked~~, flung out &
passions
jerked back, - that is what ~~feelings are here in~~
~~London~~. ~~goes on down in the street~~ life is like, in
London, for the young.

~~Waves~~. ~~The waves~~ It is curious, ~~to watch~~, ~~lie~~
lying in a boat to watch the waves. Here are three
regularly
coming /one after another, ~~regularly~~, all much of a
size; Then hurrying after them comes a fourth,
very large, ~~as if to~~ menacing; it ~~s~~ lifts the boat; as
it goes; & somehow merges, without accomplishing
anything, in the others.

What can be more violent, more desperate than the
fling of boughs in a gale - ~~yielding themself~~
the tree yielding itself all the way up the trunk &
to the very tip of the branch - streaming, &
shuddering the way the wind blows - yet broken off
sharp~~?~~ never flying in dishevelment away.
squirms
The corn ~~even bows~~ & abases itself as if it
tug out
prepared to ~~fly~~ from from its roots: yet is tied.
down.

Mrs. Flanders at the cistern,
Rebecca pumping —
Out into the orchard
The village
The Port
Paris
The cafe
The [simple life?]
Greece
└

Now it is Fanny Elmer, & next year some fair round eyed
girl from the provinces, come to learn anatomy at
University college hospital & lunching off buns ~~at~~ in
an A.B.C. shop. Now it is life itself - the days of the week,
that are blown into transparent crests over which
~~we one sails~~. ~~the~~ we are lifted; up, down: up, down.
Why, from the very windows, even in the dusk, you
~~seem to~~ see a ~~wave in~~ swelling run through
the street, an aspiration, a sizing up, as with
eyes
arms out stretched, ~~mouths~~ desiring, mouths
agape - Down, down again - ~~For to the~~ For if
the exultation lasted, we should be blown like ~~the~~
~~soft foam~~ foam right into the air. The stars
would shine through us. We should go down the
gale in ~~slt~~ salt drops. As sometimes happens.
For the impetuous spirits ~~have~~ ~~done with life &~~
~~leapt the bridge, or snatched the razor~~ - ~~have stepped~~
trifled
~~off the~~ ~~are not to be tampered with~~.
will have none of this cradling. Off they fly, from
the waves' crest; ~~never again to be sucked back,~~
~~lulled, soothed, aimlessly swaying~~, ~~straight at the~~
Never any swaying, or aimlessly lolling for them.
~~One person is different from another, always;~~
Never any making believe, or lying cosy, or genially
supposing that one ~~man~~ is much like another,
& fire warm, & wine pleasant, & extravagance a sin:
~~mistake.~~ "People are so nice, once you know them."
"Oh but ~~I couldn't speak~~ you ~~must~~
~~make allowances for her~~." I couldn't speak ill of her."
So the waves croon to us. Safe we lie.
~~The next.~~ ~~No, for them a leap from a Bridge or~~
~~a razor~~. But they ~~believe that~~. – Nick, perhaps,
or Fanny Elmer ~~for~~ ridiculously supposing that

this is the worst, the last, the end; ~~that as the other~~
leap, snatch knives, take drugs, or, prevented,
drift like wreckage across the track.
riding the crest, fling off, ~~down the wind, Heaven knows where~~,
sting the cheek on a
with sharp hail, &are seen no more, &
Perhaps - perhaps. For life, this dark eyed mother,
with all her violence, spurning us, bidding us fly,
vanish, never learn to grow old, yet if you press
close ~~cling~~ to her murmurs; ~~as a~~ some secret.
What? Only one word. Listen. Another.
No sense to it. No. But lean closer. Follow
after. ~~The The darkness gathers. A great hall,~~
~~dimly lit, with resonant, sounding. The light~~
down the great hall, dimly lit, with the curved
150
280 ceiling, - ~~noise resounding~~ Resonant with echoes;
1200 alarming; tapers blown out; ~~g~~ cold gusts
300 from what sea? Life, life, booming: ~~her~~
42,00 ~~secret~~, & the lightning; ~~&~~ ~~Terror~~ I say, how
vast it is! How musical! ~~Oh she sings~~ She draws
ground into
~~on top of the growling, what melody! like a~~ us on.
~~There he sat, sobbing; He sat~~ A question breathed
40,000 by the sea
40 . . . ~~Something laughing.~~
8. . . . There he sat with his hands on his knees ~~looking into~~
~~the fire &~~ while the tears ran down his cheeks.
150 "~~Oh said~~ Fanny, bursting ~~into the room~~, into the room.
280 They hated each other. All that evening they
1200 quarrelled - ~~infinitely unhappy both of them.~~
300 shall
"I ~~will~~ never come again" she said.
42000

XVIII

Betty Flanders stood on a chair at the top of the house,
stirring the ~~banging the side of~~ the water tank ~~cistern~~ with a broom handle.
~~The hollow sound~~ Curious ringed stockings she wore,
for, bending over ~~the tank~~, her legs were visible.
From the kitchen came at regular ~~sucking sound~~,
intervals a creak followed by a suck.
Water chuckled, & pipes groaned, but ~~nothing~~ in the water.
perhaps there was some obstruction in the tank -
~~curt~~ Betty Flanders went on banging. The
tank resounded. hollow. "~~It~~ oh" she cried. "Stop" - "There" -
This was happen~~ed~~ing precisely at three fortyfive on Wednesday
~~February March~~ the 23rd. of March.
Strange indeed are the uses to which people ~~men & women~~
put these few moments of ~~i~~ daylight; ~~for certainly~~
~~a space of this particular texture, daylight~~, this fabric
~~issued~~ of peculiar texture; which, so long as we live, we
call ~~week~~ Wednesday, Thursday or Friday -

[Margin: Wh. is strictly limited after all though somebody is always ~~using it up.~~ using it—]

And Rebecca was ~~in the kitchen had been~~ pumping in the
kitchen. She waited to hear Betty Flanders call out
from her chair at the top of the house -

Indeed when the ~~fish~~ man with the fish barrow came
round & knocked at the front door, neither of them heard
him. He came round to the back.
~~And~~ Betty Flanders got down off her chair, & descended
carrying her broom, which she held in her hands as
she examined the cod, the hake, the herring, & the
bloater. Somehow, by taking the fish in her hand, by
inclining her nose very slightly towards it, she ~~knew~~
~~its value~~. what to buy.

[Margin: made up her mind]

Something was wrong with the sucker of the pump.
Something was wrong with the oil stove. Mr.
Humphrey Piper scraping his boots went into the
kitchen to have a look. Whereupon Betty

Flanders seemed to bethink her that it was high time -
~~considering the hour~~, rather late in the day indeed -
the ~~weat~~ clouds brewing up perhaps - She put on
her galoshes, & standing the broom against the
went out
store cupboard, ~~seems~~ ~~says~~ ~~b~~ ~~bustled~~, ~~out~~ along the
~~garden path~~ garden path —
The handsome chickens were parading in the orchard. Like a
general in ~~cock~~ cocked hat the rooster walked in front.
Driven on some unknown quest the troop swept through the
long grass. Mrs. Flanders knelt by the brown earth at the
~~root~~
foot ~~base~~ of the great pear tree, & ~~drove a~~ pressed ~~a twig~~ her fingers
here & there into the soft earth. ~~Into each hole she dropped~~
a ~~tiny green seed~~. The brown lumps stuck to her finger.
Her flesh grazed the pinkish glistening coils of worms.
~~The~~ Into each hole she dropped a tiny grey seed; & that done
&
~~pressed~~ filled each hole with earth, ~~pressed it firmly~~
in a circle
& pressed it lightly on top. until ~~in a circle~~ round the pear
a ring
tree lay sleeping ~~a~~ ~~the~~ ~~a~~ ~~a~~ ~~circle of the seeds~~ of
soft blue flowers. She raised herself, with difficulty
for she was growing stout; & ~~proceeded to~~ Now she
~~p~~ ~~pinched the buds~~ gently felt the buds, on the apple trees; a
fetched a pruning hook & began ~~snipped~~ snipping
among the bushes here & there, ~~&~~ ~~her~~ the hook
squeaking ~~as she~~ each time ~~she cut a with it~~, it
opened & shut. Already the ~~blossom~~ blossom was
showed
swollen & / pinkish ~~through the~~ white. And each time
she looked up into the boughs she saw ~~the mild bluish~~
~~sky~~ them held like a pattern against the mild grey-blue
~~bluish~~ sky. Suddenly, ~~yet~~ with a thudding fulness the
~~bells~~ church bells began rumbling over the
beating out muffled & blows
scale, ~~sounding~~ with irregular ~~force~~, a fragment from a
hymn. She opened the orchard door & went out
over Garfits field ~~up~~ a little way up Dodds Hill.

The tears came to Betty Flanders eyes as she stood ~~in the orchard~~ beneath the apple tree. All the past ~~seemed to quiver which stood in her deep & tranquil was stirred into eddies by the~~ seemed to quiver in her. She felt scarcely able to contain fifty five years of life; ~~her three sons; memories; the present moment.~~ ~~Then~~ [the ~~cock led his troop on their voyage through the long grass~~.] for the random bells made the eddies in the ~~waters eddy~~ deep pool. ~~Eddy~~ Indeed she was very happy. One hundred chickens ~~were~~ . . . the potatoes had kept all the year round . . . the fruit ~~blossom~~ was ~~p~~ promising . . . nice, kind, good people in ~~the village~~. . . dear Captain Barfoot She opened the orchard gate, & walked a little way up Garfits acre towards ~~to up~~ Dodd's Hill The mother of three sons embraced / her share of the ~~whole~~ globe. She stood (to ~~she was~~ drew breath) like a rooted tree; sustenance coming to her ~~throu~~ from veins ~~veins veins~~ trickling running through the deep earth. that ~~ran through deep springs deep in the earth.~~

"Archer" she thought, will be at Gibraltar to morrow" She had heard that it was a great rock, much ~~inf.~~ infested with apes. She figured him dancing in a blue jacket with stiff gold scrolls. ~~upon it~~ And Jacob in Paris on his way to Greece. And dear little Johnnie . . . All the time the random ~~old~~ bells kept swinging ~~out~~ & the ~~hym~~ hymn tune curled about round her head. "Mr. Jarvis practising" she thought; ~~The Up~~ a ~~little further she walked.~~ ~~A few steps further on~~ The purple in the air ~~promised thunder, rain shower~~ - ~~For it was~~ became suddenly a deeper. ~~A rain~~ ~~hill above~~ She looked back at the sky ~~above the village~~ ~~at the village, lying slightly beneath her~~. ~~& saw that the~~ & saw the village laid under a leaf ~~washed~~ ~~shaped a~~ with shadow. Indeed it was half past four. The church ~~struck~~ clock was striking the half hour through the hymn tune. From all this Was there something queer in the sounds, queer in the purple,- light a little ominous? ~~The~~

downstairs
she returned. All the lamps were / in the living rooms.
The loaves were on the table. Mrs. Cranch, Mrs. Gage,
Mrs. Woolman, Mrs Garfit were all taking ~~h~~ hold of the
kettles. And from the chimneys smoke went up. regularly.
The bells enclosed the village. It seemed as if somehow,
~~could you hear it~~ a clock ticked - a heart beat - up & down
went the breast - & ~~dow~~ all the men sat ~~down~~ at the tables -
save that old Cranch was upstairs with the
bronchitis - & it was ~~half twent~~ half past four in the village,
& the village, ~~t~~ lay against the earth, trusting to it,
two dozen lights
shining out ~~very mildly~~ against the storm cloud; ~~which~~
infinitely ~~quiet~~ humble - a little community, all in
time, ~~with each other, knowing each other,~~- yes, but
~~to~~ this evening, somehow strange to Betty Flanders, as she
returned; ~~as~~ No one survives. The little company is
~~afloat on a~~ voyaging~~;~~ We who have been bound together
for so many years ~~are bound to be overwhelmed at
last;~~ will be scattered. Garfit drinks, she thought.
Betty Page is in the agony of childbirth. The ~~bells~~ bells
~~throbbed painfully~~. thudded as if it hurt them.
However there was the postman on his red bicycle
swinging off to deliver letters at the Rectory. Her door
turn - she hurried forward, ~~desiring more than~~
fearing ill news, took the little packet, shuffled through -

>——————————<

My dearest Mother,

Jacob wrote, having withdrawn to a side
table away from the others; & feeling ~~a little~~ it
romantic to ~~st~~ sit in a cafe & write ~~on paper
supplied free~~ with a pointed nib, in violet ink,
while everyone talked French.

Your loving Jacob, he
signed himself. & got up & went back to the table
where Sargeant was holding forth to Adams.

"You needn't go through all the grounds for your argument when you have to admit that its false from the very beginning" said the little American painter. He was talking very fast; Jacob was pleased to think that he had had too much to drink.

Now Flanders has finished writing to his lady said the other -

Jacob ordered absinthe; His accent was vile. Never mind. He smoked a cigarette. The marble table was stained with coffee. with ~~cream~~

Cruttendon ~~Adamson~~ had one leg ~~on~~ lying on the long shiny covered seat. A painter too. Sargeant flicked the fly off his bald head; but next moment it had settled there again. A man came slowly past the table crying La Presse La Presse. The glass cage turned & turned & let people in; ~~& through it~~ Sargeant flicked the fly off once more.

"I drink your health, Sir" he said, looking at Jacob.

~~He was muddled. Suddenly Jacob began to talk.~~

"A very fine fellow, Flanders."

"Do you uphold Velasquez?" said Cruttendon.

"By God, he does," said Sargeant.

"He always gets like this" said Cruttendon. irritably Jacob looked at him with excessive composure.

'I'll tell you the three greatest things that were ever written in the whole of literature" Cruttendon. suddenly burst out. Lie there like fruit my soul," he began.

"~~Shakespeare~~'

"Don't listen to a man who don't like Velasquez" said Sargeant.

dont give any more, to drin

"Adolphe, ~~take away~~ Mr. Sergeant's wine" said Cruttendon.

"Fair play, fair play" said Jacob. "Let

By God sir you're a damned good
painter

a man drink what he likes. You quote Shakespeare. I'm with you there, Cruttendon. Shakespeare had more guts than all the damned frogs together. ~~Lie~~ Hang there like fruit my soul" he began quoting. The devil damn you black[22] you cream-faced loon." Hang there like fruit.

~~They both burst out laughing~~. ~~Which would you rather~~" . . . . .

"~~Oh~~ Curse these flies" said Sergeant, shaking his head.

They mistake you for a ripe banana" said Cruttendon.

"Stow it, Cruttendon, said Jacob. "The fellow has no manners" he explained to Sergeant very politely. "Don't know how to behave. Wants to cut people off their drink. Look here: order me a grilled bone. What's the French: grilled bone. Grilled bone, Adolphe. Now you juggins, ~~don't have~~ ain't got such a thing? Lord what a people?

"And I'll tell you Flanders the second most beautiful thing in the whole of literature" said Cruttendon. ~~leaning~~ putting his legs on the floor taking his legs off the seat & leaning right across the table, so that he almost touched Jacob.'s face.

Hey diddle diddle the cat & the fiddle, Sergeant began, strumming his fingers on the table.

"~~Look here, what is there to eat?" said Jacob~~.

Cruttendon ~~may be~~ is a very good fellow, he remarked to no one in particular, but he ~~knows nothing about the art of painting~~. ~~makes me~~ is a bit of a fool. ~~A fool, Flanders~~. ~~He doesn't know what he's talking about.~~

X X X X X X X X

"Well, said Jacob, taking the pipe out of his mouth, there may be some sense in what you say. Only you can't deny that its the stupid art. ~~Where's your~~ Cruttendon. ~~Where's your~~ I'll just read you a passage to show what I mean.

"Well I tell you, Flanders, I'd as soon have one of Mallison's ~~Seargeants pictures as anyone's. little pictures as a~~ little pictures. as a Chardin ~~Manet~~, & ~~mind you I think Manet one of the~~ When I say that— great swells. You can buy them for an old song. - ~~But the~~ After all Chardin was a great swell. You can buy 'em for an old song now. We'll go round & have a look. A great swell - oh a very great swell."

And then Cruttendon put his brush in his mouth & began scraping paint.off his palette.

"~~A This is an~~ Its awfully pleasant ~~sort of existence~~ life" said Jacob. "Messing away ~~up here, &~~ up here with these paints. Still Its ~~a~~ the stupid art, ~~though~~ Cruttendon." He wandered off to the bookcase.

"Now my good sir are you going to settle down?" Said Cruttendon.

~~"Thats a fine By Jove thats~~

"Thats a solid piece of work" said Jacob. standing a canvas on a chair.

"~~Thats~~ Oh that? I did that so long ago ever so old" said Cruttendon looking over his shoulder.

"You're a damned good painter in my opinion" said Jacob, after a time.

"Now if you want to see ~~where~~ this is what I'm doing at the present moment in I am at the moment-" said Cruttendon; ~~He placed~~ what of the putting a canvas before Jacob. "There. ~~There~~ Thats it. Thats got nearer it. That's - " he

squirmed his thumb in a circle. round the globe of a lamp. .
You see that-"

of work straddling his legs
"~~Well thats~~ a pretty solid piece" said Jacob. upon it

"~~Thats what sp spoilt the picture to my mind~~"
what I can't see is
~~said Cruttendon~~ - "~~A little~~ "But why ~~don't you~~ painters -"
Miss Patty Carslake came into the room.

Oh Patty - heres a friend - Flanders. An Englishman.
Very rich. Highly connected. Go on Flanders-"
not quite right
"~~You see~~ its the passage there he can't get right"
said Miss Carslake. ~~They~~ All three stood looking
at the picture.

"No" said Cruttendon. "Aint ~~be~~ to be done"
He took it off the chair & stood away
He ~~put~~ it ~~away~~ decidedly with its back to them.

"Have a cigarette, Miss Carslake."

"Thank you, Mr. Cruttendon"

'Sit down ladies & gentlemen." Miss Carslake comes
from your part of the world, Flanders. From Devonshire.
Scarburgh
Oh I thought you said Devonshire. Well well, all
these extremities ~~of~~ are much of a muchness.
Yorkshire: Devonshire. She's a daughter of the
Church, ~~aren't you Patty~~? ~~She's~~ The black sheep of the
family. Her mother writes her such letters. Had
another? Its generally Sundays ~~when~~ they come.
Sort of church bell effect you know. Miss
Carslake has an outbreak on Sundays."

sitting on the

"I say - are you just ~~come out?" said Miss~~ Jenny, ~~swinging~~ table, ~~swinging~~ her legs,

"Have you met all the great men?" said Jenny, ~~sitt~~ "Was Mallinson drunk?" If you go to his studio he'll give you one a of his pictures. I say, Teddy -

"Half a jiff" said Cruttendon. "~~About our expedition~~ - " Whats the season of the year?" he looked out of the window.

"We devote the Sabbath to recreation Flanders.

Come along too?"

~~Are you agreeable~~?"

"Wont he?" said Jinny looking at Jacob. "You - "

"Yes he'll come with us," said Cruttendon.

Jinny ~~bent~~ stood on the stone rim & leant over the
pond, clasped by Cruttendon's arms or she would have fallen in.
~~She threw~~ "There! There!" she cried. ~~Right up to the~~
~~He's come~~ Right up to the top!" Some ~~s~~ sluggish
sloping shouldered fish had floated up from the depths
to nip her crumbs. "You look" she said.
fountain rough & throttled:
And then the dazzling white ~~water~~ shot up into the
air. All the water was puckered with drops -
blue
blew
~~fl~~ away
A ~~yellow~~ air ball ~~went bouncing over the pond.~~
surface.
~~lightly~~ skimmed the pond. How ~~ex all~~ The nurses
& children & old men & young crowded to the
The little girl held out her
~~e~~ edge & waved their sticks! Behind the great
arms
~~glass building~~ for her airball.

Edward Cruttendon, Jenny Carslake, & Jacob Flanders
walked in a row along the yellow gravel path.
got onto the grass; so passed ~~into the~~ under the
at the ~~pagod~~ pagoda
trees, & came out where Marie Antoinette used to
drink tea. In went Jacob & Jinny; but Edward
waited outside. sitting on the handle of his walking stick.
Out they came again.

Well?
"~~Now?~~" said ~~Jacob~~. Cruttendon.
leant
smiling at Jacob~~,"~~ Behind him, as he ~~sat~~ on his
walking stick, ~~& rolled a cigarette, lay a g~~ stood
thin green trees, ~~quite~~ straight, one ~~behind~~ after another,
~~tapering~~
vanishing away. Green dust seemed to dim the air
between them. But a sharp wedge of white sunshine
cut across.

waited;
Jinny ~~stood stil~~ & ~~so did~~ Edward waited;
& they ~~both~~ looked at Jacob. at
Well? absent mindedly
"~~Come along~~" said Jacob / ~~swinging~~ his
pressing
~~stick~~. Smiling & ~~leaning~~ both hands on his stick.
decided; &
"Come along" he ~~led~~ started off; & the others
followed.

160
280
———
0

X X X X X

"But he's quite different" said Jinny, folding her hands over the top of her glass of coffee. "I don't suppose you know what Tedd means when he says ~~a thing~~ he feels like that" she said, ~~gazing~~ looking at Jacob. "But I do. Sometimes I could kill myself."

"~~We~~ . . . Sometimes he ~~doesn't just~~ lies in bed all day long. Just lies there - . . . . ~~He's coming~~ I don't want you right on ~~to~~ the table." ~~A~~

Swollen iridescent

Pigeons were waddling round them.

"I say what a queer lot of people - lot of tramps there are in the world said Edward, looking at the black ~~figures~~ families walking across the paved courtyard. "~~Black~~" ~~he said~~.

that womans hat How ~~did~~ does she come to think of it?

isn't that superb? -that woms hat

Just look at that erection, ~~thats~~ . . . I don't believe I could live like you. Now when one walks down that street opposite the British Museum - whats it called? - ~~that thats there's always someone having a fit~~ - thats what I mean - its ~~all~~ like that. ~~And then a man calling out muffins~~ -. ~~Its something in the climate.~~"

"Everybody feeds them" said Jinny. They're stupid old things."

"Well, I don't know," said Jacob. "There's St Pauls."

"I mean going to an office" said Cruttendon.

" Hang it all" said Jacob.

"But ~~you must remember that you're practically a~~ You don't count" said Jinny; "You're mad, ~~Tedd~~; I mean you just think of painting." I cant help it.

"Yes, ~~I dont think of~~ I know." ~~But I can't help it~~. ~~I cant understand~~ ..." ~~I mean~~ ~~But~~ news you really think about things - the newspapers, ~~you know~~. ~~What's King~~ all ~~George going to do about Ireland?"~~ this What's all this in I say, in will the King give way about the Peers?"

Whats all this in the news paper?

"He'll jolly well have to" said Jacob.

"There!" said Jinny. "He really ~~knows~~"

"I wish I could ~~think about it~~, said Cruttendon. "But you see, I simply cant."

"I think I could" said Jinny. Only its all the people one dislikes who do it. At home, I mean. One gets so sick of it. They talk of nothing else. Even ~~my~~ people like my mother, ~~poor dear~~. ~~You're thought so queer if you dont~~."

What are those Tommies doing?" said Jacob.
"Oh its all kept up ~~you know~~ - rather jolly. I like that band."

The soldiers marched in under the archway. The sun shone upon the yellow brass.

"I expect you're perfectly right" said Jacob. Its all very jolly. Now if I came & lived here - What's my share? Oh very well - have your own way. What ~~shall we do now next?~~"
about these Bosquets?"

He scattered his crumbs; but the pigeons had gone to another table.

Walking up & down by the lozenge shaped bed packed with stiff ~~pink~~ hyacinths Cruttendon in the middle, Jacob on one side, Jinny on the other; turning about by common consent & marching back; ~~turning~~ turning right about & marching the ~~other way,~~ forward, the great argument ~~was de fought out~~ took place

by common... consent

The great argument is always / ~~much~~ the same. ~~are~~ whether Do we exist? Does anything ~~else~~ exist? ~~Red is~~ Then The thing itself - my conception of the thing- then "Well I don't know what I'm talking about. "~~Suddenly they st~~ Here Cruttendon stopped, & both he & Jinny said simultaneously that the colour of pink hyacinths in the shadow was ~~perfectly~~ bright astonishing - Resuming, Cruttendon said that ~~he made~~ it ~~work something like~~ out this.

violet

he had no head for philosophy, but

"~~You begin with Rembrandt~~ . ."

one began with Rembrandt/. Then ~~there were~~ he named several pictures which Jacob had never seen.

"~~Take d~~ The [Oligin?] of the Milky Way in the National Gallery?-" ~~said~~ asked Jacob.

"No, no" said Cruttendon rather irritably.

"Well take what you like," said Jacob urbanely.

And then Cruttendon named Ingres, Monet & Cézanne. rapidly one after another; &

"~~However, However, he said, I find it very~~

~~He~~ became very fluent, & a little excited. ~~His~~ He held his hat between his arm & his side, & his fair pale face, pale hair, & green eyes shone ~~in the the yellow sunlight~~. in the thin sparkling spring air

165
280
———
~~864~~ 1280
330
———
45,800

The queer thing about this argument was that it was all stuck about, ~~forever~~, in ~~all~~ their minds with pink hyacinths ; a lozenge shaped bed; a yew hedge; & the figure of Priapus, ~~which stands~~ or some other tapering White God. The hyacinths smell ~~made Jacob violently, happy~~; or ~~it was~~ the frilled waxy flowers; or (but nobody was to guess this) all these new names; or Cruttendon & Jinny & himself marching up & down up & down; ~~suddenly stopping.~~ made Jacob feel a new kind of person; And as they were all about the same age that was what they all felt. And Cruttendon knew that he was a very great genius. ~~Take it all & all, when they sat in the train they felt . . . . going back to Paris they~~

And Jacob gave Jinny a bunch of violets. And they never met again.

```
  46
   28
 ————
 368
 92
 ————
 1278
```

```
 46
   9
 —
 412
   336
 ————
```

The ~~argument~~ was new as the pink hyacinths ~~& sweet~~ & strange & penetrating as their scent; ~~t~~ lively as the emerald grass; & potent & ~~as~~ sappy as the ~~thrus~~ bird bubbling among ~~the~~ ~~gre~~ sticky white buds;

but nobody was to guess that. ~~Miss~~

They sat down upon a stone seat; they fell silent. France lay before them. Cruttendon sucked grass, thinking still about painting. Jinny - oh dear,
thinking of this. ten years later the hyacinths in Devonshire made her cry, as she hung her little boys shirts over the hissing fender.
Jacob smoked.

~~The tender &~~

Like

Then up they got & went to the station, & Jacob bought violets from a girl & gave them to Jinny.
They never met again.

Tuesday
5th April 1921

The great argument, which is always the same, has been discussed since the very earliest times ~~of all~~, is never settled, & is handed down to the next generation, ~~as the most priceless part of their inheritance~~ a . a priceless part of their inheritance, since the hours spent pacing gravel paths, are the best of all. ~~True, I am am pacing a gravel path; but are these my~~ ~~Are these legs~~? Pacing gravel paths, yes; but soon the legs disappear; & the body; & the mind ~~vaults~~ floats into the blue. What are we? & whence do we come? Those insoluble questions ~~provide~~ spread ~~an soft blue~~ their ~~immense~~ background - ~~a a~~ & against it truth is questioned & reality ~~reality? Whether objects exist; that~~ the apple tree; is scored hyacinths appear momentous; the kingdom of France fades to a green veil. ~~&~~ [The lozenge shaped bed, the yew hedge, the tapering white God, Priapus or another]

The great argument ploughs its way, & people voyage together, doing their best to find foothold, yet valiantly determined not to ~~allow anyone~~ to ~~make~~ land~~ing~~ on a false shore. ~~Such are the dangers of the enterprise that~~ The enterprise is full of danger, maybe of temper. To hear their voices ~~raised~~ as they turned right about under the grin of the God Priapus, one would have fancied a quarrel - but where people possess no bodies ~~how can they quarrel?~~- ~~th~~ only their minds can graze each other in the void. Jinny's check skirt flowed across their legs; Cruttendon held his hat pressed between his arm & his side; His fair pale face, pale hair, ~~& green eyes; I~~ he was dressed in a light tweed - made him the most conspicuous of the three.

"Well, I dont know what I'm talking about" ~~exclaimed~~ he said; ruffling his hand through his hair. & then he & they stopped Jinny both exclaimed simultaneously that the colour of pink hyacinths in the shadow is bright violet -

Jacob had vanquished.

You could see ~~t~~ so much in the way he smiled, rather queerly, & then looked at ~~the~~ France lying beneath him,

for after an argument the landscape must rearrange itself,
& people have been known to feel abashed & discomposed ~~at~~ by
the existence of good arable land, flights of rooks, steam
morning
ploughs, ~~good~~ trains & the rest of it after this ~~excursion into~~
effort to arrive at the truth. However, one may easily put too
fine a point on it. ~~Jacob was inclined for~~ a & the
~~difficulty is not~~ Our flights from solid earth are strictly
tethered. A thousand strings attach us to this & that &
~~forbid~~ the other, & only once in a hundred years does
some poet or thinker cut free. The ordinary person has
an advantage over the extraordinary in being ~~thus~~ all in a
muddle, at the mercy of instincts, responsive to hunger -
thirst ~~&~~ vanity ~~&~~ desire & kindliness, ~~& convention~~ &
~~though~~ so long as he is not smoothed over ~~in an~~
~~effort to~~ ~~by the plough, or~~ the steam roller, & brought into
conformity with the rest. ~~And this has been the~~
~~fate~~ And this has been the fate of ~~w~~ painters rather
probably it is
than of writers; explain it how you will. It was
the existence of patrons, so Cruttendon, said: ~~that had~~
~~ruined many fine fellows~~. For art had been servile
all through the eighteenth century; & was only now
But what wanted was
asserting itself ~~Then~~ they ~~talked about~~ religion, ~~&~~ how
Cruttendon
in the days ~~when it was possible to hold a~~ everything
was impossible without faith, & there was none; or
he
worse than none; & ~~Cruttendon~~ thought that men of
university training ought to see to it - ~~& Jinny~~
Then her
~~all of which~~ ~~&~~ Jinny getting up from ~~the~~ ~~chair~~ chair
(they had settled round a marble table on the terrace)
went up to the kiosk, speared a plate full of
little cakes ~~pastries~~, ~~with which she returned~~. & ~~nutmeats~~

"Which d'you like?" she asked Jacob.

And ~~later~~ later they went back to the station.

There is a wedge ~~shaped strip~~ of pavement between tramlines outside the Gare St Lazare.

Oh hang it all —

~~fellow~~

~~My good~~ ~~Sir~~, What rot you talk - Jacob broke in.

— — — — — — — — —

The

And they stood in the Gare St Lazare.

With one of those queer movements which are so slight, yet so definite, which t ~~sometimes~~ may wound, ~~or & are~~ or pass unnoticed, ~~but~~ but ~~&~~ generally inflict a good deal of discomfort, Jinny & Cruttendon drew together: Jacob stood apart. They had to separate - Something must be said. Nothing was said.

A man wheeled ~~luggage tr~~ a trolley past Jacobs legs so near~~by~~ that he almost grazed them. When Jacob ~~looked up~~ recovered his [?] balance the other two were turning away. though Jinny looked over her shoulder, & Cruttendon waved his hand.

Well, it was over.

~~XXX~~

XIX

~~The carriages~~ The carriages on Italian trains are absurdly small;
& ~~rather~~ gimcrack; upholstered in red plush; ~~&~~
~~they are~~ very high slung; ~~admitting only~~ & rickety
& shaky; & apt to get roasting hot. For April is as hot
as an ~~Italian~~ English June. For example, ~~when~~ a motor
car full of Italian officers, running along the flat ~~g~~
keeping up ~~on an equality~~ with the train raised a cloud of white dust.
There were ~~then~~ the trees laced together with vines -
as Virgil said. ~~No doubt there~~ ~~Never was there~~
~~such a flat country - all ditches & little pollarded trees~~:
Probably the peasants sitting outside the flat white ~~wine~~ houses
were drinking wine. However, here was a station: &
a tremendous leave taking going on, with ladies in
high boots, odd ~~little~~ boys in socks: They broke
in upon ~~his~~ Jacob's carriage, ~~which made him a little~~
~~uncomfortable~~; & he lifted their cheap ~~valises~~ ~~cloth~~
valises ~~bags~~ to the rack; ~~for which~~ ~~but they saw he was a~~
~~foreigner.~~ ~~The w lady & the absurd horn~~ but they
saw he was a foreigner. The station master blew a horn.
And still it was just possible to make out the
line of the mountains - the Alps. The Alps. Padua
Verona. Vicenza. Now to see them for the first time
on an ordinary Monday in April when the Italians
are travelling short distances: when there are
carts going along the roads; men sticking up posters
against buildings; this is very queer. Verona
Vicenza. Padua. Milan.

170
280
———
360
340
———
760

170
280
———
1360
340
———
4760

Sunday April 17th —— Those little stone bridges may be historical. What is the name of the river running beneath them? ~~Up on the Alps the streams had fallen~~ How the ~~waters~~ torrents had plunged as they left the Alps! & ~~once~~ the train had stopped, in a steep meadow on the Italian side, & he had distantly seen flowers & heard a bird singing. Virgils bees had gone about ~~those fields~~; the plains of Lombardy. It was the custom of the ancients to train vines over elms. Then at Milan there were actually sharp winged hawks, a bright brown, cutting figures over the town.

These Italian ~~trains~~ carriages get damnably hot. & the chances are that before ~~it's pulled~~ the engine has pulled to to the top, of the gorge the clanking chain will have broken. Up up up like a train on a scenic railway. Every ~~hill~~ peak covered with sharp trees, & amazing white villages ~~built up on the~~ crowded on ledges. Always a white tower on the very summit, flat frilled roof, & a sheer drop beneath. It is not a country in which one walks after tea. For one thing there is no grass. A whole hill side will be ruled with olive trees. g ~~in straight lines~~. Already in April the earth is ~~cl~~ clotted white between them. And then there are neither st~~y~~iles nor foot paths, nor lanes chequered with the shadows of leaves, nor eighteenth century inns, with bow windows where one ~~d~~ drinks tea. oh no: Italy is all fierceness & bareness.: exposure, dust, steepness, extravagance, precipice & torrent.

Still to be travelling on ones' own, with just so much money to spend is a fine affair. And if his money gave out, as it probably would, he would go on foot. He could live on bread & cheese & wine - ~~z~~ vino del paese - ~~what was~~ for after doing Greece he was going to knock off Rome. The Roman civilization was a very inferior affair, no doubt. But Bonamy talked a lot of rot. The Greeks were a small pastoral people. . . You ought to have been in Athens, he would say to Bonamy when he got back.

Lets to Greece

Mr & Mrs Mol~~inex~~ yneux Williams

We shall meet again

he (S.) V.

~~He would compare the Parthenon with St Peters.~~ Standing in the Parthenon, he would say: or the ruins of the Colisseum ~~are fairly sublime after all. Long~~ suggest some fairly sublime reflections. which he would write out at some length; ~~under the very shadow of the~~ his fingers actually itched for his pen. The whole thing would be put on a substantial basis. It might turn to an essay upon Civilisation - ~~with some~~ A comparison between the ancients & moderns, with some pretty sharp ~~sayings reflections upon sayings~~. hits.

A stout gentleman laboriously hauled himself in, cheap, like the valises, dusty, baggy; & Jacob regretting that he did not come of the Latin race~~s~~ himself, looked out of the window.

It is a strange reflection that by travelling for two days & nights you are in the heart of Italy. Accidental villas among olives / trees appear; ~~the~~ Victorias drive in between pompous ~~g~~ pillars. It is at once momentary & yet so astonishingly intimate. And theres a lonely hill top where no one ever comes, & yet it is seen by me, lately ~~d~~ driving down Piccadilly in an omnibus. And what I should like would be to escape by myself & ~~pick~~ take up a handful of earth - Italian earth; as indeed this is Italian dust on my shoes.

Permetto, or scusi, or something like that said the Italian gentleman lurching across as ~~the train~~ to shut the window darkness closed over the train; one lamp burning feebly. Then he took out a cigar case; & ~~Jacob~~ ~~accepting one~~ he spread his enormously fat fingers ~~to explain to~~ talking loudly, in syllables, gesticulating ~~all the time~~, to explain that he himself had connections with Ireland - horses - English horses - He gave Jacob a cigar; he gave him his card; & with his forefinger pointed emphatically ~~to~~

first to his name which was Guiseppe Bandelli & then to his address, & to the statement that he supplied the nobility & gentry with carriage horses, riding horses - here the train shot out of darkness, & on the left hand side Jacob perceived the waves of the Mediterranean peacefully breaking ~~as though there were no trains in the world~~; on a flat white shore. And, Heaven knows how, Jacob came to understand that Signor Guiseppe was going to buy a horse - was incredibly skilled at buying horses - had an establishment ~~at~~ near Milan where he & his wife would be glad to receive ~~Jacob~~ him; & always intended to go to Greece himself to see the monuments of antiquity - which were beautiful

oh very beautiful. Then he had an ~~English~~ letter from a hotel keeper in Manchester somewhere in his pocket book - ~~in here~~. The train ran ~~into darkness again - out alon~~ smoothly & swiftly along by the sea shore... The gulls of the mediterranean were standing in pools of dissolved mother of pearl; for the sun was sinking. Guiseppe Bandelli read out ~~in out~~ loud ~~in~~ with incredible ~~G guttural~~ sounds how the Manager of the Lucerne hotel ack - now - ledged - He handed the letter to Jacob. with a ~~f~~ wave of the hand. Taking it back, replacing it & ~~pu~~ Guiseppe ~~&~~ flung himself into the corner of the carriage covered his face with a yellow handkerchief, snored.

The train drew through the heart of Italy in the night. Jacob heard them ~~calling~~ crying strange names at stations:

the train stopped, he heard the frogs croaking, & ~~turning b~~ wrinkling back the blind he saw a vast strange marsh all white in the moonlight. The carriage was thick with cigar smoke; ~~& the~~ which floated ~~round the roof of the carriage, where the~~ about round the globe. with the green shade on it, through which the light burnt low. Bandelli had unbuttoned his waistcoat, & taken off his boots. &

How that torrent plunged! ~~Like a chain of water - all the links~~ water falling off a ledge like lead - & the train ran out into steep green meadow with chestnut trees. Stopping for a moment Jacob saw flowers distinctly & heard a bird singing.

& lay snoring; but Jacob could not get off. He thought of Cruttendon & Jinny, & the hyacinths, & ~~how~~ exactly how the railway goes from Paris to Milan; from Milan to Brindisi naming all the big stations one after another but ~~h worried to remember~~ he could not remember one of them. ~~And~~ And Then ~~the~~ he ~~calculated calcu~~ calculated money. He put one arm above his head, & held on to the rack with his fingers. tips and his mouth full open, & his mind jolted out words in ~~time~~ tune with the train - And all this business of going to Greece seemed to him an intolerable ~~wearne~~ weariness - ~~stan~~ sitting in hotels by oneself & looking at monuments - oh dear, he'd ~~was~~ have done better to go to the Lakes with Bonamy. And if Clara Durrant met him on a quay side wearing a hat with a blue feather it would be ... & so he actually slept,

what had he been thinking of oh he had actually been asleep; & he went off,

lying absolutely flat on his back, along the seat, with ~~such~~ a look upon his face as if life were frightfully dingy, sordid, yes, exasperating. And now & again he sighed in his sleep. And then he slept more & more deeply; & looked as if the thing was quite absorbing. Until ~~sudde~~ bits of the darkness began breaking up in front of him: ~~&~~ Oh! he protested; & ~~slept~~ a turned away: but actually Bandelli was reaching ~~down a bag~~ across the carriage.

most annoying

"Good morning"

Bandelli in his dicky, unshaven, carrying a sponge bag, was going off to wash.

So Jacob sat up: pulled up the blind; saw a lean Italian sportsman walking down a road with two dogs in the early morning light. & the whole idea of the Parthenon came upon him in a clap.

By Jove he said, we must be —? & he stuck his head out of the window.

X X X X X X X X

Nothing can be more exasperating than to feel that there are twentyfive people of your acquaintance who would ~~feel~~ say straight off ~~the~~ something very much to the point about actually being in Greece; ~~while you can feel nothing~~. about that old man waddling by in a kilt: about ~~a woman~~ the hag driving turkeys; ~~about the thing itself~~; ——— & the wine skins & the
while you ~~can~~ only ~~say~~ ~~feel uncomfortable; & remark~~ yawn & stretch & ~~re~~mark & what is the thing itself? Only a bad imitation of Paris, ~~& of~~ like most continental towns; Jacob. thought lounging through The streets of Patras that first morning. ~~That~~ So far Greece was a great fraud; unless he lacked the sort of sense that ~~other people had~~. ~~made other people T feel, straight off~~, ~~something astonishing. Wonderful~~. ~~how~~——— 0ther people had.

It is ~~perfectly true that Patras~~ This notion of

Greece

While ~~you feel~~ there is ~~t~~ a stopper on all endless [?] sensations. For after ~~bre~~ washing Jacob had followed the train lines a mile or two out, & followed them a mile or two back; thus meeting several droves of turkeys, of several strings donkeys, ~~read~~ing advertisements/ all along the road of Maggis soups & corsets; ~~but in the whole course of his walk he had not felt once This is a thing I shall remember all my life~~.
he had passed pseudo Parisian houses; he had got lost in

back streets; the children had asked him for pennys: ~~cheese smell~~ the
place smelt of ~~bad ch~~ rank cheese; & he had been glad to find
his
himself back at ~~the~~ hotel. And there was an old copy of the
on among the coffee cups
Daily Mail lying about; which he read. But what could he
do after dinner?
No doubt ~~she~~ we should be ~~m~~ much worse off than we are
our ~~capacity~~ for
without ~~this~~ astonishing ~~gift~~ ~~of~~ illusion. At the age of
gift
twelve or so having given up dolls, & broken our steam
engines, ~~Italy~~ France, but much more probably Italy, &
India almost for a certainty, ~~engages the superfluous~~
~~imaginative ardour~~. draws the superfluous imagination.
One's Aunts have been to Rome. And every one has
an Uncle, ~~a failure~~, who was last heard of in Rangoon -
~~But the~~ - poor man! He will never come back any
more. - But it is the governesses who start the
Greek myth. Look at that for a head - nose, you see, as straight
as a dart, curls, eye brows - everything appropriate to
manly beauty; while, ~~if you desire muscle~~, ~~that is~~
~~rendered~~ by his legs & arms ~~are~~ have curves on them
of the muscles
which indicate perfect development. And the Greeks
could paint fruit so that the birds pecked at it.

gloom thinks of party where he met Clara

And ~~then~~ first you read Xenophon; & then you read
Euripides. One day - ~~by~~ that was an occasion, by God! —
What people have said appears to be true; ~~strength~~ ' the Greek
Spirit'; the Greek this, that, & the other. ~~Even so~~,
thought it is unlikely, ~~that~~ by the way, that any
Greek ~~could have~~ came near Shakespeare. The
point is however that ~~ever~~ one has been brought up
with an illusion about it all.

Jacob, no doubt, thought something in this fashion; the Daily Mail crumpled ~~up~~ in his hand; his legs extended; the very picture of boredom.—

– But its the way we're brought up, he went on.
And it all seemed to him very distasteful; ~~s~~ Something ought to be done about it. [A party where people go dressed up to meet each other & to eat - ~~repulsive~~ &. Women in evening dress;- ~~yes~~, he continued,] & from being moderately depressed he became for no reason whatever like a man about to be executed. ~~And the sting of it all was that he~~
Clara Durrant leaving him ~~on the stairs~~ at a party to go & talk to ~~an man~~ American called Pilcher - And he'd come all this way to Greece & left her. And they wore evening dresses; & they talked nonsense.

In spite of its ramshackle condition, modern Greece is highly advanced in the ~~matter of~~ tramway system; so that while Jacob sat in the hotel sitting room, ~~thinking about Clara Durrant~~, the ~~bells we~~ trams were clank~~ing~~ed, chim~~ing~~ed - ~~ringing bells~~ rang, rang, rang imperiously to get the donkeys ~~or the turkeys or the old women out~~ of the way - beneath the window.

~~Yet w~~ whole civilization was being t ~~despatched~~ condemned ~~in this young man's brain~~.

The waiter~~s~~ were quite indifferent to that, too. ~~As a matter of fact there was only one waiter, as there was only one guest; & the waitress had~~ Aristotle, for that was his name, was almost carnivorously / interested in the English body, now the indifferent~~;~~ occupying the only chair — ~~No It is It is the only guest.~~

He went to the window & stood with his hands in his pockets
There he saw for the first time three Greeks in kilts.
He saw the masts of ships. ~~The idle, or~~ Idle or busy people of the
lower orders were strolling or stepping out briskly
~~confirmed~~ not the cause of his
~~But~~ Their lack of concern for him was ~~part cause~~ of his gloom;
but
~~Yet their intentness~~ on their own affairs ~~as~~ only ~~troubled~~
~~him to as it proved seemed to him to prove~~ the how ~~lonely~~
~~profound loneliness of the soul. mankind~~: everyone ~~is~~ he
thought, is completely selfish, & alone.

but some more profound conviction; not that he happened to be lonely, but that all people are. lonely.

Yet, ~~he thought to himself~~, next day, as the train
very slowly rounded a hill on the way to Olympia,
the old Greek ~~women are~~ peasant women ~~are~~
were out among the vines. ~~The~~
And ~~if it we may suppose~~ though Jacob ~~had unearthed a~~
remained convinced, he had ~~failed not. reckoned with~~
never suspected how ~~astonishin~~ tremendously pleasant it
is to be alone: out of England; ~~in Greece~~. There are very
sharp bare hills all the way to Olympia; &
between them ~~tri~~ blue sea in triangular spaces.
We~~ll now, where's the~~ Well now to go walking by oneself
all day - to get onto that track & follow it up between
the bushes - no theyre little trees - & ~~over~~ to the top
of that ~~hil~~ mountain - from which one would see
Marathon & Salamis -

Yes, said Jacob, aloud, (for his carriage
was empty. "Lets just look at the map."
~~And~~ For, blame it or praise it, ~~explain it or leave~~
~~it alone the unknown~~, every one ~~is knew~~ knows
about this wild horse in us: this impatience with
society; this ~~galloping~~, intemperate, ~~un~~
~~unkempt~~, - as for men, women - let them go hang.
f drive for galloping, ~~fe~~
Sitting down on the sand & feeling ~~utterly cut off~~,
~~as if the druids~~ as if the earth span; as if ~~human~~
humanity was over; as for

X X X X X X X X X

for the
simple &
toilworn
in particular

"I am full of love for everyone. ~~The simple & enduring are those~~
~~The world is full~~ ~~The peas~~ants stumble along beneath their
poor most of all -
burdens. ~~The~~ ~~particularly~~ for the ~~toilworn & for~~ - for
the peasants coming back in the evening with their
&
burdens. And everything is soft - vague - very sad -
~~profoundly sad.~~ ~~Everything has a kind of meaning for me.~~
a
~~now.~~ Everything has meaning" thought Sabine Wentworth

raising her
her head &
looking very
beautiful tragic
strange, & high
minded

Williams; "~~It go The sound goes on~~; ~~after it has ceased~~."
~~She stood~~ "~~It seems to me that soun~~ the world is full of
sounds ~~tonight~~" ~~she~~ One must love everything"

She held in her hand a little book convenient for
travelling - stories by Tchekhov. ~~But it was~~ ~~too dark to see~~
~~She stood in the window of the hotel at Olympia~~. as she stood,
veiled, in the window of the hotel, ~~looking at the~~ ~~which looks onto~~
at
~~out onto the hill at~~ Olympia. ~~And her own beauty~~ -
~~sorrow & infinite sympathy mounted to her eyes~~
~~she knew that she was beautiful~~;
The How beautiful it was! - & her beauty was its beauty:
~~Greece itself was wa~~ ~~The~~ ~~The statues~~ The tragedy of

the
t inevitable
compromise.

Greece was the tragedy of all high souls; ~~Som~~ She seemed to
have grasped something ~~very~~ of ~~universal meaning.~~ She
~~felt that she had life, which was so difficult,~~ -
very profound. She would write it down. And going to the
table where her husband sat reading, she t leant her
chin in her hands & thought of the peasants, of suffering, of
her own beauty, & of the inevitable compromise -
~~so that~~ Not ~~that~~ did Evan Williams say anything
banal, brutal, or foolish when he ~~looked up from~~
shut his book; put it away, to make room for
plates of soup
the dishes which were being brought in. ~~He~~
drooping
~~said nothing, He~~ Only his ~~deep~~ bloodhound eyes,
~~his cheek~~ sallow cheek
& his heavy moustache, ~~& his s~~ expressed his melancholy
tolerance, his conviction that though forced to live with
c-
circumspection & deliberation, he ~~w~~ould never
that he wanted
possibly achieve anything worth having. His
of those objects which are alone
worth pursuing

consideration was flawless; his silence unbroken.

"~~And life sometimes~~ Everything tonight means so much" said Sabine: But with the sound of her own voice the spell was broken. Her ~~mood~~ sorrow disappeared. She forgot the peasants. Only there remained ~~this~~ the sense of her own beauty, & in front, luckily, there was a looking glass.

'~~I am~~ ~~very beautiful' she thought And~~ it was true

She shifted her hat very slightly. ~~Her husband saw her looking in the glass~~. ~~And it was true~~. Her husband saw her looking in the glass; & ~~it accepted the fact~~

~~Her beauty was, perhaps, a barrier between them.~~ ~~that a beautiful woman~~ agreed that beauty is a ~~possession.~~ charge - an inheritance ~~something one e must cherish~~. one cannot ignore it. So he drank his soup, & kept his eyes fixed upon the window.

"Quails, said Mrs Wentworth Williams, & then Goat, & then ...

'Caramel Custard' presumably, ~~said~~ her husband. said in his low tone. ~~perhaps for a~~ ~~her~~ who ~~already~~ had his toothpick ready

And she put her spoon down in her soup ~~plate~~ & it was taken away half finished.

Never did she do anything without ~~dis~~ dignity. ~~The beauty of the face was in the nose, which~~ ~~The beautiful mask preserved her~~; ~~And yet~~ ~~Beauty lay upon her like a mask; straight; noble; &~~ yet ~~expressionless~~. for hers ~~It would have been difficult to improve that her~~ was the that English type, which is so Greek, save that ~~& yet~~ villagers have touched their hats to it, ~~the~~ the ~~v~~ vicarage reveres it; & ~~though the park is~~ The park has its walls, sure enough. its lean muscle comes from the hunting field. & ~~the~~ ~~As for Evan Williams~~ ~~Her~~ But her eyes moved perpetually. & Sandra's eye wandered, moved, ~~wanted something~~, watched, ~~& always~~ ~~as if she~~ wanted something - unable like Evan to accept or was she for ever trying to scramble up escape them, as her eyes wandered round the dining room at Olympia,

~~& she tried a little peevishly to remember what she~~ had
seeking the window,
~~thought ten minutes ago about sadness & love.~~

a little
fretfully
& it was
standing there
that

embraced
saw the window, & Tchekhov's stories, ~~& which~~ very ~~indeed her that~~
she had ~~found~~ discovered something about sadness & love.

But it was Evan who sighed. tranquilly, deeply, like
~~some monster in the sea at~~ night; ~~Oh yes,~~
~~Not~~ Not in despair, not in rebellion. Only he was a man
of gigantic ambition; had the political history of England at
his finger ends; & living much in company with Pitt,
Chatham, Burke & Charles James Fox could not
himself, & his age
help comparing ~~his age with theirs~~: ~~Here~~ He was now
picking his teeth in an Inn at Olympia. He had
finished. But Sandra's eye wandered.

dangerous
~~I think~~" those pink melons are ~~poisonous~~"
he said. "

And as he spoke the door opened & Jacob came in.
Beautiful but dangerous
~~Anything so beautiful~~ certainly is" said
Sandra; ~~However she had seen Jacob~~ before she
~~collected herself with that little shiver which~~

~~But~~ clearly ~~she was~~ talking to her husband in
the presence of a third person. ('An English boy on a tour')
she thought to herself
And Evan knew all that too.

Yes, he knew all that.- ~~how she would talk to that young man and~~ -
~~and~~ - ~~Indeed he envied her~~ - he admired her. Very pleasant
~~to have such enthusiasm,~~ he thought. to ~~be able still~~ to
have affairs - ~~like Sandra~~. But for himself, what with his
height, his bulk, his ~~disa~~ inability to impose his own
personality upon ~~others,~~ ~~he could not imitate her~~ ;
~~throw himself impetuously into~~ it was useless. He
straight
threw away his cigar; & went ~~straight~~ up to Jacob, & asked
~~through~~
him whether he had come straight out from England

"How very English!" said Sandra when the waiter told her
next morning that the young gentleman had left at five to
climb Mount Olympus.
of the mountain
~~And~~ stretched on the very top, quite alone, Jacob was
enjoying himself immensely. Probably he had never
been so happy in the whole of his life.
That this ~~state of mind was utterly independent of~~ ~~th~~
whatsoever
all ~~of other human beings,~~ ~~save perhaps the Greek boy~~ is
~~likely, since on coming~~
But at dinner that night just Mr Williams asked
him whether he had enjoyed himself; & then Mrs.
Williams asked him (as they strolled on the terrace
that man's
smoking, - & how could he refuse ~~that mans~~ cigar?)
whether ~~the she~~ t he had seen the Theatre by moonlight,
read Greek. & whether he knew Everard Sherborne, whether he
(by this time read ~~Greek~~, ~~loved~~ ~~liked~~ & whether he would ~~go~~
Evan had gone in)
~~next morning with them next morning to see the~~
~~Hermes of Praxiteles~~. ~~join~~ them - which of course he had to do.
& whether if he had to sacrifice one ~~civilisation,~~ it
would be the Greek literature or the Russian?
"And now, wrote Jacob in his letter to Bonamy,
her
I shall have to read ~~the~~ cursed book." ~~Tchekhov~~
~~lay on the bed table.~~ her Tchekhov, he meant;
but he meant also that ~~there was this bloody~~
~~Englishwoman~~. For she had lent it him.

2,80,00

~~Oh well~~, ~~And after all~~, Though ~~it is likely to~~
the opinion is unpopular, it seems likely enough
that bare places, the outcasts of civilisation,
fields too thick with stone to be ploughed,
tossing sea-meadows about halfway between
~~Australi~~ England & Australia ~~preserve~~
~~something~~ is suits us better than cities.

~~In short~~ There is something absolute in us which despises
qualification. [Two cats in a garden go straight to the point
without requiring introduction.] [The unhappy tigers, violent
peasants, men who curse & ~~bleed~~ groan all night tugging
at the ropes, ~~&~~ these have never compromised. Bare
places are the best. ~~As But~~ At any rate, ~~in~~ in solitude
on a steep ~~road~~ hill one is fairly matched] ~~Yet~~
~~this must be teased & twisted~~ It is this which is teased &
twisted in society. ~~Women are for ever thinking of~~
~~feelings~~. People come into a room. "So delighted,
says somebody "to meet you"- which is untrue.
And then "I enjoy the spring more than the autumn.
One does I think, as one grows older"- ~~which is~~
~~asking for a compliment~~. & ~~so it begins the perpetual~~
grading of ~~fine~~ feelings~~, with motives at the back of~~ them
unexpressed. ~~& so she grades her feelings, until~~
~~Now none of that matters~~. - ~~as if it mattered~~. ~~And~~ For
~~that is the sort of thing that~~ women are always talking
about ~~as~~ what one feels as one grows older.

True, the Greek peasants ~~do~~ live like the beasts of the
field - in mud huts, ~~with a partition between them,~~
~~& goats & turkeys wandering in & out~~. with
the cattle coming in & out:

The real question is whether Oxford or Cambridge has won
the boat race. ~~Yes, & Whether these newfangled~~
~~ideas about~~
~~As he reflected upon these questions~~, & That women are
As he walked up the southern slope of Mount Olympus
Jacob reflected ~~upon these questions~~. that ~~this was~~
~~the f~~ he would come to Greece, alone, every year for a
holiday as a way of keeping

Slapping pockets
Taking out his pipe, Jacob sat himself down in the quarry where they
cut the stone for the ~~theart~~ theatre. ~~He had to~~ for ~~walking up~~
-Greek ~~those little steep little paths, with~~ it is hot work walking up
at
hill; midday The wild cyclamen was out; & he had seen the
between the clump
little tortoises hobbling along: The smell was sweet; & the
was
sun striking on the splintered marble ~~very~~ dazzling.to the eyes.
And ~~then~~ content came over him; & ~~then~~ melancholy; & ~~then~~
boredom. But it would be a great mistake to
suppose that ~~he~~ ~~knew which~~ bothered his head much
c
about ~~that~~. And yet it was a great occasion. So vividly did
he feel himself sitting there among the splinters of
marble in the blinding light, alone.

~~Ranging the world in quest of adventure before~~
~~breakfast~~

So uncompromising was he, sitting there among the splinters
of marble in the blinding light, alone.

Ranging the world in quest of adventure before breakfast
all in white - not so very tall - but uncommonly
upright, held together, & dashing - her plumed hat
had escaped crushing , & the yellow feather was like the
crest on ~~some~~ a bird, ~~Sandr~~ Sandra saw Jacobs head
~~on~~ exactly on a level with the head of the Hermes of
Praxiteles. Before she could say a single ~~one of the~~
word, he had gone & left her. ~~alone with~~

And then she wrote in her diary the strangest stuff about
growing old, while downstairs her husband & Jacob
discussed the political situation in England, the
post having come.

She found them sitting amicably on the
terrace, when she returned, & as she broke open her
letters, she hesitated, giving a look up at Jacob -

~~& another at her husband~~.
who was in the middle of saying something; but he was very polite to her: a little awkward, but so distinguished looking.

Still, a lady of fashion travels with more than one dress, & if white suits the morning hour, perhaps ~~tawny~~ sandy yellow with ~~dark~~ purple spots on it, ~~suits the evening;~~ a black hat, & a volume ~~of Plato travels suits~~ Balzac the ~~evening~~. ~~dusk dusk after dinner~~. suit the evening. ~~At any rate~~, Thus she was arranged on the terrace when Jacob came in; ~~a~~ Very beautiful she looked; & strange into the bargain; ~~soft~~, ~~romantic~~, & yet when her ringed hands ~~lay clasped~~ were folded, &, listening to her husbands voice, she ~~scanned the hill~~, mused, ~~reflected~~, she seemed to allied herself with him; ~~she seemed loving & seductive a mistress of beautiful rooms. For if women wash their hands in scent it is impossible not to adore them.~~
~~They seemed a happy~~; ~~reflected, & at the same~~ time seemed followed the peasants ~~crossing the p valley~~ coming down with brushwood, ~~on their backs~~, & seemed to notice the shade & colours changing on the hill, & seemed to ~~speculate~~ think now of her book now of adventure alone, discriminate between one thing & another truth & false hood Jacob ~~did~~ wished that he had changed; & observed crossed his legs suddenly observing the extreme shabbiness of his trousers that his boots were ~~white with dust~~ caked with ~~white~~ dust.
~~In short~~ He was awkward, but very distinguished looking.
And Evan Williams lying back in his chair, envied them. ~~He despised himself~~. ~~Tru True, his~~ & thought that the best thing he could do would be to publish his ~~monograph~~ observations upon the age of Chatham in one volume octavo. ~~He was opposed to long books~~. ~~But this~~ the hot, queasy, tumid feeling ~~which followed~~ was ~~was jealousy. Oh Why can't one~~ was, oh ~~damn it~~ confound it, jealousy ~~again. He was~~ Oh, but confound it this tumid this which would stifle the hot queasy tumid feeling now rising ~~him~~ in him. jealousy - ~~confound it~~. jealousy ~~again~~. jealousy.

"Come with us tomorrow" he said, with

more than his usual energy, stopping ~~by Jacobs~~ his ~~lumbering~~ march.

~~And Ja~~ He was immensely relieved by Jacob's reply.; ~~No,~~ or rather by the solid, direct, composed manner ~~of~~ in which he accepted.

"Here is a ~~cha~~ young man, thought Evan Williams "who might do well in politics"

~~"These journeys, Jacob wrote to Bonamy that night~~, ~~will be neces~~sary

"I intend to come to Greece every year, so long as I live" Jacob wrote to Bonamy "~~It's the only way to save one's soul~~." It is the only ~~way to~~ chance of protect ing oneself from civilisation." That is to say he was clinging ~~to his~~ soul, though the woman had her hook in it.

Nothing could be simpler than what Sandra said as they
came down from the ~~Acr~~ mountain. She had been left
was
motherless at the age of four; & the Park ~~is~~ vast -

"One never seemed to get out of it" she laughed.
&
Of course there was the library. ~~Of course~~, there were visitors.
& then we
~~Of course~~, one heard stories about ~~the outside world~~. things outside.
~~Now a perfect~~ Jacob thought that if he had been there
he would have saved her life; for it was evident ~~from what she~~
~~said~~ that she had been exposed to ~~perils:~~ dangers: had been
lonely; &, he thought to himself, "people wouldn't understand a
woman talking ~~like that"~~ as she talks." ~~Considering~~
his
~~that she was now thirty five, ten years older elder, she~~
~~had certainly kept~~

~~Though the hill above Corinth is rough, she~~

She ~~walked~~ made little of the roughness of the hill. &, he saw,
he saw
she wore breeches under her ~~short~~ skirts. ~~Jacob felt~~
~~One owes a good deal to the aristocracy after all he thought~~

~~Very terrible~~, he thought. ~~And then,~~

"Women like Fanny Elmer don't" he thought. "Whats her name
Carslake didn't-"

She ~~wasn't an~~ a clever woman; or ~~& she might be~~
~~over thirty perhaps, but~~ ~~Bonamy~~ wouldn't see much in her.

~~He became attentive & g gallant~~, &

He was surprised by his own knowledge of the rules of
behaviour. ~~&~~ that is to say how ~~one can say~~ much more
because open:
than one would have supposed - how ~~much more~~ frank one can be.
Nor had he ~~suspected all of this~~ known himself. before.
ed
Evan join~~ing~~ them at the flat, said something of no
importance, & walked ahead by himself; ~~at which~~
~~Sandra smiled.—— For was~~
~~having seen it all -~~ oh dear yes. ~~And~~ Its not nice to
see a young man making a fool of himself. And he

can be said with a woman

was very sulky in ~~his~~ the carriage on the way back. Jacob suspected that he was not good enough for his wife.

Yet when bedtime came, Jacob had some difficulty in writing to Bonamy; He scrawled a picture postcard to Fanny. ~~He~~ Florinda ~~existed in an entirely~~ scarcely existed. No. The difficulty was about Bonamy. Bonamy didn't like women. One must say something appropriate about Salamis, which one sees. from the

~~The best thing to do~~ "I shall go to Athens all the same", Jacob decided, ~~is to go str. as I intended~~"

The ~~Wentworth~~ Williams' had done Athens already.

She knew very little about Marathon.

Evan joined them on the road, ~~on~~ looking very large, hot, ~~persp~~ perspiring & sulky; & as they drove along up hill & down hill - for Greece is ~~like a land~~ in a state of effervescence,- yet astonishingly clean cut - he scowled in his corner. with his paw upon his tweed ~~&~~ knickerbockers; grasping something; while Sandra rode the dingy fly ~~like~~ upright a Victory prepared to fling into the air;

~~When~~ "Heartless" thought Evan "Stupid" he thought. ~~Yet her vitality - !~~ Still - She had s her claws in his him side.

When bedtime came, Jacob had some difficulty in writing to Bonamy. ~~He scrawled a picture postcard to Fanny; scribbled a page to his mother.~~ ~~No, the difficulty was about Bonamy~~.

~~But~~ "Now how was he to write to Bonamy?. Ja~~cob~~ wondered.

The difficulty was to write to Bonamy, Jacob found. though he had seen Marathon & Salamis, ~~that day; & was~~ & ~~had intended~~ to ought to have had all manner of fine feelings. &

"I shall go to Athens" he decided. The

Williams' had been there already.

& ~~somehow~~ ~~the~~ upper gardeners & the undergardeners respectfully retire ~~ack~~ ~~retire~~ as she comes ~~down~~ along the broad terrace on Sunday morning with the Prime Minister, - ~~which, perhaps,~~ ~~She was~~ to pick a rose - which, perhaps she ~~tried to~~ ~~st~~ was trying to forget, as her eye wandered round the dining room of the Inn at Olympia, seeking the window where, her book lay, where a few minutes ago she had discovered something - something very profound, about love & sadness & the peasants.

But being the most ambitious of men, he had accomplished nothing ;

a
~~tree~~less land.

186 a ~~bare land where the fields~~ ~~are thin sown, fire~~
~~fiery~~, & the ~~earth is scorched~~ up ~~up, yet carved,~~ & ~~shaped,~~
& where you see the earth between the green blades, &
~~the~~ each hill ~~seems~~ cut & shaped ~~separately shaped~~, & the sea is
~~blue with a~~ & outlined against ~~soft & deep~~ sparkling ~~&~~
deep blue water, ~~islands~~ ~~floating far out like Clouds~~ -
white as sand floating ~~out~~ on the horizon -
as they drove he scowled in his corner, with his
paw upon his tweed knicker bockers, ~~as if~~
~~grasping something~~: tightly closed so that the skin
was stretched & the the little hairs rose upright.

islands
occasional groves of plane trees ~~grouped~~ standing in valleys and hills the hills. . ~~mountains~~ spotted with little olive trees -

May X X X X X X X
6th

Athens, about which so much has been written, & so much felt
should be impossible new
that ~~it is very~~ difficult to feel anything / for oneself, Athens
whose very dust has been passed through a sieve, whose
graves have been scoured, ~~s~~ & temples scraped, &
stones numbered, is nevertheless still quite capable of
impressing a young man as the ~~d~~ oddest combination,
the most incongruous assortment, ~~the~~ of gimcrack &
immortality, of cracker paste & flawless emerald;
~~for~~ ~~as one~~ no form can he find for his sensations;
one blazing afternoon
as he ~~sits~~ skips, out of the way of the royal landau,
~~which~~ which ~~comes~~ looking ~~so~~ indescribably ~~dow~~
ramshackle ~~as~~ ~~roll~~ rattles down the Parisian
saluted
cheaply dressed boulevard, ~~cheaply dressed~~ citizens ~~saluting it,~~
in bowlers & ~~a man in a thick white kilt & bandaged legs~~
&costumes, ~~of either~~ sex, ~~who~~ ~~might have pass muster in~~
though a man in a thick white kilt & bandaged legs
very nearly drives his herd of goats ~~into the royal~~
&
~~into the royal~~ into the royal horses: all the time
the Acropolis surges ~~over the~~ up in the air, ~~like a~~
~~wave~~. raises itself above the town, ~~like a wave~~.
large
like ~~a~~ the crest of ~~the~~ a wave: with the yellow
~~pillar~~ columns of the Parthenon ~~planted~~ firmly planted
upon it.

The yellow columns of the Parthenon ~~exhibit the most~~
~~absolute indifference to all word spinning whatsoever.~~
~~are to be seen at all hours of the day~~. are firmly
planted; to be seen at all hours of the day,
though at sunset, when a gun is fired, a man in a
~~fold up~~
coat ~~ca~~ coat appears, & the women ~~who have~~
who are
~~brought their~~ knitting, & the children ~~who are~~
~~running races, & scrambling about among the~~ are
have been playing hide & seek, ~~go~~ troop off down the
hill.. There they are again - the pillars, the

pediment, & the Temple of Nike, directly you unlatch your
shutter in the morning; &, leaning out, hear the clatter &
clamour & the whip cracking; there they are: standing up
~~there~~, r right, ~~high above the town~~.

The extreme definiteness with which they stand, now
a brilliant white, again yellow, & in some lights red,
concentration the spiritual
imposes ideas of durability, of the survival of some / energy,
seems
elsewhere ~~of the sort; all~~ ~~all the more that a~~ ~~picture of very great~~
dissipated ~~beauty~~ - ~~resisting decay~~ landscape
~~which, elsewhere sprinkled about, is here concentrated.~~ But this
durability ~~has an~~ exists quite independently of our
admiration. Although the beauty ~~is~~ is sufficiently
perhaps, humane to weaken us ~~with~~ - that is to say to stir us
comparisons that are personal - memories,
& ~~some~~ queer ~~personally~~, ~~as~~ with a feeling of ~~gratitude~~, something
combined with
some queer like gratitude: something quite sentimental;
feeling of ~~ind~~ separately
gratitude- the Parthenon exists ~~apart~~ from all that; & ~~is~~ if you
~~even~~ ~~very difficult to look at;~~ ~~in the~~ consider how it has
stood
~~stands~~ out all night, for centuries, & will be there still,
for centuries, one begins to connect the ~~fierce~~
~~white light~~ blaze (at midday the glare is dazzling)
~~no~~
with an idea ~~which has perhaps little~~ that
it is
perhaps ~~of~~ all beauty ~~is the only thing that survives~~.
alone that is immortal.

Added to this, compared with the blistered stucco
[wrinkled?]
~~& the hot patched houses~~, & the cheap clothes & the mobile
yet insignificant ~~but~~ faces, the place is really astonishing in its
composure; ~~its calm - its~~ which is so vigorous too,
that far from ~~being~~ decayed or aged the Parthenon
appears on the contrary likely to outlast the entire world.
of country
~~Yet~~ The oblong strip ~~of~~ which ~~app~~ fills in the
space
~~pillars~~ ~~view~~ ~~from~~ between the columns will last ~~too~~.
with it. And one must concede a blue sky: & a bee or
two; or strayed from Mount Hymettus.

280
200

56,000

"And the Greeks, like sensible men, never bothered to finish the backs of their statues" said Jacob, shading his eyes, & observing that the side of the figure which is turned away is ~~unfinished~~.left in the / rough.

He noted that slight irregularity in the line of the steps which the artistic sense of the Greeks preferred to mathematical accuracy.

He stood ~~where the~~ on the exact spot where the great statue of Athena used to stand; & identified the more famous landmarks ~~beneath.~~ of the scene beneath.

In short he was accurate, diligent, & morose. Moreover he was pestered by guides. ~~& yet,~~ But on Wednesday (~~he had arrived on Monday night) all this was changed~~.

He ~~sent~~ wrote a wire to Bonamy; telling him to come at once. And then he crumpled it in his hand & threw it into the gutter. ~~No: its no good~~ "For one thing he wouldn't come: & then, I daresay this sort of thing wears off."-

~~For it had For he had felt all the morning like~~

"This sort of thing" being that uneasy sense, that feeling ~~almost~~ of selfishness - one wishes almost that the thing would stop - it is getting more & more terrific - wonderful - ~~but I cant hold it all~~ - if it goes on much longer I ~~cant~~ shant be able to hold it - ~~No one has ever~~ but if ~~I could~~ some one else were seeing it at the same time,- ~~it would be~~ oh, I say,- damn it all - I say!" The ~~scene when~~ sight of Hymettus, Pentelicus, Lycabettus & ~~the rest~~ on one side, & the sea on the other, ~~in [?]~~ as one stands in the Parthenon at sunset seems to need a regiment of people to ~~be hold it. And they must be people of the finest~~ sensibility. Gush ~~in such a situation would be~~ intolerable. Know what it means, too. And even so - ~~well~~, there are all the [?] is thus oppressive. ~~And then Plato & Socrates & Sophocles.~~

Bonamy ~~and~~ is stuffed in a room in Gower Street-

Happily, Jacob had little sense of ~~the~~ personal association; & only in a confused way felt that he ought to be feeling how ~~her~~ it was here that Socrates ~~sat;~~ lounged.
On the other hand his sense of architecture was very strong. -
And then the hook gave a great tug in ~~at~~ his side as he lay in bed on Wednesday night, & he turned over
with a ~~huge~~ violently
~~muttering Oh curse it curse it~~" knowing ~~thinking~~ that he was in love with Sandra Wentworth Williams.

Next day he climbed Pentelicus.
The day after he went up to the Acropolis, ~~again~~, again
The hour was early, the place almost deserted, ~~& the for there were thunder clouds in the sky; against which the &~~ ~~though~~ & possibly there was thunder in the air. ~~For when there is thunder in the air,~~ ~~The marble~~ at any rate
The sun struck full upon the Acropolis.

Jacob's intention was to sit down & read; & finding a drum of marble conveniently placed, from which ~~a view of~~
Marathon
~~Salamis~~ ~~can~~ could be seen ~~obtained~~, ~~yet~~ & yet it was in the shade,
while
~~though~~ the Erechtheum blazed white in front of him, there he sat. [~~By all~~ rights, his seat should soon have ~~become untenable~~, his page unreadable; ~~for~~ yet, ~~yet Having read half a page, he~~ And after reading ~~the~~ a page he put his thumb in the book. For occasionally ~~print is so magical;~~ expands itself so in the brain; that it becomes physically impossible to admit more words un till they first ~~they~~ have marched out.
Jacob ~~had in the past few months acquired a very fair~~ Endowed with an excellent brain, which ripened slowly; ~~with the~~ indolence as the ~~of the~~ able; are; ~~by no means brilliant, yet~~ forcible rather than brilliant; in such words Jacob might be described.]

Oh to rule countries the way they should be ruled!
~~To With modern knowledge, some method should be devised:~~
~~Young men like himself~~ & ~~Bonamy~~ . . And he read again.
No doubt his position ~~at the moment~~ somehow increased his sense
omnipotence; there on the drum of marble Or it may have been that ~~in~~ a slow
capacious brain has these ~~f~~ moments of flowering.
Or he had been becoming, ~~unknown to himself,~~ more -
more apt to make up his mind about this, that, & the
other.
And then, looking up, & realising his position ~~his eye was caught by the general~~
~~look of the~~ place, & his meditations were given an
extraordinary pungency. ~~He had little sense of Plato~~ &
~~Sophocles~~ Socrates ~~in the flesh perhaps~~, ~~but~~ Greece, being over,
The parthenon a ruin, yet there he was;
~~He looked at Marathon~~ (Ladies with white &
green umbrellas passed through the courtyard. -
French ladies on their way to join ther husbands in
Constantinople~~;~~)
Jacob read on again. And, still ~~keeping his finger~~ laying the book on the ground in the
~~book; he wrote~~ began ~~, as if inspired by what he read, a letter to~~ to write
~~Bonamy, all about visiting countries, in which he~~
~~something~~ a note, ~~something that had struck him,~~ about
democracy.

And then all the French ladies appeared just ~~in~~
beneath him, opening & shutting their umbrellas, for the
weather was certainly changeable. ~~Now there was a~~
~~cloud.~~ Jacob got up & strolled across to the Temple
of Nike.

It is a truism to say that in the presence of beauty
~~particul detail~~ the personal is annulled. Yet it comes fresh each
time - ~~the sense of~~ with a little shock; possibly with
some sense (if you have been ~~making~~ thinking
very definitely about democracy, say, or money, or

a quarrel with a friend, or a some compliment or insult)
then these statues holding the pediment on their heads,
seem ~~a little~~ odd: indifferent;

There are still several women figures standing there, holding the roof on their heads; ~~The shock which beauty gives us is Instantly Jacob was chilled~~. Jacob thought - it would be more accurate to say that he ~~was~~ felt: or was he was shocked: ~~or stiffened; What, after all does anything else matter?~~ - for stability & balance affect the body first; he ~~sta~~ straightened himself slightly: ~~then came the usual feelings.~~ & then felt, as usual ~~a~~, ~~Oh the certainty of art compared with anything else!~~ What ~~nobody has ever succeeded in saying.~~ people are never able to say. - ~~a little de~~jected ~~perhaps~~, ~~to think what a heat he had been in about his ow into among the rest;~~ & with it all a little bewildered by the ~~strength~~ ~~of his own~~ ~~w with which one feeling followed another.~~ shock power of one sensation after another.

These statues annulled so much

[raised?] He looked up ~~into their faces~~ at them. Then He turned; & there was Madame Lucien Gravé, standing on a marble fragment with her Kodak pointed at ~~his head.~~ him Of course she jumped down, in spite of her age, her figure, & her tight boots; - the elderly Frenchwoman giving up the fight earlier than ~~their t~~ the English, accepting the fact but not before he had seen her ~~a &~~

"Damn these women - damn these women" - oh, how they ~~spoil things~~ interfere! he thought. And ~~he~~ went to fetch ~~had left~~ his book / wh. he had left lying on the ground. in the Parthenon.

~~Again; precisely like a book, or something which Love, his love for Sandra wrenched down his side. The landscape all become blank; his own feelings~~

They spoilt things. He pondered leaning against one of the
pillars ~~holding~~ pressing his book tight~~ly~~ between his arm & his side.
(As for the weather, no doubt the storm would break ~~soon; the~~ soon
~~for the plain was~~ Athens was under cloud)

~~Sandra perhaps was left in one excepted when he~~

To think meanly of the race ~~is a~~ may be ~~a~~ nothing but a habit.
And suddenly ~~real~~ real feelings confirm the lazy theory; &
then from being quite tolerable the belief is ~~odious~~. odious.
~~bet bitter; the~~ ~~Yet to hate despise women~~

entirely different from a theory

It is however part of the process of growing up: & (were we
~~able~~ scientific) ~~there~~ this violent disillusionment
might ~~be a~~ generally be expected ~~of~~ in ~~those who at~~ ~~its~~ vigour
young men of twenty four or five ~~who enjoy their lives~~ at the height of physical ~~vi~~ lives,
have ~~all~~ every gift & power, & will mature into
~~the~~ happy fathers of families & ~~the~~ directors of banks.

"~~But women are despicable~~ It is these damned women" thought Jacob.
~~a~~ without any trace of personal bitterness,
but rather with sadness; & disappointment.
that what might have been should ~~never~~ not be.

~~How people can be so inconsistent is inexplicable; but,~~

Nnow that the French women had taken themselves
off, ~~Jacob~~, taking the precaution to look well
round, strolled ~~once more~~ over to the Erechtheum,
~~almost surreptitiously, for he~~ & looked, rather

After a time ~~Now~~ & seeing that the Frenchwomen had gone Jacob

furtively at the Goddess on the left hand side, with the corner of the roof on her head
~~who~~ she reminded him of Sandra. ~~she had~~ You don't
look at the statue squarely, under these circumstances;
you ~~look at her get~~ snatch a glimpse of her, side ~~face~~ ways, & turn away.
This he did several times; & then took the precaution to
make sure from his guide book at what date the
missing figure was stolen by the English. This
was a tribute, to Bonamy presumably, - to
Bonamy mugging up Roman law in his rooms
in Gower Street - to Bonamy who couldn't fall

||||

in love, he said with any woman, & had such fine taste in the classics.

~~Still~~ -

Still, He was terribly romantic - if it is romantic to walk very rapidly for fifty yards on the strength of one glance at a battered Greek nose: & ~~to imagine that somehow or other gre & Sa Mrs. Wentworth Williams is a tremendous success with Bonamy, who says - but then to go back & look again: & then to & to~~ & then take another look, ~~& go on in the same way imagining & think,~~ then start imagining ~~that you are so~~ Yourself all ~~sorts of thing brave, noble, strong, Proud~~ a hero, dying - no, making the finest speech that ever was ~~heard~~ made - & then winning a race. Oh such nonsense! as Jacob himself said; but ~~that did not~~ then he was off again. [And then he pulled himself up, ~~& stared at something or other very particularly.~~] & so on.

And ~~then~~ is it romantic, under these circumstances, to ~~start off~~ for a very long ~~walk t&~~ ~~Probably it~~ is; & ~~in the perfect state these this expenditure of energy~~

walk will ~~be~~ right up Hymettus, ~~in fact~~, in the heat?

So was Sandra Wentworth Williams - very romantic.
~~One means by this, perhaps, that~~ Both ~~were~~ were apt to become ~~fa~~ hot-blooded sentimentalists, but with this difference, that Jacob's mood / ~~vanished~~ went, left him glum, & Sandra's ~~left~~ lingered, & ~~went off in~~ & left her peevish.

The enormous aloes which are planted in the Square ~~seem c~~ curving like scimitars through cigarette smoke; ~~the~~ & the band; & the the dragging of feet; & the ~~the China~~ sky; ~~against the yellow~~ & the horses: all this became so significant to ~~San~~ M[rs.] Williams, after her cup of coffee, that ~~her~~ she began ~~thinking of in a kind of rhapsody about her own~~ dramatizing her the story of ~~beautiful kindness to the poor old / American lady at Mycenae;~~ ~~for such a~~ the impulsive & noble English woman, (~~so Sandra a mad it ran in Sandra's head) had gone~~ ~~offered Mrs. Duggan~~ a ~~seat~~ in ~~the~~ her ~~carriage~~. & the old American lady at Mycenae. - not altogether a false story, but ~~Sandra had could not be~~ - & yet so concocted that that it disregarded the fact that Evan was bored to Evan, for example, would scarcely have recognized it: But then Kubla Khan was written under some such stimulus. And Sandra floating from the particular to the universal, lay back in a trance;

The curling leaves of the aloes, & ~~the~~ the flight of time. ~~&~~

Kubla Khan was written under some such circumstances.
~~The~~ The flight of time - which hurries us so tragically
~~with it~~, along - but Sandra ~~was~~ felt that she was on
the front of that wave - ~~& a the then though brief~~
~~it was for life~~ is ~~the brief spurts of [dram?] yellow in~~
the intensity - ~~like those oranges in the~~ which is
like brief spurts of yellow among green leaves (she was
looking at orange trees) ~~emotions~~ - lines on lips that are
to die - the world turning, turning in mazes of heat.
sound - though to be sure there is the quiet evening -
with its lovely ~~lights~~ pallor & so on 'for, I am sensitive
to every side of it" she thought - "~~haven't I wasn't~~
~~I perfectly charming to Mrs. Duggan?~~ - "I ~~encour~~
~~I made~~ Mrs. Duggan ~~love me~~" -~~Now~~ and the royal
band stirred her to wider rings of emotion, &
~~in the midst of them~~ - indeed life ~~must be considered to~~
is something ~~one learns - one is infinitely~~ the
mount & courageous ride out to sea on - the hair blown back -
~~plucking the fruit~~ - so she envisaged it - tempestuous,
white foam~~ed~~, ~~when she saw Jacob~~ & herself
bursting through in the van - when she saw Jacob.
He was standing in the Square, with a book under
his arm.

[margin: will write to me for ever - I shall write to Mrs Duggan for ever -]

[margin: with its]

That he was heavily built & might become stout in
time was a fact.

But she suspected him of being a mere
bumpkin. ~~She smiled a little bitterly~~.

"There is that young man, she said, peevishly - Mr. Flanders -
I dont see him" said Evan looking about.
Where ~~is he?~~"

"Never mind. We ~~shall~~ are sure to run into him" -
& so of course they did.

But how far ~~he was~~ was he a mere bumpkin,
~~romantic, - at least now & again~~ -

now & again seized by ~~a kind of~~ emotions; then his love of books - what did that amount to? [?] was Impressionable, ~~yet~~ at the same time / very sluggish. ~~He was~~ It is no use

it is certain that he was

trying to sum people up in one glance. One must follow hints - not exactly what is said, nor yet entirely what is done - Some ~~say that~~ it is true take ineffacable impressions at once. Others dally - loiter, & get blown first this way, then that. Kind old ladies assure us that cats are often the best judges of character.

~~"Now~~

A cat will always go to a good man, they say; but then, Mrs. Garfit, Jacob's landlady, loathed cats.

There is also the highly respectable opinion that character mongering is much overdone nowadays. After all, what does it matter - that Fanny Elmer was ~~all sentiment &~~ all sentiment & sensational & Mrs. Durrant hard as iron? - that Clara, owing (so the character mongers say) largely to her mother's influence never had the chance yet to do anything off her own bat, & only ~~in~~ to a very observant eye displayed deeps of feelings which were positively alarming - ~~to showed~~ showed an awful power of being hurt, & covering it with silence: ~~&~~ would certainly fling herself away upon someone unworthy of her, unless, as the character mongers said, she had a spark of her mother's spirit in her, latent up till now: was some how heroic. But what a term to apply to Clara Durrant! Simple to a degree, others thought her; ~~perhaps a little obstinate;~~ And that is the very reason, so they said, why she attracts Dick Bonamy - the young man with the Wellington nose. Now He's a dark horse if you like. And there these gossips would suddenly pause.

Obviously they meant to hint at his peculiar disposition.

"And ~~one's seen a great deal of harm come of it" one of them would~~ say.

"But" "~~And~~ But sometimes its precisely a woman like Clara that men of that temperament need to ."..

"Well, the other would reply "It may be so."

For however long the gossips sit, & however ~~swollen the characters~~ they stuff out their victim's characters, till they are swollen & tender as the livers of geese exposed to a hot fire, ~~their they yet leave things dark~~. they never come to a ~~conclusion~~ decision.

Take any man in a bank - take Lord Kitchener at the Home Guard, ~~take~~ or the Prime Minister; or ~~for the matter of that the policeman on point duty at Ludgate Circus~~, - ~~the Ferryman whose~~ the policeman or the surgeon - all of these being occupied with facts, ~~must make up their minds~~; must act; ~~& thus~~ their faces clean of all wrinkles; have ab~~out them~~ a mastery, an authority,

&

to a decision.
"That young man, Jacob Flanders," they would say, "is so very awkward
distinguished looking - ~~& yet such a bumpkin"~~ - "but he & a bit of a
bumpkin too", thus they would apply themselves to Jacob,
& vacillate eternally between the two extremes. ~~Women~~

doesn't know how to come into a room yet" —

He rode to hounds –; after a fashion, ~~for~~ he hasn't ~~a~~ a penny.
Did you ever hear who ~~what~~ his father was? And his mother? - ~~She's~~
somehow connected with the Rocksbiers. ~~That is where~~ the
~~looks come from~~. I believe. [I find his silence very
intrigueing. ~~some one would say~~ ~~He Obviously he~~
~~he is one of those~~ ~~Jacob Flanders~~ He is precisely the type of
young ~~man~~ / they say to fall headlong in love with a pretty girl -
But he doesn't take his profession very seriously:
I ~~should be sorry to see that~~. — ~~for there were certain~~
~~people who held that Jacob~~ Anyhow His friends are
very fond of him. Dick Bonamy, you mean?
~~Well, I didn't mean that~~ ~~Not in that sense~~.
~~for evidently~~ I always take it for a good sign when I
hear that a young man likes country walks. ~~His~~
~~ignorance of~~ the social amenities is ~~sometimes very~~
dis~~tressing though. I don't call that a bad sign~~ - ~~not in a~~
~~boy of his age~~. -

He has good a head piece, so they say.

& repent it for the rest of his life

No evidently, its the other way with Jacob

How utterly superficial, negligible & worthless all this was -
like the crawling of winter blue bottles over a face, ~~which~~
~~For all their~~ though they ~~had seen Jacob~~, been in the same
~~room~~ with Jacob ~~him~~ [~~severa~~?] half a dozen times, & filtered
him assiduously through their fingers at least twice as
often, they had not touched a single spring. ~~he was~~

So we are driven back to see what the ~~od~~ other side
means when they say that character drawing is a
frivolous fireside art, accomplished with pins and needles
essentially feminine, ~~feeble~~ ~~leading~~ ~~all~~ cloistered ~~off the~~ ~~sequestered &~~
~~& beside the point~~. ~~Are nations ruled by~~
futile, ~~a~~

The battleships ray out ~~shoot out~~ over the North Sea,

with flawless precision. At a given signal all the guns are
trained on a target, which, the moment after, ~~flames &~~
flames up ~~goes up~~ in splinters. ~~Equally~~ With equal nonchalance
a dozen young men in the prime of life descend with
composed faces into the depths of the sea; & there
impassively - (though with a perfect mastery of machinery)
~~await the~~ accept their fate. So, too, like tin soldiers in
army covers
blocks the ~~army~~ cornfield ~~is covered with an army~~
~~rel~~ reels this way & that
which moves up the hillside; stops; quivers slightly; lies
dead - or with only a little ~~piece here and there~~ it is
lies still flat & rigid
quiver here & there in one of its pieces. ~~For all these~~
~~precise & orderly movements men in are responsible~~
Without these precise & orderly movements, ~~of~~ civilization
would not advance; ~~&~~ To take the pen & strive with its
pin point to delineate the eddies, crisscrosses, &
~~quiv~~ currents which ~~underlie~~ perhaps ~~direct the~~
statesmen, the bankers, the merchants, the
sailors soldiers, keepers of lighthouses, & others
doing punctually difficult & dangerous tasks, is

These actions, together with the ~~wh~~ incessant commerce of
banks, laboratories, chancelleries & houses of business,
supply the gossips with little material for their favourite
~~pursuit~~. pastime. The strokes which oar the world
forward are dealt by men as smoothly sculptured
as the impassive policeman ~~at~~ at Ludgate Circus.
But you will observe that far from being padded into
rotundity his face is immobile from force of will, &
so
lean from the effort of keeping it ~~so~~. When, his
right rises
straight for ~~therefore~~, his arm ~~goes up,~~ all the force in his veins flows into
~~straight~~ into it. ~~which no gossip of them all could perceive~~
shoulder to
finger tip. ~~frittered away into~~ not an ounce is diverted into
~~mere likings & dislikings~~, sudden impulses,
sentimental regrets, ~~fine~~ wire drawn distinctions,
The buses punctually stop. Nothing is

more baffling to the character mongers. As soon could they
take the spiritual diagram of Mr. Peabody's statue at the
Bank as write this man's character. Thus they
boggled at what was most obvious in Jacob Flanders;
as it was obvious too in Clara Durrant, her brother
Timothy, M^{rs}. Durrant, Bonamy, Sandra Williams,
the
and all the rest. ~~For those~~ ~~that~~ natural unseizable
force in people, ~~which~~ ~~which~~ Take the quietest street in the
placidest
suburbs. Select the ~~dreariest~~ old maid. ~~You might~~
climax
~~suppose that the~~ sole tragedy & cata~~strophe of the~~ week was
robin flower bed
that the ~~cat sat~~ upon the ~~carnation~~ & broke ~~its head off:~~
the pink carnation. Yet in truth ~~she is driven from~~
~~street to street~~ the same unseizable force drives her ~~from~~ a
~~street to street from shop to shop~~, that impels the
down fr. Oxford, with political ardour
young man with a brilliant career. She, for no reason,
that anyone could discover, quietly blew her brains out
one day on a seat in Richmond Park: & he becomes
Prime Minister: the ~~char~~ gossips can never tell us what
~~the~~ force ~~is behind this.~~ inspired them. Thus,
unfortunately for the character dealers, life is all action
&
Even the quietest, ~~the~~ least eventful; & though some
try to reason it out, directly the clock strikes even the
philosopher has to ~~act~~, pull on his boots, nor can his
affect
meditations much alter the flow of the unseizable force.

where
you might
suppose to be
that

152

"Oh, said Fanny, bursting into the room, three quarters of an hour late in keeping her appointment with Nick, because she had been hanging about the neighbourhood of the Foundling Hospital in order merely to see Jacob. ~~& if possible~~ — walk up the street, take out his latch key & let himself in
All that evening Nick was glum; & Fanny peevish.

"I'll never come again" she cried at length.

"Dont then" said Nick, ~~walking~~ &

off she ran without goodnight,

XVIII

"Archer, said Mrs. Flanders with that tenderness which mothers often display towards their eldest sons," Archer will be at Gibraltar tomorrow."

The post for which she was waiting (strolling up Dodds Hill, while the random church bells swung a hymn tune about her head, the clock striking four ~~straight~~ straigtly [h] through the circling hymn tune; the purple in the air deepening under a storm cloud, & the village huddling [cowering] up, infinitely humble, a little community against the earth) the post with all its variety of messages, ~~han~~ envelopes addressed in bold hands, in slanting hands, stamped now with English stamps, again with colonial stamps, ~~an~~ or some times hastily dabbed with a yellow bar, - the post was about to scatter over the world a myriad ~~envelope~~ message ~~all sorts of news:~~ Whether we gain or not by all this communication is not for the living to say. ~~For us things~~ But that letter writing is practised mendaciously nowadays, particularly by young men ~~as their~~ foreign travel~~ing is~~ in foreign seems ~~obvious enough~~. likely enough.

For example, take this scene.

Here was Jacob Flanders gone abroad, & breaking his journey in Paris. (Old Miss Birkbeck, his

~~Having~~

mothers cousin, had died last June & left him a hundred pounds -)

Cruttendon "you needn't repeat the whole damned thing over again" said Mallinson, the little bald painter, who was sitting at a marble table, talking very fast - & undoubtedly more than a little drunk.

"Well, Flanders, finished writing to your lady" said Cruttendon as Jacob put down his pen & dabbed the blotting paper over an envelope addressed to Mrs. Flanders near Scarborough. England Jacob ordered vin rouge.

157.

Well; not a word of this was ever told to Mrs. Flanders.

Then here is another scrap of conversation; the time being eleven in the morning, the scene ~~in~~ a studio, & ~~where Cruttendon was at work~~ - & the day Sunday.

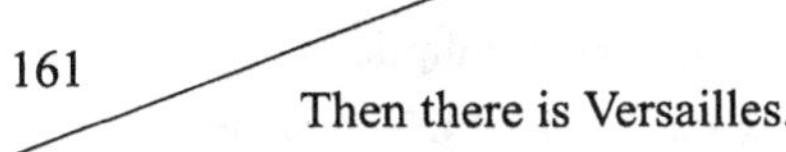

161 Then there is Versailles.

162.

And finally, there was Jacob standing on the terrace at Versailles looking rather queerly at the landscape, as people do after ~~an argument~~ ~~beatin~~ getting the better of an argument -

And then they stood

Mrs. Flanders was told none of this, ~~a~~ though ~~it is safe to say that these experiences, were of the utmost importance to Jacob.~~ Jacob felt, it is safe to say, that nothing in the world was of greater importance, & as for Cruttendon & Jinny he thought them far & away the most remarkable ~~couple~~ - people he had ever met - being of course unable to foresee ~~the future~~ how it [?] fell out in the course of time. Cruttendon ~~alas capitulated to the crow crowd~~ & took to painting orchards; had therefore to live in Kent, & must one would think, see through apple blossom by this time~~s~~; ~~&~~ since his wife, for whose sake he did it, has eloped with a novelist; but no: Cruttendon ~~is~~ still paints orchards savagely, & in solitude, in Kent, & gets 30 pounds a piece. Then Jinny Carslake after ~~her being very badly treated by~~ her affair Lefanu, the American painter, ~~found~~ took to Indian philosophy, & now you find her in Pensions in ~~Perugia~~, Italy, cherishing a little jewellers box containing ordinary pebbles off the road. But if you look at them steadily enough, she says, ~~everything becomes one~~, multiplicity becomes unity, which is somehow the secret of life, though it does not prevent her from following the maccaroni as it goes round the table, & sometimes, ~~perhaps, she losing her head~~ on spring nights bursting out in the strangest way altogether ~~with young men on~~ spring ~~All this~~, nights with ~~awkward~~ shy young ~~English~~men.

All this, infinitely more than all this, was quite unknown to Betty Flanders - who had her own affairs to think of - her orchard, her chickens, her curious intimacy with Captain Barfoot, ~~not to &~~ which, now that M^rs. Barfoot was ~~almost entirely~~ hopelessly ill - ~~it~~ her disease was ~~now known to be cancer~~ diabetes - ~~took on a~~ had become ~~a little different~~ more serious. ~~She~~ People ~~believed that people gossiped~~ had begun to talk for the first time. - [At any rate though she held a letter ~~from~~ which Jacob ~~pos~~ had posted at Milan in her] Yet Jacob had nothing to hide from her. It was only that ~~his~~ he could make no sense himself out of his excitement.

He wrote to Bonamy from Patras - to Bonamy who couldn't love a woman & never read a foolish book -

~~For reading in good books~~ ~~The good books are very~~ There are very few good books, after all - for we can't count profuse histories, travels to discover the sources of the Nile, ~~lives of good men~~ ~~lives~~ - ~~mere bundles of bills tied together with red tape - or~~ ~~the~~ lives - mere bundles of bills tied together with red tape - or the volubility of fiction. ~~One~~. "I like books whose virtue is all drawn together in a page or two. I like sentences that don't budge though armies march over cross the them. I like to ~~think that this~~ the inalterab is ~~inalterable~~. Such were Bonamy's opinions, & they had won him the ~~to think that~~ words ~~whose~~ ~~which endure-don't~~ to be hard." Such were Bonamy's opinions, & they won him the hostility of those whose taste is all for the fresh growths of the morning, who throw up the window & find ~~all~~ the poppies spread in the sun, & can't forbear a great shout of jubilation at the astounding fertility of English Literature. That was not Bonamy's way at all. That his taste in literature ~~much~~ affected his friendships & made him silent, secretive, suspicious & only quite at his ease with one or two young men of his own way of thinking was the charge against him. But then Jacob Flanders was not at all of his / own way of thinking, - far from it, Bonamy sighed laying the thin sheets of note paper on the table & falling into thought about Jacob's character, ~~not by any~~ ~~by any~~ not ~~means~~ for the first time.

[Margin: that is to say not to give yield the least drop of [their?] virtue however often.]

The trouble was this romantic vein in him. He would fall in love. [But not only that. He was a little stupid. ~~perhaps.~~ "He is oddly at the mercy of his moods", Bonamy reflected;] And mixed with the stupidity which leads him into these absurd predicaments, ~~which are really too grotes~~que", thought Bonamy, "there is a ~~vein~~ of course the sublime. ~~what, he did not say, but he sighed; not only he did not~~ he ~~sighed~~. He ~~gets sees through it all~~, - ~~anyhow for moments~~ [at] /" thought Bonamy; for ~~Jacob was subject to moods~~ of And the fact remained that he ~~adored him~~. was fonder of him than of anyone. in the whole world. And yet he was provoking enough; & wrote just like a schoolboy;

Anyhow at moments he sees through it all

He has extraordinary moods of depression" thought Bonamy.

~~Jacob, having written his letter to Bonamy,~~

Jacob sat in the hotel at Patras, the Daily Mail crumpled in his hand, his legs extended, the very picture of boredom.

"It's the way we're brought up" he thought to himself.

&

who enjoyed things, was romantic, not very analytic -

~~yet mysterious, Bonamy thought;~~ though he gave one the

impression, Bonamy thought, that he was capable of a

yet

great ~~good~~ deal more than he had / done.

"He will fall in love," thought Bonamy.

"Some Greek woman with a straight nose" he thought. ~~bitterly~~.

It was this kind of bitterness which frequently led him to

read Chaucer. - if not Chaucer some other of the

ancients ~~who~~ - Donne perhaps or Ben Jonson -

for though a number of people write well enough nowadays,

what we have lost entirely is vigour of language.

There is a scene for example in Bartholomew Fair of a

fat woman scolding which could not be pieced together

by twenty of our young men writing in concert; & then

~~this~~ when this torrent of language gets its way,

that

the chances are it sweeps down with it something

~~lovely~~ - ~~somethin~~ - ~~as & phrase like a flash of lightning~~.

astonishing. Bonamy turned the pages.

~~"He will fall in love" he thought again.~~

"It would be just like Jacob" he thought, "to

marry a woman with a straight nose - & ~~then~~

~~they'd have children with even straighter noses~~ -

H~~e was t~~hinking of a peasant woman, someone

strapping & inarticu~~late, w~~ho would sit on the

a ham

other side of the fire place smok~~ing~~ & saying

nothing, & ~~Jacob would say nothing.~~ Jacob

~~would be lost for ever~~.

But after all it takes a week for a letter ~~to~~

from Greece to reach England - the gulf is one of those
which blurs ever feature in ~~the~~ a friends face.
And then, however we may disguise it, can we deny
the deep chasm which separates us? On this side of it -
that is within Bonamy's room, all is acute even to
distraction - the boys shouting in the mews - the tick of the
clock - & the ~~silence~~ quality of the silence - ~~on the
other~~, but Jacob ~~is far away on the other side~~, a ghost
at the end of a thread of memory which falters before it
reaches him -

Those who complained that Bonamy could find comfort in
books were quite right - He could read & he could stop &
he could read again -

There is a consolation in literature, after all.
The ~~emotional readers take up a book &~~ serious readers
brush everything else aside, & ~~set themselves sternly to~~
read a play at a time, without stopping, or
a
stopping only to make ~~sure that they~~ ~~their~~ note, ~~so that~~
certainly [?] [?]
of the ~~the to~~ line, say, ~~which~~ was influenced by Marlowe -
the emotional readers on the other hand, like Sandra
Wentworth Williams are for ever running ~~ove~~
off the page ~~"saying to themselves "~~ onto the
landscape thus -
"I

— Bonamy would have said, ~~with some truth~~, that
this was the sort of thing that made him uneasy -
when Jacob got in to ~~his grumpy~~ the doldrums - looked
like a mogul boatman out of a job - or ~~Dr Johnson~~
aristocr
~~after~~ or a British peer - ~~or~~ quite uncivilized - ~~very fine of~~
course; but you couldn't make him understand a word
when he was in a mood like this - One had better
im~~posing~~
leave him. He was dull -

The water fell off . . .

200
280
——
1600
400
——
5600

"Goodness knows what he means by that" Bonamy said,
And as he never said a clumsy thing himself, these dark sayings
of Jacob's ~~impressed him, &~~ made him feel that ~~a great force~~ was
blundering about the world, ~~his own nature~~ & impressed
as
him, his own nature and being, ~~as we have said~~ ~~all~~ ~~definite as~~
the the
a ~~blade steel blade~~. all for the exact, ~~compact~~, definite, ~~&~~ rational.

Nothing could be much simpler that what Sandra said
as she descended the acro-Corinth, keeping to the little
path, while Jacob ~~sprang along~~ strode over rougher
ground by her side . . She

Bonamy must have been alarmed by ~~Jacobs~~ what
Jacob wrote or did not write, for it was on this same
afternoon that he went to tea with Clara Durrant.
~~simply in order to talk about Jacob~~. ~~in~~ in the square
behind Sloane Street, where on ~~sprin~~ hot spring days
room
there are striped blinds over the drawing windows;
Victorias
single horse ~~broughams~~ standing outside the doors; &
~~&~~ pretty ~~nursemaids take wheeling perambulators;~~
~~while I the~~ elderly gentlemen in yellow waistcoats
ringing bells at those same doors, & stepping in very
politely when the maid demurely replies that M$^{rs.}$
Durrant is at home.

~~Thus Bonamy had some talk with Clara alone.~~
~~wh with~~
Bonamy had Clara alone in the sunny front room; ~~with while~~
with
~~the organ piping sweetly outside, & the~~ The organ
piping [pi...?]
~~played~~ outside. The carriages ~~dashing~~ jingling; & the
~~stripes the parquet floor striped with silver, white,~~
all the silver & ~~white &~~ chintz & ~~green boughs~~
red ~~old~~ rugs on the floor & vases full of
~~of the daffodils~~ ~~green leaves~~ in ~~the vases~~ green
boughs
oddly striped with ~~sunshine~~.
yellow bars.

But the insipidity of what was said needs no illustration, -
Bonamy kept ~~on~~ gently ~~returning~~ ~~making his observations, while~~
~~Mrs. Durrant was~~ returning quiet answers or ~~dis~~ ~~until Clara~~
~~feeling sorry for the simpleness the good an existence~~
&'accumulating amazement' at on ~~convention~~ existence
all forced & emasculated within a white satin shoe (
Mr. Durrant meanwhile enunciating ~~such~~ strident
politics ~~in~~ with Sir Somebody in the back room)
until ~~there~~ ~~on top of his pity~~ ~~while~~ then ~~lay besides~~ ~~he~~ ~~pitying~~ ed ~~Clara~~, ~~her~~
he ~~feel~~ ~~her he began to suspect that~~ ~~this her simplicity~~
~~some~~ ~~in its candour~~ ~~in its candour~~ ~~appeared to him so~~ ~~natural that~~
~~honest that~~, ~~until she said something so~~ ~~hones~~
~~natural that he began to suspect that the viriginity~~ of her
soul ~~had protected~~ a the virginity of her soul appeared to
him candid & he would have mentioned Jacob's name, had he
not ~~begun to~~ be good felt positively afraid ~~of her~~ that Clara
Durrant ~~felt~~ things ~~& would indeed have been~~
~~worth knowing~~, ~~if~~ ~~so~~ as girls presumably do ~~who~~
loved him ~~felt~~ ~~very deeply~~ things; - ~~And one pities a girl who has no~~
chance of expressing ~~herself~~. & What's to happen to a
~~girl who cannot can do nothing whatever?~~ -

He ~~guessed it, Heaven knows how.~~ & could do nothing
whatever, ~~She was so still, so ingenuous.~~
~~And he knew that Clara Durrant had something like his own~~
a~~larm~~

"Nothing whatever! he said to himself; & for a
man of his temperament, which was ~~one~~ positive & unmystical,
Got a very queer feeling, as he walked home through ~~the pa~~
~~Hyde~~ Park, ~~of carriages, & people's lives; of roar &~~
~~disorder; of~~ most of ~~the~~ these carriages being driven ~~by fate~~;
~~in~~ by men in masks. & that the policemen ~~were~~ was
a dummies; ~~who~~ & the beds of hyacinths laid out in
meaningless patterns by an insane God without eyes.

the average mood, ~~the~~ the weather wh. is neither wet nor fine

Long before Jacob descended Hymettus his romance had faded & left him glum; yet happy enough too, - & ~~I mean~~ quite able to carry on with life, - It is useless to attempt to give a name to that sort of mood. - Presumably his was coloured a little by the emotions of the morning; & those who can't help feeling themselves part of the ~~every~~ landscape would have been aware of the new ~~great~~ ~~hills~~, ~~the~~ & ~~Athens~~ of the craggy

nears hill ~~with the~~ of the [Harpies?] above the white scattered homes

~~Athens on the plain;~~ but how far Jacob was ~~at the~~ ~~in~~ influenced by such things one cannot ~~it is impossible~~ ~~to~~ say - Mrs. Wentworth Williams was romantic in the sense that ~~a~~ walz music, a cup of coffee, a private view of an evening party stimulated the tips of her nerves to such an extent that she improvised ~~views~~ emotions of the most sweeping character, on the gust of which she said some very foolish things & some charming ones; & astounded comparative strangers by the intimacy of her confidences & ~~But~~ Her romance ~~faded & left h~~ lingered & left her peevish.

The orange trees which flourish in the Square of the Constitution; the band; the dragging of feet; the sky; the houses; ~~like white & yellow~~ all this became so significant to Mrs. Wentworth Williams after her second cup of coffee that she leant her head back on the bamboo chair & began dramatising the story of the noble & impulsive Englishwoman - that is herself ~~of course~~ - who had offered a seat in her carriage to the American lady at Mycenae, & had made: a friend of her for life.

"I am putting the story of Father Damien into verse" ~~Mi~~ Sally Duggan had said; in answer to Sandra's questions; but Sandra never laughed at what people told her. "I have never told anyone what I have told you" said Sally Duggan at the end of the evening - & now Sandra, floating from the particular to the universal, lay back in a trance.

The flight of time which hurries us so tragically along; the eternal drudge & drone now bursting into a fiery flash, like those brief bursts of yellow among green trees (she was looking at the orange trees) - kisses on lips that are to die - the world turning, turning in mazes of heat & sound - though I am also sensitive, she thought, to the quiet evening & its pallor - Sally Duggan will find me walking on ~~the~~ terrace among the roses - Here ~~the band struck up~~ Soldiers marched past ~~with the~~ carrying the National flag & stirred wider rings of emotion - "And indeed life is something that the courageous mount & ride out to sea on - the hair blown back -' She envisaged ~~it~~ ~~tempestuous with white foam, & herself breaking through~~ a tempestuous ~~ocean~~, ~~with then~~ sea, & herself ~~pul~~ plunging, emerging, scattering spray, when she saw Jacob. He was standing in the square with a book under his arm looking rather vacantly about him.

Therefore the

It is a frivolous fireside art, they say, a matter of pins & needles, exquisite outlines enveloping vacancy, ~~&~~ flourishes & mere scrawls. The strokes which oar the world forward are dealt by men as smoothly sculptured as the impassive policeman at Ludgate Circus. [But you will observe that far from being padded to rotundity his face is immobile from force of will & lean from the effort of keeping it so. When his right arm rises, all the ~~force~~ blood in his veins flows straight from shoulder to finger tips; not an ounce is diverted into sudden impulses, sentimental regrets, or wire drawn distinctions; t the ~~bus~~ omnibuses punctually stop. [There is an unseizable force in us; an unknown force in us. The novelists stretch ~~all~~ their nets to catch it; but it tears a great hole.]
~~Thus we~~ It is thus that we live; driven
It is thus that we live, they say, ~~plunging forward, doing things more by instinct than by reason; flooded~~ ~~&~~ driven by an unseizable force. They say that the novelists ~~art has never~~ never catch it. ~~but have contrived exhibit a network of~~ ~~but it goes~~ & that goes hurtling through their nets ~~like~~ leaving them ~~torn &~~ rent & useless. ~~They say that you have only to pick out~~ ~~It is no good making these~~

Yet of course, so they say, ~~one everybod~~ it is what we live by -

Jacob, walking ~~rapidly down Hermes Street~~ ran straight into the Williamses ~~at~~ the corner of Hermes Street. Sandra's face lit by the sunset hung in the air like ~~some~~ a Chinese lantern~~; &~~

They asked him to dinner. They gave him an excellent dinner, with real butter, a quantity of fresh rolls in a silver basket; & meat that might have been English.

'Oh' cried Sandra with a cordiality which she certainly felt.
And ~~Jac~~ Evan added 'What luck!"
The dinner which they gave him in their hotel which looks onto the square of the constitution was ~~admirable~~ excellent.
Plated baskets contained fresh rolls. There was real butter.
And the meat scarcely needed the disguise of innumerable little red & green vegetables, in ~~the thick~~ brown sauce.

veiled as usual

It was strange enough. ~~to see~~ There were the little tables set out at intervals on the scarlet floor. Sandra dined in her hat. - ~~Evan had the travelled manner to perfection,~~ -
& ~~some diamond flashed in the her white lace.~~
~~Evan was imperturbable yet supple.~~ It was strange.
For they were English people come together in Athens on a ~~certain~~ night in May. - dining together; ~~t perhaps it was the sense of England behind them, that was strange.~~
but ~~not knowing each other at all;~~

Evan looked this way & that over his shoulder - & sometimes sighed.

And Jacob ~~talked with a~~ felt perhaps ~~as people feel when they learn to ride a bicycle. He felt perfectly assured.~~
helping himself to this & that answered Evan intelligently; yet with a little excitement; ~~For one thing the service at the hotel was admirable, then the English meeting in an hotel in Athens,~~ without ~~& yet they it was strange,~~ The Williamses were going to Constantinople ~~by the f~~ early the next morning. they said.

"Before you are up" said Sandra -
Then Jacob felt that ~~he would be left a~~
if this were so he would be ~~left alone~~. lonely
Turning very slightly Evan ordered something.
~~He It was for Jacob a~~ bottle of wine.
from which he helped Jacob. ~~And And Evan smiled saw that Jacob was excited~~ He was excited; as Evan saw; ~~but then~~
so were ~~they all~~ the talk was all about
Greece - the ambiguities - the hotels, the exchange, the ~~rate~~ peasants, & how the land is cultivated, &

And you have been to the Acropolis? asked Sandra.

'Yes' said Jacob. And they moved off to the window together, while Evan spoke to the head waiter about ~~the~~ calling them early next morning.

"It was astonishing" said Jacob~~, in~~ His voice was almost gruff.

Sandra opened her eyes very slightly. Possibly her nostrils were just opened.

"At half past six then" said Evan coming towards them ~~with a~~ looking as if he faced something in facing ~~the~~ his wife & Jacob standing with their backs to the window.

Sandra smiled at him.

And as he went to the window & had nothing to say, she added, ~~rather falteringly~~, in broken half sentences

"Well but why - how lovely ~~if it were fine~~ wouldn't it be ? - -

The Acropolis, Evan - are you too tired?"

At that Evan looked at them. Or, since Jacob was staring ahead of him, at his wife, surlily, sullenly, yet with a kind of distress - not that she would pity him, Nor would the implacable spirit of love, ~~for~~ for anything he could do; cease its tortures.

They left him, & he sat in the smoking room of the ~~hotel which~~ looks onto the Square of the Constitution.

~~"Oh~~ yes, said Sandra, I think my father was one of the very few people to whom Mr. Gladstone spoke without reserve. He had a face like alabaster, she said. White. Wonderful. Evan of course is the other way of thinking. I think he gets more & more so.

One wants things for one's husband

One's [is] ambitious for one's husband. But what does

~~one really~~ want ~~want for peop~~ matter ? le? ~~Only~~ T that / ~~people~~ they should be happy -

~~He stood for~~ Will he stand again? said Jacob

"I ~~think~~ Perhaps so," ~~she said~~. But where are we going?"

You said you wanted to ~~see~~ go to the Acropolis, said Jacob.

"Shall we ever get there? . . . I love crowds. But I want to know . . . Tell me" she began, - being brushed off the pavement by men parading - I want to know ~~what~~ ~~about~~ what you ~~are~~ ~~mean~~ were to be."

Oh he hesitated for a very long time. You came to Greece all alone without a friend" she said. Evan tells me that you care for politics -

Yes, said Jacob, twisting his stick in his hands. I dare say it would be all right."

And again, Sandra's nostrils opened slightly. Do I ~~believ~~ You distrust me! she cried

No, ~~no~~ no of course I dont" he replied hastily

~~If one could ever say what one wants to say" she~~

I never remember ~~what~~ who people are when I'm talking to them. ~~I might have known you al~~ways. ~~Here we are~~ What does it matter? ~~It is what we feel~~ after all." -

We feel -

"I cant say what I feel' awfully difficult to talk, - Jacob brought out.

Oh she said stopping & looking about her & waving his hand - In the dark there were the great hills: stars rippling like ~~wat~~ deep water; & ~~the~~ red & yellow gauzy lights over the town. — Oh - look - She touched his arm.

~~Somehow he looked as if he flinched -~~ & he looked drawn; "Foreigners ~~seem~~ are so different from us" he said

out of doors like
You would never get people sitting ~~about like~~ this in London."
At this Sandra was silent.
But what did she want?
Evan is happier alone," she said ... [Reading the paper -]
We have been separated from our papers - Well, it is
better that people should have what they want -"
~~What~~ You have seen all these wonderful things since we met ...
What impression - I think that you are changed ..."
You said you wanted to go to the Acropolis" said Jacob.
~~Then we ought to go~~ Up here ~~on~~ them -"
I ~~think it will alter the whole of one's life!~~ said Sandra.
"One will remember it all one's life"
we
"Yes said Jacob. I wish you could have come ~~up here~~ in the
daytime.

"This is more wonderful" said Sandra.

~~Look she said,~~ ~~looking~~ waving her hand. ~~In the~~
the
Against the sky were the great hills; stars rippling like
deep water; & a gauzy red & yellow light ~~over the great main~~
Street ~~which they had just left~~ -

Jacob looked vaguely.

in the daytime
But you should see those ~~statues - &~~ the Parthenon
itself" he said. You couldn't come tomorrow - it would be
too early - ?

sat
"And you have <u>been</u> there for hours & hours by yourself - "
"Oh there ~~was a~~ were some awful women this
morning said Jacob -

'Awful women' Sandra ~~re~~ echoed
they're
~~Yes~~ Frenchwomen. I think ~~they are~~ the worst"
"But tell me said Sandra - Something
very wonderful has happened."

"Yes" he said.
"When one is your age - when one is young. ~~But~~ What will
you do? You will fall in love - oh yes! - But
don't be in too great a hurry. I am so much older. ~~that~~
I feel that I can see your life as it is, ~~now;~~ - I see
~~how~~ more than you can. It is one of the compensations.
She was brushed off the pavement by parading men -
Is this too tiring? Jacob asked.
No
~~Oh~~ let us go on" she insisted. For she could not stop
until she had told him - or heard him say - or was it
required
some action on his part that she ~~wanted?~~ ~~Indeed,~~
Far away on the horizon she discerned it, & could not
rest. ~~That was~~ ~~Yet she~~
in the street
"You never find English people sitting out/like this" he
~~said~~

"They are too comfortable ~~at home~~" she said
contemptuously. "Dont make compromises.
~~Don't forget~~ - ~~when you are in England~~, ~~don't~~
What fatuity possessed them? Why was the same belief
~~so firmly~~ set in each of them - that there is a definite
thing which happens, perhaps when one reaches the
top of Acropolis - Yes, it is then that it will
happen; but only if we never stop, ~~ever~~ all the
way up the hill to strive for it."

"You never find English people sitting in the
Street ~~like this~~" he said

"They are too comfortable - ~~Never~~
~~compromise~~, Jacob. When you get back to
England, ~~be~~ remember ~~how you~~ ~~sat~~ this -

Come with us to Constantinople?"
Oh but then -"
(The light from the wine merchants window
showed Jacob's strained terrific face, ~~as gave on~~ a
~~desperately set~~ -) I ~~mean Mr. Williams won't want me~~.
Sandra sighed, ~~like some one free sailing ship~~ & swished
off, like a sailing ship on a new tack -
"We are very happy, Evan & I.
what
(Then ~~why~~, she asked herself, ~~if that is so~~, ~~am I~~
can this man give me? - It is something that I have
missed"

~~Her soul was not mean. She was had indeed~~
~~forgotten herself; she who she had~~ & yet she
was not egotistical; ~~or~~ nor vapid; at the moment;
~~she was~~ but exalted & without self-consciousness.
Nor was she a silly woman, nor a ~~ba~~ cruel one.
That she told lies was true, but only with her mind,
which was unstable; & sometimes she was
~~come to~~
extraordinarily sincere, & would ~~come to alone~~
~~with Evan~~ show great insight into her husbands
character.
with something brazen when
—— an aristocrat too, for the matter of that.
She would not be beaten. Or if beaten she would ~~never~~
~~own to it~~ hold on her way.
"You will get there about six o'clock in the evening" she said,
You will ~~There will be an eagle. hanging over the gorge~~ - see
the eagles, as we did - ~~You go up & up -"~~
Eagles? said Jacob.
as
And then you go up & up ~~& up~~" she said.
I shall write you an account of it" he said.
He looked desperate enough by the light in ~~the~~ at the
street corner: & yet composed. He was suffering

perhaps; He was ~~infinitely~~ credulous. Yet there was a
~~simplicity about him~~. & something caustic about him - He had in him the
seeds of extreme disillusionment, which would ~~come~~ be come to him
from women ~~from women~~ in middle life; ~~to be from knowing women.~~
~~And this Sandra felt.~~ But now, Sandra felt, ~~they were~~
This had not happened. Perhaps, if one strove hard enough,
to reach the top of the ~~Acropolis~~ hill, it need not happen.
~~He was simple, he willing~~.

~~You love poetry~~

" ~~Might~~ May I write to you from Delphi?" he ~~said~~.asked.

Oh "Please ~~do~~." ~~Still, it was not~~ But 'then' was no
use; it was the present; this moment; this very moment;
~~For, aristocrat~~

~~And he~~ ~~Such was his feeling~~. ~~which~~
~~tantalised them both -~~

"~~Tell me exactly what you feel there" she said~~ -
~~But as for doing anything, as for saying anything, she~~
~~But she was~~ She was

~~Well, it happened~~.

"But the hotel is awful - she said ~~perfectly vile, she said.~~
The last visitors had left basins full of dirty water.
~~Imagine my feelings~~. ~~I am in their bedrooms.~~
There is always that ~~contrast~~ ... ~~Evan minds it~~
~~more than I do.~~ ~~There~~ is in life - nothing seems
~~as one wants it~~ - Perfect. [Except ~~a few~~
children - & one or two people.] ~~Nights like this~~ -
~~And even this is — no, this is good," she said.~~
"The people one meets are beastly," Jacob said.
His excitement, his extraordinarily ~~chivalrous~~ trust in
Sandra, [who was infinitely ~~the~~ superior ~~of~~ to the
Frenchwomen, was so daring,] together with
capacity for quite other things - for jolly laughter, for

her love of pictures
being a fool, for carrying a whole household on his back,
This was clear enough —— ;

~~The~~ ~~But are we going the right way? she asked.~~

Write & tell me all about it - she said

I ~~will, certainly~~ -

She was disillusioned, momentarily. She
And tell me what you feel, & what you think
tell me everything."

[~~But~~ had it happened, for either of them? - that]
The night following a stormy day, was extremely dark.
There was no moon. It is true that a gauzy light
hung over Athens, & one or two houses were
plainly visible. ~~But~~ The Parthenon was

"I should like to, awfully" he said.

"~~Then~~ when we get back to London, ~~she said~~, ~~we shall meet~~"

~~You will come & see us~~:"

. . . . . .

"Yes"

But it was now; the present; this very moment.

"There is so much more - how little one says - A post perhaps - Do you feel it - too - this bewilderment. ~~not being able to~~ express We are ~~so~~ very ~~happy - Evan~~ & I. After all, here we are alone in Greece, ~~after & we were~~ married 10 years ~~ago~~ -"

~~It is not But life~~ - ~~It is these moments~~ -

Oh but the waters slipped by - unmarked. There must be something one ~~can~~ could hold to~~?~~—something enduring~~?—real?~~

"This is so real" she said. "~~To be out here~~, ~~alone at~~

to "I suppose they do leave the gates open ?" he asked.

But she

I suppose they leave the gates open" he said.

We could climb them up this she ~~said~~ answered

[~~You always do what you want he said.~~

He had already climbed them lifted her over, broken them down - a flight of fancy; Then he ~~sighed~~

If there was anything real - ~~& that of course is the gravest doubt~~ - ~~The~~ they ~~possessed it. saw~~ grasped it -

At last she drew ~~that queer~~ the sighing ~~breath.~~ ——~~She floated a a few seconds~~

"One can pretty nearly always get one's way in this country" he said.

~~Oh you get your way~~ -

"Breaking the gates, or jumping them?" she laughed.

~~Well~~, we could - he said. "You would - &

~~The waters~~ Time no longer slipped by unmarked.

They grasped ~~something~~

The stream raced.

~~But it they~~ [?] [like?] [to?] [?] their [?]

~~Certainly~~ She was half maternal. ~~Yet~~ a "Its all slipped away, she thought, years & years; & ~~then~~ have slipped Yet ~~all the time it~~ was there. all the time it is ~~there~~ here" she sighed as he said that he could knock up some Johnny. Reality of some sort she meant; & felt [in the soft dark ~~how strong~~ its strength, ~~passion~~; its ~~fearful~~ rough excitement.]

~~They had no wish for to~~ To kiss him - ~~would have been enough: she had no wish beyond it.~~ She might have wanted that - ~~but scarcely more.~~

~~"There's the Parthenon right enough" he said.~~ no - not that.

To kiss her? - no. not that. What then?

Presumably they both wished only for one thing - ~~to be not for this th she~~ certainty ~~that something~~ ~~Certainty not of~~ That something survives, still means, yes even in the charms of dark years the thing we ~~saw~~ felt.

Presumably wha~~t they~~ wanted was that something ~~should~~
happen so ~~definitely~~ ~~that~~ there it would always ~~be~~
They wanted certainty; ~~they wanted~~ separate, they wanted
that the thin shell ~~between~~ dividing them should break. ~~Then~~ Once
~~united~~ united, ~~be~~ something even in the waste of chaos,
survives. She sighed. Oh ~~this was~~ now it was easy, &
fluent, & now - now - at least for a few seconds, for her; &
now he talked to her as if grateful to her, ~~so grateful for~~
that ~~the—it should be possible for him, a man, to~~
~~beli be sure of the delighting in~~ rejoicing in life,
though perhaps ~~there never be~~ never altogether putting
aside ~~an~~ something defensive his armour. Obscuring the moon, &
altogether darkening the Acropolis, the clouds ~~which~~
~~were had gathered after the sultry day~~ passed
from ~~fr West to~~ East to West. ~~leaving the~~
The clouds solidified; the vapours thickened; the
trailing veils stayed & accumulated.

It was dark now over Athens, except for gauzy red
lanes, where the streets ran; & the front of the palace was
cadaverous. from ~~it~~ arc lamps. At sea the
the piers stood out, ~~the~~ ~~separate dots~~ marked by
separate dots. ~~for~~ the waves ~~were~~ being invisible; &
promontories, ~~the~~ & islands ~~were~~ only ~~outlines~~ dark humps,
with a few lights.

~~I fel~~ I ~~think if he might come & see you~~ it
~~would make "There's a great deal~~

Yes I should love to bring him. ~~At his age~~
It would make all the difference " said Jacob.
And if ~~I could~~ then perhaps meet your mother, ~~you have only to~~
Greece was dark; & somewhere off Euboea ~~the~~
some cloud must have touched the waves, &
shattered them, but the dolphins, seeking deeper &

deeper. Violent was the wind now ~~racing~~ rushing ~~between~~
down the Sea of Marmara, between Greece and the plains
of Troy.

~~D~~ "~~I will lend you~~ ~~Do read~~ ~~Write~~ I should
love to read it in your copy - where you have marked the
poems" said Sandra -

"I will give it you" said Jacob - & the
wind buffeted them both & ~~it~~ made all the
Venetian blinds in the residential quarter rattle,
So that Greek merchants ~~who had just gone up to bed~~
~~went to the window to—And the~~ ~~talking~~ unbuttoning
their waistcoats stopped. In Greece, the uplands of
Albania & Turkey, what can the wind do but
drive ~~chase~~ the sand & the dust? sowing itself thick with
particles? And then it pelts the smooth domes
of the Mosques, & makes the ~~stiff~~ cypresses standing
turbaned tombstones
by the ~~graves~~ of Mahomeddans creak.

Sandra's veils were swirled about her
head. ~~She kissed him,~~

this respect she was always to the [some?]

"I will give you my copy, said Jacob. "Here. Will you keep it?"

(The book was the poems of Donne.)

~~Far off The agitation of the air uncovered a racing star—star;~~ & ~~the~~ all the ~~lamp~~ lights had now mounted ~~from the lower~~ high in the houses; had diminished; had gone out; & ~~leaving the [mass of?] the city dark black as rock.~~ ~~The~~ The ~~clouds~~ dark which ~~raced~~, which ~~brooded~~, washed over dark cities, dark, seas In this Flying over enormous tracts of land went light, & darkness followed; & the ~~the~~ spires & domes ~~only dipped in the themselves in the air~~, &

& it was odd that Jacob should read Donne, t ~~considering how difficult his he~~ is: & ~~to~~ carry him about ~~too~~; & ~~know~~ like him)

~~However~~ Now the agitation of the air uncovered a racing star; now it was dark. Now, ~~the~~ one after another, lights were extinguished. Now ~~the the cities were~~ Great ~~dis~~ towns were black as rock; Waterways might be distinguished perhaps~~;~~ In England the trees were heavy in leaf. Here, perhaps, in some Southern wood, an old man ~~long~~ lit his fire; & the birds were startled. The flowers in gardens swayed one towards the other. The ~~cows asleep in the meadows c~~ sheep coughed in the meadows. The English sky is milkier, softer, than the Eastern. Into its atmosphere has passed something ~~soft~~ gentle from the rounded hills, ~~or v~~ vaporous from the ~~vegetation~~. ~~And~~ thick leaved woods. ~~Not that~~ Often after midnight ~~it~~ the sky is pearly, & mottled.

(No I.)

March 12th 1922

Jacobs Room

March 12th (added chapters IX a)

Abide with me,
Fast falls the eventide,
The shadows deepen,
Lord with me abide -

"At my place we used to have ~~a hymn~~

Gulls rode gently swaying in ~~little~~ ~~gro~~ groups of two or three quite near the boat; the cormorant ~~skimmed~~; as if following his long strained neck; skimmed from bay to bay, for the coast was folded into little bays, where the waves break forever unseen, though the drone of the tide in the caves comes across the water, low, monotonous, like the voice of some one talking to himself.

in eternal pursuit

Rock of ages cleft for me,
Let me hide myself in thee

~~H~~ Public schoolboys have the old testament almost by heart; nothing pleases them better than to cap quotations; & thus loosen the bands which as little boys ~~were~~ ~~tightly~~ tied ~~t~~ them tight: now they are men. They can dare the gods:

Like the ~~too~~ blunt tooth of some monster a rock broke the surface; brown; overflown with perpetual waterfalls; ~~th~~

Rock of ages,

Jacob sang, lying on his back, ~~with his~~ looking up into the sky at midday; which every shred of cloud had been from with drawn It was ~~immaculate~~, eternal, ~~as if~~ like something permanent, ~~with the~~ displayed with the cover off.

But the longest day was already past; &
by ~~five~~ six o'clock ~~the~~ a ~~breeze~~ cold breeze ~~from some~~
~~different world~~ blew in from some different world; &
by seven the water was more purple than green; &
by ~~eight after~~ half past seven there was rough gold beaten
skin all round the ~~Si~~ Scilly Isles, & ~~looking up,~~
Durrants face, as he sat steering, was of the colour of a
red lacquer box, polished ~~by~~ for generations.
By nine all the fire & confusion had gone out of the sky,
~~&~~ leaving wedges of apple green & pale plates of yellow,
& by ten, the ~~boat was~~ lanterns on the boat were
making twisted colours upon the waves, ~~& the air~~
~~being fine & blue & starlit; but without a moon~~.
The ~~lighthouse~~ beam from the lighthouse strode
rapidly across ~~the waves~~; them. But the sea was
black; the land was dark; There was ~~a whiteness in~~
~~the sky from the stars~~; but no moon; & the
~~wav water sl~~ ~~sea~~ slapped the boat, & crashed with
~~an~~ appalling solemnity against the rocks.

Jacob had nothing to hide from his mother. It was only that he cd make no sense

XXX

"He left everything just as it was," Bonamy marvelled, "Nothing arranged. All his letters strewn about for any one to read. What did he expect? Did he think he would come back?" he mused, standing in the middle of Jacob's room.

The eighteenth century has its distinction. A rose or a ram's skull carved above the doorways; ~~& the~~ the panels even

though smothered in raspberry paint

Bonamy took up a bill for a hunting crop.

"Seems to be paid" he said.

The panels even though smothered in ~~raspberry-coloured~~ paint have their distinction.

Bonamy took up a bill for a hunting crop.

~~That~~ " Seems to be paid" he said.

There were Sandra's letters. M[rs.] Durrant was taking a party to Greenwich.

One fibre in the wicker arm chair clicked, though no one sat there.

Bonamy crossed to the window. ~~All the voices of the August morning were in full cry.~~ ~~The~~ Pickfords van swung down the street. The omnibuses ~~were~~ palpitated blocked together at Mudies Corner. ~~Innumerl~~ Innumerable wheels turned, & carters, ~~sent~~ jamming the brakes down, ~~tu~~ ~~tugged at their~~ pulled their horses back. ~~Again & again~~ A man's voice ~~was heard~~ cried out cried out, harsh & distinct, saying but inarticulate. And then suddenly all the leaves seemed to raise themselves , & ~~Jacob~~

Jacob, Jacob, said Bonamy, standing by the window.

"Such confusion everywhere!" said Betty Flanders, opening the bedroom door.

"What is one to do with these, Mr. Bonamy?" She held out a pair of Jacob's old shoes. ~~They both laughed.~~

~~The room waved beh~~ind her tears.

~~She~~ Bonamy turned away from the window.

"What is one to do with these, M[r.] Bonamy?" said Betty Flanders.

She held out a pair of Jacob's old shoes.

38

"Poor old Topaz", said M$^{rs.}$ Flanders, as he
stretched himself out in the sun, & she smiled,
thinking how she had had him gelded, & how
she did not like red hair in men. Smiling
she went into the kitchen.

Jacob drew rather a dirty pocket handkerchief
across his face, in order not to catch Archer's
eye. (They/both guessed that M$^{r.}$ Floyd had loved
their mother).

He went upstairs to his room.
The stagbeetle dies slowly, but, let us hope, painlessly.
Even on the second day his ~~limbs~~ legs are still supple, which
may ~~prove~~ show that the poison pot ought to be ~~taken into~~
recharged. But the butterflies were dead.
A whiff of rotten eggs had vanquished the pale clouded
yellows which came pelting over the potato field,
& so across the orchard & over Dods Hill &
away on to the moor, now lost behind a furze
bush, & then off again helter skelter in the broiling
sun. A ~~peacock~~ fritillary ~~butterfly~~ ~~sunned~~ basked itself on a
white stone in the Roman camp. From the
valley came the sound of the church ~~bells~~ clock.
They were all eating roast beef; it was Sunday.

The death's head moth had been found by
Rebecca clinging to the zinc blind in the larder.
It was Sunday when Jacob caught ~~the~~ ~~twelve a~~ pale clouded
yellows in the clover field ~~far from home~~
eight miles from home.

Rebecca had caught the Death's Head Moth in the kitchen.
A strong smell of camphor came from the butterfly boxes.
Mixed with the smell of camphor, was the unmistakable
smell of sea weed. Tawny ribbons hung upon the door.
The sun beat straight upon them.

~~A~~ The upper wings of the moth which Jacob held
were ~~und~~ undoubtedly ~~sprinkled~~ marked with kidney shaped spots.
~~But the~~ of a fulvous hue. But there ~~specimen was rubbed~~ was no —
crescent upon the underwing ~~was almost rubbed out.~~
The tree had fallen, the night he caught it. There had been a
volley of pistol shots, suddenly, in the depths of the wood.
And his mother had taken him for a burglar when he came
home late.

"An extremely local insect", M^r. Morris called it. "which
~~has been recorded only in the~~ occurs in damp, or marshy
places, — not further north than ~~Norwi Nor~~ Suffolk."
~~But once or twice Jacob had put M^r. Morris right.~~
That may be so
Morris is sometimes wrong. Sometimes Jacob, choosing a very
fine pen, ~~ann~~ ~~wrote his~~ made a correction in the margin.
It was John/who had started the beetles, but he must find some
way of de/stroying them for himself. ~~They had only one
stink pot between the two of them.~~ ~~Moreover~~ Also they attract
insects. ~~The moth~~" [?] Holtwood, ap. 26th..

The tree had fallen, ~~the night he caught it.~~ ~~though~~
though it was a windless night ~~& after the sudden report,
he Jacob had heard twigs pattering to the ground~~
& the lantern stood upon the ground had lit up the still green
leaves & dead beech leaves. It was a dry place.
A toad was there. And the red underwing had flashed through
the light & ~~gone lit on the tree~~ & gone. He had never
come back, though Jacob had waited. It was ~~past
midnight~~ after twelve when he crossed the garden & saw
his mother sitting in the bright ~~hot~~ room, ~~& she had
taken him for a burglar~~ playing patience, sitting up.

cried
"It was so inconsiderate", she had said to him
not to have to have gone off without telling anyone — She
had thought something dreadful had happened.
And he woke Rebecca, who had to be up so early.
There he stood, pale, just come out of the depths of darkness,
in the hot room, blinking at the light.

No, it could not be a straw-bordered underwing.
The mowing machine always wanted oiling.
And Barnet always turned it under Jacob's window, &
it was always creaked — creaked, & rattled, &
across the lawn & creaked again — which reminded him
apparently to Barnet was mowing the lawn. &
Therefore if Jacob wanted his pony seen to, he had
must do it himself himself.
And now it was clouding over no doubt for rain.
Back came the sun, dazzlingly.
It fell, like an eye, upon the stirrups, & then in
suddenly & yet very gently, rested upon the bed,
& then again upon the antlers ameri alarum clock.

The red underwing had settled for one second
upon the bark. If only Jacob had had the nerve to wait!
But he had moved, & the red underwing had flashed
round his head & gone. And the grasshopper
gr grasshopper had crawled up to the lantern; the
daddy long legs: & t the toad stuffed with moths, as
It was so white. Sometimes a twig pattered to the ground
Something sighed then. The tree had fallen.

Only a moth Ar Archer was in the
Pacific;

But Mrs. Flanders would never go to bed
until Jacob was indoors.

And After all, it was only a wretched Har
Heart & Dart, — a battered one He
so rubbed, it might be anything.

far away. ~~The dark night was sunlight for hi~~m.
The
& then upon the butterfly box, stood open.
The pale clouded yellows had pelted over the moor.
across
They had zigzagged ~~over~~ the purple clover. The
fritillaries flaunted along the hedgerows. The blues
~~se~~ settled ~~on rabbits skulls~~ or little ~~bl~~ bones
lying in the grass with the sun beating down on them;
& the painted ladies & the peacock. seated upon
entrail dropped
~~the~~ bloody ~~cra~~ scraps left by a hawk.
among teasles
Miles away from home, in a hollow,/ beneath a ruin,
he had ~~com~~ found the commas, ~~nearly~~ He
circling
had seen a white Admiral ~~going~~ higher &
higher round an oak tree, but he had never caught it.
An old cottage woman, living alone, high up ~~on hi~~
had told him of a butterfly which he took to be a
purple Emperor. The fox cubs played in her garden
in the early morning she told him. And if you got up
at dawn you could always see two badgers.
Sometimes they s~~eemed to play together, she said.~~
knocked each other over like two boys fighting, she said.

The sun fell upon his purple blazer, & upon his
shoes.
~~She~~ was late for Bramham, as usual. She

– – – – – – – – –

And how ~~dist~~ ~~t~~ exquisite it was — that
dress in Evelina's shop off Shaftesbury Avenue!
It was four o'clock on a fine day, early in
April, & was Fanny the one to spend four o'clock
on a fine day indoors? Other girls in that very
street sat over ledgers, or drew long threads
~~rather~~ wearily ~~from~~ between silk & gauze; or,
festooned with ribbons in Swan & Edgars
rapidly added up ~~farth~~ ~~yards~~ pence & farthings
on the back of the bill & twisted the yard &
three quarters in tissue paper, & ~~then~~ asked "Your
pleasure?" of the next comer.

In Evelina's shop off Shaftesbury Avenue
the parts of a woman ~~w~~ were shown separate.
In the lefthand corner was her skirt. Twining
~~too~~ like a soft serpent round a pole was a
~~b~~ feather ~~f~~ boa. Ranged like the heads of
malefactors on Temple Bar were hats.
Wreathes of flowers circled them, or deep dyed
feathers drooped. The whole stands upon
pointed golden shoes, or patent leather slashed
with scarlet.

Fanny eyed it.[?] Feasted upon by the eyes of
women since nine o'clock that morning the clothes
should have been flyblown as sugar cakes ~~in~~
exposed in a bakers window. ~~Desires~~ Waking

desires for ~~love~~ money, for admiration, tightening lips, narrowing eyes, the clothes hung in Evelina's window, like ~~a~~ the nightshade or the brilliant mushroom ~~which poison the~~ of the forest.

Fanny eyed it.

But coming along Gerrard Street was a tall man in a shabby coat.

A shadow fell across Evelina's window. It was not Jacob, but it was his shadow ~~nevertheless:~~ ~~The shadow of truth, thought~~ & Fanny, ~~walking~~ walked along Gerrard Street wishing that she had ~~been educated at College & had~~ read books; ~~& had was 'real';~~ but Nick never read; never talked of Ireland ~~on~~ or the House of Lords; & as for his finger nails! She would learn Latin & read Virgil. She had been a great reader. She had read Scott; she had read Dumas. At the Slade no one read. But ~~there was a Fanny~~ no one ~~kne~~ knew ⧺ Fanny ~~really — the~~ at the Slade, or guessed how empty it seemed to her. These earrings, these dances, & ~~have~~ working for Tonks & Steer when it was only the French who could paint Jacob said ~~But~~ For ~~wh~~ the moderns were futile; painting the least respectable of arts; & why read anything but Marlowe & Shakespeare, Jacob said, & Fielding if you must read novels?

(for she had a heart)

"Fielding", said Fanny when ~~M^r^~~ the man in the book shop asked her what she wanted.

"Tom Jones cost three & six.

At ten o'clock ~~in her~~ in the morning, in a room which she
shared with a school teacher, Fanny Elmer read Tom Jones —
that mystic book. For this dull stuff, (Fanny thought) about
people with ~~odd~~ odd ~~absurd~~ names, is what Jacob likes. Good
people like it. Dowdy women who don't mind how they cross
their legs, ~~really~~ like ~~this sort of thing, better than shop windows, &~~
~~& pearls & sugar cakes.~~ [?] ~~it.~~ read Tom Jones — a
mystic book; for there is something ~~a distinction~~, Fanny thought,
~~that~~ about books, ~~good books~~, which "if I had been educated
I could have liked — much better than earrings & flowers & all
that" she sighed, thinking of the corridors at the Slade &
~~of~~ the fancy dresses. She had nothing to wear at the dance next
week. But Tom Jones. "They are real" thought Fanny Elmer,
~~tapping~~ setting her feet against the mantelpiece. Some people
are ~~real, she th~~ought. Very few. ~~None of her fri~~ends. Nick perhaps ~~was~~
only ~~but~~ he was so ~~too~~ stupid. And women never — except ~~strange~~
Miss Sargent, but Miss Sargent ~~never looked~~ as young but
~~picked up her things & went off at lunch time~~ ~~went off at lunch time &~~; gave herself
~~people called her haughty,~~ airs ~~never talked to you~~.
~~& went off~~ alone. There they sat quietly of a night, reading;
she thought; Not going to music halls; not looking in at
shop windows; not wearing each other's clothes like Robertson,
who had worn her shawl & she had worn his waistcoat. ~~The~~
~~other night.~~ which Jacob would ~~never~~ only do very
awkwardly for he liked Tom Jones. There it lay in
her lap, in double columns, price three & six, the
mystic book in which Henry Fielding, ever so many
years ago, rebuked ~~Fanny Elmer.~~ ~~frivolity~~.
Fanny Elmer in perfect prose, Jacob said. For he
never read modern novels. He liked Tom Jones.

"I do like Tom Jones" said Fanny, at five thirty that same day,
took out
early in April. When Jacob ~~having finished his tea~~, ~~lit~~ his pipe.
alas, alas. Women lied.
And It was a lie, ~~alas~~. ~~And alas that women should have to~~ lie.
But Clara Durrant never lied. A flawless mind; a candid nature;
off Lowndes
a virgin chained to a rock (somewhere near ~~Sloane~~ Square)
~~for company~~
eternally pouring out tea for ~~elderly gentlemen in~~
. . . .
~~white waistcoats, —~~ twisting her dance programme
her ~~w~~
round her looking glass, & ~~putting on the~~ chair white satin,
white stockings, white shoes — of all women, Jacob
honoured her most. But ~~they~~ to sit at a table
with bread & butter ~~in a saucer;~~ [to sit at a table] with
~~silver spo~~ dowagers in velvet, & never say more to
Clara than ~~the~~ Benson said to the parrot, when old
Miss Perry poured out tea was an insufferable
outrage upon the ~~decency of~~ liberties &
decencies of human nature — or words to that effect —
for Jacob said nothing. Only he glared at the fire.
Fanny ~~shut~~ dropped Tom Jones.

She stitched or knitted.

What?" asked Jacob.

For
"The dance at the Slade"

And she ~~went~~ fetched her headdress; her trousers; her
shoes with red tassels ~~v~~. What should she wear?
~~Jacob said he was going to the New~~ Forest.
Paris
"I shall be in the ~~New Forest~~" said Jacob.
And what is the point of fancy dress dances? thought Fanny.
You meet the same people; you wear the same clothes.
~~Robertson takes you on his knee.~~ Mangin gets drunk. [?]
She
[?] Florinda sits on his knee. ~~Florinda~~ flirts
outrageously. with Its Nick Bramham just now.

"In Paris?" said Fanny.

"On my way to Greece" said Jacob.

For, he said, there is nothing so detestable as English society.
~~We have outlived the great age & dally on,~~
~~The age of reason is~~ You dance. You meet the same people.
The age of reason is over — ~~of argument & common sense.~~
Here undoubtedly, he put before her a page
which is harder to read than ~~Tom Jones~~. any in Fielding
~~She would be alone~~. He would forget her.
A sparrow flew past the window trailing a long straw —
a golden straw, a straw from one of a stack stood ~~in~~
by a barn in a field. The old brown spaniel
snuffs at the base for a rat. Already the thin upper
branches of the elms are blotted with frail nests.
The ~~young leaves are~~ chestnuts have flirted their
[ǂǂǂ] ~~green~~ fans. And in ~~the New Forest~~ the butterflies are
crossing the rides in the New Forest, & who knows? —
perhaps the Purple Emperor is feasting, as Morris says,
putrid at the base of an oak tree
upon a mass of ~~putrid~~ carrion — ~~that is the only~~
~~chance of gett catching him.~~

Jacob sighed for you ~~can't take Fanny~~
Elmer riding in the New Forest

Fanny thought that it all came from Tom Jones —
a book in
He could go alone with ~~Shakespeare~~ in his pocket to
Inns & watch the badgers. He liked the talk of
~~verderers & tufters; &~~ men in public houses. He would
take a train at half past eight and walk in the forest all night.
He saw fire flies & glow worms. He knew tufters &
verderers, & bought toys for their children. He
would hunt with the New Forest Staghounds. There was
his story of the great red deer which was killed in the
quarry. And she sighed, thinking how it
all came from Tom Jones, & he would go to Paris,
to Greece, with a book in his pocket, & forget her.

~~However, she rigged him up in a silver turban & a~~
~~She gave him her handglass.~~
She fetched her handglass. There was her face.
A ~~thin girl~~ And suppose one wreathed Jacob in a
silver turban? There was his face. She lit the
lamp. But as the daylight came through the window
~~it was indeed so strange;~~ only half was lit up
by the lamp~~light~~. And though he looked
terrible & magnificent, ~~like a~~ & would ~~take her on~~
~~his knee, &~~ chuck the forest, he said, &
come to the Slade, — be a Turkish knight or a
Roman Emperor, — (& he let her blacken his
~~lips~~ lips & ~~looked~~ clenched his teeth & ~~looked~~
~~in the~~ scowled in the glass) still — there
lay Tom Jones.

"Jacob's letters are so like him," said Mrs. Jarvis,
"Indeed he seems to be having" said Mrs. Flanders, &
paused for she was cutting out a dress & had to
pin down the pattern — "a very gay time."
At her back
Mrs. Jarvis thought of Paris. The window was open, for it was a
even
mild night, a calm, ~~muffled~~ night, when ~~even~~ the moon,
~~though free from clouds~~ seems muffled, & the
apple trees stand ~~perf~~ perfectly quietly.

"I never pity the dead" said Mrs. Jarvis,
shutting the curtain at her back, & ~~looking~~
clasping her hands behind her head.
Perhaps Betty Flanders was not listening.

"~~I think that~~ They are at rest" said Mrs. Jarvis.

'And we spend our days ~~in trivial occupations without knowing why."~~ doing
why
unnecessary things without knowing ~~the reason~~".
Indeed, Mrs. Jarvis was not really liked in the
village.

walk
"You never ~~walk go out~~ at this time of
night?" she asked Mrs. Flanders.

"It is certainly wonderfully mild" said Mrs. Flanders.
it
Yet was years since she had opened the orchard
gate & gone out on Dod's Hill after dinner.

"~~N~~ow everything smells so sweet" said
Mrs. Jarvis, as they shut the ~~do~~ orchard door
& stepped on to the turf.

"I shan't go very far" said Betty Flanders.
"Does Jacob say when he ~~expects to go on to Greece~~?"
is leaving Paris? she asked. " You know

he is going to Greece. & then perhaps to Rome on the way back.

"Jacob was always my friend" said M^rs. Jarvis. Not so easy to live with as the others" said M^rs. Flanders. "Perhaps one is a little hard on boys. though" she added. "First it was butterflies; then it was ~~animals~~ beasts; ~~?~~ now he seems ~~[?]~~ given ~~interested in~~ over to books.

"One of these days he will bring you a daughter-in-law" said M^rs. Jarvis. "Now, my dear I am going to turn back" said M^rs. ~~Ja~~ Flanders. They had reached the Roman Camp.

~~"Oh but I go much further than this" said M^rs. Jarvis.~~

~~It~~ The rampart rose at their feet; the smooth circle surrounding the ~~grave~~ camp or the grave. How many needles Betty Flanders had lost there! & ~~once~~ ~~a~~ her garnet brooch.

"It is much clearer than this sometimes", said M^rs. Jarvis standing upon the ridge. There were no clouds, & yet there was a haze over the sea, & over the ~~Dow~~ moors. ~~&~~ The lights of Scarborough flashed ~~with a watery brilliance,~~ as if som~~ebody wore~~ one wearing a diamond necklace ~~&~~ turned her ~~he neck~~ her head fr. side to side this way & that.

"How peaceful it is!" said M^rs. Jarvis. M^rs. Flanders was thinking of her brooch, ~~&~~ rubb~~ing~~ed the turf with her toe.

Indeed M^rs. Jarvis found it difficult to think of herself. There was no wind; there was nothing racing, flying, escaping. Black shadows stood still over the silver moors. The furze bushes stood perfectly still. Neither did M^rs. Jarvis think of God. There was a church of course. There! It was striking ten. Did ~~they~~ the ~~ten~~ strokes reach the furze bush? or did the thorn tree hear them? M^rs. Flanders could never resist looking for her brooch. She was actually stooping down and picking up a pebble. Sometimes people do find things, M^rs. Jarvis thought, & she ~~began st~~ put her hand on the grass. ~~She sat do~~ It was so dry. She sat down, for ~~M^rs. Fland~~ Betty Flanders was poking about — & yet in this queer hazy moonlight it was difficult to see anything, except bone, & little pieces of chalk, that looked white.

Jacob ~~saved up his po~~ bought it out of his own money" ~~said M^rs. Flanders~~. ~~"~~ I & ~~came~~ brought M^r. Parker up to show & [his?] [this?] M^r. Parker up to the view & then I lost it." M^rs. Flanders murmured.

The church chimed the quarter.

~~"I've never been able to keep anything" M^rs.~~

~~She straightened herself~~.

And there ~~on~~ the grave or in the camp M^rs. Flanders

M^rs. Jarvis no ~~longer~~ wished she wa wished to escape, or to gallop with the horses that galloped ~~on~~ wild, days when the sea was white & black & then she was content.

Did the bones stir, or the rusty swords? Was
M[rs.] Flanders' twopenny halfpenny brooch for
ever part of that ~~richness~~ accumulation; & if
rubbed all the ghosts flocked thick ~~in that circle,~~ &
shoulders stood in the circle with M[rs.] Flanders would she not
have seemed perfectly at her ease, — a live an English
matron, growing stout?

The clock struck the quarter.

They returned.

The frail waves of sound broke ~~tinkled~~ among the stiff
gorse & the ~~thorn~~ hawthorn twigs, as ~~for~~ the
church ~~named the hours, & even the quarter~~s,
~~precisely~~, ~~distinctly~~ — divided time ~~the hour~~ into
quarters, ~~distinctly, all night,~~ ~~an~~ of an hour.
Immobile, & very stately, the moors received the ~~that~~ statement
"It is a fifteen minutes past ~~ten"~~ the hour."
~~The only sign~~ ~~M~~ ~~What~~ answer do they make ~~I~~ unless
the wind breaks a branch, ~~as~~ ~~for There is no other~~
~~change; no protest; no~~ Yet, even in this light, the
legends on the tombstones can be read, voices of
~~protest~~ protruding from the earth, like arms &
crying, ~~We are not dead~~. "I am Bertha Ruck"
"I am ~~Fred/Hammond~~ ~~erick~~." ~~Tom P~~ Thomas —"
Tom ~~Ga~~ Gage". They speak, indeed, some
~~beautiful words, & some old~~ snatches of doggerel.
And they say when they died; & ~~they~~ the New
Testament says something for them very
proud, very emphatic, or consoling.

The moors accept all ~~all~~ that too, soundlessly.
But the moonlight also falls, like a pale page
upon the church wall; & illuminates the
~~tablet with the~~ kneeling family ~~effigies~~, & the
tablet set up, in 1780 to the squire of the parish

who was manly, sincere, ~~obeyed the laws of man & God~~,
&
relieved the poor, befriended the fatherless; ~~&~~
so
~~&~~ the measured voice goes on down the marble page,
~~very composed & articulate~~ as though it could impose
free
itself upon time & the ~~open~~ air.

Now a fox steals out from behind the gorse
bushes.

And often, even ~~in the m~~ at night, the ~~pew~~ church
seems full of people. The pews are worn & greasy,
& the cassocks in place, & the hymnbooks on
the ledges. It is ~~like~~ a ship with all its crew
aboard. The timbers strain to hold ~~so much~~
~~life.~~ - the ploughmen, the carpenters, the
cooks, & scullions, & dairymaids; ~~& sexton~~;
the fine ladies; the foxhunting gentlemen, &
paw impatiently in the ga
the farmers, whose nags are tied up further down
in
the road. Their tongues join together
syllabling the ~~clear out~~ words. which ~~do~~
battle so lustily ~~that~~ with time & the broad-
backed moors. Plaint & belief & elegy;
triumph, ~~now & then~~ despair; but on the whole
sense & ~~energy~~ & jolly indifference go
trampling out of the windows anytime these five
hundred years.

Still, as M[rs.] Jarvis said ~~not an ho~~
stepping on to the moor, How quiet it is!

Quiet at midday, except when the hunt scatters across it,
quiet in the afternoon, save for the drifting sheep,
perfectly
~~now~~ at night the moor is ~~perfectly~~ quiet, ~~as if it~~
pads
A garnet brooch has dropped into its grass. A fox ~~foots it~~
on its edge
stealthily. A leaf turns ~~aimlessly~~. M$^{rs.}$ Jarvis, who is
~~past~~ fifty years of age, reposes in the camp.
id
"...and, sa~~ys~~ M$^{rs.}$ Flanders, straightening herself, up,
I didnt care for M$^{r.}$ Parker" ~~was not a~~

"Neither did I" said M$^{rs.}$ Jarvis; ~~&~~ They began to walk
home.

for
But in their voices float a little ~~longer~~ on the
~~still air~~, above the camp; ~~&~~

The moonlight destroys nothing. The moor accepts
everything. Tom Gage cries aloud so long as his
skeletons
tombstone endures. The roman hair pins are in
safe keeping. Betty Flanders darning needles are
safe
~~there~~ too. And sometimes at midday the moor
the
seems to hoard little treasures, like an old nurse.
But at midnight — ~~the church clock strikes twelve~~ —
who
~~how~~ can ~~one~~ tell?

Would it not be wiser to change your
shoes?" said M$^{rs.}$ Flanders...

up to bed
But M$^{rs.}$ Jarvis waited till she went home.
moving between her
There was her light in her bedroom & the bath
room
window. ~~And there was M$^{rs.}$~~
G. for the moors — are ~~is it not beautiful~~?
~~& heartless, & indifferent, &~~ lying there in the
moonlight, right at our very doors, so that
the passionate can vex it with questions; & the
sit down in it?
~~weary~~ tired ~~sleep on it — but~~ is it not
wise, & kindly? The Church clock strikes twelve
Beautiful it is certainly,

At midnight nothing moves upon the moor. The thorn tree is perfectly still.

But at midnight when ~~it is perfectly still~~ & no one speaks or gallops, & ~~from~~ nothing stirs, the thorn tree is perfectly still, & the clock strikes twelve [& the rectory lamp is extinguished & the Mrs. Flanders lies down:] then it would be foolish ~~espe~~ to vex the moor with questions, ~~or to say anything now that It makes no reply~~. Let The church clock strike~~s~~ twelve.